HOT & COLD

SHAYNA ASTOR

Edited by HEARTS FULL OF READS
Edited by NICE GIRL NAUGHTY EDITS
Cover Designer COFFIN PRINT
Formatting GARNET CHRISTIE

Hot & Cold

FROM THE AUTHOR

Hot
&
Cold

ŞHAYNA ĄSTOR

Hot & Cold is a full-length, stand alone that features strong language, mature situations, and explicit sexual scenes. Reader discretion is advised, and this book is intended for readers age 18 and up.

Thank you so much for reading my novel! I hope you enjoy reading it, as much as I enjoyed writing it!

To my husband—

My very own college sweetheart.

CHAPTER 1

"I can't believe we're never going to see each other again." The wistfulness of Lauren's voice doesn't match the death grip she has around my shoulders. A warm breeze wraps its delicate tendrils around us where we sit in a secluded section of the park, the only sounds the gentle waves and distant squeals of children.

Carefully, I push her off. "What are you talking about? Of *course*, we'll see each other again. We're just going away to college."

"I know, but it won't be the same. It won't be every day."

"No, it won't be, but we can talk daily, right?"

"It's not the same." Tears shimmer in her hazel eyes. Lauren's always been so emotional, having cried at least once every week all summer due to our upcoming departure for college. Which, surprisingly, is only a few days away. However, I'm not as emotional of a person. Of course, I'll miss my best friend, but if I cry about it, it won't be until I'm in my car driving away.

"But it will make it so much better when we're together again," I try to offer her a tiny morsel of happiness.

"We've seen each other every single day for fifteen years."

Though exaggerating a bit, she's right. Fifteen years ago, I moved to our small town in upstate New York. My parents and I met the family down the road who had a little girl a few months younger than me. We instantly clicked and haven't parted ways since. Even when we didn't have classes together, even when we fell into different social circles in middle school that inevitably rolled into high school, we always had each other.

Flinging my arm over her narrow shoulders, I hug her close. "We'll visit, and we'll talk every day. It won't be the same, but it will be great."

"Please, just promise me you'll meet some guys. I won't be there to introduce you."

"Introduce me? Don't you mean *force* me?" A smile spreads across my face as I bump my shoulder into hers.

"Force is a strong word."

"Is *surprise* better?"

"Eh, maybe. Oh, Lexie, I just want you to not be such an introvert all the time. Parties are fun. Boys are fun…or at least they can be, if enjoyed properly." A wicked smile stretches across her lips as she winks at me.

I roll my eyes. Partying or the company of others, especially of the male variety, has never sounded as appealing as a good book to me. The tendency to put my foot in my mouth and blurt something truly embarrassing around them is usually profound. Especially, good-looking ones. That is, of course, when I can say anything at all. Sometimes I get so nervous I'm basically a mute.

"I promise I'll try." *Try* being the key word.

"I guess that's all I can ask for."

I giggle before turning somber. "There's the slightest chance I'll miss the sneak attack set-ups, though."

"Don't think I won't be coming for an early visit and doing some recon work to figure out who to set you up with."

Lauren points a long finger at me, her purple nail polish impeccable.

"Oh, I'd never doubt you for a second."

Tilting our heads together, her straight blonde strands and my dark brown curls overlap and weave together in the wind. Lauren and I have been talking about this day for years.

How we would want to spend our last days together before we head to college. *Separately.*

Sitting on the edge of the park, looking out over the river with our end of summer treat was our top priority. We've done this every year since we were five, when our moms brought us to this very park and bought us ice-cream from the same shop a week before we started kindergarten. It became our tradition, something we both looked forward to before every new school year.

This year, it's bittersweet.

While we still have a few days until we leave for our respective schools, family obligations and packing are the priority, which doesn't leave us a lot of time to spend together. In fact, today is our last day.

We sit in silence, eating our ice-cream, watching the gentle waves lapping the shore, the ripples spanning the water. Every so often, a boat will pass by. There are kids yelling and playing on the playground a few yards away, but it's calm and peaceful, this quiet observation of the ebb and flow below us, while orange and pink hues decorate the sky.

We've spent a lot of time staring out at the river, either at this spot or a few others we like to frequent. This place sports as our destructive playground—we visit here to talk, to throw things into the dark abyss after one of Lauren's heartbreaks, and much more. The water is forgiving, understanding. You can disperse your thoughts, troubles, and fears into it, and watch them disappear.

Looking at the rise and fall against the rocks, I think about my fears. I'm going off to a brand-new school where I know nobody and can be anybody. I'm excited, but I'm also really nervous. The two emotions work like strings through my body, twisting into a ball, sitting heavy in my stomach and leaving me with a slight tremor.

Lauren won't be there to help me break the silence that tends to exist between me and others. Can I do it on my own?

I know nothing about my roommate. Despite reaching out repeatedly, I've gotten nothing in return. Not even when I said I wanted to try to plan for a fridge and TV. Instead, my parents bought me both, figuring I could at least have my own. Closing my eyes, I let my fears shroud the water, as Lauren and I have always done. It makes us feel better—this superstition.

After dark settles around us and chirping crickets mingle with the soft sounds of the waves, I drive us back to my house. The large colonial sits on its own small hill as we linger in the driveway for a few minutes, not knowing how to say goodbye now that the time has finally arrived.

How do you say goodbye to your best friend of fifteen years and consider it enough? Sure, we'll see each other and talk all the time, but it's going to be so different. The confidence I felt while at the park washed away with the tide.

Thankfully, Lauren never lets me feel awkward and unsure for too long. Running around to my side of the car, she wraps me in a bear hug, pulling me close to her. "Oh, Lexie, I'm going to miss you so much!"

"I'm going to miss you too, Laur." The sting in my eyes surprises me.

She pulls back and pushes my curls behind my shoulders, a move I've always claimed something a sister would do. "Please promise me you'll try to make friends. I know you're shy and nervous, but you're such an amazing person and friend. Let other people get to know you. And I don't even mean boys. I mean, yeah, you should definitely include some, but just don't be a recluse. Meet people. Please."

"I will, Laur. I promise."

She looks at me skeptically, brows knit together, and hazel eyes narrowed.

"What? I will! I promise the first week, I'll try my hardest to make a friend."

"Okay. But trying also means things like leaving your door open and talking to people."

"I know what it means."

"And your roommate doesn't count," Lauren's quick to add this stipulation.

"Um, okay. Fine. I'll agree to those terms."

Her lips stretch into a tender, triumphant smile. I know she's going to be fine at school. She has no problems talking to anybody and everybody. But she's nervous to leave home, having never gone anywhere before. And I know she's worried about me. Lauren thinks she's the only reason I have any friends, though I have many aside from her that I'd managed all on my own. Sure, I'm shy; I prefer to be alone a lot, but I know how to socialize, even if I'm a little awkward during the process.

Taking my hand, she traces her finger over the wave tattoo on the inside of my wrist as I trace the one I know is on hers. "We'll be okay, Laur. We knew it was coming."

"But so many people lose touch in college. Look at what happened with Theo."

"You said Theo and his friends still get together when they're home."

"Yeah, when they're home! When was the last time you saw Theo home?"

It has been a while since I've seen her older brother. "Alright, that may be true. But we're not Theo. We're not boys. We're us!"

Even though she bobs her head, I can see giant tears welling in her eyes, causing a laugh to rise from my chest.

5

"Lauren, we'll talk all the time. And we'll see each other in a few months."

Although hesitantly, she nods again. "Okay, you're right. I'm excited, I am. It'll just be so weird not seeing you every day."

"You mean I'll finally get a break? I can't wait!" I'm only partially kidding. I love her, but she can be a bit overbearing at times.

Lauren shoves me gently. "Remember our agreement. You know I'll be checking up on you."

"Yes, I know."

She pulls me into a hug. "I love you, Lex. You're the sister I never had."

"I love you too, Laur." With that, she backs away and starts walking home. When she's turned the bend in the road, I spin around and walk into my house, knowing that the next few days will be filled with some more lasts before I leave. Sure, I'll be back at breaks. I'll be back over summer, but it won't really be the same.

The familiar scent of lilacs infiltrates my nose as I walk into my house. I know I'll miss it all, but I'm amped up about leaving, about going to an unknown place where nobody knows me. I can be whoever I want; I don't have to live in Lauren's shadow. Most of my other friends have already left for school, so we've already said our goodbyes. Besides my parents, Lauren was the last one.

Walking into the living room, I find Mom asleep on the couch. She always tries to stay up for me, and even though it's only ten, she's usually zonked out by now. Smiling, I know that she'll end up waking in an hour or so, checking in on me, and then doing something until the wee morning hours. It's the little things like this that I'll miss the most.

I head up to my room, still decorated like it had been when I was a kid, with a teddy bear border against pink walls, and pack a few more things. Logging in to my computer quickly, I check to see if I have any response from my room-mate. Nothing. Sighing frustratedly, I shift to my bed and try to busy my mind with thoughts of all the things waiting for me.

New friends. New environment. New me.

CHAPTER 2

Three days later, Mom and I pile into my car while Dad drives theirs. Mom sits behind the steering wheel as I stare out the window, biting my cuticles, my knee bouncing relentlessly.

"How about some music?"

"Sure, Mom."

"Oh, honey, I know you're nervous, but it's going to be so wonderful! You'll have an amazing time."

"I know. It's just a lot of changes at once."

"Thinking back, my college days were some of the best of my life. You know Mady, we still talk all the time. We met our freshman year." She keeps talking, but I tune out.

The thumping in my ears overpowers her words, the radio, and the whirring of the tires beneath me. Trees and other cars whiz by me, but I barely take in more than their color. The farther from home we get, the more my heart tries to pull me in the opposite direction, like the string that always connected me to home is being stretched. I wonder if it will snap or if it can reach all the way to Bleeker University.

Mom's hand on mine startles me so much I nearly jump out of my seat. "Sorry, sweetheart, I couldn't get your attention. We're going to make a stop for some coffee and maybe something to eat." Her voice is low and calm, like how she used to talk to me when I was sick.

"Okay. Does Daddy know?"

"We just had an entire conversation. Where's your head at?"

"Oh, uh, I don't really know. I guess I'm just really anxious. Thinking about what to expect and all that."

A thousand images have flashed through my mind, both good and bad. Anything from what my roommate might look like to the classes I'll be taking. Which is hard, considering I don't know about any of it.

"Well, have you ever thought about going in with no expectations?"

My eyes narrow and my brow scrunches as I look at her. "What do you mean?"

"I mean, maybe try going in not expecting *anything* and just waiting to see what happens and how things go. Allow the process to take over."

"I still don't really understand." How do I do what she's suggesting? I don't even see how it's possible to go in so openly like that. The jitteriness that's been settled in my bones for the past few days only increases.

"You may deny this, but I'm your mother, so I know you pretty well. You put high standards and expectations on things, like college. I know you're nervous because it's new, but I think part of it is also you're afraid it won't live up to what you've pictured in your mind. Maybe let those images go. Let the pieces fall where they may."

"I don't do that. Do I?" Shifting in my seat, I tug at my pants and thrum my fingers against my thighs at this revelation.

"I seem to remember you getting upset because you weren't wearing your lucky shirt when your acceptance letter came in. And that we had a dreary day for orientation instead of the bright sunny skies you'd hoped for." She gives me a sidelong glance as her lips turn down on one end.

"The whole college experience is the same thing. Four years is a long time, and that's before grad school, which you'll need as well. Don't place too much pressure on yourself, *or* school to be perfect."

"I guess I just don't see what I set for myself."

"That's understandable. I'm just saying try to live it day to day. Don't get caught up in what should be or could be and miss out on life. Go to parties, date, make friends."

"Mom, are you telling me to drink and spend time with boys?" I want to say *have sex,* but I can't bring myself to say the words out loud.

"In a way, maybe I am. Listen, Alexis, college is a time to have fun, to try new things. Does that mean drinking? Maybe. I'm not foolish. I know you've gone to parties, hell, I've picked you up at one in the morning." Mom pauses and glances at me with a raised eyebrow.

"And I don't know about your experiences with boys, and while on some level, I'd like to think you feel comfortable enough talking to me about these things, I prefer to stay ignorant of the details. However, I don't want you to turn around in twenty years and have regrets about how you lived during these college years."

Looking at my lap, I nod, trying to digest what she's saying.

While it really sounds like Mom is suggesting that I get wasted every day and sleep around, I understand what she means. If I think about it, I have had the intention of holing myself away in my room or the library, and reading or studying regularly. It'd probably be better if I didn't do that.

As Mom pulls off to the service stop, I glance at the clock. We've been driving for three hours now. Somehow, I've managed to distract myself for the better part of that time.

Once we get back on the road, we'll have about two more hours to pass.

The nausea that had settled is again rising in my throat, ready to break free.

"Come on, sweetheart. You'll feel better after some coffee and a snack."

"I don't have much of an appetite right now."

"Well, you'll have to try."

Mom doesn't give me much choice as she gets out of the car. I can stay, but she knows I won't. Dragging my feet, I follow behind her. Coffee does sound good. Maybe it will give me the attitude adjustment I need to be excited for what lies ahead. Doubtful. But worth a shot.

TWO HOURS LATER, WE PARK IN THE CIRCLE IN FRONT OF MY dorm. It isn't much to look at, merely a concrete square with windows, but it's separated from the rest of the campus with three other dorms, and a spacious grassy area across from the entrance. With a gasp and an inward squeal, I notice that the lake is fully visible from the front door. I can only hope that my room has as breathtaking of a view. Grabbing a bag, I stare up at the four-story building.

Though I feel Mom standing next to me, I'm unable to tear my eyes from the building, the flutters of anxiety rising in my chest.

"You ready?"

All I can do is nod due to the giant lump in my throat. Crossing the threshold, we follow the signs for checking in. These first two days are only for freshmen, with everybody else moving in over the weekend. The only people here already are staff and athletes. Taking in my surroundings, I note the chairs right in the entryway. There's a small hallway with in-wall mailboxes to the right, a large room behind them, at the front of which is a half wall that has **FRONT DESK** scribbled across it.

Being able to see straight to the back of the large room, I find couches, a pool table, and ping-pong table all pushed to the sides. This allows room for there to be three large fold-out tables in the center of the lounge.

People sit behind each one in matching blue shirts; I assume they're RA's. Making our way through the assembly line, I'm handed my own matching t-shirt; keys for the front door, my room, and the mailbox; and lastly, a folder with maps of campus and the dorm layout, my class schedule, as well as the dining hall menu.

There are more staff members standing to the side waiting to take newcomers up to their room. Giant rolling bins are out front for everything that needs to go upstairs. Everybody seems good-natured, but I barely register any of it, the apprehension overtaking me.

As Mom and I are following an RA with a light blue pixie cut, I notice a guy taller than those around him enter from outside. Aside from a quick glimpse of dark hair and muscles peeking out from the sleeve of his t-shirt—the same one everybody surrounding me has on—I can't see much of him. I quickly turn away as heat creeps up my neck and catch up to pixie cut, Tracy, I think she said, as she walks through the door that leads to the stairwell.

Tracy keeps chattering on a bit, and I'm able to pick up things here and there. "And the dining hall is connected, so just go down the stairs and—"

Her voice starts to fall away as I can't keep my mind focused on what she's saying, but out of the corner of my eye, see Mom bobbing her head. Something about being open certain times, many nights opening again after dinner with a much more limited menu. She mentions a few get-togethers over the weekend for freshman and then a few things for the following week. They allot a few days before classes start to give some time to acclimate and get books from the bookstore for classes. All things I know from orientation, but I'm sure is just a reminder.

"And make sure you get your photo ID as soon as you can. Well, here you are!" She extends her hand toward an open room. Nobody else is here, which means I made it before my roommate, Kimberly. And just as I'd hoped, I notice the window looks out over the grassy area and to the lake. A smile spreads across my face. "I know, nice view, huh? I'm so jealous, mine faces the other way. There's a pond and stuff, but it's definitely not the lake. So your RA is Julie, who's pretty cool and lives right next door. Go ahead, get yourself situated. We'll be floating around or downstairs if you need anything." With a perky smile, she's off, leaving my folder on the desk closest to the door.

Deciding that side of the room is as good as any, I'm determined to make it mine, so I toss my bag on the bed.

"Well, this is nice," Mom says, looking around. "Not as small as I remember from our tour in the fall. And you get a view of the lake. How lovely."

"Yeah, it'll feel more homey being able to see the water from here." My fingers absentmindedly run across the tattoo on my wrist.

Mom wasn't thrilled when I came home with it earlier this summer. Lauren and I had gone after she turned eighteen in June, my birthday already having passed in March. We went running into the house to show them to Mom. For a minute, I thought she might faint, but she swallowed it and smiled, albeit tensely.

"I bet Lauren's fine, sweetie."

"Man, that elevator is slow." Dad pushes a giant bin up to the doorframe of my room. "Let's get unpacking!"

We spend the next hour and a half unpacking together, mostly in silence, as my nerves steal my voice. Dad makes a second trip down to get more stuff while Mom and I make the bed.

A sense of calm washes over me when I take out some books and arrange them neatly on the top shelf of my desk.

I'm in the process of setting up my computer while my mom puts some of my clothes away when there's a knock at the door. We both freeze and turn to look. A girl about my height, with a high ponytail of straight blonde hair, and deep blue eyes, stands in the doorframe.

"Hi! I'm Brittney. I live just around the corner." Leaning back, she points her finger to the left.

"Hi, Brittney. I'm Alexis Harper, I go by Lexie." I walk over to shake her hand, then immediately feel like an idiot. Do people do that? And I told her my last name, but she hadn't done that. "This is my mom."

"Nice to meet you both. How are you settling in? Finding everything okay?"

"Um, I haven't really looked yet, just been unpacking." My voice is shaky, and I break eye contact as I look around the room. I wish Lauren was here to break the ice and awkwardness.

"I'm actually a sophomore. I'm here for field hockey, but if you need anything, let me know." The smile hasn't left her face since she first said hello. It helps ease my nerves. A little.

"That's really nice of you, thanks."

She leans into the room a bit farther and meets my eyes again. "Your roommate here yet?"

Scrunching my shoulders, I slide my hands into my back pockets. "Not yet."

"What's she like?"

"I have no idea. She never responded to my emails."

Brittney's brow furrows. "Really? That's kind of weird."

Uh-oh. That makes my nerves jump right back up.

Reaching behind my back, I pull at my curls, hoping she

can't see my unease. "I wasn't really sure what to make of it myself. My only hope is that she's nice."

"It will probably be fine. Most people have at least decent roommates."

"Have you met yours?"

"No, she's not here yet either, but we chatted a little over email. She seems alright. She has a boyfriend or something, so she said she may not be around much? Works for me!" She shifts on her feet and leans into the doorjamb.

"That does sound nice. So, any tips or tricks for the place?"

"Not really. Most people leave their doors open the first several days to just get to know people as they walk around. Many times, people just kind of gather in the hallways to chat or stand in their doorway. It's nice the first week or so before classes start. Once things get under way, there's more closed doors."

I nod, feeling like a fool, but can't seem to make myself stop. "That makes sense."

"Hey, listen, I have to go change for practice, but if you want, we can meet for dinner later?"

"Um, I think I may be having dinner with my parents. But, thank you." I gesture with my thumb over my shoulder toward my mom, who's still putting things away.

"You're welcome to join us, Brittney! It'd be nice to be able to hear a little about your experience last year," Mom speaks up for the first time since Brittney stopped by. To invite her to dinner. It makes me feel the slightest bit pathetic.

"Oh, I don't want to impose."

"Nonsense, we'd love to have you. You can help us figure out where to go too." Mom always invites those she feels have nowhere to go. One year, our Thanksgiving dinner was fifteen people. Our extended family isn't more than eight. She had heard of friends and far distant relatives who had nowhere else to go and invited them all.

A big smile spreads across Brittney's face. "Thank you, that's very kind of you. I'd love to."

"Okay, wonderful. Is six alright? Will you be done with practice by then?"

"Absolutely, it should be short. Coach worked us over yesterday, so she's promised a shorter practice today."

"Excellent, we'll see you then."

"See you then." With a quick pat at the doorframe, her ponytail bounces off down the hall.

"Well, she seems sweet," Mom comments as she goes back to hanging up some of my clothes.

"It was kind of you to invite her to dinner. But I don't need you to make friends for me." Though in this case, maybe it won't be the worst thing.

"I wasn't doing that, dear, you were doing just fine on your own. And she invited you to dinner first; I don't want you to miss out on opportunities because we're here. So, we'll still go eat, and we'll just have a guest. No big deal."

"Okay. Well, it was still nice of you." Around four-thirty, when we've finished unpacking, my parents head back to their hotel to get ready for dinner. A surge of sadness overtakes me. My roommate still hasn't arrived and while we have two days to move in, I had chosen to come the first day. I have to assume she's coming the second.

"I had a feeling you might be alone." A voice makes me turn toward the hallway. It's Brittney, leaning against my door with a smile on her face, her hair falling long and straight over her shoulders. I get the feeling she's always happy, or at least smiling, since I've seen her twice now with the same expression.

"Yeah."

"My parents did the same thing my first day. This year, they basically dropped me off, helped me bring stuff up, and left." Rolling her eyes as she walks in, she juts her chin over to the other bed. "Still no roommate?"

"No. I guess she's coming tomorrow?"

"Most likely. Kind of late for her to decide to show up today." Walking over to the empty bed, she hops up, resting her hands on either side of her and swinging her feet.

"Yeah." I realize I'm not saying much. "Sorry, I don't really know what to say and am a bit nervous too." At this point, she has to know how awkward and boring I am.

She laughs a little. "Totally okay. I remember it well. Granted, I'm not often nervous, but I get the concept. New place, new people. I'm very confident with myself and will say hi to anybody and everybody."

Flipping some hair over her shoulder, she continues, "But my sister is not at all like me. She had a rough start. I promise I can talk enough for the both of us. I also tend to not really have a filter, so I'm sure I'll say something embarrassing at some point and stick my foot in my mouth that will make you feel comfortable enough to talk to me." I can't help but laugh. "See? We're already getting there."

Brittney's right, I feel comfortable around her already. I bet it's the ease she seems to exude. "So, you play field hockey?"

"I do. I don't love it as much as I used to, but it's still something fun to do, helps me stay active in the fall. It helped me keep off the 'freshman fifteen' last year." Her eyes widen and she shows a grimace of perfectly straight white teeth. "You into any sports?"

"Not really. I actually did play field hockey during my sophomore year of high school. And that was about it." While I had been pretty decent, I wasn't good enough for anything to come of it and didn't really enjoy it terribly much. I'm not an athletic, or frequently even well-coordinated person.

"I definitely wouldn't say it's a passion, but it's fun. It's good exercise and for getting out all that pent-up rage."

"I do remember that."

Following her gaze around the room, I notice her eyes

settle on my shelf. "You have a lot of books. Are you an English major?"

Glancing over at my desk, I take in her observation. There aren't *that* many there, only about a dozen. "Uh, no, education major, actually. Though I do have a concentration in English." Really, I just enjoy getting lost in another world.

Brittney nods as though that explains everything. "Well, I guess there's that. I'm still undecided. Though I'm leaning toward business, but I'm just not sure. My advisor has me taking all the prerequisites now so that once I finally declare, which she said I have to do by middle of this year, I'll be able to just jump right into the major classes." When she rolls her eyes, I get an overwhelming sense that Brittney does that a lot. "I don't know. I'm not like passionate about any of it, ya know? Nothing screams at me that *that's* what I want to do for the rest of my life." She also gestures with her hands as she talks.

I've wanted to be a teacher for as long as I can remember, but I nod anyway.

"So how nervous are you really?" Her voice is hesitant.

"About what?"

"School starting!" The way she says it is like there could be absolutely nothing else she's referring to. Not the new people I'm going to meet, not the fact that I'm away from family and my best friend for the first time ever. Not what I'm sure is to be a very different course load. Not even that from my under-standing boys in college have different…expectations.

Maybe she said school because it encompasses all of those things.

"A little, I guess. Maybe a lot. It's a little strange, being in a new place, not knowing anybody or where anything is. Or what to expect, really. But I'm kind of looking forward to it. I know it's going to be different and difficult, but I'm kind of excited for the challenge."

"That's good. It can get busy and hectic, especially around

midterms and finals. The first few weeks are pretty fun, though, especially this first part of the week with no classes. Pretty much everybody keeps their door open unless they're changing or sleeping, and even then, some don't care. And lots of parties. Like tons."

I give a tight smile. "That sounds fun." Kind of.

"The open doors are so you can meet other people who live near you. They recommend it, but you can really get to know some good friends that way. You may have a song playing or something on TV that somebody hears and they like the same band or show, so they poke their head in, and bam… You're insta-friends."

"Sounds nice."

"Or some random person just pops in." Shooting me a wink, she leans back against the wall and crosses her arms over her chest. "Sorry, I talk a lot. You can totally cut me off. Hope it doesn't bother you or anything."

Oh no, I've offended her in my shy, reserved way. "No, no, you're fine. Sorry, I'm not great at talking to people who are new. I never really know what to say, so instead, I just say nothing. Though sometimes, I ramble aimlessly, so prepare for that."

"That's okay. Like I said, I can do the talking for the both of us." The smile she gives me makes one spread across my face as my chest floods with emotions. Could I actually be making a friend? On my first day here?

I glance over at the clock. "We can probably head down and wait for my parents. They'll be here any minute."

Just as we walk out the front doors, my parents pull up to the curb. "Well, look at that timing," Mom says as she rolls down her window. "Hi Brittney, it's nice to see you again."

"You as well, Mrs. Harper. Thanks again for inviting me to dinner, I really appreciate it."

"You're welcome sweetie. Come now, girls, get in, I'm

hungry!" Climbing into the backseat, I watch more people moving in. "So, Brittney, any suggestions on where to eat?"

"Well, if you wanted to stay in town, there are two Italian places that are decent, a few of the chain restaurants, a diner, and then there's a few Chinese buffets and pizza joints. Otherwise, everything else is about a half hour away."

"Hm, not too many choices," Dad grumbles from the front.

Brittney just shrugs. "College town." She says it like it's the explanation for all things. It probably is.

"Well, Italian it is!" Mom sounds excited. She has a way of making anything more upbeat.

The food at dinner is alright, and the restaurant is cute with small tables and dim candlelight. My chicken parmesan is a little tasteless, but Dad claims his is too salty and his vegetables are undercooked.

Brittney is great. Her presence brings a calming of the swirling butterflies for the time being, and she answers all of my parents' thousand and one questions. That, in turn, makes me feel less worried about school.

Funny anecdotes from her freshman year have us in stitches. One of them is about a time early on when she accidentally tried to go to the wrong room, wondering why her key didn't work. Thankfully, she doesn't say anything too crazy or about parties that may make my parents worry. I'm able to learn a bit about Brittney and realize she's definitely somebody I can be friends with.

When we get back upstairs, I still have no roommate. Being late in the day, I hadn't expected her to come while we were at dinner, but I also hadn't anticipated spending the first night of school in solitude.

"You going to be okay here alone?" Brittney asks as she lingers by my door.

I nod slowly. "Yeah, yeah, I think so."

"Alright, well, I'm just around the corner in 453 if you

need anything. And Julie's pretty cool; she and I chatted for a while the other day."

"I appreciate that. I'll probably turn the TV on for noise or something." I gesture toward the set that sits atop my mini fridge in front of the window.

"Okay, well, like I said, I'm here if you need anything. I imagine you'll be getting breakfast with your folks, but let's make a plan for lunch, yeah?"

"Yeah, that'd be great."

"Okay, lunch it is." With a pat of the doorframe, she starts off toward her room.

"Hey, Brittney?" I call after her.

Her head pokes back into the frame. "Yeah?"

"Thanks for tonight. You've made things feel a little less scary."

A wide, toothy smile spreads across her face. "Absolutely! Happy to. I'll see you tomorrow."

"See you tomorrow."

Not quite sure what to do with myself, I get ready for bed, flip on the TV, and find something to watch. Being truly alone as things start to quiet down allows my mind to go haywire. It starts to spiral around the various scenarios of my MIA roommate, settling a tickle in my chest. I toss and turn in the new bed, trying to ease the tremble set in my bones.

Eventually, I settle in and fall asleep. My first night in college, and I'm ready for whatever tomorrow brings.

CHAPTER 3

The next morning, after breakfast at the diner, I return from a teary goodbye with my parents to find I still don't have a roommate. Anxiety bubbles in my stomach. I know there can be benefits to living alone, not having another person to worry about, but I hadn't expected it. So many people have told me that their roommate became a good friend. It tends to happen when you spend so much time together.

I'm sitting on my bed looking around the room, not really knowing what to do with myself, when Brittney appears in the doorway. "Knock-knock!"

"Hi, come on in!" Oops. That came off as overly excited.

Walking in, her brow knits together as she looks over at the bed on the opposite side of the room. "Still no sign of the roommate?"

I shake my head as I knot my fingers together, trying to quell the queasy feeling rising in my stomach. "Nope, nothing. I'm getting a little worried."

"Why? No roommate would be awesome! Think of all the guys you could have here. And you could push the beds together to make it even bigger. Oh, man, it would be awesome." A wistful look pulls at her features.

"Uh, guys?"

"Well, yeah, for sex?"

Heat rushes to my face as I try to burn holes into my comforter with my eyes. "I haven't had sex yet." It's an odd thing to say to a stranger; I'm aware of that, but I don't know how else to answer her.

Glancing up at her, I see her jaw hanging open, but she quickly recovers. "You haven't? Why? How? You're gorgeous! Aren't guys just lining up for a taste?"

I flinch at the crassness of her statement. I know enough about sex; Lauren has gone into more than enough detail for me, but it never fails to elicit a reaction, including a burning face. "Not really."

"Well then, all the boys from where you lived are stupid. I'm sure you're going to have a ton of guys interested in you here. But trust me, not having to worry about a roommate? It's perfect. You can bring boys back whenever you want."

"I don't think I'll be bringing back too many." Or any at all.

"We can work on that." She looks at the empty bed for a second. "OH! That reminds me. There are a lot of parties tonight. We should go to at least one!"

"A party?" My face scrunches into a grimace as trepidation starts to tingle through my extremities. I've gone to plenty, but I'm not a big fan of them, mostly sticking to the sidelines and watching.

"Yeah! There's always a ton of semester kick-off celebrations once everybody's moved in. They're usually pretty epic because classes haven't started yet, and everybody still has the money their parents gave them or put in their account to get things."

"I mean, I guess we could." Shrugging my shoulders, I

glance back at the ground. I don't want her to regret bringing me when she realizes how *not* fun I am.

"Wow, way to sound enthusiastic."

"Are you sure you want to take *me?* I'm not a huge party girl."

"Well, I can't change that if you don't come with me, can I?"

My light laugh fills the otherwise quiet room.

"What's so funny?" she asks as her eyes narrow at my snickering.

"Oh nothing, you sound just like my best friend back home is all." So much so that I almost think they've somehow done a soul switch. I flip my hand at her, a wave of sadness cresting over me as I miss Lauren.

"I'm sure she's awesome, then. You'll have to have her come visit at some point."

"She certainly plans to."

"Sounds like it'll be a super fun time, filled with alcohol and boys. Lots and lots of boys."

"I bet she would love that. She may come just for the boys, forget me and the alcohol."

"Definitely a girl after my own heart." Her hands fly to her chest, covering her left breast, as she laughs. "Okay, let's go get some lunch."

It's my first meal in the dining hall. Brittney shows me the ropes of the lines.

"This one's for the hot meal, which is on the menu we get in our mailboxes every month. The other one is for sandwiches and sometimes other cold items. It's also the one open for the midnight meal. That's really just the thing that opens a little after dinner most nights." She explains it all as we wait in line for our popcorn chicken and french fries.

Brittney does most of the talking while we eat, and I mostly stare at my plate.

People keep stopping by our table to talk to Brittney. It seems like she knows everybody. She's always kind enough to introduce me, especially to any guys that happen to come over.

After one particular pair of boys departs, she turns to me, eyes wide. "Did you see how Greg looked at you? He totally thinks you're hot!"

I roll my eyes as I pick apart a fry. "I hadn't noticed."

"Oh, Lexie, you need to pay more attention if you ever want to get laid."

"Who says I do?" My tone comes across a little more snarky than I intend it to. Boys just make me feel itchy in my own skin. I don't know why, never have, it's a discomfort I can't explain.

"So what, your plans involve staying celibate forever?"

"Well, no. But I'm not going to just have random sex."

"Why not? It's fun." Her eyebrows dance up and down as a wicked smile spreads across her face.

What's left of my fries gets the brunt of my discomfort as I decimate them, shaking my head. "You and Lauren will get along swimmingly."

She laughs a full belly laugh. At least she finds me amusing. "You'll have to have Lauren come sooner as opposed to later, then, so we can plot."

Despite how unsettled I am, I can't help but laugh in response, especially when she starts tapping her fingertips together.

Hitting the table, Brittney stands to grab her tray. "Come on, let's go back upstairs."

As we're walking up the stairs, Brittney has me cackling, doubling over and grabbing at my sides. She's going into great detail about an extremely embarrassing story of her being in the wrong class the year before and the verbal lashing she got from the professor for standing during her two-hundred-person lecture while all eyes were obviously on her.

"I swear I thought I was going to be known as the girl who

didn't–" She stops as we stand in front of my room, door open. There are bags and boxes all over the place. We look at each other, suddenly incredibly somber.

She juts her chin forward, and I walk in quietly. A girl I assume is my roommate, Kimberly, is by her closet, her back to me. At a loss for what to do next, I turn to Brittney, my arms raised in question. Pointing at the stranger, she mouths to me to greet her.

When I clear my throat, the girl stiffens and grunts. I'm slightly taken aback but try to brush it off as her being nervous.

"Hi, I'm Lexie, your roommate." She still doesn't turn around or acknowledge my presence. With desperation sprawled across my face, I glance over at Brittney for assistance when she just shrugs and shakes her head, eyes wide, looking almost as shocked as I am. With her ability to make anybody feel comfortable and talk to absolutely every-body, I'm hoping she can pave the road for me, so I desper-ately wave her in.

Hesitantly, she enters. "Hi. I'm Brittney. I live around the corner. This is my sophomore year here, so if you need anything, feel free to ask! Lexie's pretty cool, I think you guys will get along."

That's when the girl, who I'm still not sure is even Kimberly, turns to look at us. She looks back and forth between us before scoffing. "What are you, the Sluts Unite welcoming committee? 'Cause to me, you look like two girls who like to get on your knees."

My jaw drops as my stomach clenches. *That* is the first thing she chooses to say to me?

"Wow," Brittney exclaims it before I can. "Well, welcome." She turns to look at me. "Good luck with this one, Lexie. Dinner, then party, yeah?"

I nod, still stunned at the words of this rude girl. "Sure."

With Brittney gone, I'm not quite sure what to do, but I

hope that this girl, who hasn't been so kind as to share her name, will warm up. I decide I may as well try to make conversation as I hop on my bed. "Well, as I mentioned, I'm Lexie. I'm assuming you're Kimberly?"

Her long, wavy red hair swirls around her as she whips her head to look at me. "Wow, you're so brilliant." Her tone is anything but kind.

I'm not exactly sure what I've done to offend her. I have a hard time believing she's just this unhappy of a person. Not that I'm all rainbows and sunshine, but at least I'm not *mean*.

Maybe if I keep talking, it will make her feel more welcome. When I'm uneasy, I have a tendency to either say too much or nothing at all. Guess I'm going the word vomit route today. "I'm an education major with a concentration in English, probably part of why I read a lot." Waiting for some sort of response and getting none, I puff out a breath, not really sure what else to do or say. "I'm from downstate. How about you?"

She growls and looks at the ceiling before turning her angry green eyes on me. "Look, we're not going to do this whole '*get to know me, let's be best friends*' crap. We're here for school, and that's it. I have zero intention of being your friend. So, drop it, 'kay?"

My eyes almost bulge out of my sockets as my stomach free falls. She's certainly blunt. It must be why she never responded to my emails. She does *not* want to get to know me at all.

I decide to try again anyway. Maybe I'm a sucker for punishment, but it's going to be a long year, away from home, living together in a very small room. It'd be nice to at least be able to be *friendly*. "I wasn't sure if you were bringing a fridge or a TV, so I brought both, but you're welcome to use them, of course. I have some waters and sodas in there now, but I can take some stuff out if you need room."

Chewing the inside of my lip, I look around the room,

feeling awkward. "There's a party tonight somewhere that Brit mentioned. I'm sure you could come with us if you want to."

She flips around to look at me. "Look, I don't know what I have to say to get you to just leave me the fuck alone, but I don't want to talk to you. I don't want to be your friend. I don't want to party with you. I don't care what you do, how you do it. Just leave me alone and don't bring guys back while I'm here. And just so we're clear, I don't plan to leave much, so you may want to make other arrangements."

"Well, first of all–" The hatred seething from her stops me from continuing. Patting my thighs, I glance around, gaze settling on the door. "I'll let you unpack."

"Thank God," I hear her mutter as I walk out.

Not really being sure where to go or what to do, I walk around the corner to Brittney's room. She's sitting at her desk, scrolling on her computer. Her eyes flash up as I hesitantly tap on the doorframe.

"Didn't go so well, huh?" Her brows scrunch together.

"Uh, no. Can we go for a walk or something? I'd really rather not be in here and risk even running into her."

Closing her laptop, she quickly stands. "Sure, let's go. Do you have your ID and money? We can go to the campus center to get some coffee."

"No, but I'll grab it on our way out." I'm feeling defeated. Not the start of the relationship with my roommate that I was anticipating.

"Are you sure that's safe?" She's trying to make light of things.

"Ha, honestly, I'm *not* sure. But I'll have to find a way to live with it, right?"

"Unfortunately, yeah." When we're almost at the bottom of the stairwell, Brittney snorts. "I thought I had it bad with Nadia, but man, you have it *rough*." On the way down, I'd told her how Kimberly has made it exceptionally clear that she wants absolutely nothing to do with me and somehow seems even less thrilled with the set-up than I am.

We push through the doors into sunshine that melts away the ice that had settled over me upstairs. It's the very last weekend of August, and while we're so far upstate we can literally see Canada across the Great Lake, it's still a beautiful day. The sunshine feels warm and refreshing after the frigidness that exists in my dorm room. A smile naturally creeps its way across my face, realizing that I've already made a new friend.

CHAPTER 4

B rittney and I are walking arm in arm around the corner of one of the dorms, leaving Kimberly to unpack for a bit, when I bump right into a tall, solid wall of warmth, knocking books out of his arms.

"Ohmygod, I'm so sorry!" I stammer as I bend down to help him pick up his belongings. When I raise my eyes to look at him, my cheeks immediately heat as I tuck a lock of hair behind my ear. He's crouched down as well and is looking at me with piercing blue eyes, his sandy blond hair feathered across his forehead.

"It's alright. I don't mind being knocked into as long as it's by a pretty girl. So you're in luck." A brilliant pearly-white smile greets me. "I'm Liam."

"Hi, Liam. I'm Brit." Interjecting, she extends her hand down to shake Liam's. Though he closes his hand around hers, he doesn't take his eyes off of me.

"And you? What's your name?" His question is directed at me. Suddenly, it's hard to take a full breath as anxiety grips my ribs.

"Oh, sorry. I'm Alexis, Lexie, rather." I shake his

outstretched hand before I pass him some of the books I had knocked to the ground.

"Well, Lexie and Brit, it's nice to meet you. Where do you live?"

"We're just over in Hogan. How about you?" Brit is, of course, doing all the talking. In this moment, I am very appreciative of her outward personality as I'm sure I'd be a fish out of water.

"I'm right here, in Lafayette." He points at the building to our right.

"Ah, so you live in the suites. Nice." Brittney continues to speak for both of us. Thank God.

"Yeah. So, Lexie, I haven't seen you around campus before. What year are you?"

"I'm a freshman."

"Ah, interesting. How are you enjoying things so far?"

"Not too bad. Granted, we're only a few days in and classes haven't started yet. Ask me again in a few weeks and it may be a different answer." Did I just inadvertently suggest we talk again in a few weeks? And more so, did I actually put two coherent sentences together in front of a very good-looking guy?

"You finding everything okay?"

"I think so."

"I'm a senior, so I'd be happy to take you on a tour and show you where your classes will be."

"Oh, I don't–"

"She'd love that!" Brittney interrupts me. While I was planning to politely decline his offer, it seems Brittney has other plans for me.

"Awesome. How about tomorrow? I can meet you outside your dorm around one. Just bring your schedule so we know what buildings to walk to."

"Sounds great, Liam. She'll see you then. And I promise I won't tag along."

"Nice to meet you, ladies. Lexie, I'll see you tomorrow."
With a smile, he's off.

"Brit! What are you doing?" I spin on her before she can
start walking again.

"A super hot guy just offered to take you on a tour of
campus. You were about to say no. I made sure you didn't.
You're welcome." She has a giant smile plastered on her face.

"I don't want him to have to waste time giving me a tour. I
can find the buildings myself."

"Oh, Lexie, Lexie, Lexie. It's not about his time. Hell, it's
not even about showing you the buildings. He thinks you're
hot, which you are. Embrace it. Let him take you on a tour.
You told me you promised Lauren you'd meet some guys.
Now he may not be mister wonderful, he may not be your
future husband, he may even be a total bore, but at least you'll
be meeting somebody and spending time with a member of
the opposite sex *alone*. It's not a date, it's just walking around
campus. It's harmless. And who knows? Maybe you'll actually
end up liking him."

Though I roll my eyes, I can't deny that she's right. I *had*
told Lauren I'd meet some boys, and this does seem harmless
enough. It's just a tour around campus. And he's pretty nice to
look at, which will make it not as bad. Giving in, I sigh heavily.
"You're right. Thank you."

"Stick with me, kid. I'll have you hanging out with a
different guy every weekend." She puts her hands on my
shoulders as she talks.

"That's quite alright. I'll stick with the one for now."

"Hey, your loss is my gain."

Looping her arm through mine again, she drags me
toward the campus center.

AFTER WE GET BACK FROM GETTING COFFEE, IT SEEMS LIKE everybody is out in the hallway or standing just inside their doors. It's packed. And loud.

"Everybody's trying to get to know each other, I bet," Brittney says next to me.

Within a few minutes, we're standing in the hallway, making conversation with Steve and Lucas, some neighbors of mine, Brittney doing most of the talking, of course.

Everything freezes as I see him walking down the hallway. It's the RA from move-in day, the one who towered above everybody else.

I quickly close my mouth, hoping nobody noticed my jaw was on the floor a second ago.

"That's Josh Roberts. We call him the hot RA," Brittney whispers in my ear.

Tall, dark, and handsome is a phrase invented for a guy like Josh Roberts, whose shaggy, chocolate hair curtains his eyes that appear to be a hint lighter than obsidian. Taking him in now, he still stands inches above everybody in the hallway. His shirt fits so perfectly that you can see the ridges of muscles in his shoulders and chest. My brain almost can't comprehend the gorgeousness as I continue to stare like a love-struck puppy. Heads turn to look at him down the hall. He either doesn't notice or doesn't care. Looking like he does, he's probably used to it.

"I can see why you call him that," I mumble, still unable to tear my eyes from him. That is, of course, until he lifts his gaze from the clipboard in his hand and looks right at me. I quickly turn away, heat rising to my hairline, but not before I notice a lopsided smirk on his face.

I try to pay attention to what Brittney is saying next to me, but I just can't help stealing another glance at the gorgeous man just a few feet away from me. When I look over, I'm stunned to find that his eyes are still fixed on me.

"I'm going to go back to my room." I'm not sure what else

to do aside from fall over from embarrassment. He noticed me staring, likely with a wide-open mouth and drool pooling in the corners.

Once back in the safety of my room, I turn on some music, low, so as to be able to overhear some conversation out in the hall, and start reading a book.

"Good song." I jump, dropping my book to the floor. Turning toward the deep voice, I find none other than Josh Roberts, standing in my doorway, clipboard in hand.

"Oh, yeah, it is."

"You ever see them live? It's an awesome show."

"No, but that sounds amazing!" That came out a little too excited and giddy. I try to take an unnoticeable deep breath to steady myself and my racing heart. My awkwardness is showing in vibrant colors, and I need to tone it down.

"It really is. I'm Josh, by the way. I'm the RA down the hall. I know Julie's right next door, but if she's ever not around and you need anything, feel free to come knock on my door."

"Lexie, and thanks."

With one hand holding on to the top of the doorframe, his arm bent sharply at the elbow, he leans into my room, smiling widely as he juts his chin toward my desk. "You got a lot of books there."

I'm suddenly a furnace, and a bead of sweat drips down my back. Yup, a hot guy making me nervous. No surprise there. "Yeah, I like to read a lot."

"On top of the reading for class?"

"Yeah? I mean, I'm not sure, I haven't really had to read for class yet."

"You may not like it as much once classes start."

I shrug, not sure what else to do with myself. "Maybe. I'm often guilty of reading for pleasure instead of for class. At least I did in high school. Though I guess the stakes are a bit higher here."

"What's your major?"

"Education. With a focus on English."

"Ah, hence the books. I'm an education major too." My shocked expression must have been quite noticeable, despite my attempt to hide it, as Josh lets out a low chuckle. "I know you don't often meet a lot of male educators. But I worked a few summers as a camp counselor and spent a semester tutoring students at the elementary school, and I enjoyed it. Figured I may as well do something I enjoy."

"I think that's really respectable. Schools definitely need more strong male teachers."

"Thank you." He shifts on his feet slightly, almost like I made him uncomfortable.

"What's your focus?" This is the longest I've ever held a conversation with a man I just met. Or really any person in general where I actually participated and they didn't do the lion's share of the talking.

"Math."

"Ah, see that's where you lose me."

"Not a math person?"

I giggle. "Not at all."

"See, there ya go. I'm not really an English person. I enjoy a good book here and there, but not like what I hear the classes and teaching are like. Plus, all those old books...not for me."

"Okay, well, now you're just dissing the classics." I'm truly shocked at the ease of this conversation. Never once have I been able to so seamlessly talk to a member of the opposite sex for this long without putting my foot in my mouth.

"They're just so old and out of touch."

"They're classics for a reason though."

Josh smirks as he glances at the ground before resting his gaze on me. "You sure you don't want to go to law school?"

"Trust me, you're not the first person to ask me that. But I've wanted to be a teacher for as long as I can remember."

He nods as I hear somebody call his name out in the hallway. "Well, Lexie, I need to be moving on." Tapping the door-frame, he slowly stands up straight. "Let me know if you'd be interested in hearing some more bands like that one. See you around."

"Yeah, see you," I say breathlessly. The thrumming in my ears tells me my heart is still racing, but I can't even feel it anymore.

"Were you just talking to Josh?" Brit pokes her head in.

"Yeah."

"Oh my God, what is he like? I mean, I know a little from what I've heard, but I haven't been lucky enough to get more than a 'hi' here or there." Moving farther into my room, she leans back against the door.

"He liked the song I had on, said they were a good band. We talked about school a little, he's also an ed major. That's really it." I want to keep the part about him offering to show me more music to myself. Though I'm not sure why, aside from thinking Brittney will pressure me into trying to find more time immediately.

"Did he offer to tutor you?"

My brow pinches together. "Did he what? No. Why would he do that?"

She giggles a little. "Oh, nothing. Not sure your virginal ears can handle it."

I'm regretting having let that tiny detail slip. Especially when she decided her new mission is to take me to as many parties as she can to make sure I meet some boys in the process. She hopes to take Lauren's place as my bad influence. "Just tell me."

"Well, he has a bit of a reputation. He says he'll tutor you, usually in Italian, but really, he fucks you. And from what I hear, he's damn good at it." Leaning forward as she says it, it's almost as if she thinks she's sharing some huge secret instead of what sounds like, at the very least, dorm gossip.

My face is now burning hot. I'm sure if I looked in the mirror, I'd closely resemble a tomato with dark curly hair.

"See, told you, you can't handle it."

"I'm fine, I'm just surprised he'd do something like that."

"Why? Have you seen him? He's *gorgeous*. He could have any girl he wants. Why not have those he does?"

"I don't know. It just doesn't seem professional."

"Lexie, he's an RA. He's not a professor or something. And trust me, that happens too."

"I know, it's just... he lives in the same building. Isn't that awkward?" I feel awkward just talking about it.

She shrugs, looking flippant. "Only if you let it be. If everybody has fun, who cares?"

"I guess." I look down at my desk. "Just not my thing."

"I'm aware." She chuckles lightly. "I'll see ya later. We'll get dinner."

And just like that, she's off, floating down the hallway again.

I'm not sure how I feel about everything that just transpired. Josh had been friendly. Was he expecting me to want to *study* with him at some point? Was he laying some groundwork, saying hi, being friendly, to invite me to come down in the future so he could get my pants off? That is certainly *not* the sort of attention I'm trying to find at school, especially not in the first week. Not wanting to end up in the bed of somebody who will push me aside the next day, I decide it's best to avoid Josh Roberts.

―――――――

AT DINNER, BRITTNEY CONVINCES ME TO GO TO THE PARTY. Aside from being able to make conversation with anybody, which I'm pretty sure also includes a wall, she's also exceptionally good at convincing you to do something you don't want to do.

"Haven't you ever been to a party? I mean, come on, Lexie!" She's sitting on my bed as I stand by my closet.

"Of course, I have, but this is a college party. There are different...expectations." The nerves for the start of school haven't ceased. If anything, they ebb and flow, getting much higher when things like parties and hot guys possibly wanting me for sex arise.

She waves me off. "No such thing. Dress hot, that's all you need to know. Any short skirts?"

"I'm not wearing a short skirt to my first college party." Kimberly laughs behind me, and I do my best to ignore her.

"Okay, tight jeans?"

"Why do they need to be tight?"

"Really? Are you really asking me that question?" She sounds exasperated.

I sigh, just as exasperated with her. "I'm not having sex with anybody, Brittney."

"Just because you're not going to doesn't mean you don't want the boys to want to. Just trust me, would ya?" Walking over to my closet, she starts pushing things aside, wrinkling her nose at a few articles of clothing. Smiling, she pulls out a pair of light-wash skinny jeans and a low-cut dark teal tank top.

Lauren had given it to me as a farewell present, saying, *"Your boobs would look awesome in this shirt. Every guy would be drooling."*

Certain I'd left it behind, since I have no plans to actually wear it anywhere, I'm not even sure how it ended up being packed. I'm convinced Lauren stowed it in a bag somewhere before we parted ways. "Brit, no."

"Um, one hundred percent yes. Are you kidding? This outfit with your curls hanging down? The guys will be lining up. Listen, babe, you don't need to do anything with them. But you're in a good position if they want you."

"What if I don't want them to want me?" I wouldn't even

know what to do if somebody *did* want me. It's just easier to
steer clear.

"You do."

"I don't."

"Yes. You do. Just get dressed. Please?"

With a growl, I yank the outfit from her grasp. "Fine," I
say as I turn around to get dressed. There really isn't
anywhere I can go for privacy. The bathrooms don't give
much space to change. I've always been self-conscious in front
of other people; even girls. Brittney has no shame, tearing her
clothes off in front of me, with the door barely even shut. I'm
much more uncomfortable with Kimberly also being here.

Fully dressed, I spin back around. "There, happy?"

"Damn, you look *hot*. I'll get guys talking to me just so they
can get a close look at you. Damn." I have no idea what she's
talking about. Brittney is definitely extremely pretty in her
own right. Tonight, her blonde hair falls in a straight sheet
down her back and her glittery eye make-up draws attention
to her blue eyes.

I turn and stand on my toes to look in the mirror. My curls
are looking great, and the shirt does compliment my coloring
nicely. As usual, Lauren knew better than me, though her
motives were questionable. I'd let Brittney do my make-up
earlier. She had said the deep hue, while subtle, would accen-
tuate the dark brown of my eyes.

The overall look is surprisingly acceptable, and even a bit
pleasing. "Okay, so where is this party? I don't have a fake ID
or anything, so I sincerely hope that won't be an issue."

Brittney huffs at me, like it's the craziest thing she's ever
heard. "Please. It's college. If you need a fake ID, you're in the
wrong place." She waves her hand in the air. "It's an off-
campus house. We could just walk down some of the more
prominently college housing streets and pop into any house,
but this one's a yearly tradition. From what I was told, last

year, it's actually a townie that started it when he went here. He still owns the house but rents it out to students because it was like ten years ago and it'd be kinda pervy if he was still around. But they've all kept up with hosting."

When we get there, I can immediately see she's right. There are people crammed together inside the house, which is surprisingly large for a student residence. We push our way through the throng to get to the kitchen where the drinks are.

"It's nice enough out now that some people will be outside. Come winter, it's worse," Brittney yells against my ear. We can barely hear each other over the music and voices.

Once we get into the kitchen, it's a bit quieter. She walks over to the keg and fills two cups, handing me one.

"Cheers to your first college party," she says as she bumps her cup into mine. Tipping her head back, she drains half of the liquid.

I take it a little slower, taking a few small sips.

We walk around talking to people Brittney knows. Standing behind her, I look on as she happily entertains half the men's lacrosse team. She'd been right; I feel the tingle of a *lot* of eyes on me. Thankfully, nobody is brave enough to talk to me, aside from those in the group Brittney's chatting with.

I lean into her ear. "I'll be right back. Need more." Shaking my empty cup at her, I point to the kitchen, in case she didn't hear me.

She glances back at me. "Will you be okay on your own?"

Since I've already stepped away from her, I nod at her.

Pushing my way through the crowd, I try not to step on anybody or get stepped on. Turning the corner to a small alcove that leads into the kitchen, I bump into something hard but warm. It's a chest. Josh Roberts', to be exact. So much for avoiding him.

His dark eyes sear into me as he takes a slow sip from his red cup, gaze drifting slowly over my body. "Lexie."

Chills run down my spine as he utters my name disdainfully.

"Hi, Josh." I try to make my voice sound steady, but it comes out choked and much more meek than I was hoping for.

"I see you're getting your feet wet already."

"Yeah, thanks to Brittney. She's around here somewhere."

He nods, his penetrating eyes never leaving mine. Uncomfortable under his gaze, I fidget with my shirt. "Did you need something or…?" His voice holds nothing but irritation.

"Oh, no. I just…was saying hi, I guess. I'm on my way to get a refill when we bumped into each other. I just thought maybe…" What had I thought? He'd been so nice when we had met earlier. I guess I'd been thinking he'd be friendly and make conversation. But he seems to want absolutely nothing to do with me.

"I'm not your RA here, Lexie, so I'm not sure if you were hoping for me to hold your hand to get you through this party, but that's not going to happen. In fact, don't expect me to do much for you. I like my residents to bother me as little as possible, and those who aren't my residents, to not bother me at all."

The shock of his words almost stings against my skin. "Well, okay, then. I'll be off. See you around." Pushing past Josh, my shoulder grazes his arm, electricity shooting through me.

"That shirt looks good on you," he murmurs, finger trailing down my back, just as my body passes by his. My heart hammers at his words and touch.

I whip around to look at him, but he's walking away, already lost in the crowd. Deciding it's a lost cause, I finish my trip into the kitchen to refill my cup.

When I get back to Brittney's side, I've already finished half my drink. "What happened to you? You were gone for ages."

"Long line," I lie. The sensation of eyes boring into my back causes me to turn around to find Josh glaring at me again. One thing is for sure, Josh Roberts is the king of mixed signals.

CHAPTER 5

The next morning, anxiety is rippling through me, causing me an inability to keep still. To get the nervous energy out, I pace around my room. It doesn't help that I still have a slight headache—even after some aspirin—thanks to the previous night's festivities.

"What is *your* problem?" Kimberly barks at me.

I roll my eyes. "Nothing."

"Well, could you stop then? It's annoying."

All I can do is sigh. Kimberly is anything but a pleasant roommate.

"Sure thing." I sit at my desk, but I'm unable to concentrate on anything, my leg jiggling as I get a side-eye stare from Kimberly. Growling, I stand to leave. "I'll just go down to Brittney's room then."

"Finally," she mumbles under her breath.

I close the door a little harder than necessary. Rounding the corner to Brittney's room, I see the door is wide open.

"Lexie!" she squeals when she sees me. Way too much excitement for me at this very moment. Though she acts like she hasn't seen me in days, it's only been a few hours since we parted ways after brunch.

"Brit," I whine as I shuffle into her room.

"No. You are going. You are taking a walk around this gorgeous campus with a gorgeous boy. If you hate him after that, fine. But you're at least taking the chance." I grumble in response. She points one finger at me and very quietly says, "I will call Lauren on you."

I hold up my hands in surrender. "Okay, okay, I'll go." I know she'd call Lauren. And calling her means she'll show up and drag me around campus, talking to every guy even remotely good-looking, and introducing me as her virgin friend, who has an unleashed crazy sex drive that just needs the right guy. She'd informed me of all the things she'd say and explain in-depth after I told her about my fears.

"Good." Her tone has changed to a more tender note. "Come on, Lexie, what have you got to lose? He's handsome and appears sweet. It's one in the afternoon and you'll be outside walking around campus. He's not going to try anything during the day, in public. And if he invites you in after, just say no if you don't want to go. Maybe it will be awful and uncomfortable, and he'll be terrible company. Or maybe, just maybe, you'll actually like him. You could certainly do worse."

"You're right. I just, I'm missing the gene that you and Lauren seem to have. The one that just makes you feel comfortable and carefree around guys." I've pushed myself up onto her bed and am swinging my feet, eyes trained on them as they move forward and backward.

"It's not a gene, babe. It's confidence." A quick turn of the magazine page in front of Brittney draws my attention momentarily.

"Well, whatever it is, I'm missing it."

"I don't understand how. You're hot. You're also oblivious, but you're hot." She waves a hand down my body.

"How am I oblivious?"

"Do you not see how guys look at you? How they give you

a quick once-over? Did you not see *all* those guys last night who were ogling you?" Flipping the magazine shut, Brittney looks at me intently.

"No, they don't. They weren't." There's one who comes to mind, but he's clearly not interested in me. I pick at invisible lint on my jeans, feeling uncomfortable.

"They do. They absolutely do. With your dark coiled hair and your chocolate eyes? Not to mention you have an awesome ass."

I raise my eyebrows at her. "You sure you're into guys?"

She shrugs hopelessly. "I'm sure, but I can tell sexy when I see it. And you, Lexie, are sexy. You just need to embrace it. You have a rack others would kill for. Hell, I'd kill for your hair. I can't even get mine half as curly with a wand or iron. And here you are, perfect dark curls with a hint of copper in the right light, and you don't appreciate the appeal they have on men. Or any of your fine *ass*ets."

Glancing down at my knotted fingers, which rest against my thighs, I'm not sure how to respond.

"Confidence, Lexie. It's attractive. At least pretend. Wear your favorite pair of jeans and a top you feel good in. Maybe not something that makes you feel sexy, but something that you feel good in."

"So I can wear sweatpants?" Looking at her, I raise an eyebrow. I'm only sort of teasing.

One corner of her mouth tips down as she locks her gaze on mine. "You know what I mean."

"Yeah, I do. I'm just nervous. It's been a crazy few days."

"Ah, but you've met me and that's all you need." Smiling warmly, she puts her hands under her chin.

"That's true." Brittney and I only met a couple days ago, but it feels like we've been friends for years. It's probably because she reminds me so much of Lauren. They are so similar, from their outlook on life, and guys down to tiny mannerisms. They even look alike. I'm slightly convinced they're long-

47

lost sisters or at least distant relatives. "Can I hang out here for a bit?"

"Kimberly driving you nuts?"

"Of course, she is."

"It's been two days and she hasn't changed at all?"

"Nope. I swear my very existence makes her contemplate murder."

She shakes her head. "I'm not sure what she was expecting. I mean it's college. You get a roommate."

"I guess she applied for a single? I didn't even know they had those." I'd been able to get very few details out of her in one short-lived exchange.

"So, so few. One dorm in mid-campus has singles. But only like fifteen or something crazy. Mostly if you want to be a single, you become an RA, junior year."

"Unfortunately, until then, I'm stuck with her." My insides twist, thinking about how long that will be.

"Nadia's not great, but at least she's rarely here."

"Yeah, where is she? It's noon on a Sunday." In the three days I've known Brittney, I have yet to meet her roommate. And we spend a lot of time together.

"The gym. Then she was going to go to her boyfriend's."

"Well, either way, she's not here and you're lucky."

"When she's not here, I am. When she is, it's not so pleasant. She's by no means as bad as Kimberly, but certainly not somebody I'll be keeping in touch with after this." Brittney picks up a pen and starts twirling it between her fingers.

"Why didn't you room with a field hockey buddy?"

"I like them well enough as teammates, but I don't really want to room with any of them. I figured a stranger was fine. It worked out well enough for me last year. I actually had a pretty good roommate; we were friendly enough, did a few things together. But she decided not to come back this year." Disappointment coats her words at the memory. She huffs a tendril of hair off her forehead before shrugging.

"I gotta say I'm super thankful for you. If we hadn't met, I don't know what I'd do."

A wide smile crosses her face. "You'd have to hunt all those good-looking guys on your own." Turning away from me, she looks at the clock on her computer. "Want to grab a bite before you go meet Liam?"

Just his name sends anxiety rippling through my body. "I don't know if I can eat."

"Then, you can keep me company while I eat." She hops up from her chair and slides on her slippers, grabbing my arm and pulling me out the door.

AN HOUR LATER, I WALK DOWNSTAIRS, SMOOTHING MY SHIRT and taking a deep breath before heading through the double doors. Liam is standing by a tree just outside the dorm, and he turns around as the door shuts behind me, a smile slowly spreading across his face.

It makes me smile in return as butterflies take flight in my chest, and I look down at my shoes, tucking some hair behind my ear.

He takes a step closer. "You ready?"

Pulling my schedule out of my back pocket, I hold it up. "Yup!" Though I try to keep my voice level, I hear the tiny crack in it, and hope it doesn't show the nerves ready to burst out of me.

I fall into step next to him. He stays close enough that every so often, his arm grazes mine and his citrus-scented cologne wafts into my nose. My whole body is tense and tight, but his smile and the lilt of his voice make my muscles start to loosen within minutes.

I'm thankful he takes charge of the conversation, diving right into talking about the campus. Trying hard to focus on what he's saying—and not the thumping of my heartbeat in

49

my ears or what to do with my hands—takes a lot of concentration.

So far, I'm eternally grateful his questions mostly only require one-word answers, because I'm not sure I'm listening well enough to give detail.

As we get to the quad, Liam slows. "Most of the buildings for your classes are going to be here."

Holding his hand out, I take a minute to grasp what he's asking for. "May I?" When I do, I pass him my schedule. He shows me each building I'll need, tells me some funny anecdotes about some of the teachers he'd had or interesting lectures he sat through.

"One class, a buddy of mine brought a metal water bottle. Doesn't seem like a big deal, right? Need to stay hydrated. So, we were about halfway through class when he sneezed and knocked the water bottle off his desk. It bounced down the amphitheater steps, which are concrete, and made such a loud noise the whole way down. It was almost like slow-mo because it rolled until it reached the next step down. We didn't get back into the lesson after that. And my buddy started bringing both plastic waters and leaving it in his bag on the floor."

Covering my mouth with my hand, I giggle at his story. My body is almost completely relaxed and I'm feeling at ease. While Liam still doesn't require too much input from me, I'm only slightly worried about saying the wrong thing. He has a kind of calming effect on me.

As we move through campus, his stories change as he points out various spots on campus where he or his friends had interesting things happen. "And that plant over there? That's where I puked after my first big dorm party over in the lake dorms. Tequila can be a bitch."

We walk around most of campus, going beyond where the majority of my classes are, ditching the schedule halfway through. I mostly listen to his stories about classes and friends, about the memories he's made so far. Excitement builds within

me as I hope to make my own memories to share with somebody one day.

Liam walks me to the farthest classroom building on
campus, explaining as an ed major, most of my classes will
end up in this building at some point.

Glancing up at it, I'm finding myself very okay with that.
It's beautiful, with large pillars by the entrance and a clock
tower at the top. Many of the other buildings are basic
concrete squares or rectangles. But this one has much more
character.

"Alright. I'm sorry. I got distracted from showing you your
buildings and got into details about myself. Let's make sure
we've covered everything."

As I pull out my schedule, he steps behind me to peer over
my shoulder. He's close enough that I can feel his breath on
my neck. It makes me shiver slightly, but surprisingly, I don't
feel uncomfortable or awkward.

"I see you have a class in the satellite building. How'd you
swing that? They don't usually allow freshmen to take classes
there."

"I was able to place out of a class from some high school
credits and internship type work. I had to write an essay about
what I learned." I fiddle with my paper in my hands as he
moves to stand in front of me again.

"Oh, so you're some sort of genius then?" It sounds like
he's playfully teasing me, and he does have a smile on his face,
but I'm not entirely sure.

"I wouldn't say that. I just know what I want to be. I took
the course and the internship on purpose. I wasn't sure the
credits would transfer as anything more than just some generic
credits, but when I spoke to the class advisors, they mentioned
the class and paper. It was up to the ed department, though. I
guess they felt I learned enough to place out." Lifting my
shoulders, I try to seem confident, but any time I think about
classes starting, my stomach drops.

"Did you?"

"I don't really know. We haven't started classes yet." And that one class has me in knots with worry. What if I didn't learn enough?

He nods next to me, a smile sweeping his face. "Pretty and smart."

Heat rushes to the nape of my neck as I look down and tuck some hair behind my ear.

"You don't take compliments well, do you?"

"I have been told that I don't." I'm not sure how he would know this after a day except for the clearly nervous habit I just exhibited.

A small chuckle releases from his chest. "Hey, how about dinner? I'll take you somewhere off campus."

For what feels like eternity, but is likely only a few seconds, I stare at him, mouth agape. I wasn't expecting him to ask me out. Maybe to his room, but not dinner. I'd been so worried before meeting him, but things have gone so smoothly, and he's made me feel comfortable enough. "Yeah, dinner would be nice." Fisting my hand, I stop it from flying to my mouth. I'm not sure I fully thought it through before answering.

Liam's smile spreads farther, showing off a set of perfectly straight, white teeth. "Let me walk you back over to the dorms. It's a little early for dinner. Can I pick you up around five?"

"Yeah, five sounds good." *What* did I just agree to? I suddenly feel like I can't catch my breath and my lungs are being squeezed.

As we walk back across campus, he helps fill in the gaps looming in the conversation.

"Tell me about your family."

"Um, I have my parents, who've been married for twenty-five years. But I'm an only child. My best friend, Lauren, she's like a sister, which is nice. We've been friends for fifteen years. It was really hard leaving her, since we've seen each other basically every day for most of our lives. She was concerned for me and—" I stop short, realizing I'm rambling. Maybe I'm not as comfortable as I think. Clearing my throat, I turn it back to him. "How about you?"

Hands in his pockets, he turns to me, chuckling lowly at my abrupt pause. "I have three older brothers."

My eyebrows fly up to my hairline.

"Yeah, things could get, uh, intense, in my house when we were growing up. Punches have definitely been thrown. My oldest two, Paul and Steve, they got into it *bad* one year over some girl. I don't really remember too much, but there were black eyes and holes in walls involved. My parents both lost their shit. Took their cars, phones, and computers away." He shakes his head at the memory.

"That certainly sounds like something. The best part of not having siblings was not having to be stuck in a house with somebody you were fighting with. But it was lonely."

"I was certainly never lonely. At least not until Mike, the brother closest in age, left for college. Then it was just me. The quiet was really weird and hard to get used to." There's a far off look in his eyes when I glance over at him, but he quickly shakes it away.

I just nod, not really sure what to say, my awkwardness around boys showing tremendously right now, though I'm happy it's the first time it's shown this afternoon. Thankfully, the doors to my building are only a few feet away.

As we stand in front of my dorm, he puts his hand on my lower back, causing my heart to jackhammer. "I'll see you at five. I'm looking forward to it."

"Me too." I smile at him as he turns to walk away. Suddenly, my nerves are back full force as I run into the dorm and up the stairs, taking them two at a time to the fourth floor.

By the time I get to Brittney's door, I'm panting a little. "Brit," I say, hand against the door frame for support.

She hops off her bed, looking concerned, and walks over

to me slowly. "You okay? Everything okay? You were gone for a while."

Still out of breath, I lift my face up to meet hers. "He asked me out on a date." It comes out just above a whisper.

She throws her head back in laughter. When she finally calms down, she tilts her face back to mine, wiping tears from her eyes. "Oh, man, you had me there for a minute. I take it you had a nice time?"

My heart rate has returned to normal, but I still feel like I can't breathe, so I walk in and sit on her bed. "We did. And he asked me out to dinner. And I said yes. What the *hell* was I thinking? I can't go to dinner with him!"

"And why not?"

"Well…because!"

"That's not a reason." Her voice is too calm for my liking in this very *not* okay situation.

"What if he expects something?"

"What if all he expects is a nice dinner with you?"

I stare at her incredulously. "Do you really think after a tour of campus and then dinner, he won't expect anything from me?"

She looks at me like I have no idea how human interaction works. "I'm not sure where you get these ideas that *all* guys at college are morally corrupt and are only after sex, but that's not how it is. Yes, there are many. But not all."

"And what if he's just one of the many?"

"Then he's one of the many. But that doesn't mean anything has to happen. He can have all the expectations he wants. That doesn't mean something will or has to happen. You can have a perfectly nice dinner and decline his invitation upstairs. Don't invite him to your room. You can back away from a kiss if you so choose to. But maybe you'll go on the date and see that he's a nice guy who just wants the pleasure of your neurotic company."

I throw a pillow at her but smile a little. "I'm not neurotic,"

I mumble under my breath. The truth is I know I am. It doesn't matter that Liam and I have already had a relatively nice time together. I'm sure the next won't be the same.

"Just be yourself. You're friendly and smart. We've been able to get to know each other in less than a week. Granted, we spend the majority of our time together, but still. He clearly saw something he liked in you during the tour. Even if he does just like your looks, who cares? Get a free meal out of it and see how it goes."

"Do I change? Should I not be wearing the same thing?" I've never really dated before. I don't know how it works.

After giving me a quick once-over, she shrugs. "Maybe change your shirt?"

I run a hand through my hair, groaning. "Why does this have to be so hard?"

"It doesn't. You're making it that way. It's *just* dinner. Have you really never been on a date before?" Her eyes narrow as she holds a pen between her fingers.

I just stare at her.

"Really? Never?"

I shake my head, tightlipped. "I mean, I've gone on what I guess would be double dates with Lauren, but that was really more something she planned. Not something where the guy was interested in me and asked me on a date."

Her shoulder quirks up. "First time for everything. You get to pop your dating cherry tonight." She laughs as I roll my eyes. She and Lauren are like two peas in a pod.

A memory from last night slams into the forefront of my mind. I'd let Lauren and Brittney talk. I had drunk dialed Lauren, telling her I'd made a friend she'd like because she wanted to fill my life with debauchery just like Lauren had. She insisted I let them talk and, in my inebriated state, I let it happen.

Eyes wide, I turn to Brittney. "You talked to Lauren last night."

She bursts out laughing and falls back onto her bed. "I did. You forgot?"

I nod slowly, too shocked for my eyes to return to their normal size.

She sits up, wiping tears from her eyes. "Oh, yes. We had a long talk about all the ways I need to add fun to your life and all that I need to be sure to expose you to. We came up with some grand schemes."

"I hope nothing you actually expect me to follow through with."

She softens. "Or maybe you can just trust that your best friend knows you and told me to treat you like a timid animal. She was excited you were allowing yourself to go on the tour today. You should probably let her know about dinner."

Grumbling, I sink my head into my hands. "Ugh, dinner."

Brittney is suddenly standing in front of me, shaking my shoulders. "Come on, it'll be great! Here, think of it this way. It will give you extra time away from Kimberly."

At that, I perk up. "Well, that is a nice benefit at least."

"See? If you look at it positively, it will be great."

"But what do I *say*?"

"Just be you! I know you won't believe me, but you're actually a pretty cool person. You're honest and you speak your mind. Run with it. Maybe he'll carry the conversation. Let him fill in the gaps. Change the subject if it becomes uncomfortable, be honest if you don't know about something, and don't try to lie. If he brings up, I don't know, football? Don't be all: '*Oh yeah, I love football, especially when the goalie scores a homerun.*' He'll probably just want to get to know you."

I sigh. "Okay. I guess I can do that."

"Atta girl."

I roll my eyes and we both start laughing. Taking a deep breath, I shake out my arms. "Okay. I'm going to go get ready, maybe read to relax a little. If it's really awful, can I call you or something?"

"How about this, if it's awful, text me, and I'll find a reason to call you to get you out."

"What should I text?" I shouldn't feel excited at the possibility of an out.

"Whatever you want. But try to give him a chance before you decide you're going to hate it. You had a good enough time on the tour to agree to go."

"True. But what if he was good then and won't be at dinner?"

"Then he's not. Maybe he's a small doses kind of guy."

"A what?"

"A small doses guy. Maybe he's only good in short increments of time. Dinner may be too long."

I nod, shaking my whole body. "Okay, I'm going to go. I'll see you later? Or tomorrow?"

"Text me when you get back, see if I'm still up."

"Okay. See you later, then."

"Good luck!" she says as I walk out. "Oh, and, Lexie?" I poke my head back in her room. "Don't do anything I wouldn't do," she says with a wink.

CHAPTER 6

That Wednesday, after my first day of classes, I'm down in the laundry room, distracted, thinking about my date with Liam a few nights before. It turned out to be a really nice date. He made me feel at ease, and his smile was both infectious and left a warmth spreading through my chest every time he flashed it my way.

I'm replaying our conversation about our interests and hobbies. Liam was surprised when I told him I read *a lot*, saying he just doesn't understand people who read on top of schoolwork.

The slamming of a laundry basket pulls me out of my reverie and causes me to jump.

I whip around at the noise and find Josh standing near one of the tables, his glare searing through me. Three different colored sets of sheets sit in his laundry basket.

He glides up beside me as I try to push out the thoughts of why he might be washing his sheets after only a few days. Classes only started today; is he already *studying* with somebody? Or somebodies?

"Lisa."

I flip to look at him. "It's *Lexie*." He knows my name. He'd said it at the party the other night. At least his voice isn't dripping with disdain this time.

"Oh, right, my mistake." There it is. I'm not exactly sure what I've done to make him dislike me so much. We've barely spoken. And that first time, he'd seemed so nice.

Maybe it's me, since I get it from both Josh and Kimberly. I've barely interacted with either of them.

I put a few things in the washer, with Josh standing so close I can smell the muskiness of his cologne, making my heart rate increase. I'm usually almost mute around guys, but for some reason, he fills me with a combination of rage and something I can't put my finger on. It makes me want to call him out.

I turn to him. "You know what, no. It's not a mistake. You know my name. You said it at the party the other night."

"The party?" Is he playing dumb? Or does he actually not remember? "Yeah, the one where you said my shirt looked good?"

A slight blush coats his cheeks. So…he *does* remember.

"I guess I forgot between then and now." His voice is lower and less confident.

I roll my eyes. "Sure, okay."

As I'm angrily throwing clothes into the washer, I can feel his gaze on me. It's the same prickling sensation I felt the other day in the hallway. I'm not sure if he's playing some sort of game with me. Spinning on my heels to look at him, I raise my eyebrows. "Can I help you?" I ask him rudely.

"Are you mad at your clothes or something? You seem to be taking your anger out on them."

"Nope, I'm perfectly fine," I say as I slam the door shut. I put in my detergent and pull the quarters out of my pocket. My mom had been shocked the laundry is still run by quarters and not somehow linked to our IDs.

As I'm filling the slots, I notice I'm a quarter short. Confident I had grabbed five, I frantically search my pockets, when

Josh holds one up in front of me and places it in the empty slot, pushing the drawer in as the washer comes to life.

I'm not sure why he's helping me, and I fight the heat burning inside me at my embarrassment. "Thank you, you didn't have to do that," I mumble.

"Not a problem." Is he being nice now? Or does he just feel bad for the poor freshman who didn't bring enough money to wash her clothes? He's leaning back against his own washer, arms crossed over his broad chest. I'm not sure if he's expecting more out of the conversation or just wants to make me squirm some more.

"Okay, well thanks again." I slowly start walking away to see if Josh says anything or comes to walk upstairs with me. As I get to the doorway and realize he's doing neither, I turn back to look at him. His eyes are trained on me, muscles in his arms taut. It sends shivers down my spine.

I take the stairs two at a time, seeking solace in my room. Pulling out my book, I wait to head back down to the laundry room, mentally preparing myself to see Josh again.

AN HOUR LATER, I MAKE MY WAY TO THE LAUNDRY ROOM TO put my clothes in the dryer. I was warned at orientation to get down there as soon as it's done, or clothes could end up on the floor as other people don't want to have to wait.

But as I walk in, I notice my clothes aren't in the washer where I'd left them, a new load started with something bright red and sparkly spinning around, which is not anything I own.

"You weren't here, and somebody needed the washer, so I tossed your stuff in the dryer." Josh is suddenly right behind me, his voice low and gravelly, close to my ear. Normally, I'd be jittery, so close to such an attractive guy. So why, instead, am I imagining him putting his hands on my waist?

Flipping around to face him, I notice exactly how close

he's standing. "Thank you." My voice comes out low, but I'm proud of myself that there's no tremble to it.

"You're welcome." While he's several inches taller than me —definitely at least six foot compared to my five foot five— he's close enough for me to smell the mintiness on his breath. I have a strange urge to taste it.

We stand there for what feels like an eternity, but is more likely only seconds, before Josh clears his throat and takes a few steps back. The second he's out of my bubble, I immediately wish he'd come back.

"You have to make sure you get down here in time. Your clothes could have ended up on the floor." There's a cutting edge to his voice that wasn't there a few moments ago.

"Sorry, I got distracted." Now that he's out of my personal space and not distracting my senses, it registers that he moved my clothes. I'm immediately thankful it was just some pants, shirts, and washcloths, and no intimates.

"Don't let it happen again. I won't always be here to save your clothes."

"Right. Well, thank you again. Can I pay you back for the dry? And the quarter from before?" I point to my dryer to indicate what I'm talking about, though, of course, he knows.

"It's fine. Just don't leave your clothes in the machines. You need to pay attention to what you're doing."

I nod. He's being unfriendly again. I suddenly have whiplash from his rapid mood changes. One minute, he's cold and pretending he doesn't know my name; the next, he's offering me a quarter. His eyes have held nothing but contempt, but then he stood close, so close, that I could feel his warmth. The way my body reacted confuses me even more.

Pulling out my phone, I look at the time on the dryer. Setting an alarm, I slide it into my back pocket.

"Okay, I just set an alarm for a few minutes before the dryer finishes. I guess, I'll, uh, see you later, or something."

Josh doesn't even answer me as I walk out of the laundry room. I consider finding Brittney, getting her thoughts on what just happened. But part of me wants to keep it to myself. I don't want her to think I'm being silly.

My book can't hold my interest while I wait for the timer to beep. Instead, I find myself checking the clock regularly, and not to make sure I'm there before it's finished.

I'm back in the laundry room before my timer even goes off. I was anticipating seeing Josh again, though unsure which Josh I'd see, the one who makes butterflies flutter in my stomach or the one who makes me feel tiny and insignificant. I'm not really sure I care as long as I get to see him.

Yet when I walk into the room, I quickly notice that he's nowhere to be found. I'm frustrated at the feeling of disappointment that spreads through my chest. I'm not even sure if his things are still in the dryer.

My dryer slows to a halt while I watch and release a heavy sigh. As I start pulling my clothes out and bend to place them in my basket, I feel a brush against my back, causing me to stand straight up and stiffen.

"Glad to see you made it this time. Would have hated to see your nice clean clothes all over the floor." The ice hangs off his words again.

"I was early, in fact."

"Ah. Well, at least you learned something."

"Actually, I've learned a few things."

"Is that so?"

"It is. I've learned you like to make residents nervous as you tower over them, glaring down your nose. You like to make people feel smaller than you. And you corner residents at parties, acting like you have zero interest in them, and then compliment their attire as you walk away." I'm shocked at my outburst. I don't talk to people this way, and certainly not boys. Something about him just makes me able to find my voice.

"Excuse me, but if I'm not mistaken, *you* bumped into *me.*"

Slamming the dryer shut, I grab my laundry basket. "Asshole," I mutter under my breath as I storm out, rage making my blood boil.

His deep laugh follows me down the hallway to the stairs. Before I even reach the first floor, I decide I need to avoid Josh Roberts at all costs.

AVOIDING JOSH TURNS OUT TO BE PRETTY EASY. UNTIL Tuesday of the first full week of classes when I walk into the satellite building and see him sitting in the second row.

He notices me as soon as I'm through the door and a scowl spreads across his face.

Looking at the ground, I tuck hair behind my ear as I walk to the back of the classroom, finding a seat as far from him as I can. I try to keep my head down, getting my books out and ready, but glance over at him once, finding he's gazing slyly back at me. The shade of his irises seems to be directly related to his mood, something I've noticed in just the few times we've spoken. The more displeased the mood is, the darker his gaze becomes.

His eyes dash forward when he sees me look over.

The professor walks in then, standing at a table at the front of the room and putting down a few different packets of paper. "Good afternoon. I'm Professor Carp, I'll be your teacher for this semester of English. We're going to work on how to get English Language Arts into the classroom in varying ways and reaching different learners. This class meets Tuesdays and Thursdays.

"I have some packets up here; I'd like you to please come take. The first here is your syllabus, we'll go over that this class. You'll see a few papers and a partner project, which is to be done early on. If you're in this class, it's because you've

64

completed some level of course work or hours toward your education credits. Come on up and get these packets please, then we'll get started."

We all stand to get our packets. I'm slow getting into the line, not wanting to be too close to Josh. Based on his face, he doesn't seem too happy that I'm in the class with him.

I haven't timed things as well as I had hoped and end up waiting right in front of Josh's desk. While I'm paused in front of him, he sighs loudly. As much as I try not to look at him, I can't help myself.

His dark eyes glance up at me. I can't read what's hiding in them, but a scowl still resides on his face. Twirling some hair behind my ear, I look away as I worry my lip between my teeth.

I'm not sure why Josh doesn't like me. Honestly, I'm not even sure he doesn't, but the way he looks at me most of the time certainly makes it seem that way. He'd been so nice when he introduced himself, then at the party he was anything but, confusing me with his compliment. And then there was the laundry, which I don't even know what to think of. I was worried that *I* would have to avoid *him* because I didn't want him thinking I was some easy freshman he could invite down to his room to 'study' with. And instead, it's pretty clear that Josh wants nothing to do with me.

I'm able to get most of what Professor Carp talks about during the class, taking notes and marking things on my syllabus, but a few things I'm unable to grasp as I'm lost in my head, staring at the back of Josh's, wondering what I could have done to make him dislike me.

I end up rationalizing that maybe he's just been in a bad mood, each and every time I've seen him, that he doesn't know me well enough to dislike me and maybe he'd be friendly and say goodbye or we'd walk out to leave together. I know I shouldn't care, but I hate the thought of somebody hating me for no reason. Not to mention, he's an RA in my building. What if I need something from him? He has no reason to dislike me, so surely, he can't possibly.

I realize I'm very, very wrong when at the end of class, I catch up to Josh. "Hello." I try to put on my best friendly voice, though it comes out airy. For some reason, I can hardly breathe.

Without even meeting my eyes, he turns to me. "Hi." One gruff syllable is all I get before he turns and leaves the building.

One thing is clear. Josh Roberts does not like me.

CHAPTER 7

A week and a half into classes and things have started flowing for me. Brittney and I are together all the time. Nothing has changed with Kimberly. I relish the times she's in class. Thankfully, our schedules are relatively opposite, and I get a decent amount of time in my room without her during the day.

My date with Liam went well enough that I've seen him a few times since. Brittney and Lauren are both over the moon with the development. I have to remind them both regularly that we're just hanging out, casually, though he's taken me to dinner twice more since our first date. He's also joined Brittney and me in the dining hall a few times.

"So, give me all the updates. How are things with Liam? Brittney? Oh, and what's that RA's name? Josh, right?" I'm on my bed, having my weekly call with Lauren. We'd hoped to talk daily, but as it turns out, things got a little hectic once classes started, and our daily calls have gradually lessened.

"Oh, boy. Well, things with Liam are good. He's sweet, and I feel comfortable around him, which is such a head spinner. Brit's great. She's so much like you, I swear. And yes, Josh." I take a deep breath before I dive in.

"Things with Josh are…interesting. I don't know, Laur. I could swear he hates me, but for the life of me, I can't figure out why. I've thought back to our first conversations and run-ins and can't put my finger on it. But in class, *if* he looks at me, it's with a deep glare that makes me want to shrink into myself. I haven't seen him in the halls in over a week. It's all incredibly distracting and taking up way more space in my brain than it should." Leaning back against the wall, I pull my knees to my chest.

"It sounds like you feel something for him."

"What? No way. Nothing but confusion at least." The tingle that settles in my chest tells me I'm lying. But I brush it off, sure it's just the nagging worry of why he hates me.

"I told you about the party and the laundry room. Hell, even when we met for the first time, he was friendly. Was I supposed to ask him about the music? Like, was that some sort of invitation that I royally screwed up?" I don't even know that I care. I have Liam, who's kind and wonderful. But something keeps nibbling at me and I can't seem to let it go.

"I mean I'd say no. It doesn't really sound like you two have interacted enough for whatever is going on. I don't know, it's weird."

"Ugh, well, that's less than helpful. Distract me, tell me about you. What have you been up to?"

"Well, I went to that party last weekend and…"

Lauren's voice melts into the background as I start to zone out. I catch bits and pieces. Something about the party being good, a boy she met there, that they're still talking. She continues the conversation, but my mind is stuck on the one thing I wish I could stop thinking about. Josh Roberts.

"Lex. Did you hear me?"

"Huh? Oh sorry, I, uh, heard somebody out in the hall." I twirl a curl around my finger at the discomfort of my lie as I readjust myself on the bed, shoving a pillow behind my back.

"I asked when you're seeing Liam again."

"Oh. Today, actually."

"You've seen each other a lot in the past two weeks." There's a hint of something in Lauren's voice that I can't quite place. Probably because I'm distracted.

"Yeah, he's nice. Attractive."

"Think you can get me a picture?"

I roll my eyes and smile at her. Of course, that's the sort of question she'd ask. Actually, she's asked more than once about both of the guys we've talked about today. "Ha, I can try."

Just then, Brit waltzes into my room like it's her own, earning a scowl from Kimberly. I watch with amusement as Brittney gives her a giant smile and flips her off. "Hey, Laur, I gotta go. Brit just walked in and we're headed to the bookstore to pick up some stuff."

"Okay! I miss you, Lex."

"I miss you too. So much."

"Try to get that picture for me."

"I definitely will. Love you."

"Love you too. Bye."

Hanging up, I slide my phone into my pocket as I hop off the bed and grab my ID and sunglasses. I don't even give Kimberly a glance back as I hook my arm in Brittney's and we walk out the door.

"So, how's Lauren?"

"She's good. I feel bad because I was a little distracted as she talked about some guy she met at a party. I'll have to ask for details again next week and apologize for my drifting mind."

"Was it drifting toward anybody…exciting?"

Squinting as we push through the doors, I flip my sunglasses down over my eyes. "I have no idea what you're talking about," I grumble.

"Uh-huh. Sure, you don't."

"Liam invited me over for a movie tonight." I figure a change of subject is in order.

"Did he now? And are you going?"

"Yeah. Why wouldn't I?"

"I don't know...guy you're seeing invites you over for a movie. That usually means he wants it to lead somewhere. Have you kissed yet?" With the slightest turn of her head in my direction, her gaze slides over to me.

Bile rises in my throat at my stupidity. She's right, of course. How could I not have seen it? "Um, no. No, we haven't."

"Do you want to kiss him? You have kissed a boy before, right?"

"Yes, I have." I'm not a *complete* recluse. "And I don't know if I'm interested in kissing Liam. I mean we seem to be in a good place, but he hasn't asked me to be his girlfriend or anything. I don't know. I'm not sure how I feel about it."

"Well, you should make up your mind before you go. And is it like, a self-written rule to be in a relationship?"

"Not necessarily."

"What about the guys you kissed prior?" My arm being linked with hers prevents me from twisting my fingers. This topic isn't something I'm overly comfortable talking about. I loop some hair behind my ear instead.

"One was a boyfriend, the only boyfriend I've really had. The other was a close friend."

"Just think it through. Don't let him pressure you. It's okay to say no." Brittney says *no* with some extra force as she yanks the door open.

"Should I not go?" Turning my face toward hers, I pull my bottom lip between my teeth. She's the slightest bit taller, so I feel like I have to look up to her.

"That's up to you. I wouldn't say not to; he may just want to spend time with you."

Quiet and caught up in my head, I follow Brittney through the college store while she gathers what she needs. I take any opportunity she offers to leave the dorm, especially when

Kimberly is around, which is, as she said it would be: very infrequent.

Brittney bumping her hip against mine not only almost sends me to the ground, but breaks me from my daze. "Hey, don't think too much about it. Maybe you'll want to decide in the moment."

"Sure, maybe." Really, I don't want to decide at all. I want it to be an easy choice, like it is for people like Brittney and Lauren who know what they want when they want it. I'm sure they'd both have already kissed Liam by now. I'm thankful he's been patient with me for taking things slow.

Glancing at the clock on the wall, I note that it's four o'clock. I told Liam I'd be over at seven, which allows me time to have dinner with Brittney. That gives me three hours to stress and worry about what the night means and what's going to happen. *Fantastic.*

BEFORE KNOCKING ON LIAM'S DOOR, I SHAKE MY LIMBS OUT and exhale a deep breath. He pulls it open within seconds, a smile breaking across his face. It causes my queasy stomach to flip-flop and my shoulders to lower ever so slightly. I spent the last three hours stressing myself out, despite Brittney's constant reminders that I don't have to do anything.

"Hey, beautiful. Come on in."

I've never been to Liam's suite before. The door opens to a large room with couches and chairs on either side of me. It's big enough to separate into two sections, each of which contains a large TV. There are three doors opposite where I stand just inside the entrance—I'm assuming the bedrooms.

"Where are your roommates?" It takes me a moment to realize I don't see or hear anybody.

"They're out. Dinner, then a party."

My mouth goes arid, and I suddenly find it exceptionally

hard to swallow. Roommates not being here makes me wonder if he has more thoughts than just a kiss.

"You didn't want to join them?"

"No, I'd rather spend time with you." Giving me that megawatt smile, he puts an arm around my waist, leading me farther into the common room. If he can see my unease, he's ignoring it. "I'd show you my room, but it's a bit of a mess right now. It's that one though." He points to the middle door. I hope not showing me inside his room is a good sign.

"Oh." I don't know what else to say.

"Here, sit, get comfortable." Leading me over to the couch, he sits down, pulling me with him. "Lexie, relax. I just want to spend time with you, watch a movie. I'm not expecting anything. I said we could take it slow. I meant it."

Nodding, my muscles loosen as I sit close enough for our arms to be touching. Flipping through a few channels but eventually giving up, he switches to his streaming device, finding a romcom and pressing play, without asking if I'd like to watch it.

I don't mind, really, I like romantic comedies, but it's still nice to be asked. It makes me realize he does that a lot—makes decisions without asking me.

We sit mostly in silence, and Liam moves his arm over the back of the couch, his fingers gently grazing my shoulder as I lean against him ever so slightly. It's enough that my body jostles when he laughs.

I'm starting to relax more, getting out of my head and enjoying the movie, which is actually quite funny, when Liam shifts closer. Every muscle in my body immediately goes rigid. The warmth that had been pouring off of him is now like fire scorching my skin. Convinced my heart is going to hammer out of my chest, I cross my arms tightly against it to keep everything contained within my body.

His lemony scent drifts over me, this time, mixed with

something earthy. Taking a shaky deep breath, I run my hands down my thighs.

"Hey."

I turn my head to Liam's low voice. My eyes are wide, and I can almost feel my anxiety rising.

"Lexie, please relax. If you're uncomfortable, I can sit on another couch."

"It's fine." My voice is an octave higher, a pure indication of how not fine it is. It's not so much that I'm scared to kiss Liam. There should be some sort of pull, some sort of desire, an irresistibility. For me, right now, there isn't.

Still, he's very attractive and kind. I appreciate his willingness to take things slow, and I've never really felt pressured in any way. I'm fully aware that everything in my head right now is my own doing.

Taking my hair in his fingers, he starts twirling it around them as he continues to look at me. "Lexie, I like spending time with you. You're cute and sweet. I don't want you to be uncomfortable around me."

"I'm not."

"It kind of seems like you are. My roommates not being here wasn't exactly by design. I was kind of hoping to introduce you to them, but I am glad they're gone because we can be alone. But I'm not going to suddenly go back on what I've said just because I have you here with nobody else around." His voice is low and gentle, soothing.

"I'm sorry." I look at my hands, now resting in my lap.

Liam links his fingers with mine and moves his other hand from my hair to rest against the side of my neck. I'm sure he can feel my pulse skyrocket under his fingers. "I wanted you here to spend time with you. But I'd be lying if I said I wasn't hoping to kiss you tonight. I've been thinking about it for a while now, probably since the first day I met you. But I've been trying to be respectful of you. And if you tell me no, or that you don't want to, I'll understand, and we can watch the rest of the movie in silence, or you can even leave if you need to."

I swallow roughly. While I have wondered what it'd be like to kiss Liam, I'm not sure I'm ready for him to take the initiative and move in for it. Brittney said he has a kissable mouth, whatever that means. I look at him for a moment as he keeps his gaze on mine. It's time for a decision.

Shifting my body toward Liam, I rest my hand on his hard chest, my heart fluttering.

Taking the hint, he slides his hand up to cup my jaw and leans in. His lips brush against mine briefly and he pulls back for a moment, I'm assuming to read me, as his gaze dances along my face. When he leans in again, his mouth moves against mine with more pressure.

His tongue slides cautiously just between my lips, and I part them for him. I haven't made out too many times before, and in the back of my mind, I hope I'm doing it right. I'm sure Brittney and Lauren would both scold me for worrying about such a thing, but I can't help it.

After a few minutes, Liam slowly pulls away, leaving a small kiss on my bottom lip and another on the tip of my nose. Leaning back against the couch, he slides his arm around my shoulders and pulls me into him.

Sighing contentedly, I settle in for the rest of the movie. *That wasn't so bad. And it wasn't so scary either.*

CHAPTER 8

W hile Professor Carp is giving out teams, I'm doodling in my notebook. It's Thursday of our fourth week of classes and we're doing the group project she had mentioned, though it really seems to be more of a partner project.

"Roberts and...Harper." I freeze, pen stilled on the paper. I look up and over at Josh, sitting in the second row. Raising his head, he slowly turns to look at me. Rolling his eyes, he sinks lower in his seat, long legs stretching out in front of him as he shakes his head. He seems less excited about the prospect of working together than I am.

Quickly, I avert my eyes back to my paper and my doodle. How are we going to work together when we can't even look at each other?

When the professor releases us, I rapidly gather my books and try to leave, head down so as not to catch his eye. I'm not so lucky.

"If we have to work together, we may as well make the most of it. Come over tonight; we'll go through the project and start working on an outline." He's fallen into step beside me.

"Maybe we can just ask for a partner reassignment."

He's standing close enough that I feel him tense next to me. "I can be professional about this if you can. It's just a class project."

Stopping, I turn to look at him. His eyes have a softness to them that I haven't seen until now. It sends tingles racing through my body. "I can do that." A twinkle flashes across his eyes. In the light of the sun, they're a softer brown with amber flecks throughout.

"Good. Tonight. My room. Say eight?"

"So late?"

"I have to work the desk before then."

"Oh, okay. Sure. Eight, it is."

Giving me a tight smile and a quick nod, he walks off. Utterly frozen in place, I can't help but stare after him. I know what he does with girls when they come to his room to study. Will he be expecting the same from me? I'm sure sex trumps hatred.

Working with Josh is all I can think about on my drive back to the dorm. Being so wrapped up in my own head, I hadn't even noticed I was back until I pulled onto campus, driving on autopilot.

"Hey!" I jump at the sound of Liam's voice, close by. "Sorry, thought you heard me calling you. What's wrong?"

Shaking my head, I force a smile. "Nothing. Just a partner project in class. Not thrilled with my partner."

"You can always ask the professor for a change if you're really not comfortable." Resting his hand against the top of my car, he leans toward me slightly.

"Nah, it's okay. We're going to start tonight and I don't want to cause waves. It'll be fine." It *will* be fine.

"I'll tell you what. Why don't we grab some dinner first? Your choice, my treat."

"Dinner, sure." My mind is so distracted I can barely put together a coherent sentence. *I wonder if Josh will eat first. I hope we don't cut into his dinner.*

Liam laces his fingers through mine as we start off toward the dorms. "So what do you think?"

If he's coming right from work, will that make him extra grumpy? Am I going to get mean Josh or nice Josh tonight? I really hope nice because I can't work with him the other way.

A firm squeeze of my hand pulls me from my mind. "Huh?" I hadn't realized that Liam had been talking.

"Dinner. What are you in the mood for?"

"Um, how about burgers?" I don't even want burgers; it was just the first thing that came to mind.

"You sure? Burgers are kind of…heavy. Maybe something a little less than burgers?"

"Okay, um Chinese?"

"Eh. How about Italian?"

Just the word makes my stomach do flips and my heart start beating faster as my brain makes the instant connection to Josh. "Uh, sure."

"Want to go now?"

"No, let me change first. I just threw this on this morning." I gesture a hand down my body.

"I think you look great." Leaning in, he gives me a peck on the cheek. Of course, he thinks I look great; I'm wearing skinny jeans and a tight semi low-cut shirt, figuring it can't hurt to make Josh think I look good too. Maybe then he'd be nicer, as horrible as it would be for that to be the reason.

"Thank you. I'd just rather change. I don't think this is right for Nona's. I'll be quick, I promise."

"Alright, let's meet in an hour, then. I'll pick you up out front." We're at my dorm. How had we already gotten here?

"Okay, see you then." A small part of me hopes I'm not so far behind Josh that I may be able to catch a quick glimpse of him. Maybe he's hanging out in the hall. After running up the stairs, I notice his door is closed.

The deflation in my chest both confuses and frustrates me. I want to see him. I want him to see me. But I don't really know why I do. It isn't lost on me that he's not happy about being my partner on the project. Yet for some reason, I haven't been able to stop thinking about him, for weeks, and I know I need to get him out of my head. It's like I have whiplash going back and forth between emotions of longing and disdain for the same person.

I don't realize how hard I throw the door open until it hits the wall, making me jump. Kimberly is nowhere to be found. Walking over to the mirror, I stare at myself. My eyes are wide, cheeks flushed. I look crazed. All over somebody who seems to want nothing to do with me. It shouldn't bother me; it's just a project and I know that not everybody will like me. But the issue lies in the way his glance, those brief moments of nearness weeks ago, make my insides light on fire.

"NO WINE? ARE YOU SURE?" LIAM POINTS HIS GLASS IN MY direction with a raised eyebrow.

"Yeah, had a little too much this past weekend. I'll stick with water."

Liam shrugs. He's all too happy to order alcohol for me, but it makes me feel wrong since I'm only eighteen. Though I've told him more than once, he doesn't seem to understand.

"So, how was your day? I know you're nervous about that project." His eyes stay on his plate.

"I don't want to talk about that. My day was fine. How about yours?"

I can barely focus on what Liam is saying. I'm so apprehensive about seeing Josh in just a few hours. There are a few things I catch that I'm able to give more of a response than an 'uh huh' and 'oh wow' to, but not enough to really absorb anything. I hope none of it comes up later.

"So, for Halloween, do you know if you have anything

going on?" He suddenly has my full attention. Halloween? That's over a month away.

"Uh, I'm not sure since it's pretty far away, but Brit probably has something planned or will. She mentioned a few things, but no specifics. I've already told her I'll go with her, but if you'd rather do something, I can cancel. I'm sure she'll know plenty of people there that she won't even notice." At this point, I'm just pushing the pasta around on my plate, my stomach too fluttery to eat.

"No, that's fine. I was actually going to apologize that I couldn't be with you. I'm heading out of town. It's my buddy Nate's birthday weekend, and I go visit him. He always throws a rager. It's going to be a rough weekend." I'm not sure why he's apologizing. We don't spend that much time together and haven't yet on a weekend, both of us usually doing our own thing. Plus, this is still so far away. Who even knows what will be going on with us by then.

"So, when do you leave?"

"I'll be heading out Friday after classes. Be back sometime late Sunday, it takes me a while to be up and sober enough to drive. At least from what past experience dictates for the weekend." He chuckles as he takes a sip of his wine.

"Sounds like you'll be having a lot of fun." I give him a tight smile. I realize I should feel something about him being gone, but I don't.

"I'm sorry, I'd rather spend it with you. But you sound like you'll be having a good time with Brit anyway. I just wanted to mention it now so that you could be prepared."

"I appreciate that." Liam is always thinking about the future. I'm not sure what he sees with us, but I know that this isn't the first time he's talked about things weeks ahead. I've yet to see them pan out.

"But this weekend, let's do something. I'm sure we can find a party, or make one at the suite. We can hang out—you and I, whatever you want."

"Can I let you know? Brit said something about a movie? I'm also not sure what will happen with the project with Josh tonight and how much we'll be able to get done between now and then. We only have a week to finish. Plus, all my reading for my other English class."

Liam picks up my hand and kisses it. "You'll be fine. No stress."

I smile a little at his attempt to calm me.

"We can keep it open. If something comes up, I'll let you know. And even if you do need to work with Josh, would it be that late? I mean, it'd be kind of weird to work later in the night with him."

I shrug like it's no big deal, because to me, it isn't. "He works weird hours since occasionally he has to do the desk or sit out front to check IDs on the weekends. We'll likely be having to work whenever we can. Like I said, though, I don't know. He doesn't seem to like me, so we may not even do that much together in person."

"Well, he's crazy for not liking you. But at least I know I have no competition there. He's not worth it anyway." The words don't sit right with me, and there's something in his eyes I can't place. Something mixed with victory, like he's won me. But we haven't been together that long, not even officially dating so much as hanging out. Not to mention, I can't ignore the things that I feel when I'm around Josh, that I *don't* feel around Liam.

Before I have a chance to ask what he means, he takes my hand and pulls me to stand. "Come on, let's get out of here."

After Liam pays, he walks me over to the passenger side to pull the door open, but before he does, he leans into me, pushing his body against mine. "You look beautiful tonight," he murmurs in my ear. Then his lips are on mine. Sweet, gentle, brief. He pulls away, smiling. "Did I tell you that yet?"

"You have. But thank you again. And thank you for

dinner." Liam is good about ignoring some of my awkwardness.

"You're welcome." He opens the door for me as I climb in.

His car still has that fresh smell, and everything is shiny. Driving toward campus, I stare out the window at the passing lights as Liam drones on about one of his classes and the professor, who everybody seems to hate. It's not just nerves making me drown him out, but his words swirling around in my head, wondering what he meant, and leaving a sour taste in my mouth.

Liam parks in the parking lot and walks me over to my front doors. "Good luck on the project. Give me a call tomorrow, let me know how it went." Leaning in, he gives me a kiss on the cheek, then squeezes my shoulder and walks away.

Before he's even across the road, I turn and walk in the door. The time with Liam hasn't distracted me much, but it's better than being alone with my thoughts. Or with Kimberly.

That's when I notice who's behind the desk. Somehow, I'd forgotten Josh said he'd be there. He glares at me, piercing me with his dark eyes. While I quite can't read what's behind them, it *feels* like hatred. Spinning on my heels, I run up the stairs, dreading what's coming tonight.

AN HOUR LATER, I TAKE A DEEP BREATH BEFORE KNOCKING ON Josh's door. I give a small smile as he opens the door.

"Come in." Moving to the side, he allows me to pass, closing the door behind him.

I try to swallow around the lump in my throat. Does the closed door mean he expects something more than our project to happen? I wiggle my toes in my Converse to try to take away the tingles. Not only am I in a room, closed door, with probably the most gorgeous guy I've ever seen, but he has quite the reputation that I do not plan to be a participant of.

81

Sitting down at his desk, he points to the bed. "You can sit there."

I look between him and the bed a few times. "The bed? Are you sure?"

"There's nowhere else for you to sit and I want to be able to check the computer if I need to."

"Maybe we should go to the library then."

"You can't sit on my bed for an hour while we get some work done?" His tone is biting, and it makes me want to disappear.

Taking a deep breath, I climb up and rest my books in my lap. "So, where should we start?"

"I haven't really had a chance to look over the assignment yet so let's start there."

"Sure." Silence fills the room as we both read over the instructions. We're supposed to take a children's book and make it a small group activity, each group having a separate task to teach the rest of the class something about the book. There's a lot of freedom with how we can do this. Our imaginary students can do their part of the assignment any way they want to, from a poster, to a diorama, to a computer presentation.

"Okay, well, there's a lot of flexibility here."

I'm happy he speaks first. It allows me another minute to get my bearings.

"I guess the first step is to pick a book. Any thoughts?" Being stuck in a small room with him gives me the ability to really see how handsome he is up close.

His dark hair is shaggy, hanging the slightest bit over his ears and forehead, curling up a bit at the ends. The lines of his jaw are sharp and covered with stubble. I'm not sure if he shaves regularly or not. I've never paid much attention. The black shirt he's wearing is tight against his chest and arms.

"I guess we should decide what level first?" Not wanting to step on toes, I ask, unsure of myself.

"I think it'd be easier to do a chapter book and upper elementary. Gives a little bit more meat for the projects."

"Okay, sure." I think for a minute. "Why are you in this class anyway?" My hand flies to my mouth; I hadn't meant for that come out. "Sorry, that was rude."

I shouldn't be so quick to jump to conclusions. I'm only in the class because of the internship, and so far, I feel wholly unprepared.

Chuckling, he runs his hand along the back of his neck. "I have to take a certain number of elementary-geared English classes, and I'd been putting them off. Not big into English, like we discussed." His eyes meet mine for a minute and it sends my heart soaring high. "So now I'm in a few to get the requirement finished."

I just nod like a fool.

"Lesson to be learned, don't delay something you can do freshman year." A serious look flashes across his face. "I actually wasn't an ed major when I started school, so I'm playing a bit of catch up."

"What was your major?"

"I came as a culinary major." He chuckles.

"What's so funny about that?" The corner of my lips ticks up.

"Nothing, it's just...I've never told anybody that before." He flashes me a crooked smile.

My pulse flutters at my neck and I rub my finger along it, drawing Josh's gaze. "I think that sounds like an exciting career choice. Why'd you switch majors?"

The smile vanishes, replaced with a seriousness that's undeniable; a darkness and emptiness has taken over his eyes. "My dad. He said there was way too much uncertainty and struggle in the culinary world. That unless you're remarkable from the beginning you don't get anywhere."

"But education is pretty uncertain too. And who says you wouldn't have been a remarkable chef?" Despite putting my

83

foot in my mouth to start the conversation, I'm happy I did, as I'm learning a bit about Josh. The nerves are almost completely gone and I'm enjoying the ease I'm feeling talking to him.

"He said that he didn't work so hard to make sure I got into a good school for me to throw it away and come live on his couch. I made sure he understood that education can also be very uncertain. I'm not guaranteed a job when I finish school or even in the next few years, but he felt like it was more secure in the long run. Once you reach tenure, you're set. He wanted me to do more but felt that education was an acceptable option."

"Your dad sounds strict." Looking up at him through my eyelashes, I find him staring at the notebook in his lap, pen between his fingers.

"He's a good father and a good man. He struggled a lot growing up. Things were hard when I was young, financially, and he wants more than that for me."

"I can understand that." Though really, I can only understand the thought behind it. I've come from a very different financial background, at least from the sound of it.

"How about you?"

"Oh, I've wanted to be a teacher forever. I've always loved kids. I started babysitting when I was twelve, worked at a summer camp since I was fourteen. There really is no other option for me besides teaching. At least none that I can see."

"It's nice to have a goal from early on."

"It is. I feel like I have a sense of where I'm headed. I only applied to colleges with strong education programs."

"Yeah, I got lucky there. Had they not had a good program here, I'm not sure what I would have switched to." He taps his pen on his notebook. "We should probably get back to this."

We spend the next hour going over the details of our project. Josh hops on the computer and finds that the library has a few copies of a chapter book he remembers from when he was younger and puts one on hold for himself. "Here, why don't you come log in and reserve one for yourself. I don't think it's terribly popular, but you never know." He moves aside so I can sit at his computer.

The hairs on my neck and arms stand up, a chill running down my spine at how close behind me he stands. Hoping he doesn't see my shaky hands, I reserve the book for myself. "I'll swing by after my class tomorrow to grab my copy and start reading since I haven't read it before." Wincing at the weakness of my voice, I hate that he intimidates me so much with his nearness. Especially because tonight, he's being nice.

"Alright. I'll grab it tomorrow too. Here's my number. Let me know how far you get, so we can try to keep pace." The piece of paper he slides toward me has his cell phone number scrawled across it.

"Yeah, okay." I gather my papers and notebook in my arms, hugging them to my chest. "I'll, uh, see you around then."

Josh holds the door open for me but stands close enough that I brush against him on my way out. "See you around," he murmurs.

I walk quickly down the hall and straight into my room, leaving the door open as I flop into my chair.

"Did you just come from Josh's room?" Brittney comes walking right in.

"Yeah." I feel breathless, though I have no reason to be and can breathe perfectly normal.

"Ohmygod! Did you guys have sex?"

"What?! No!" The chair nearly tips over, I push it back so quickly.

"Oh." Her voice is thick with disappointment. "Why were you in there?"

"You know some people can sit together in a room and actually get work done."

"Yeah, but not with Josh."

From what I've heard floating around, she's right. Does he not find me attractive? Shaking my head, I dismiss the thought. That's not something I care about. I'm there to work. And I have Liam.

"All we did was talk about our assignment. Sorry to disappoint you."

"Maybe next time." I'm pretty sure she can tell by the look on my face and my attitude that I don't find her amusing at this very moment. "Oh, come on Lexie, lighten up!"

"I'm fine. We just worked." If I keep telling her we didn't do anything but our assignment, she's going to think that something *did* happen.

"Alright, alright. How was dinner?"

I had almost completely forgotten about dinner with Liam. Had it really been only a few hours ago? "It was fine. You know, nothing exciting, just dinner."

"You just went from good to fine. What's going on with you?"

"Nothing, just a bit distracted. I have a lot of work this week." I'm lying through my teeth, hoping Brit doesn't notice. What's really going on is that my mind is stuck on Josh.

The fact that he told me about being a culinary major. The way my skin warmed as it brushed against him. The uptick it caused in my pulse.

"It tends to set in around this time. Let me know if you need any help or anything."

"Sure. Thanks. I just need to focus and use my time well."

My attention is drawn to my computer as I hear a ding.

I'll get my book tomorrow. Let's meet again, same time as tonight.

It's a message from Josh. The air sticks in my lungs, and I have to reread it.

"Again, tomorrow? You lucky girl."

I can't tear my eyes from the computer to look at her.

"Nothing happened, we just talked about the project." And his major change. I don't know why I'm keeping that to myself.

"I believe you, but you're still lucky to sit in close quarters with somebody who looks like he does."

"I guess." If I give her more, she'll have a field day, but yes, I am very lucky to be able to look at him.

"You guess? Oh, Lexie, sometimes I wonder about you when it comes to boys."

"We're just working. He's made it pretty clear he doesn't have any interest in me."

She shrugs. "Maybe he doesn't like the virginal type."

Heat rushes my face. "How would he know that?"

"I mean, he probably doesn't, but you don't exactly exude sexual confidence. It's not a bad thing, but he likely realizes you're not the hookup type."

"Whatever. Listen, I don't want to be rude, but I have a lot of work to get done here. Breakfast tomorrow?"

"You know it. Wake me if I'm not up by ten."

"Like I could!"

With a smack on my arm, she's off down the hall.

Is that why Josh seemed like he couldn't stand to be near me for weeks? Because I'm "virginal" and that somehow goes against what he's interested in? I don't really know why I care. I have a boyfriend. Kind of. We haven't really given it a title. It's just going to make working with Josh that much more difficult. Despite feeling like Josh doesn't like me and it's going to make working with him hard, I'm excited to see him again.

87

CHAPTER 9

At 7:55 the next night, I find myself eagerly awaiting the clock turning to eight so I can head down to Josh's room again. I'm wondering which Josh I'll see tonight. The nice one who makes casual conversation and shares things with me, or the one who talks down to me and looks at me like he hates me.

"Would you *stop?*" Kimberly barks at me.

"Huh? Oh, sorry." Apparently, I've been banging my pen on my desk, a nervous habit I didn't realize I was doing. I know it's irritating, but my very existence still seems to annoy Kimberly.

"Aren't you going somewhere?"

"In a few minutes."

"Can't come soon enough." Agreed.

"It's fine. I'll go now." Gathering my books, I head down to Josh's room.

"Thank God." I just roll my eyes on the way out of my room.

His door is open. Knocking lightly, I step inside the slightest bit.

"Sorry, I'm early, roommate troubles." I venture quietly, pulling my bottom lip between my teeth.

"It's fine. Come on in." He closes some books on his desk. "Shut the door."

Walking over to the bed, I wait, not wanting to sit without his invitation.

"You can sit on the bed again." He juts his chin toward it, not making eye contact. Sitting in his desk chair, he pulls his books out, uncapping a pen with his mouth, leaving the cap between his lips, gently blowing through it creating a small whistle sound. He taps the pen against the notebook a few times before looking up and catching me watching him intently. My cheeks burn as I look away, but not before seeing him smirk. "How far did you get?"

"I read the whole thing."

The pen cap drops out of his mouth. "You read the whole thing?"

I have the slightest swelling of pride that I surprised him. "Yeah? It wasn't that long of a book, and it was better than doing my other work. I liked it, though. Good choice."

"Thanks, yeah, it's a good book. I remember loving it. So, you actually do like to read, huh?"

My heart palpitates as I realize he remembered that part of our conversation. "Yeah, I do."

"I mean, I know you told me when we met a few weeks ago, but I wasn't sure how much."

"Oh, a lot. I'm always reading something. Lately, it's been a lot more for class, or at least trying to, but this worked out well because I liked it and it *was* for class. It just means I didn't get much of my other reading done, but that can be tomorrow's problem."

"Dangerous outlook to have. Waiting for tomorrow."

Glancing up, I find he's staring at me intently. "I wanted to be prepared for you." For a brief moment, I level my gaze with his and stop breathing completely.

"Let's get to talking about the book. I didn't finish it, but I think I remember enough to be able to get through."

We spend about a half hour talking about the book and the ways we could assign things for a group of students. Being newer at education courses, I'm afraid to give too much input in terms of how it should work in a classroom.

"You have good teaching instincts, don't be afraid to share your ideas," he says flippantly at one point.

Busted. "I'm not."

"I feel like you're holding back. Don't."

"I just haven't had any real education-related classes. I don't want to overstep."

"I mean, that's what this is all about, right? They let a freshman in the class for a reason. Don't be afraid to take chances." Josh fixes me with his stare again. There's something behind his eyes I can't figure out. Directing his gaze back down to his notebook, he adjusts his posture by slouching lower in his chair, long legs stretching out in front of him. "So, the guy I saw you with last night, he your boyfriend?" At first, I'm not sure I heard him correctly, and his eyes haven't left his notebook.

"Liam? I mean, I guess? I'm not sure. We hang out some-times, but he hasn't really asked me to be his girlfriend or anything. He lives over in the suites. He's a business major." I don't know why I'm giving him so much information besides just a simple yes or no.

"Yeah, I know Liam." The way he says it harps on a chord that reminds me of what Liam said.

"You do? I told him I'd be studying with you last night. He didn't mention that he knew you." I wonder why he did that. It gives me a sinking feeling that this may end up causing problems I hadn't anticipated.

He snorts. "That doesn't surprise me."

My brow knits together. "What do you mean?"

"Liam and I knew each other freshman year. We lived in

the same dorm, had a class together. We hung out every so often. We're just…different people, and he liked to make sure I knew it."

"I'm still confused."

"He has a lot more money than I do. He made sure that was known."

"That doesn't sound like the Liam I know. Granted, I don't know him that well, but still…"

"He's not like that around beautiful girls. He does and says what he needs to, to impress them, shows off his fancy car." As though he needs to push away the idea, he waves his hand through the air. "You been together long?"

There's a tightness set in his jaw. And a sense of swirling butterflies in my chest. Did he call me beautiful?

"No. We met the week before classes started, bumped into each other outside the dorms. He offered me a tour of campus that Brittney was kind enough to accept for me. We've really just been hanging out here and there. He's taken me out a few times, last night being one." I shrug. "He's sweet to me." I flash my eyes at Josh. "How about the women who come in here? Do you know them well?" I'm being bold, and I don't know where the bravery is coming from.

His eyes meet mine. "I'm not sure I understand your meaning."

"The girls, who come in here to *study*."

One side of his mouth quirks up. "What about them?"

"Do you know them well? I can't imagine you're dating all of them."

"I'm not dating any of them. We just study."

"So, you're saying you don't sleep with any of them?" Why is my heart beating erratically, my palms starting to sweat at the thought?

"Well, I didn't say *that.*"

I don't like how this crushes me slightly, drawing the air

from my lungs and blood from my veins. I shouldn't care. "You know you have a reputation, right?"

"I'm aware. I've also been told that I hold up to that reputation."

Heat floods my cheeks, and I look down at my lap at the mention. Not only have I been told that he has sex with these girls, but that he's good at it. When he chuckles quietly, I know he must see the pinkness in my cheeks. "As long as you're aware. Interesting reputation to be interested in having."

"I didn't say I was interested in having it. I'm just aware that it exists. It's college."

"I'm so sick of hearing that. 'It's college.' Like it's some excuse for bad behavior and depravity."

He gives an exaggerated shrug. "I mean, it kind of is."

My mouth hangs open for a minute before I gather myself. "You can't possibly mean that."

"Isn't college the time to explore things? To make choices and mistakes?" It sounds eerily similar to what my mom had said. "In high school, you're with your parents, and it's frowned upon. After college, you're expected to be an adult, hold down a job, get married, start a family. College is the time to try new things." Leaning back in his chair, he twirls a pen between his thumb and forefinger of both hands.

"I guess, for some people," I mumble, doodling on my paper.

"But not you?"

"No, not really."

"So, you're not doing any new things? You're exactly who you were in high school?"

"Well, no. I mean, I went to parties, but I didn't really drink, so I'm drinking a bit more. But that's really it."

"And no meaningless sex?"

Try as I might by digging my nails into my palm, I can't help reddening again. Nor can I help but notice Josh's chuckle. My propensity to blush is my biggest tell, and I hate it about myself. I'd be a terrible poker player. "No. Not my style." As though I have the moral high ground, I tip my chin up slightly.

"You're one of very few. But I guess it's not meaningless if you're in a relationship."

"I'm not...Liam and I aren't...I'm still a virgin." My hand flies to my mouth, and my eyes grow to the size of saucers. I didn't mean to say that. Falling backward on his bed, I cover my face with my notebook. "Oh my God, please let me just die right here," I mumble. If he wasn't sure I was virgin before, he certainly is now.

Josh is quiet for a few minutes. I'm not sure if that makes things better or worse. "There's nothing wrong with that, Lexie." His voice is so quiet and calm that it draws me in.

Sitting up, I look at him to find nothing but sincerity in his eyes.

"You don't have to let college change you. This is my second year as an RA. I've seen college change a lot of people. Many not for the better. I know a lot of people get things together as they go on, once out of school. But it can also derail some. It's rare to meet somebody like you who has kept true to themselves."

Giving him a tiny smile, my eyes drop back to my notebook as I play with the fray of the torn-out pages. "Thanks. It's not like a life choice. Just hasn't happened. I'm just not interested in giving it up to get it over with, you know?" I snort. "Actually, I'm sure you don't know, seeing the girls filing in and out of here."

"I told you, I don't sleep with all of them."

"Not all of them is not the same as none of them."

With tight lips, he nods slightly. "I can tell you don't approve."

"It's not really any of my business. Just not something I'd be interested in on either end. I can't see myself sleeping with multiple people, nor can I see myself being one of the many.

Or few. I don't need to know numbers. I guess I consider myself a one-man woman and would prefer to be the one woman for the man I'm with. Maybe that's not college, but I'm sure real relationships can be found."

"With Liam." The slightest octave increase at the end makes it sounds almost like a question.

Curls fly around my face as I shake my head. "I didn't say that. But yeah, he is who I'm with…right now. And while you may have your issues with him, he's always been kind to me."

"That's good. It's good that you feel he treats you right. Maybe he's changed, I don't know." He wiggles the mouse on his laptop and the screen jumps to life. "It's getting pretty late."

I start closing my books, planning to leave.

"You want to go down to the dining hall and grab a coffee? We could talk out a few more details."

Excitement rushes through me. I'm not ready for our time together to end. "I'd love to."

"You do drink coffee, right?"

"Oh, yes, much coffee."

We bring our notebooks with us to the dining hall, getting a cup of coffee each and finding a table. We spend another forty-five minutes talking, but our notebooks sit open to blank pages. Instead, we get to know each other more, conversation flowing as we talk about our childhoods.

He has two older siblings, his parents are divorced, and he and his home-friends are all still close even though college took them to different states.

I tell him about my family, what it's like to be an only child, my high school experience, Lauren. It's not until I get a text from Brittney asking where I am that I realize the time.

Josh walks me back to my room. When we get there, he stops, hand on my elbow. Tingles spread through my body. "Let's keep working tomorrow night. Same time?"

"That sounds great." With a smile, he's off down the hall.

Entering my room, I have a feeling I can't place coursing through me. It's excitement mixed with something else. The main thing is, it seems as though Josh may not hate me after all.

I CAN'T DENY MY EAGERNESS TO SEE JOSH AGAIN. I'M STARTING to enjoy his company, crave it even. While I'm not sure if he doesn't actually hate me or is just really good at acting, I don't care either way. Even if he just pretends so he can get an A, works hard, plays nice, puts in the work, it will all be worth it.

Part of me does feel terrible. I'm shrugging off Liam to work with Josh. I've told him we're just working on our project, which isn't entirely inaccurate. We *are* doing our project, but we're also talking and getting to know each other. Not to mention the feelings for Josh that I can't deny I'm developing.

Brittney has asked me what exactly is going on. I've given her the same party line I'm giving Liam. We're just working on our assignment. While I'm not really sure what *is* going on besides that, nobody else needs to know. Especially if I'm making something out of nothing.

At 7:45, I can't wait any longer and decide to try my luck venturing down to Josh's room. Surprisingly, Kimberly isn't shooting death glares at me, but I figure I can say she's giving me trouble anyway. Stacking my books, I glance in the mirror, hating myself for wanting to look good for a guy who is not my sort of boyfriend.

Trying to drag the minutes along so I don't irritate him by being early, I make sure to walk slowly. I'm not even sure he's in his room. As I get closer to his door, I notice it's open, making my heart hammer against my sternum. At the room next to his, I take a deep breath to steady myself.

"Here for me?" Josh's voice is low and right against my ear.

My heart, which had calmed to a normal rhythm, is now threatening to beat out of my chest. I'm acutely aware of just how close he's standing behind me, my body thrumming at his nearness.

Before I can answer, he slips around me and into his room, fingers ever so slightly grazing my hip. Taking another deep breath, I follow him while he closes the door behind me.

I take my seat on the bed, but this time, Josh sits next to me. He's close enough for our knees to touch, sending a shock through my body. Josh clears his throat, adjusting his position, but instead of moving farther away, he shifts closer to me.

His hands are down on the bed, close enough to mine that if I just stretch my fingers...

Josh's eyes catch mine as my fingertips touch his. Electricity crackles at our connection and through the air between us. Ever so slowly, he leans in. Every part of my body freezes, including my lungs and the ability to breathe.

The second his lips gently brush mine, though almost hesitantly, my body jumps back to life, the blood coursing through my veins with newfound vigor. They're warm, soft, and nothing else matters.

It lasts for all of thirty seconds, but I'm caught in a daze and seeing stars.

Sitting up, he clears his throat. "Lexie, I have to put this out there now. Nothing can happen between us. I'm an RA, you're one of my residents. We could both get into a lot of trouble."

"I'm not your resident. I'm Julie's resident." Why am I even arguing? I have a boyfriend. *I have a boyfriend.*

At least, I think Liam's my boyfriend.

"It doesn't matter. The school doesn't look at it that way."

"But why is it okay for you to *study* with all those women." He winces when I say 'all those women.'

"First of all, it's not as many as you may be thinking. Second of all, it's a onetime thing. They know that; I know that. Relationships are different. Harder to hide. A buddy of mine got fired last year for starting a relationship with a girl on a different floor. She got kicked out. The rules exist and they're harsh. And the school is not afraid to enforce them. It happens at least once a year on campus. I need this job, Lexie, to afford staying here. You don't want to get kicked out." Sighing heavily, he looks at the ceiling as if talking to himself. "Nothing can happen."

Fighting away the sting of disappointment and ache of sadness that's welling within me, I nod and swallow despite my suddenly dry throat. "Okay. I understand. We can keep it professional. I promise."

Nodding, he gives me one last longing glance before looking down at his notebook. The rest of the time is spent working on our project, talking about that and only that. Every so often, I take a peek at him and find him looking at me.

When it gets to be ten, we close up our books.

"Let's do eight again tomorrow night. But, uh, try not to come early. Please."

Clutching my books to my chest, I look up at him. "Yeah, sure. Sorry."

With a tight smile, Josh opens the door and says good-night. Hurrying down the hall to my room, I'm not sure what to make of everything that just transpired.

Josh kissed me. It had been the slightest tiny little thing, but it had happened. My breath shortens against a smile as I remember.

It's gone just as quick as a weight settles in my bones. That kiss was immediately followed by his rejection.

My mind knows it makes sense, that I need to put my feelings for Josh away and let them go. But my body does not. My lips are still tingling from the sensation of his on mine.

Though there's a range of emotions running through me, I manage to fall asleep. Disappointment weighs heavy in my heart that we can't be together. Anger bubbles under my skin at the stupid rules. There's even a sense of distrust that it's the true reasoning and not a disinterest in me that he's blaming on the school so as not to hurt my feelings.

But the one in the forefront, the one that's heavier and stronger than the rest...is wanting. For Josh.

THE NEXT NIGHT WHEN I GET TO JOSH'S ROOM, I'M MET WITH a different Josh than who I've seen the past few nights. Quietly, he invites me in, not making eye contact. I sit on the bed, the place he's been suggesting I sit for days, but he looks at me with such a forceful expression that I get down.

Sliding off the bed, I move to stand away from it, ankles crossed. "I'm sorry, I just assumed." My voice is low and tight, uncomfortable again in his presence as I look at the ground and loop some hair behind my ear.

"It's fine. Go ahead and sit. I really want to finish today."

"Alright, we can achieve that." We haven't really gotten a ton of work done outside of ideas. I'm worried it means a late night.

Instead, it means we don't talk about anything but class and work. He barely makes eye contact; no conversation gets sidetracked to anything remotely outside of the assignment. I don't say anything related to what happened last night. I keep looking over at him, trying to get a glimpse of something, a quick flash of the guy I had been with the past three nights. He's not there. If he is, he's not anywhere I can find him.

Dejectedly, I focus on my notebook, working on the project, not saying anything personal, barely getting any response back. We mostly sit in silence while we think up ideas or write notes.

"So, if you could do the packets, I'll work on the slideshow. We can send it to each other. I don't think we need to work on it together." It's abundantly clear that he wants to stop having to spend time with me.

My blood crystallizes in my veins. "Sure. Whatever you want." I collect my stuff to leave, hugging my books to my chest. But before I can, I need to know something. "What happened?"

"What do you mean?"

"The last three nights, things have been easy between us. Nice even. We had good conversation, we got to know each other. We went for coffee the other night and talked about ourselves instead of school. You kissed me."

He stiffens from head to toe. "That was a mistake. We shouldn't have done that; we should have kept it about school and only school. I told you, nothing can happen."

Dropping my chin to my chest, I nod, a gaping wound where my heart had been. Of course, he can't have any interest in getting to know me. Of course, he regrets kissing me. For a second, I had thought maybe, just maybe, he's interested in pursuing me. Now I know I was wrong. "Oh. Right. You're right. Okay. I'll just go, then."

He lets me leave without another word. I don't look back. I don't ask any more questions, either.

But I'd be lying if I said my heart didn't break the tiniest bit.

CHAPTER 10

Hopping off my bed, I run to answer the knocking that pulled me from a deep midday slumber.

Whipping open the door, I breathlessly answer, "Yeah?" I can feel my hair sticking up at funny angles, my face flush with warmth.

"Sorry, did I wake you?"

"Liam, hi. I was just taking a nap." I gesture my thumb over my shoulder toward my bed, my heart racing like I've been caught doing something wrong. Maybe I have been.

"Having a nice dream?" I was, in fact, very nice. But how do you tell your boyfriend that you were having a sex dream about another man? You don't. You lie.

"No, scary, actually. I was running away from something I couldn't see." Worrying my lip between my teeth, I hope he doesn't pick up on my tell.

"Ah, well, that explains the flushed face." The icy tendrils of guilt start to twist through my veins. Just another fib in the sea of lies I've been telling Liam lately.

Since the strangeness with Josh, I've been avoiding Liam, saying I'm busy with homework or Brittney, when really, I haven't been doing any of those things. Instead, I've been locked away in my room, sorting through the events of the past weekend over and over. Especially the kiss that I hate myself for wanting again.

"I came to see if you wanted to go grab a coffee."

"Yeah, definitely!" I say it a little too eagerly, but sincerely hope that Liam doesn't notice. Or if he does, that he'll at least think it's eagerness to see him, not to escape my bedroom and the dirty dreams that haunt me while here. Though I'm not really sure I want them to stop. "Let me just get changed. I'll meet you downstairs?"

"Sure thing." Smiling, he leans in to give me a peck on the cheek.

Taking a look in the mirror, I surprise even myself. My hair is standing up at impossible angles, my cheeks still pink. I have what I've come to recognize, from Lauren and Brittney, as sex hair, though I haven't even had sex.

Sighing, I pull my hair out of the tie holding it somewhat in place. I'm able to smooth it back a bit, tapping down the flyaways. The problem with curly hair is you can't just pull a brush through it, that only makes things worse. Short of washing it, this is the best I can do for now.

After changing into a fresh pair of jeans and a long sleeve shirt, I take a final look in the mirror. Not too bad. My hair is tamed nicely, up in a neat pony, the tail curling at the ends even though the top is a bit of a mess. If I had time, I'd refresh, but I want to get downstairs to Liam. A sense of guilt, like I'm looking at the scene of something scandalous, nibbles at my mind as I take one last look at my bed. Grabbing a lightweight jacket, I take a deep breath and head out the door.

When I get downstairs, Liam is sitting in a chair in the main lounge. Standing and grinning as soon as he sees me, he walks over to place a hand on my hip and a kiss on my cheek. "Shall we?" He extends his elbow for me to take, which I do giggling.

"Where are we going?" Confusion takes over as he leads me out of the building.

"For coffee."

"I thought we'd just go downstairs to the dining hall."

"No, no, let's go to the shop in the campus center. The coffee's better. Plus, it's a nice day for a little walk." Turning to me, he gives me a quick once-over and I hope the rosy hue is gone from my cheeks.

He's right, the coffee in the campus center is *way* better. But it also costs money while the dining hall is free.

"Don't worry, my treat." It's as if he's reading my mind. "So how are classes going? Are you enjoying things so far?"

Remorse bubbles under my skin as I think about the fact that it's been several days since I've done more than send him a text. I'm pretty sure he's asking about the project more than classes, but thinking back, we haven't really talked about school much recently.

"Yeah, I guess I am. It's a *lot* of work, and I'd expected a lot, but it's more than I'd anticipated. I'm having to read complete novels in a week for one of them. On top of all of my other classes." I shake my head.

"I mean, I'm a reader, I love to read all day everyday, but it's a lot even for me. And they're not necessarily books I enjoy or would choose for myself, so that makes it a little harder. I'm longing for my books of choice. Not to mention all the work can make it a little harder to have a social life." Heat creeps up my neck. It hadn't made it harder to see Josh. In fact, thanks to our English class, it made it easier. Not that he's given me even the slightest lick of attention since then, but I can still see him.

"It's okay, I remember how overwhelming freshman year can be, especially the first semester." Liam reads my flushed state as embarrassment that I'm not spending enough time with him. Good. "The guys and I are having a party tonight. I'd love if you could come."

"Sure. I'd love to." I'm not as enthusiastic as I probably should be. I'm not entirely sure I want to go, but I can't keep avoiding him. Can I?

"You can bring Brittney too. And Kimberly." I groan at the sound of her name. "Still not going well between you two?"

"Not even a little. I don't know what I did to get punished with such a horrible roommate." I do actually. Though, I had the roommate before anything happened between me and Josh. Maybe it was a proactive punishment; the universe knew I was going to do something wrong and started the retribution early.

"It happens. I got lucky with good roommates the first two years. We all decided to room together in the suite, but Jason's roommate the first year? Phew, he was a doozy. He almost never left the dorm. And you know Jason, he, uh, likes the ladies." I'm not quite sure why he says it like this. I *don't* know Jason. In fact, I barely know his suitemates at all.

"He couldn't bring any back because his roommate was always there and wasn't exactly pleasant to any of the girls he brought over." Liam laughs for a minute, as he looks off into the distance, a glazed look in his eyes. "He actually yelled, like really yelled, at one of the girls to get out of his room. That was when Jay stopped bringing girls over."

"Jason wasn't a roommate of yours?" I turn to him, brow furrowed. We're in the quad now, almost to coffee.

"No, actually, I met him in a history class freshman year. He's the only one though that I didn't room with. I thought I told you that?"

"Maybe it slipped my mind. Sorry." I'm pretty sure he hadn't, but these days, my mind isn't exactly retaining much about Liam.

"No worries, just thought I'd told you. But long story short, you'll make friends. And Kimberly doesn't have to be your roommate again next year. Have you thought about putting in for a roommate transfer?" Putting his hand on my lower back, he guides me toward the campus center.

Confusion pulls at my features, scrunching my brow and narrowing my eyes as I look up at him. "A roommate transfer? What's that?"

"You can fill out a paper at the desk asking for a roommate switch. You can choose to have a new random person or find somebody you want to room with who would want to switch as well and live with you. You can ask Brittney, but it's not always a good idea to room with a friend. Even me and the guys, we're buddies, but it can get a little sticky. Thankfully, we have the common room so if anybody's not getting along, there's a couch or two to choose from."

"I didn't know you could do that. Thank you so much, I'll have to look into it. I don't know if I can last the whole year with her." For the first time since I met Kimberly, I feel the slightest glimmer of hope rising in my chest.

"You haven't really told me what's so bad about her, just that she's awful. She seems to not be there much."

"You just happen to show up at times she's not hanging around. Probably because our schedules are fairly opposite. When she's there, she's just so rude and passive aggressive. She turned off my alarm one morning because *she* had a late night." There's an ache in my fingers that makes me realize how tightly my fist is balled.

Relaxing my grip, I continue, "She took a note left for me off the door and I found it in the trash. I'm glad it was just something stupid from Brit about dinner, which she came to tell me anyway, but still." I have to take a deep breath to tamp down the rage boiling in my blood.

"She's always mumbling under her breath and it's often pretty mean. I actually thought she and Brit were going to get into the other day because Brit was over, telling me about some guy and I could have sworn Kimberly said something about Brit being a whore."

Liam sighs and slides his hands into his pockets. He's probably sick of hearing me complain, but right now I can't seem to stop.

"The good thing about Kimberly is she doesn't seem to like confrontation, so when Brit very loudly said 'excuse me' Kimberly got up and left. I don't even want to think about what Brit would have done if she hadn't."

Liam stays quiet through my whole rant as we walk up the ramp to the center of the building.

"I don't know, maybe I'm making it seem not so bad, but everybody on the hall agrees that she's just hard to deal with."

A shrug is given in response. "Sounds like she can be difficult, I guess. Check out the roommate transfer. May be worthwhile."

"I will, thanks."

As we get our coffees and Liam pays, I'm left thinking about the paperwork. Could there really be a way out from dealing with Kimberly for the rest of the year? I'm not exactly sure, but if there's an option, I have to try. Rooming with Brittney could be fun, but it could definitely also have its downfalls. I wonder if they're more likely to grant it when there's a set somebody who agrees to room with you versus having to find a new random person.

OUTSIDE OF EACH OF THE DORMS, SURROUNDED BY ROADS that cut through campus, are big grassy areas. People use them to study, play Hacky Sack, Frisbee, and football.

It's a little after noon on a warm Saturday in late September, a few days after my talk with Liam and six weeks into the semester. Brittney and I are walking past one of those large green stretches of space on our way to the bookstore. There's a group of guys playing football by our dorm and my gaze immediately zeroes in on Josh amongst them.

Catching my eye, he smirks as he notices me staring, and reaches behind his head, pulling off his shirt and tossing it to the side. The light sheen covering his chest catches the sunlight, making his taut muscles glisten. All I can think about is running my fingers and tongue over them.

My tongue? I've never had thoughts like that before.

"Lexie!" Brit's voice snaps my attention back.

"What?" Slightly dazed, I turn back to her.

Her eyebrows sit high on her face. "You're practically drooling." She shakes her head. "He's not worth it, Lexie. He's not a relationship guy. At all."

"I don't know what you're talking about. I have Liam."

She cocks her head to the side. "Well, maybe you need to remind yourself of that while you're wetting your shirt staring at Josh."

My body is suddenly an inferno, knowing she's absolutely right. "I was not."

"Okay, whatever you say. Just be more discrete at least. I mean I was staring too, but you wouldn't know it."

"Right. Sorry."

Hooking her arm through mine, she starts pulling me toward the quad again. "It's okay. You're still new to such amazingness right at your fingertips. College is a whole new world, baby!"

I roll my eyes. "It may be a whole new world, but I'm still the same old Lexie."

She shrugs at my thought. "For now. We'll see how you are when I'm through with you."

"If it didn't work for Lauren for the last fifteen years, I doubt it will work for you."

"Ah, but, sweet Lexie, this is college. And all things are different in college. You'll see."

"Like I said, I have Liam. Who's no slouch to look at himself."

"He certainly isn't. But he isn't *that*," she says as she points at Josh. No, Liam certainly isn't Josh. He's good-looking in his own right, there's no denying that. But Josh stands in a world all his own. And he knows it.

Shaking my head, I try to rid the thoughts of Josh and his gorgeousness as we round the corner, literally putting him behind me. He's already told me nothing can happen. And outside of class, I haven't seen him since that night almost two weeks ago, let alone talk to him. "I don't need that. I wouldn't even know what to do with that."

She laughs. Loudly. "Trust me. Not only would you figure it out *very* quickly, but you'd have an excellent tutor."

My mouth goes arid at the thought of his guise. "Alright, enough of this. Let's go get your book and drop this subject, please?"

"Whatever you say, Lexie. You know you have to be able to talk about sex to have sex, right?"

"Who says I'm ready to have sex?"

"Nobody, I suppose, but you will at some point, right? Unless you plan to join a nunnery."

"I guess," I mumble. "I don't see a rush. What does it matter when I have sex?"

"It doesn't. But it's fun." Her eyebrows wiggle across her forehead.

"So how are things with Nadia?"

She laughs, understanding I'm making a quick subject change. "Eh. Not as bad as you and Kimberly, but still not great. Like I said, I'm thankful she's not around much. She's really not that smart; I don't know how she got in here, but try to correct her, and wow. Watch out. She's just not friendly. I try and try and get nothing in return."

"You know, Liam mentioned a roommate swap to me. He said that there's some sort of paperwork we can fill out and ask to switch roommates. If you'd maybe want to live with me."

"That would be amazing! I know they say not to live with

108

your friends, but it has to be better for both of us than what we have right now."

"I wholeheartedly agree."

"Think you'd be able to handle my social life, though?"

I know what she's referring to and while it does make me squirm a bit, I'd rather figure it out than continue with Kimberly. "I think we would have to establish some sort of system for that."

"Yeah, a scrunchie system. I have one already. Yellow is proceed with caution, possibly some clothes off. Red is *definitely* clothes off so enter at your own risk. Black means definitely do not enter."

"Why don't we just have black?"

She giggles a little. "Whatever your virginal self would prefer. But consider it for yourself as well."

"We should swing by the desk when we get back to get the paperwork. He said it can take a while to go through, if at all, but can't hurt, right?" Glazing over her suggestion helps ease my discomfort on the matter.

"Definitely can't. And who knows, maybe we'll get lucky."

"I hope so. I'm not sure how much more of Kimberly I can take. I feel like I'm doing something wrong just being in my room."

"The only thing you'll be doing wrong when we're roomies is *not* bringing boys back." Playfully, she tugs at my arm.

"Boy. Singular. One boy." To emphasize my point, I hold up one finger.

"But you may actually bring him back? Oh, yay, little Lexie is coming out of her shell!"

"Ugh, I can't win with you, can I?"

"Ha, nope. I'm kidding though. You know that, right?"

"Of course." Regardless of what Brittney may do in our room, she'd be far better than Kimberly.

When we get back to the dorm, we grab the paperwork

from Lisa, one of the desk attendants. It takes her a few minutes to find the correct form.

"We don't get too many of these," she says as she hands us the papers. "Good luck."

We fill them out together and bring them downstairs immediately. Lisa beams as she puts them in the hall director's folder. Crossing our fingers, we hope for the best.

CHAPTER 11

"No, no, please no. Don't do this to me!" I smack the steering wheel. "Stupid car." What am I going to do now? How am I supposed to get to English? Resting my head against the leather, I gently bang it repeatedly. I'll have to miss class while I wait for a tow truck to come.

A car horn sounds next to me, drawing my attention. It's none other than Josh, likely on his way to the satellite building, two towns south of campus. Where I'm *supposed* to be on my way to.

Getting out, he rests his arm on the lip of the door, so, I too, step out. "Having car trouble?" He juts his chin toward the front hood.

"It won't start," I respond dejectedly.

Tightlipped, he nods and looks across the top of his car like he's searching for answers there. "Okay, get in."

I quickly close my jaw from hanging open, eyes wide. "What?"

"Get in. I'll drive you to class."

"I'm not—I don't think that's a good idea."

"You think it's better to miss it?" He narrows his eyes at me as he gauges my reaction.

I chew the inside of my lip. I really don't want to miss English. But I also really don't want to sit in the car next to Josh for half an hour.

Class wins out over my discomfort. "Fine." Grabbing my bag, I close and lock my door, giving the tire a good kick before climbing into the passenger seat.

Positioning my body close to the door, I look out the window. I feel the tingle of his eyes on me every so often.

"You have car problems a lot?"

"No," I grumble out. I'm not mad at him; he's driving me to class. I should be nice.

"If you want, I can take a look at it when we get back."

Glancing over at him, I soften as a warmth spreads through my chest and defrosts the rest of me. "You know about cars?"

Keeping his eyes on the road, he lifts one shoulder. "A bit. I can change a tire and battery, maybe a few other things. I'm not a mechanic, by any means, but can maybe at least figure out what's wrong or if it's something simple that somebody could fix without a shop."

"That's impressive." I'm not sure I know anybody who can do that. Not even my dad. He may be handy with tools, but not so much with cars.

He shrugs again, fingers rubbing against his lip. It immediately draws my attention to his mouth, my own tingling in response at the thought of his brushing mine. "No big deal. It's good to know some things. What's it doing?"

"Not starting."

"Well, I know that. But is it making a sound? Does anything come on?"

Blankly staring at him, I blink repeatedly.

Giving a quick glance over at my dumbfounded expression, he chuckles lightly. "I'll take a look at it if you want me to."

"That would be very nice of you."

"Happy to." Turning to me, he offers a slight smile. His eyes trail over my body before going back to the road, the smile on his face widening.

"Why did you offer to drive me?"

His brow furrows, and he adjusts his pants as if getting more comfortable. "Why wouldn't I?"

"Because you hate me?"

Sitting up straighter in his seat, his eyebrows shoot up. He looks between me and the road a few times before answering. "I don't hate you." His voice is very quiet.

"No? Could have fooled me."

"What exactly have I done to make you think I hate you?"

"The way you look at me. We'd done a few days of working peacefully together, getting to know each other a bit. Then the last night, you barely spoke to me. I was worried I'd done something to offend you or something. And, yeah, okay, maybe we kissed, but it was like thirty seconds. You haven't even looked at me since."

"Are you paying attention to whether or not I'm looking at you?" Josh's gaze dashes in my direction quickly.

Heat rushes to my face as I swoop some hair behind my ear. "No, but I can notice when it seems like somebody is intentionally trying *not* to look at me." I try to make sure my voice doesn't hold a trace of the shakiness I feel.

This time, *his* face reddens. "It's just not a good idea."

"Knowing each other?"

He stares at the road for a minute. Repeatedly, his jaw tightens and relaxes. "Knowing each other as more than RA and resident. Or classmates."

"RAs and residents can get to know each other, can't they? And certainly classmates."

There's an expression on his face that I can't read. "I just think it's better to keep things less."

All I can do is nod. Maybe he doesn't hate me, but he

doesn't want to know me. "I understand." I don't, but it's easier to just say I do.

We drive the rest of the way in silence. I keep sliding my eyes sideways to look at him. His stay trained on the road, face giving away nothing. When we get to the satellite building, he finds a spot, hops out and waits at the front of the car as I gather my things, though I'm not sure why. We walk quietly into the building, his arm grazing mine every few steps, sending a strange zing through me. He holds the doors as I walk under his arm. Without a word, he takes his usual seat in the front, not even looking over at me.

Sighing, I drop my head and shuffle to the back to take mine.

As class wears on, I'm distracted by the thought of the drive back with Josh. The drive here had been awkward. The drive back, I'm sure, will be no less uncomfortable. Despite trying to pay close attention to Professor Carp, I can't focus on what she's saying. I wonder if anybody else in class could drive me back, but I don't really know them. Sliding my phone out, I slyly text Liam.

Me: *Do you know anything about repairing cars?*

Liam: *No. That's what mechanics are for.*

Me: *Ok. Thanks. Any chance you can come get me from the satellite building?*

Liam: *Busy. Sorry.*

Well, okay, then. Guess I'm stuck with Josh. It's only a half hour. I'll make the most of it. He'd offered to look at my car, which would be helpful because I'll at least have some idea about what's going on.

When class ends, Josh packs up his things and comes to stand by my desk, adjusting the backpack hung on one shoulder, other hand in his pocket. "Take your time," he says quietly as I rush to load up my stuff.

"All done." Standing, I throw my bag over my shoulder.

Moving back a few inches, he holds his arm out, signaling

for me to go first. He falls into step next to me as we walk in silence out to his car.

We're on the highway, almost halfway back, when he finally speaks first. "Sorry, my car isn't as nice as you're accustomed to other guys having."

"Sorry?" My eyes narrow at him. Is he somehow insulting me?

"I'm just saying, I know it's not as nice as Liam's."

I furrow my brow. "I don't care about that. I just appreciate the ride. You made it so I didn't have to miss class." Looking back out the window for a moment, I turn to him again. "Do you think I'm shallow or something?"

"Shallow?"

"Yeah. Why would your car matter to me?"

"I just know it matters to some girls."

"Well, I'm not one of those girls. Have you seen *my* car?"

"For one, your car is nicer than mine. For two, there are plenty of women who drive shitty cars, but prefer guys with nice ones."

"That's not something that matters to me."

He nods. "Good to know." I'm not really sure of the purpose of this conversation. Josh told me on the way down that we aren't going to get to know each other. So why does he care if I like what he drives? Maybe he's just being self-conscious about it. "I'm happy to still check your car when we get back, if you want."

"Yeah, I'd really appreciate it."

He gives me a small smile before turning back to the road. We drive the rest of the way back to campus with just the sounds from the radio filtering through the air.

Once we're back in the lot, I practically jump out of the car before he's done parking.

"Okay, let's take a look. Hop in and pop the hood for me."

I do as I'm asked, taking a second to find the lever.

"Try to start it."

Again, I do as I'm asked.

"Okay. Mind if I sit for a second?" Josh appears next to the open driver's door.

"Be my guest."

He does a few things, tries a few times before looking up at me. "Your battery's dead. I can replace it for you."

"Are you sure? Isn't that a big deal?"

"No, not really. I've done it plenty of times."

"I can just bring it to a shop. I don't want you to have to waste your time."

"A shop will overcharge you. They see beautiful girls like you coming from a mile away. I don't mind. It's not a waste of my time." My heart leaps when he calls me beautiful.

"Okay, if you're sure."

"I am." Taking the keys out, he shuts the door, then the hood. "Come on, I'll drive you over to the auto-shop to buy one."

As we drive across town, he actually talks to me, asking about my other classes, how I feel things are going now that we're almost six weeks into the semester, a few things behind me. Contentment swirls through me as I realize I have nice Josh here with me.

"Still enjoying reading?"

A tiny tendril of shock wraps around my mind, but a much larger one of excitement wraps around my chest. I can't believe he remembered that. "Um, not as much. I haven't had a chance to read for myself since classes started." There's a sadness in my tone that I'm just now realizing I feel.

"That's too bad. Sometimes, it's hard, sometimes, it's doable. You'll find a rhythm in upcoming weeks or next semester."

"That book we did for the project was pretty decent. It was a nice change."

"Good, I'm glad it helped a little. You did a nice job on that."

The air is pulled from my lungs. "Thanks. You too."

Clearing his throat, he pulls into the parking lot. "I'll run in and grab what we need."

Without another word or looking back, he's out of the car and striding across the lot.

He's only gone for a few minutes when he returns with the battery. "Alright, let's go fix it."

When we get back to campus, he parks near my car, grabbing some tools from his trunk. I wait outside the car, letting him take over. Utterly unashamedly, I stare at his butt as he leans over the open hood. It sends a rush through me that I know it shouldn't. I have to look away.

After about twenty minutes, he stands up, wiping his hands on a rag. "Okay, come try it."

I hop behind the wheel and take a deep breath, turning the key. The car starts immediately. I'm floored, and eternally thankful. And a little turned on. "How can I possibly thank you?"

He shrugs. "Don't worry about it."

"How much was the battery?" Grabbing my purse, I pull out my wallet.

He waves his hand at me. "Don't worry about it."

"No, please, you have to let me at least pay for it. You fixed it for free too."

"It's fine. Really, I don't mind."

I tuck some hair behind my ear as Josh's eyes catch mine. I'm aware it's the first time since we got back to campus. "Well, I really appreciate it."

Shutting the hood, he winks at me, completely melting my insides. "I'm going to just put these away."

Waiting for him to return, I lean against the door. The chime that indicates a text from Liam has come in sounds, and I pull my phone out.

Liam: *Something wrong with your car?*

I roll my eyes. Two hours after the fact isn't going to help me now.

"Something wrong?" Josh asks as he rounds my car.

"Nope, nothing," I say as I push my phone back into my purse, falling into step next to him. Looking up at him, I take a second to note the lighter tones as the sun shines on his hair. "I want to thank you again. It means a lot to me."

"I'm happy to help you out. Really."

"Just know I would have been completely stuck without you. And not just for class today."

"Really, not a big deal." I can't tell if he's being modest or just truly doesn't mind helping. Maybe he does this a lot. As we step onto the sidewalk in front of our dorm, I notice Liam walking over. Josh does too, as he stiffens. "I should go. I'll see you around." Giving me a tight smile, he gently puts his hand on my arm, before disappearing inside.

Warmth emanates from his hand through my body.

"Hey, babe. I wanted to check on you. Sorry it took me a while to get back to you." Leaning in to give me a kiss on the cheek, his eyes glance over my shoulder into the dorm lobby.

"That's okay. I'm good."

"Yeah? Anything I need to know about?" There's a biting edge to his tone that I don't exactly appreciate, when I was stuck and he was less than helpful.

"My car died?"

"I mean, anything with you and Josh."

Trying to seem nonchalant and act like nothing happened, I lift a shoulder breezily. Aside from having feelings that I know I shouldn't have, nothing *had* happened. Today at least. I choose to focus on that. "He gave me a ride to class. It's the one we have together, and he saw me yelling at my car."

"That it?"

I look at the ground. "He also fixed it for me," I mumble.

Liam's silent. I have to look up to see his face. He's just

nodding slowly, chewing his lip. Shaking his head, he looks at me, a smile on his face, like he's forcing away whatever thought he had. I catch the tail end of an iciness as it leaves his eyes.

I'm a little surprised by his reaction. I know Liam doesn't really care much about Josh; he hadn't even mentioned he knew Josh until I brought it up a few days ago. Despite his comment a week ago, Liam made it seem like Josh was just another guy on campus. Though that was hardly the impression I'd gotten from Josh.

"It's okay. Sorry, I couldn't be there to help you out."

"It's fine, everything worked out." His quick change has me feeling a little on edge.

"Want to come over?"

"I have some work to finish. Maybe later?"

"Sure." Leaning in, he gives me a kiss on the cheek, lingering for a second. "Call me tonight and let me know."

He's off before I can answer him. It certainly feels like he's not so okay with what occurred. I don't want to press it, though. If he says he's okay, I'm going to let it be. He hadn't been there to help me out. What could he expect from me? Besides, Josh and I are just classmates.

If that's really the case, why do I have to say it to myself repeatedly?

ON THURSDAY, I'M WALKING TO MY CAR FOR CLASS WHEN JOSH catches up to me.

"Hey," he says breathlessly. It almost seems like he ran.

"Hey." There's a hint of questioning in my voice. I'm not sure why he's talking to me when last time we spoke, he'd made it clear we shouldn't get to know each other.

"Can I drive you to class today?"

Shock freezes my muscles in place, and I come to a halt.

Josh stops a few feet ahead of me and turns around. "Why?" I ask with narrow eyes.

His shoulders slowly rise and fall. "I just figured since we're both coming from the same place and going to the same place, we may as well go together. Save the planet and all that." He runs a hand through his hair, his shirt sliding up slightly to show his tight stomach underneath.

My breath catches at the sight, a smirk spreading across his face.

Shaking my head, I clear out the fuzziness that seeing his toned stomach brought on. "Sure. That's nice of you to offer." I follow him to his car, where he holds the door open for me. My eyes meet his as I slip in. "Thank you."

Sliding into his side, he stretches out his long legs as much as he can. We drive to the satellite building, making small talk about classes even though it's only been two days since we last discussed them. He asks if I've driven my car again, which I haven't, since it's only been two days.

"Just make sure you turn off your lights. And don't sit in it with just the radio on."

My face burns, and instantly I look down at my lap, tucking hair behind my ear.

"What?"

"That's probably what happened, then. I just…it's so awful with Kimberly! She's so miserable. Every so often I just pop out to my car to have a little alone time, music loud, drowning everything out. I can't deal with her. For some reason, I'm being punished with a terrible roommate." Sighing, I look up at the ceiling.

"Sorry, you probably don't want to hear about this; you deal with this stuff all day long." My anger quickly fades to a guilt that twists through my stomach as I realize I just exploded my brain all over him.

His hand is at his mouth, finger running along his lips. I've noticed he does that when he's thinking. "I don't mind hearing about it from you."

A tingle starts at the nape of my neck and sprawls through my body. He's being nice to me again. I hadn't realized how upset it had made me when he wasn't welcoming until this moment. Last time I was so preoccupied with my car and figured he was just being nice because I was stuck. The whole damsel in distress thing.

"I won't go into detail. I don't need to unload on you. I put in for a roommate switch, but I know it can take a while to go through, if at all, so I'm not holding out any hope. Guess I'm just stuck with her." Slamming my head back against the seat rest, I look out the window, not having realized we were here already until Josh pulls into a spot.

Shrugging, he turns off the car. "You never know. Sometimes those things go smoothly." His gaze stays locked on mine in an odd sort of staring contest, where neither of us move to get out.

Blinking and turning away, he exits the car first.

When we get inside, instead of Josh heading to his seat in the front, he walks toward the middle, glancing back at me with a question in his eyes.

Following him rather than taking my usual seat at the back, I make note of the small smile on his face as I sit at a desk next to his. Stretching his long legs out, he reaches one out into my space a little. Instead of turning away from him, I tilt toward him, my knee grazing his. His smile spreads more, pen at his mouth to try to hide it.

Professor Carp walks in and starts class. Throughout the hour and a half, I repeatedly glance at Josh. Every so often I'll notice him looking at me and quickly avert my gaze to my desk, my hair a curtain between us. His leg shakes as he laughs quietly at my embarrassment.

When we get back to the parking lot on campus, I thank him for driving me. He walks me back to the dorm, silently walking up the stairs to our floor. When we step out of the stairwell, I stop. His door is to the left, while mine is to the right. This is where we part ways.

"Well, thanks again. See you Tuesday." I turn to leave but his voice stops me.

"If you ever want to study together, let me know."

Is this one of those invitations he gives girls? I turn on my toes to face him. "Study or *study?*"

A knowing look flashes across his eyes before they drift briefly to my chest. "I mean study, like books, words, flashcards. But I'll happily do the other too." One corner of his mouth ticks up.

Huffing, I roll my eyes. "I may be interested in the studying, books and flash cards style, if you think you can keep it to just that."

Snapping his feet together, he holds up his hand, all fingers pressed together. "Scout's honor." Relaxing to a more normal pose, he laughs lightly.

Shaking my head, I roll my eyes again, though, really, I just want to laugh. I like this side of him when he's willing to show it to me. "If you can't take it seriously, then never mind." Turning away from him, I start to walk to my room.

But Josh grabs my hand, stopping me. I spin to face him, eyebrows raised, no sign of amusement on my face.

"I'm being serious. If you ever want to study, really study, let me know. I'd be happy to work with you. We did a good job on our project." His voice is low, serious.

I'm not really sure why he's saying all this. Just two days ago, he had told me we shouldn't be getting to know each other. I guess, classmates study together without discussing personal details, though. He'll probably make sure we stick to just books, like we had during our last meeting for our assignment. "Sure. I'd like that. This class is a little harder than I thought it would be."

A smile spreads across his face that makes me want to melt into the floor. "Okay, good. Let me know. Any time."

"I will." With that, he lets go of my hand. I hadn't even noticed he was still holding on to it, but immediately, I miss his warm hand around mine. Giving him a small smile, I turn for my room. When I'm just outside my door, hand on the knob, his voice stops me again.

"Oh, uh, just not this weekend. Let me know if you need help next weekend."

"Sure thing." Taking a deep breath, I look at the ceiling before opening the door, knowing that Kimberly is going to be in there as she doesn't have any classes on Thursdays.

She makes a noise as I walk in and put my books down on my desk. Glancing over at her, I wonder what higher power I've pissed off to get stuck with such a bad roommate. Or why she seems to hate me even though she doesn't know me at all. She barely speaks to me enough to find out anything about me.

Sitting at my computer, I start working on a paper for my history class when a message pops up from Liam.

Liam: *Sorry, something came up. I'll call you tomorrow.*

Great. The out I was going to have to get away from Kimberly for a few hours just fell apart. I would go down to Brit's room, but she's in classes for another four hours, since Thursdays are late days for her. Deciding it's too soon to take Josh up on his offer to study, I resign myself to a night of Kimberly.

CHAPTER 12

I freeze, key in midair. There's an envelope with my name on it tacked to the corkboard on my door. Looking both ways down the hall, I almost expect to find who left it, but on some level, I know that that person has to be long gone as I'm alone in the hallway. It is after eleven at night on a Thursday, after all.

After the message from Liam, I decided a trip to the library was warranted. It gave me the opportunity to finish my paper in peace and not have to deal with Kimberly's frequent huffs and puffs in my direction.

I pull the white rectangle off gingerly, like it may burst into flames if not treated carefully, before opening the door and stepping inside. Thankfully, Kimberly is nowhere to be found. I have no idea where she is this late, but the thought isn't going to bother me for more than a half second.

Tenderly opening the envelope, I pull out a ticket to the Switchfoot concert. I've been wanting to go but have nobody to go with. It's not really Brittney's style of music, and Liam had told me before I even brought it up that he'd join me if I really want him to, but I could tell by the way he said it he'd really hate it. I don't want to be owing him any major favors.

A little note goes floating down to the floor.

Go with me?
-J

My heart hammers against my breastbone. He knows I'd want to go. This is exactly the sort of music he knows I like; that first conversation sneaking into my mind. I flip out my phone.

Me: *Yes.*

Josh: *Good.*

At the immediate ping of his text, I hold the phone to my chest, unable to contain the excitement. I'm not sure if I'm more excited about the concert or the company I'll be attending with.

Josh and I don't talk about the concert again after those texts. Two days later, not even knowing if we're still going, I get myself ready and walk over to the athletic building where the concert is, figuring I'll just wait for him outside.

After forty-five minutes of waiting, and missing the first song of the opening band, I stand up from the curb, ready to go home. That's when I spot him, head down, hands in his pockets. A tall, dark figure walking toward me. My breath catches, barely even seeing him, but knowing he's coming to see me.

"Sorry, I'm late. I was stuck doing...something," he says when he comes to stand before me.

"Or someone." I try to say it quietly.

"Huh?"

Not quietly enough. "Nothing."

"No, you said *'or someone.'* Is that in reference to something?"

"Just, you know, the studying. We've already had this discussion."

"I haven't *tutored* since that conversation."

I'm shocked, needing to pick my jaw up off the floor. I feel like I've noticed fewer girls in and out of his room. But he's an RA, his room is always busy, always people knocking. "Why?"

The sincerity in his eyes blazes, even in the darkness. "I have my reasons. Come on, let's go in. I'm sure we've already missed a song or two, and I wanted to hear the opening band."

Following him in, I can't stop glancing up at him every few minutes. We show our tickets at the door and head into the large gymnasium, converted for concerts. It's pretty packed close to the band, not as much farther back, but so loud I can hardly hear myself think.

Josh points toward the stage, and I nod. We push our way through people to get closer. Finally spotting a small opening, we can actually see the band. We're standing close enough that his musky cologne swirls in my nose and every so often our arms graze. The music is thumping so intensely that I feel it thrum through my body, which makes it impossible to know what my heart's doing, though I'm sure it's pounding away at Josh's nearness.

Somebody walking toward the exit bumps into me on his way back, almost knocking me over. Josh's hands are on my hips before I can fall, steadying me.

"You okay?" His lips are right against my ear, sending a shiver racing down my spine.

All I can do is nod.

He stands up straighter but keeps his hand around my waist. Looking up at him, his eyes lock on mine, the tiniest smile spreading across his lips. Taking a chance, I move the littlest increment closer to him, my shoulder brushing his chest.

We stand there, rocking a little to the music, his arm around me. Another two songs in and somebody pushes by on his side. He steps to stand directly behind me, putting his other hand on my waist. As he starts to move back to the side, slowly pulling his hand away, I place mine on his, stopping him from removing it. Tilting my head up to look at him, there's a twinkle in his eyes as he bites his bottom lip and moves to stand behind me, wrapping his arms around my waist. Leaning back into him, I feel his heart thumping quickly, too fast to be the bumping of the bass.

Without feeling it, I can say for certainty that mine is doing the same.

I have the briefest thought of Liam. I know I shouldn't be standing here, like this, with another man. A man who could get in trouble if caught. But it's dark and so busy in here I feel confident that we'll be okay. And I don't want to be standing here with anybody else but Josh.

We stand pressed together for five songs. Josh's arms get a little tighter around my waist with each one, pulling me closer and closer against him. Resting my head back against his shoulder, with his chest warm at my back, I enjoy the feeling of him up against me.

Then I hear the opening chords for one of the band's ballads. I have a moment of panic. Is Josh going to push me away? Standing pressed together, not looking at each other, is one thing; slow dancing is another. Though, honestly, I'm not really sure I see the line at this point. Maybe because I'm already across it.

The moment of panic is over quickly as Josh takes my hands and spins me around to face him, roping my arms around his neck, his hands settling on my lower back, pinkies reaching into my back pockets. We spend the first verse of the song just swaying together, not making eye contact. But when the chorus starts, there's a vibration in his chest.

Looking up, I find his eyes on me, mouthing the lyrics of the song. I can't hear him, but I know the lyrics by heart. I know the words he's seemingly singing to me. They're about wanting, longing, desire. My eyes inadvertently drift down to his lips, wanting to feel them pressed against mine again.

His mouth closes on mine in an instant, pushing my mouth open as his tongue slides across mine. His hand trails up my back, wrapping in my hair, palm against my ear.

I've kissed other boys before, including Liam. But this kiss...this one makes everything around me fade away. There's no more concert, no other people. I'm not worried about what I'm doing or if I'm doing it right or how to spell my name in cursive, a trick Lauren had sworn would always work. This kiss makes me forget anything else exists.

Until he pulls away, hand settling on my hip again, giving a tiny squeeze. Leaning my head into his chest, I listen to his heart pounding around the humming of the song, all breath stolen from my lungs.

We stay that way even after the ballad ends, even as the last song comes to a close and everybody cheers. When the lights flick on, we jump apart, eyes locking on each other.

"Come on, I'll walk you back." Josh jerks his head toward the door as he shoves his hands in his pockets.

We walk back to the dorm in silence, arms bumping every so often. He unlocks the doors for me, holding them open so I can go first. He walks me to my room and places the gentlest kiss on my temple, so small I'm not sure if I'm imagining it.

"Good night, Lexie. Thanks for coming with me. I had a nice time."

"I did too. Thanks for inviting me. Good night, Josh."

I step into my room before he reaches his, closing the door and leaning against it, trying to catch my breath.

"What is wrong with you?" I almost forgot that I'd left Kimberly here, fully expecting her to still be here when I got back, considering she basically never leaves the dorm outside of classes and meals.

"Nothing." I glare at her as I put my stuff away. Taking the ticket stub out of my pocket, I tack it to the corkboard on my desk. "I'm going to sleep."

"Whatever."

Grabbing my things, I take them to the bathroom, brushing my teeth and putting on my pajamas. Once back in my room, I give one more glance at Kimberly sitting at her computer and climb into bed.

I'VE BEEN LAYING IN BED FOR OVER AN HOUR, UNABLE TO SLEEP. It's one in the morning at this point. The events of the night keep running through my mind. The lyrics of the song that Josh had sung. The kiss. *The kiss.* I know how I feel about it. But I also know that I shouldn't feel this way. I have a boyfriend. Sort of. I have Liam. Liam, who had offered to go with me even though he very clearly didn't want to.

To make me feel worse, I get a text from him while working through the night for the hundredth time.

Liam: *Hey babe! How was the concert?*

How was the concert? I can't possibly tell him. I hadn't even told him I was going with Josh, instead telling him I was going alone. Now I feel a surge of guilt. I lied to my boyfriend. I had thought it was an innocent white lie at first, I didn't want him to feel like he had to come with me and convinced him I was totally fine going by myself, knowing I wasn't.

But Josh has made it clear we can't be anything, so I figured it was innocent to go together, as friends, or whatever it is we are.

Me: *Amazing.*

What else can I say? It was amazing. But not for the reasons Liam would think. I put my phone on my desk and close my eyes before getting his response.

CHAPTER 13

I don't see Josh outside of class for almost a week, and while there, he won't even look at me. It isn't necessary for me to talk to him to know that he regrets the night of the concert, what happened between us. Despite the guilt I feel about it, I don't regret it. In fact, I dream about it, and more.

The very brief phone call I had with Lauren makes things even muddier. She thinks he's stringing me along, and maybe he is, but my heart tells me there's more here, there's more going on. The pull that I feel toward him, I can't be alone in that. Can I?

It makes my head spin. I've known I'm attracted to Josh from day one. Who wouldn't be? We've shared a few small moments, and he's made it clear he's not boyfriend material; that I'm not somebody he can be with. Maybe not even somebody he wants to be with despite the kissing. Maybe the other night he realized what little bit of him may be attracted to me was very, very wrong, and he's decided to steer clear. Or maybe it's just that stupid rule again. He's made it well known, yet it hadn't stopped him from bringing me to the concert. Or kissing me. Again.

The thoughts running around in my head are so distracting, I don't hear Professor Carp release us. Looking down at my notebook, I realize I missed the entire class, not taking a single note. *Crap.*

Quickly scooping up my books, I scoot right out, not making eye contact with anybody.

"Hey." I'm so startled I almost trip, Josh's hands wrapping around my waist before I can fall forward. "Whoa, there. Sorry. Thought you saw me?"

"No, sorry. Been a bit distracted." Clearing my throat, I adjust my bag on my shoulder, and take a minute to stare at the ground before glancing in his direction.

"Listen, I'm sorry about the other night. I shouldn't have…we shouldn't have…I shouldn't have kissed you. It's not fair to you. It was a mistake."

A coolness starts in my heart and extends through my veins.

"I can't give you what you want. Liam can. I need to step back; take myself out of the picture."

"How do you know what I want?"

He's taken aback. His mouth starts moving, trying to find the words, then closes again. "You're a relationship girl, Lexie. That's why you're *in* a relationship. Let's not forget that. What happened the other night, it was wrong. You're with somebody!"

"I know. And I feel guilty about that. But I also don't regret what happened." His jaw tightens and his Adam's apple bobs up and down.

He looks at me with a sadness in his eyes before sighing and looking at the sky. "It was wrong. That's all there is too it."

"That's not all there is to it."

"It has to be. Lexie, we *can't* be together. We just can't."

"But if we could?"

He looks back at me, dark eyes penetrating mine.

"Then I would want to be." He's so quiet I have to lean in to hear him. When it registers, my heart flutters. "But it doesn't matter. Because we can't be. That's not going to change. We're a month and a half into the semester, the year. There's a lot of time left. Be with Liam, be happy."

"I never said that he makes me happy."

"But if I were out of the picture, you could be."

The thought of him being gone steals the breath from my lungs. My heart thuds against my sternum and his eyes dash to my neck and back up again, a tightness settling in his jaw.

His fingers flutter at his sides, as if he's fighting some internal battle against moving them.

We stand in the parking lot staring at each other for a long time, barely blinking or even moving more than a shift of our feet. It's like we're in a battle of wills to see who will turn away first.

Enough is enough. Clearing my throat, I break the silence that's blanketed us. "And what are we going to do? Pretend we don't know each other? We live down the hall from one another; I can literally see your door from mine. And we have a class together."

"We'll avoid each other. Our current seating arrangement works fine. We don't see each other in the hall a lot anyway."

Running my tongue across my teeth, I try to stop the shake wanting to overtake my body. "Fine. If that's what you want."

"I think it's what's best." He doesn't say it's what he wants. I decide to hold on to that fact, because I can't cope with the loss of Josh, in whatever small capacity I have him now. "I'll see you around."

"Sure." And with that, he's off, leaving me standing feeling disregarded, cast aside. In this moment, I feel a surge of anger rising in my veins like a tidal wave. I'm angry at the school, angry at their stupid rules, and angry at Josh.

HUFFING MY WAY BACK UPSTAIRS, I THROW MY BAG UNDER MY desk with a growl.

"Well, hello, there sunshine."

I whip around at Brittney's voice. I'd left the door open in my rage. Josh's words had played over and over in my mind on my drive back, the anger boiling under the surface.

"Hi."

"Want to talk about it?"

"No."

"Fine." Waltzing into my room, she hops up onto the bed. "I can't make it to Liam's on Saturday."

Jumping up on the bed next to her, I pull one leg under me as I turn to face her. "Why? You said you'd come to be my guardian or whatever." Not that I feel I need one, but at the same time, I don't exactly think it's the worst idea.

"It's Taylor's birthday. She's a shitty captain, but we always go big for birthdays on the team. I have to go. I'm sorry," she grumbles her way through her words.

"It's okay. I understand. I'm sure I'll be fine."

"You can come with us if you want to."

"No, Liam's expecting me. Really, it's no big deal."

"So why did you come storming in and take some anger out on your bag just now?" Her eyebrow quirks up as she looks at me.

"Rough class." I can't tell her the truth. Not only could Josh and I get in trouble if anybody found out, though I trust Brittney not to say anything, intentionally, but she'd probably tell me I'm being foolish letting him pull me in time and time again.

"Want to go grab a coffee? That should brighten your mood."

"Absolutely." I'm hopping off the bed and heading for the door before she's even moved an inch.

Though deep in my soul, I know this is something even

coffee can't help. Maybe I need a trip to the lake, or a call to Lauren. Some part of me knows those things won't help either. That the only thing to make this feeling of wanting to claw out my own heart go away, is the boy who put it there in the first place.

CHAPTER 14

Tripping over my own feet on my way out of Liam's building and onto the sidewalk, I laugh to myself, happy I didn't fall. My dorm is only about ten feet away. I drag my feet through the drive that separates the two dorms and up to the door.

That's when I see him. Josh's tall frame, sitting on the couch behind the door, another RA by his side. His dark eyes lock on mine immediately, fire burning in them.

After fumbling with my keys, I'm able to open the door before reaching into my pocket to show my ID. My gaze stays on Josh's, which causes me to barely hear what the other RA says.

Taking a few steps forward, I stumble a bit, putting my arms out to try to regain my balance.

Josh exchanges a look I can't quite make out with the guy next to him, handing over the clipboard that's in his lap.

I'm almost at the staircase when Josh's arm loops around my waist, pulling me into him.

Jerking away, I fall into the wall. "What are you doing?" It comes out more slurred than I would like.

"Helping you upstairs." His voice is low and calm, but there's an edge to it.

"I don't need your help."

"You're drunk."

Waving him off, I keep moving. "I'm fine." I pitch forward a bit. Oops.

Sighing, he wraps his arm around my waist again and opens the door to the stairwell.

He helps me up the first set of stairs. Once we get to the second floor, I push him off again. "I said, I'm fine."

Staying close behind me, we walk up the second flight of stairs. A few steps up the third set, I trip forward, sure I'm going to smack my face against the stairs, when a pair of hands firmly grab my waist, righting me.

Turning around, I find his jaw tight, eyes blazing. I can't tell if he's angry at me, the situation, or both. I'm sure helping me up the stairs is the very last thing he wanted to be doing tonight.

He makes sure I'm on my feet and steady before loosening his grip, though not letting go completely.

After I successfully make it the rest of the way up the stairs without falling, and throw myself an internal party, I pull open the door to the fourth floor a little too hard. The force of it has me tripping sideways. Josh is able to stop the door from slamming into the wall with one hand, grabbing my bicep to keep me from crashing into it with the other.

"That's it," he murmurs under his breath as he whisks me up into his arms. I lean my head against his shoulder as he carries me down the hall.

"Why are you being nice to me?" I'd blame the alcohol for my lack of filter, but I've never had much of one when it comes to Josh.

Looking down at me, his gaze penetrates straight through to my soul. If I wasn't drunk, I'd want to shrink in on myself. The reason it's called liquid courage suddenly makes all the sense in the world. "What are you talking about? I'm always nice to you."

"You mean, ignoring me is being nice to me? Interesting."

When he huffs, I look up at him, swaying a bit as I do, causing his arm to tighten around me.

"You're taking care of me. Why?"

"Because you're a beautiful young woman and you're drunk. I'm getting you back safely."

"There's nobody out here, everybody's asleep." I move my arm out around me for effect. We haven't run into another person since we started up the stairs.

"You never know. Plus, you may end up falling down the stairs." Well, that's certainly true.

"But you're not usually nice to me. You're only nice when you want something. Otherwise, we're strictly RA and resident. Right?"

His eyes flash back to mine. "My job *is* to take care of residents, make sure they're safe."

All I can do is nod, though part of me is sure that doesn't include carrying them upstairs. I choose to keep my mouth shut on that part.

"Hey, that's my room!" I squeal as he walks right past it. Reaching behind his back, my arms extend toward it.

Josh ignores me and keeps walking. When he stops, we're outside his room. Propping my butt up on his knee, he reaches into his pocket for his keys and unlocks his door, carrying me inside, pushing the door closed with his foot, and bringing me to the bed.

"Why are we here?" The slurring is getting worse.

"Just...lie down. Rest." His voice is low and gentle. Soothing.

Without argument, I lay my head against his pillow. It's cool and feels nice on my warm skin. It also has the musky scent of his cologne mixed with a crispness of soap. I'm vaguely aware of him gently taking off my shoes and pulling a blanket over me, tenderly brushing some hair off my face before I fall into a deep sleep.

With a start, I sit straight up and look frantically at my surroundings, not remembering where I am or how I got here. A throbbing slams my head as my hand flies up to my temple, eliciting a groan.

That's when I notice a dark figure sitting near the foot of the bed. He's slouched down in his chair, long legs stretched out, bent at the knees. The fire in his eyes is still aflame, and they never leave mine as he brings a beer to his lips and takes a slow sip.

We sit for a few minutes, eyes locked on one another, his blazing with an anger that I can clearly make out, despite the darkness of the room.

I know I have to be the one to break the silence. "What am I doing here?"

"I wanted to make sure you were safe."

"You brought me upstairs. You could have left me at my doorstep to know I was safe."

"Do you understand how hammered you were tonight? You're lucky you haven't puked. I mean, Jesus, Lexie, what were you doing?"

As his voice rises and hits a level that's too much for the pressure in my head, it elicits another groan from me. "I went to a party and had too much. I would have been fine."

"Why did you come back alone? Where was Brit?"

"She didn't go with me. I went by myself." My voice is low to match the need for my head.

"You went to a party alone? Are you crazy?" His voice is loud, causing me to wince.

A heavy breath pushes from my nose. "It was at Liam's." I hadn't wanted to tell him.

Josh tenses as he absorbs the information. "And Liam let you leave, alone, as drunk as you were?"

My head drops, chin hanging over my chest. "He wanted me to stay," I say quietly.

"He what?" His voice is quiet, coated in anger. The opposite of what I expected, already curled into myself to protect from what I thought would be yelling.

I raise my head up to look at him. "He wanted me to stay. With him. I declined. He got mad. We argued, and I left."

His free hand balls into a fist. I can feel the tension rolling off of him from a few feet away. "So he pushed drinks on you all night, then wanted you to stay with him, wasted?"

"I wouldn't say he *pushed* the drinks. But, yeah, that's the gist of it." I can tell that he's doing everything in his power to control himself, control his anger as his chest rises and falls, his hand opening and closing again. "Why do you care?"

Hurt flashes across his face. "Because I do. And you know that I do."

"No, I don't. You run so hot and cold I never know what you're thinking from one moment to the next. One minute, you're kissing me, holding me at concerts. The next, you don't talk to me for days, just glare at me from across the room, telling me that kissing me was a mistake. I can't keep track of whether you like me and want to be with me but can't, or you hate me but like my body or the way I feel, so you come around when you want to get something. Though, you know you can and have had any woman you want on this campus, so I'm not sure why you're messing with me." It all comes out with one long, exasperated breath as I use what courage I have left to get my point across.

The rage fueled the words. The alcohol helped me be brave enough to get them out.

Placing his beer on the desk, he crosses the room in a second, cupping my face with both hands and pressing his lips to mine. Though the kiss starts gentle, it quickly intensifies as he slides one hand to the back of my neck, tipping my head back as he parts my lips with his, his tongue slipping over mine. His hand glides down my back, pulling me against him.

It takes my body a minute to respond, still a bit out of sorts from the alcohol and sleep. Looping my arms around his neck, I pull him closer, closing the tiny bit of space that still exists between us. He slowly leans me back on the bed, keeping his mouth against mine, to lay over me, his hand running down the side of my body. Wrapping his arm around my waist, he pulls me flush against him. I can feel the muscles in his chest against mine, his heart hammering.

We lay there pressed up against each other, mouths moving in sync, until my lips are swollen. When Josh ends the kiss, he rests his forehead against mine, breathing heavily. Tenderly, he touches the tip of his nose to mine, leaving a gentle kiss on my bottom lip, then placing tiny kisses along my jaw.

"I want you. But I can't have you," he whispers against my ear. Dread settles deep into every nook and cranny of my body. He's going to tell me we can't do this, that I have to go. But I want nothing more than to stay here with him.

Instead, he rolls over to lay next to me, turning me on my side, facing away from him. Taking my hand in his, he places it on my stomach and pulls me tightly against his chest. "But for tonight, let's just pretend I can."

With a racing heart and warmth flowing through my veins, I fall asleep in Josh's arms, his face nuzzled into the back of my neck, his steady heartbeat the last sound I hear.

THE INCESSANT POUNDING IN MY HEAD IS WHAT WAKES ME. Slowly opening my eyes, I look around, sitting up slightly. I remember being in Josh's room. My gaze searches for a clock, finding one with bright red numbers telling me it's five-thirty in the morning.

Turning my head, I find Josh sleeping soundly next to me, one arm thrown over his head, his shirt pulled up the slightest bit to show the indentations of a V at his waist and the slightest bit of a hair trail. I bite my lip and turn away from him, desire stirring in me.

As I start to slide away, a pull against my thigh makes me suddenly aware he still has a hand there. Ever so gently, I release myself from his grasp.

There's nothing I want more than to stay in bed with him. To snuggle up close and breathe him in and fall back asleep listening to the steady rhythm of his heart, my head rising and falling with his breaths.

But I know I can't. I know staying and waking up when or after he does will only lead to heartache. So, I quietly climb out of his bed, grab my shoes and key, and silently let myself out, feeling an ache spread from my chest through my body.

Nobody will be up this early on a Sunday, so there's no worry of being seen leaving his room in the wee hours of the morning. It's a little eerie walking down the silent hall when I'm so used to it bustling with noise and life.

I slip quietly into my room, Kimberly still fast asleep. Not wanting to draw attention to myself, I put my things down as gently as I can and change quickly into pajamas, having still been in my jeans and long-sleeved shirt from the night before. Climbing into bed, my heavy head hits the pillow, and I'm asleep within seconds. All the while wishing I was still down the hall.

THE DOOR SLAMMING OPEN MAKES ME BOLT UP IN BED. Turning toward the sound, I find Brittney standing there.

"Why?" is all I can moan, hand leaping to my head. I flick

143

my eyes over to the other bed, noting that Kimberly is nowhere to be seen, so kindly leaving the door unlocked in her absence.

"How was the party?"

I shake my head. "Bad. So very bad."

"Hangover?"

"Of epic proportions."

"Here." She holds out two Tylenol and grabs a water from my fridge.

I look up at her with amazement. "You're my angel."

This elicits a laugh, thankfully low decibel. "Take those and get ready. Food and coffee will help."

All I can do is groan. I not-so-gracefully get out of bed, sliding my feet into my slippers. "Let me run to the bathroom to freshen up a little," I mumble as I grab my caddy of toiletries.

The cool water on my face feels good, helping the headache a bit. Looking in the mirror, I'm happy to see that despite a rough night, my hair isn't *too* terrible. Curls lay flat in some spots, sticking out in a few others. A few spurts of my refresh spray and a little water, plus come scrunching, make the curls twist nicely. I give a quick shake and they bounce around my face. Not great, but good enough. It helps me look not quite so hung-over. I can't do anything about the tired look settled into my eyes.

I shuffle back to my room. "Okay. I'm good. Or at least as good as I'm going to get."

At this moment, I'm thankful for having left my bra on when I changed to go back to bed.

Mental images from the night before play like a movie through my mind as I follow her down the stairs. That's where Josh scooped me up, that's where he grabbed my waist to stop me from face planting into the staircase. Brittney's voice is more of a whir in the background as the throbbing hasn't quite subsided and the memories with Josh send my feelings reeling, mind spinning.

We get down to the dining hall, which is attached through the lower level of our building. I'm eternally grateful for that today, as I'm not sure my head could handle what appears to be a bright sunny day. The line is always long for brunch on the weekends, since it starts later in the day and there are no classes. Any loud noises, amplified by the hallway we wait in, cause me to flinch.

"Head still throbbing?" Brittney ventures quietly.

"It's a little better, but this noise doesn't help."

"Get ready, you know it will only be worse inside."

I groan, knowing it's true. It's not just the volume level of the voices. There's always plates, cups, and silverware being dropped.

We finally make our way into the dining hall, grabbing trays to get our food. "Get pancakes. It'll help with any sour stomach."

"My stomach's not too bad. My head though..."

"Coffee. Lots and lots of coffee."

"Never a problem here." With the pancakes on my tray, I take the largest cup they have, filling it full of dark deliciousness. Coffee is an any-time-of-day thing for me, but especially in the morning. And especially with this hangover.

We find a table near the corner of the room, away from most of the noise.

"So, good night?" Brittney is grinning at me from behind the rim of her coffee.

"Not really."

"Well, you certainly seemed to have had enough to drink. What happened?"

I dive into the story. I tell her about the party, the drinks, how Liam kept me close to him the whole time and kept putting drinks in my hand. I tell her how he pushed me against the wall, and kissed me before I realized what was

145

going on, a detail I intentionally left out from my retelling to Josh. "And he asked me to stay."

Brittney sinks back into her seat, two hands wrapping around her paper cup as she narrows her eyes and looks at me. While she wants me to break out of my shell, to loosen up and have fun and finally have sex, she also knows me and is protective. She wouldn't have wanted it to be like that.

"No," is all I have to say to make relief spread across her face as her posture relaxes and she drops her head for a second.

"So you walked yourself back?"

I try to keep myself calm while the butterflies flutter in my stomach, remembering Josh's hands on me, the way his arms felt as they carried me, the ease with which he swooped me up. His lips on mine. "Yeah. It's not far, and I wasn't *that* drunk." There's no way I can tell her that Josh helped me both upstairs and that I spent the night in his room. She found me in mine, she'll never know the difference. Nobody needs to know.

"What's the deal with Liam now, then?"

"I don't know. I mean, I didn't *like* it, but he wasn't demanding. He was drunk too. He wasn't pleased I didn't stay, but he didn't try to force me to, he didn't try to force anything on me. He just kind of assumed I'd say yes if he poured enough alcohol in me and was not super happy that he was wrong." Swallowing, I duck my head, hoping she won't see the redness that's invaded my face.

Although I'm telling her it's not a big deal, I'm not quite sure what to make of it. The thought of it makes me uneasy, shaky with anger and fear. Is he going to be mad at me? Do I care if he is?

Her mouth straightens into a line, lips tight. "I don't like it."

"Before you jump to any conclusions, let me talk to him." I

raise my hand as I pull my cup to my lips, the warmth running through my body as a sense of peace washes over me.

She shakes her head. "No, I don't like it. I don't like that he knows you're a virgin and tried to get you drunk so he could get you to stay and take advantage of you."

"You don't know that that's what was going on. Maybe he just wanted me to stay to be near him."

"Guys don't do that," she says with the flip of her hand.

Some do.

There's no stopping the memories from flooding my mind again. The kiss, the kiss that made my pulse speed and my lips sore. It's like I can feel the weight of his arm around my waist, hear his heart beating in my ears. Or maybe it's just the residual pounding in my head.

Lifting one shoulder, I try to regain my composure. "Either way, I'm going to give him a chance to explain. He's been nothing but respectful until last night."

"Want me to go with you?"

"No. I don't think I need a babysitter, but thanks. He won't be drunk anymore. Probably." Honestly, I'm not sure. He'd had a lot the night before, and he was still drinking when I left. Who knows what time the party actually ended.

"I'm around if you change your mind."

Nodding, I jut my chin at her to change the subject. "How was your night? Didn't you end up at some frat party?"

"Ugh, not great. Better than yours apparently. But not great. We all went over to the party, and it was just a sloppy mess. They'd clearly started at like noon. We didn't stay long. Slobbering drunk before I get there is not the sort of party I want to attend."

"Wait, was it the frat of that guy in your history class?"

She nods resolutely, but her face gives nothing away. "The very same."

"Not good?"

"Nope. He was just as bad as everybody else there. I don't want to be with a guy that can't wait for me to come over."

"Sorry. I know you were interested in him."

She shrugs like it's no big deal, but she'd been excited about him. "He isn't my soul mate or anything, but he looked like he would have been fun in bed."

The corners of my lips tip up at her candor. Brittney's outgoing behavior no longer makes me redden. I like to consider it progress. "Come on, let's go." We clear our trays, with minimal wincing from me, and I swing back to refill my coffee before we leave.

When we reach the main level, I start to go through the door to get into the lobby instead of up the rest of the stairs before Brittney stops me. "Where are you going?"

"It's Sunday." I respond like it's the only possible logical answer.

Brittney rolls her eyes at me. "Oh, right, mail day."

"I have to check it. Excuse me for liking to have my mailbox empty for the next week."

"We barely get any mail."

"I get stuff here and there. My dad still likes to write me letters. It's my routine, leave me alone." Lauren had always made fun of my odd routines too.

"Fine. I'll be upstairs."

I walk over to the narrow hallway, with a door to a stairwell at the far end, mailboxes to the left, a blank wall to the right. I'm flipping through the few things when I sense somebody right behind me. He's so close my hair shifts with his breath as my heart races.

"You were gone when I woke up this morning." His voice is low, just next to my ear, shivers shooting down my spine. Josh gently takes a curl in his fingers and pulls it straight, letting his knuckles graze down my back.

Letting out a sigh, I fight the urge to lean my head into his shoulder. I ache to feel his body against mine.

"I thought it would be better if I didn't stay. Not making any mistakes. Right?" My voice is low as I turn my head slightly toward his. We're close enough that if I shift the tiniest bit more, I can feel his lips on mine again, the very thought of which makes them tingle.

His breath is warm against my shoulder as he exhales a heavy breath, fingers trailing against my waist as he pulls away, stepping back to stand against the opposite side of the small hallway.

"You're right. Doesn't mean I didn't want you there, though." His voice is quiet. I turn around to see a glimmer in his eyes. It's gone just as quickly as it appears. "How are you feeling this morning?" Now his voice is at a normal level, no emotion to it, no sign that anything happened between us, last night or ever.

Just like that, I know we're back to RA and resident mode. "I'm good. Had some breakfast, have my coffee." I hold up my cup as if I need to prove it to him.

"Good, good. Glad to see you're doing alright. Last night was…I didn't like seeing you that way." The words are cold and edged, but his eyes hold compassion and longing.

I try my best to give him a warm smile. "I'm fine. I'll be okay." I hope the smile is enough because all I want to do is rush into his arms and feel his warmth, hear his heartbeat in my ears again.

He nods, but it seems like he's reassuring himself more than me. "Good." Moving away, he opens the door to the office. "Lots of water," he calls from over his shoulder before stepping inside.

And with that, he's gone, into the office, behind the desk, back in his professional role. With nothing left down here for me, I start back upstairs, head hurting again, but this time for different reasons.

CHAPTER 15

Once I get back upstairs, I decide it's not a good idea to take Josh up on his offer to study this weekend, despite my lack of note taking earlier in the week. I'm not sure how I feel about the whole situation, but I do know I don't want to rehash anything from last night.

The way I feel around Josh isn't appropriate, considering I have a boyfriend. A boyfriend that I spent most of yesterday with, watching movies before the party. A boyfriend who doesn't sleep around. A boyfriend who also doesn't give me the butterflies that Josh does. My head is all sorts of confused. Or maybe it's my heart. I can't tell anymore.

The fact that my headache persists, and I fall asleep for a few hours after brunch also helps in keeping me from calling Josh.

Brittney comes by around five-thirty to go to dinner. Thankfully, Kimberly left an hour ago. Nothing's better with her and every day I hope for word on the roommate transfer.

"I just need to finish this paper for history and then I'll be ready." I don't even look at her as she comes in, focused only on getting my work finished as soon as possible.

I'm in the zone, fingers moving with fury over the keys, when there's a knock at the door.

Turning toward it, I see Liam, hands in his pockets. He's all kinds of disheveled-looking, shirt wrinkled, hair standing up in odd places. It doesn't look like he faired too well today.

Glancing behind me, I catch Brittney shooting daggers at him, but thankfully keeping her mouth closed.

"Uh, hey, Lexie. Can we talk?"

"Sure." I don't get out of my chair but do turn toward him. As the day progressed, my frustration with him compounded and I don't feel like giving him any grace.

"I just want to apologize for last night. I shouldn't have gotten mad. You don't owe me anything. And that kiss was over the line. I'm sorry."

I'm quiet for a minute as I look him over. His posture is lax, his eyes wide and pleading. He seems sincere. And he apologized for everything that turned me off. "It's okay."

"Yeah?"

"Mhm. Brit and I were going to go to dinner in a few minutes. Want to join us?"

She grumbles behind me, but I choose to ignore it. She can continue to hold it against Liam if she wants to, but I'm not going to. He came over here and apologized; that's enough for me. Besides, I have my own things I should be asking forgiveness for that I'm not.

"Oh, no, that's okay. Not sure I can keep anything down. Been a rough day. I just wanted to make sure I came by to say that. This is the first I've been able to get out of bed all day or I would have come sooner."

Brittney snorts behind me, and I turn to give her a stern look. While I was mad, still am a little, I did something worse last night, and my own hangover was bad enough this morning. I don't want him to be sick.

"Alright, well, call me later or something." Liam slowly backs away and is off without another word.

"Ready to eat?" Brittney jumps off the bed with a huff.

"Sure." I could get into it with her, but it's not really worth it. She's not going to change her mind. If she wants to be mad at Liam, that's her choice. And in reality, I'm glad I have her in my corner looking out for me.

WHEN I WALK OUT OF THE DORM ON TUESDAY TO GO TO class, Josh is leaning against the wall waiting for me. "Hey."

I jump, hand flying to my chest. I was so distracted about what I'd say to him if he decided he was going to talk to me today that I hadn't recognized it was actually *him* against the building until he spoke to me.

"You didn't call to study this weekend."

"No, I uh…I was fine." That's a lie. I'm not. A lot of the education stuff confuses me still. Not taking notes last week didn't help. Though I had been able to place out of some earlier classes, I'm realizing it was a bad idea to skip them. This class really expects you to know a lot of what would have been taught in the ones I didn't take.

"Oh. Well, maybe another time. Come on, I'll drive you again." It isn't a question—he's not asking if I want a ride. He's expecting me to follow him.

And I do. Because as much as I know tomorrow, or even after class, he may be telling me we shouldn't be talking, I want what time I can get. Even though I know I shouldn't because of Liam, I can't help the excitement I'm feeling about the prospect of that time with Josh.

We talk about the weather on the way to class, it's starting to get chilly even though it's only the middle of October. Josh tells me one year they had a decent snow fall around this time. It's boring, but it's safe.

When we get to class, he waits for me again, walking a little closer so that our arms brush with every step. It sends a shock through me every time, my body awaiting the next one. As a repeat of last class, we sit in the middle, his leg reaching into my space. Again, I don't lean away, my knee resting against his.

Every so often, when I glance over at him, he's looking back at me. This time, I smile, but still look down at my paper and tuck hair behind my ear.

Thursday is the same routine. I haven't called him to study and have no plans to. While the offer is nice, and the time with him would no doubt be something I'd enjoy, I like where we are right now. He's talking to me, actually being nice to me. I don't want to ruin that by studying with him, and he decides we're spending too much time together.

On Friday, I don't have a choice. I'm in my room, working on a paper for English and notice my notes are almost nonexistent. That's what I get for obsessing for over a week. I have no idea how to write the paper with no notes. All I can do when looking at my notebook is think about Josh and the feeling of his knee against mine, the glimmer in his eyes when I'd catch him looking at me, the rush through my veins I'd get when he did.

It's convenient to take him up on his offer. I haven't been able to suppress the need intensifying in me to see him more. It's almost like water, rising around me and it's currently sitting just below my chin. I'm about to drown and I don't know what it means when that happens.

Me: *Hey. It's Lexie. I'm kind of embarrassed but I'm struggling with this paper. My notes are lacking. Any chance I could come see yours?*

Taking a deep breath, I reread it quickly to make sure it sounds like I only want to study. Pressing send, I put my phone down, anticipating it'll be a while before he gets back to me.

Josh: *Sure. Come on down. Door's unlocked.*

An immediate response was not what I had anticipated. Gathering my books, I try to quell the tremble that's settled into my extremities, walking into the hallway without giving Kimberly a second glance.

I knock on the door as I turn the knob and open it, not waiting for a response.

"Hey. Come in. Shut the door behind you." He glances up from his desk for a moment. Walking in, I stand next to the bed, not wanting to assume I should sit there.

"Go ahead and sit, I'm almost done with this." Josh's fingers are flying across the keys on his laptop. He hits the last few keys with a bit of force, clicks a few times and closes it. "Okay, sorry, had to finish an email to somebody." Collecting his books, he comes to sit next to me on the bed. My breath catches as his knee touches mine. I hadn't been expecting him to sit with me.

I open my notebook to the pages I have from the week. "This is all I have. I wasn't listening so well." Heat prickles the back of my neck, knowing Josh probably understands why I wasn't paying attention. To class at least.

Flipping open his notebook, he leans his head in close to mine as he looks between the two notebooks. His musky cologne wafts into my nose, making a tingling sensation slowly crawl through my body. Turning, he looks at me, his face close enough that I can feel his breath warm on my skin.

Having him so close to me, I can't help but sigh.

Clamping his eyes shut, it gives me the feeling that he's trying to fight something; a thought, an action. "We should study." It comes out tight and forced.

"Yeah," is all I can say in return. Neither one of us turn away.

Tapping his notebook with his pen, he pulls us both out of the trance. "Let's just get you caught up on notes."

"Sure." To fight the prickles inching up my spine, my fingers find their way under the cuff of my shirt, tracing idly over the wave on the inside of my wrist.

Josh juts his chin toward my busy fingers. "What's that? I saw a little something last time but not enough."

I pull up my sleeve. "What, this? It's just a wave, pretty simple."

"I like it."

"Thanks. My best friend, Lauren, has the same one, same spot. We'd always go to the river when we had something sad or dramatic happen, or just needed to think. We like to think that we can cast our fears, anger, hurt into it for an absolution of sorts. It's part of why I loved this campus so much, the lake being right there."

The thing with Josh is that while he shuts me out, every time he lets me in, I want to give him as much of myself as I can. He didn't ask for more; I gave it willingly because I want him to *know* me.

He nods resolutely. "We should focus." His gaze falls back to his notebook, and he says nothing else that's not related to our English class.

Josh lets me copy some notes, giving a bit more explana-tion when I'm not sure what something means. He gives me a bit of the background information that I would have gotten had I not placed out of the few classes. I try not to be both-ered when he shifts away a bit, our knees no longer touching. But I hold on to the fact that every so often when I look up, his gaze dashes to my mouth.

It makes me wonder if he's remembering the pressure of my mouth against his, the way our tongues and hearts warred. If he wants it to happen again, like I do.

"Thank you, Josh. Really, I feel better now. I would have been really lost without you."

"Happy to help, Lex. It's why I offered." My pulse skyrockets when he calls me *Lex*. Only people super close to me have adopted that nickname; not even Liam or Brittney use it. And I'm extremely okay with the way it flowed out of Josh's mouth.

"Well, I guess I should be getting back to my room now. Thanks again." Scooping my books, I stand to leave, Josh rising with me. I almost wish he'd stay sitting, then he doesn't tower over me.

Before I can take two steps, he grabs my hand and pulls me against him, my books falling to the floor as my fingers rest gently against his chest. He runs his hands slowly up my arms to rest on my shoulders, brushing my hair behind them. My whole body feels like it's ice cold, but where his hands touch burns with fire.

I'm not sure what's happening, but I know I don't want him to take his hands off me. His eyes are locked on mine. We're standing in some strange cat-and-mouse game. He's caught me, now what is he going to do with me.

All at once, he cups my face, fingers tangling in my hair, while the other hand slides to my waist, pulling me tightly against him. His mouth closes on mine in an instant.

Lacing my arms around his neck, my mouth parts for his as he slips his tongue in. Keeping our mouths connected, he turns, pushing me backward until my tailbone hits the edge of the bed.

Pulling away, he puts his hands on my waist and lifts me onto the mattress, climbing up, his mouth colliding with mine as he slowly leans me back to rest against his pillow.

I'm vaguely aware of the screaming in my head that this is going somewhere, somewhere bigger than just kissing, but I quickly tune it out. I want him to keep going; I want more than just his lips on mine.

As he starts kissing with a new urgency, his hand makes a slow slide up the inside of my shirt, leaving a trail of fire in its wake. Brushing his thumb over my bra, he gently cups my breast, as though he's memorizing its feel in his hand.

A moan rises from my throat as he reaches a finger inside the cup to run along my hardened nipple.

Removing his hand from my shirt, leaving me wanting

more, he quickly slides it to the top of my jeans. Leaning back, he looks at me as he slowly undoes the button and slips his hand under the waistband to run over my panties.

"Is this okay?"

Keeping my eyes on his, my throat arid, I nod slowly. My head is fighting itself, pulling in two directions. One part of me wants to tear my clothes off and let him have me, all of me, at this very moment. The other part is screaming it's too much.

Not knowing the battle raging in my head, Josh pushes my panties to the side, his finger touching me.

My eyes grow wide as my breath hitches. "I've never…" I can't finish the thought. It's too embarrassing as he stares into my eyes. He knows I'm a virgin, but that doesn't mean he knows I've never done *anything* besides kissing. Well, with another person, that is.

"Do you want me to stop?" he whispers against my lips.

"No," I breathe, too quickly to even think. His mouth crashes on mine again, tongue tangling with mine for a hurried kiss.

"Lexie, if you want me to stop, you can say so at any time. Do you want to do this with me?"

"Yes." I appreciate him double checking. But I'm not going to change my mind. I don't exactly know what *this* is, but I want it, all of it, everything.

As he slowly slides in one finger, then another, I gasp at the feeling.

Kissing along my jaw to my neck, he deftly moves his fingers, making me feel things I didn't know were possible. Writhing underneath him, my hands claw and grab at his shirt as his mouth presses into my neck.

With my fingers twisted into his shirt, I pull him against me as I cry out his name. My entire body tingles and my breath shallows out.

Smiling against my neck, he places a tiny kiss there before

pulling away. He sits up as I button my pants and adjust my shirt.

Sitting up beside him, I pull my lip between my teeth. What do you say after something like that?

But he knows what to do, what to say. Brushing some hair behind my ear, trailing his hand to my chin, he draws me in, placing a tiny kiss on my lower lip, resting his forehead against mine. "I'm sorry, I couldn't help myself."

I push my forehead into his a little. This closeness is nice. "It's okay. I liked it." That sounds corny and wrong, but I've never been in this situation before and don't know what else to say.

And just like that, Josh changes. Dropping his hand, he pulls away and looks at the ground. "*Fuck.* It shouldn't have happened. I shouldn't have done that. I'm sorry."

My heart plummets to my feet, and with it, my head droops, and I nod. I know the line. I know the rule. I don't care. Silently I stand, grazing Josh's shoulder with my fingertips, picking my books up from the floor, and leave his room without another glance in his direction.

Josh doesn't drive me to class on Tuesday, sending me a text explaining why it's better for us to steer clear of each other. Though, he does ask that I reach out if I have car trouble again.

Walking into English, I find him sitting in his seat in the front row. I try to ignore the drop in my stomach as I walk toward my spot in the back. As Professor Carp walks to the front of the room, I sigh heavily, ready to take notes, being thankful for the time I had in his company.

CHAPTER 16

Trudging across campus, I decide to stop into the café after an exceptionally boring and long lecture. I'm waiting in line, third from the register, when my phone buzzes in my pocket.

"Hello?"

"Where are you?" Brittney is breathless.

"I'm getting a coffee."

"Get back here now!" She's practically shouting.

"What's wrong, Brit?"

"Just get back here!"

"But…coffee."

"We'll go for one after, get your ass back to this dorm immediately."

Worried something's wrong, I get out of line and make my way back as quickly as my legs will carry me.

Throwing the door open, I find Brit sitting in a chair, waiting for me. "What? What was so urgent that you couldn't wait until I got my caffeine boost?"

Jumping out of her seat, she thrusts a paper so far into my face I have to back up to see it. Taking it gently from her hands, I look at the beaming smile on her face with a touch of apprehension.

"Dear Miss Pruit, we are informing you that your request for the—" I begin to read out loud.

"It's our roommate transfer! It went through!" She's practically jumping, she's bouncing so much.

Skimming the rest of the paper, I see she is in fact right, that it was approved.

"Oh my God." Thrusting the sheet back into her hand, I run to check my own mailbox, finding the envelope from the rooming department containing the same letter.

My jaw hangs open in astonishment. I can't begin to wrap my head around not only that it's happening, but that it's happening so quickly. I was expecting at least a spring switch, if it happened at all.

"I just, I can't believe it," I say it almost more to myself than to Brit, who's now moved on to actual jumping around as she clamps the paper in her hand and has a giant smile plastered to her face.

"It's going to be so much fun to live together!" She practically screams in my ear as she throws her arms around my neck.

"Wait, whose room are we going to move into?"

Her excitement drops a little as we realize we hadn't gotten to that part of the paperwork. Giving mine another quick read, I notice it doesn't really have any specific information. Glancing at Brittney's, I see hers doesn't either.

Shrugging, she walks over to the desk. "Hey, Trina. Lexie and I got these letters about our request for a roommate transfer being approved, but it doesn't say whose roommate is moving out. Any chance you have info on that?"

"Sure hon, let me check." Trina's a junior but she calls everybody "hon" or "doll". It makes me squirmy. Pulling out a large binder, she starts flipping through. "Fourth floor, right, girls?"

We both nod and give a light 'mhm.' I'm not sure if Brittney is as jittery as I am, but it takes all my strength to keep my knees from bouncing.

"It looks like a Kimberly Westole was also approved to move." Leaning closer to us, she wiggles her fingers for us to do the same. "You know, I heard somebody got kicked out of their single in the Pineville dorm and she was able to switch over there. Somebody pushed it through." Trina's also a terrible gossip. While she speaks quietly, I'm sure she'd tell anybody who would listen.

After a minute, the dust settles, and I realize what Trina just said. "Wait. So, Kimberly's leaving? The whole *building*?"

"Mhm. Hon, she got her letter and went right upstairs to start packing. This says she can move in by the weekend. Which means the two of you can too."

There's such a strong lightness in my chest I grab onto the counter, afraid I might float away.

It's immediately filled with a weight as Josh walks into the office. Our eyes lock for all of ten seconds, but it's enough to send my heart off to the races.

Taking a steadying breath, I catch Brittney glance over at me. We haven't talked about Josh more than his looks and the project we worked on together. She doesn't know that we kissed, that I let him touch me, that we went to the concert together. She doesn't even know that I dream about him nightly and think about him all the time.

After a hesitation that probably goes unnoticed by everybody but me, Josh walks over to the desk. "What do you have there, ladies?" Taking the letter from my hands, his fingers graze mine, sending electricity zinging straight up my fingertips and down to my toes. His eyes lock on mine momentarily before turning down to the paper.

"Wow, roommate transfer. Congratulations, these are hard to come by. When's the big day?"

"Kimberly can be out by this weekend, so we'll probably

get Brit's stuff ready to move in for then too. I'm sure Kimberly's going to run out of here as fast as she can." It's a wonder I'm able to say anything without my voice wavering. I certainly don't feel as steady as I sound.

Nodding slowly, he glances up at me again. I, on the other hand, haven't been able to tear my gaze from him. "Nice and fast. I bet that's going to be appreciated. I was just dropping some paperwork off. Trina, Brit, I'll see you around. Lexie, I'll see you at class." Slapping his fingers on the desk, he turns and leaves.

It wasn't exactly an awkward conversation; he was plenty friendly and personable. I just wish it could be more. There's so much sexual tension between us, at least on my end. When his hand touched me, I didn't want him to stop. Instead, I wanted him to slide his hand up my arm, over my chest, and down my pants.

"Lexie?"

"Huh?" Uh-oh. Brit caught me daydreaming.

"Let's go upstairs, check in with Kimberly, and then start talking stuff over."

"Yeah, sounds good. Thanks, Trina." Turning on my heels to leave, heat rushes my face. These thoughts are so atypical for me. And Brit has caught me daydreaming more than once recently. I need to get a handle on this before it becomes a problem.

Thankfully, Brit doesn't call any attention to it.

Once we get upstairs, we decide to chance going into my room, hoping two are stronger than one. Opening the door, we find that Kimberly has already packed up all of her clothes in the closet and cleared her desk of everything but her laptop and some books. She's also nowhere to be found.

"Well, I guess she's ready to go." The swell of excitement rising in my chest is almost too much to contain. Kimberly will finally be gone. Weeks and weeks of her absolute hatred of me, for doing nothing more than simply breathing. Finally, I'll be able to feel comfortable in my room, even have fun with my roommate. And have real conversations.

"Okay, so we'll figure out what day she's actually leaving. I'd assume it's absolutely as soon as possible, and then I'll start moving in either that day or the next day. If that works? Do you need a day alone or anything?"

"No, of course not. You can even bring some smaller stuff over that I can keep on my side." Looking around, the space is tight but there's a little room under the bed, in the closet. If she keeps it to not much, I can hold on to it.

"Oh, even better! Let's go look at what's in my room that I can maybe bring now. I have an away game tomorrow. I'll be gone for the night, but if Kimberly leaves, we'll bring as much as we can before I leave, and I'll do the rest Sunday."

We start looking through her things, finding a few outfits she doesn't think she'll need in the next day or two. It's not like we're so far apart she couldn't come grab it.

The whole time, I have a nagging feeling in the back of my head. There's a sensation of confusion nibbling at my mind.

How had this happened? We'd been told most don't go through at all, and if they do, it takes months and certain circumstances. Yeah, the person in Pineville had gotten kicked out, but that just doesn't feel like enough of a reason for all of it to go through. And so quickly. I'm a little uneasy about it all. I don't want to bring it up to Brit because she's so excited, and I am too, but I can't squash the unsettled feeling in my chest.

Dropping a few things in my room and finding no signs of Kimberly, but seemingly fewer boxes, I demand Brit get me the coffee she promised. Grumbling slightly as we leave, she perks up once we exit the building. There's an earthiness in the air, and the sun feels like warm kisses against my face. It's like I'm seeing the world through a new set of lenses.

"So why are you dragging me to coffee?"

"Um, you promised when you insisted I get out of line and return to the dorm." I look at her with a furrowed brow. She should know better than to try to deny me coffee.

"But I had exciting news!"

"Yeah, not getting a pass."

Hooking her arm through mine, she pulls me closer. "I'm so excited. It's going to be so fun."

"Brit, we're together like all the time."

"Yeah, but now, we can have late night movies and not have to deal with getting side eye and eye rolls and huffs and all that other nonsense that happens with Kimberly in the room."

"Very true."

"And we can gossip all the time without having to worry about who else is around and may walk in." This part, I'm far less excited for. "Speaking of, how are things with Liam?"

I wave my free hand at her. "You know, fine. I don't know. Weird, maybe? We don't spend a lot of time together anymore, but we talk pretty regularly. I don't even know what to call what we are. He will say girlfriend, but he's never really asked me, and he only says it when certain people are around. Otherwise, he just introduces me as Lexie."

"I'm sure it's nothing to be concerned about. But have you asked if you're exclusive?"

"Should I be worried about that?"

"I mean, if you're not technically dating, maybe? I obviously don't know him like you do, so I don't know if he's the type of guy who would be with more than one girl at a time, but it may not hurt to ask."

Though I could never say it to Brit, I'm not really sure I actually know Liam that well.

"No, no, I don't think he's with anybody else. I think it's just me." With resolution, I nod, but my stomach flips nonetheless. I'm not as confident as my words say I am.

"And in terms of things in the bedroom...any progress in that area?"

My cheeks burn at her question. Not only are Liam and I *not* doing anything aside from the occasional kiss, but I can't tell her about what's transpired between me and Josh. Brittney will jump on it so fast I won't be able to keep up and will surely spill something. I trust her, but there's too much on the line to risk it. Not to mention, I'm putting it to bed. I'm done with Josh and his back and forth. I think. I decided at the desk when I wanted more of his hands on me and then remembered the hurt of him saying it was a mistake.

"Um, no, just kissing."

"Then why are you bright red?"

"Just uncomfortable with the line of questioning." Guilt pangs in my chest, and I hate myself for lying to Brittney, my only real friend here.

We walk in silence for a few minutes and when she speaks again, I nearly shriek. "Okay, I have to ask. What's the deal with you and Josh?"

My heart pounds and a deep breath is hard to come by. "What do you mean?"

"I saw you guys at the desk. There's something there."

Frantically, I shake my head, which makes me look way more guilty than innocent. "No, we've just talked a bit here and there, gotten friendlier. He drove me to class those few times. I told you about that. It's thirty minutes each way, so we chatted a little."

Turning to look at her, I'm met with narrowed eyes. Putting a smile on my face, I try to sell my story, telling myself again that she wouldn't say anything if she knew the truth but ultimately deciding keeping it close to the vest is better.

"I don't know if I believe you, but I won't push you either." There's an edge to her voice that I can't find a reason for, but I'm thankful she's dropping the subject. "We should celebrate tonight. Chinese and a movie?"

"Yeah, yeah, that sounds nice." I'm not as enthusiastic as I should be, my words coming out lackluster. I'm thrown by her astute observation.

If Brit can see it, does that mean everybody else can too?

CHAPTER 17

I had been nervous to come to the party, being it's in the dorm. But Brit was right. I'm having a great time. The music is so loud I feel it pulsing through my body. While the room is a bit spinny from the alcohol I've consumed, it's all doing wonders to help me forget about Josh.

That is, until he walks through the door with two other RAs, breaking up the fun. His eyes lock on mine the second he steps in the room, widening as his brows shoot up. Then they scrunch together, and I can see his jaw clenching from the opposite side of the four-walled square we're in.

The three of them start walking through the very crowded room, having everybody gather to the side. In all the commotion, Josh walks over to me and wraps his arm around my waist, sweeping me out the door.

"What are you doing?" My voice is higher than it should be, shock and a few too many drinks inhibiting my ability to be normal.

"I'm saving you from getting in trouble. What the hell are *you* doing? A dorm party? Really, Lex? I thought you were smarter than that." Anger ripples through his words.

"I thought I was smarter in a lot of ways. I guess I'm not."

Josh tenses beside me. "You can let go of me. I'm not drunk. I don't need help walking back to my room."

Slowly, he slides his arm out from around me, fingers lingering for a moment on my lower back. I manage to take two steps away from him before I stumble, and two strong hands grab my waist. "Or maybe you do need my help."

Sighing, I let him wrap his arm around my waist again. I *do* like it, that's not the problem. Or maybe it is, because I shouldn't. I *can't*. Leaning into him, I take a deep breath, the scent of his musky cologne swirling in my nose. "Mm, you smell nice." It doesn't help me trying to push him from my mind. Instead, it makes desire twist through my body, desperate to feel his hands and lips everywhere on my body.

He chuckles, and the sound vibrates through me. "I think you're more drunk than you realize."

I shrug. "Maybe. But you still smell nice. You always smell nice." Looking up at him, I waver a bit as I tilt my head back. "Why did you take me out of the party? Can't you get in trouble?"

Josh inhales a deep breath before exhaling. "I could, yeah, but these guys are friends of mine. I trust them to keep it a secret." He's quiet for a minute, then adds, "I couldn't let you get caught. The campus patrol are on their way, we have to call for a party. I had to get you out of there."

Leaning farther into his side, I hear his heart racing as I wrap my arms around his waist.

He stops in front of my door. Disappointment weighs down my lungs as I realize this time won't be like when I came back from Liam's. There will be no sleepover.

After letting me fumble with the keys for a minute, he carefully takes them out of my hand, fingers grazing against mine, and smoothly gets it in the lock and twists, the loud thud reverberating in my ears.

I smile up at him. "Thank you."

"Think you can get yourself to bed alright?" His eyes narrow as he takes me in.

"I told you, I'm not drunk. Maybe a bit tipsy. But I'm fine." The fact that I'm standing what I think is perfectly still says enough for me.

Leaning against the doorframe, he slides his hands into his pockets. Damn, why does he have to look so sexy when he does that? "If that's what you want to believe."

Before I can stop myself, I push up on my toes and kiss him. He jerks back quickly, a stern look on his face.

"Come in," I whisper, my mouth close to his.

"No. You're drunk."

"I'm *not*, for the hundredth time. And even if I am, who cares?" I certainly don't.

"I'm not doing this with you, not like this. I don't take advantage of drunk girls."

"If I'm inviting you in, you're not taking advantage. Like vampires, it's okay if they're invited in." Everybody knows that, right?

"It's still taking advantage if you don't know what you're saying."

"I know exactly what I'm saying. I know exactly what I'm doing, what I want. The alcohol has made my mind a little looser now to be able to say it." Why won't he meet my eyes? Reaching up with both hands, I tilt his head down until his eyes lock on mine. Longing and desire swirl through their darkness. So, I take a shot and kiss him again.

This time he reacts, kissing me back with ferocity, his arms looping around my waist as he opens the door and pushes me inside, his lips never leaving mine. He kicks the door closed behind him as his hands reach down to slip into the back pockets of my jeans, yanking me closer to him.

"Brit?" he asks breathlessly against my mouth.

"She's away for the night." A smile spreads across his face and his lips are back on mine with a newfound urgency.

171

And just as suddenly as this all started, it stops. Spinning away from me, he runs a hand through his hair, making it stand up in all different directions. "Dammit!"

My feet are glued in place, my bottom lip between my teeth. I don't know what to say, what to do, but I'm suddenly feeling much more sober.

"You keep telling me that we can't be together, that it's not going to happen. You've told me to be with Liam, that he can make me happy and you can't. Yet you keep showing up, inviting me to concerts, saving me." Despite the pain and need raging through me, I keep my voice low and calm, free of emotion.

"You say things you shouldn't be saying, and we do things we shouldn't be doing. Things you tell me are a mistake and shouldn't have happened, and that you're sorry. But here you are. *Again.*"

Josh whirls around and his mouth closes on mine with a forcefulness I wasn't expecting. Hesitating for all of a second, I give in, hooking my arms over his shoulders. I don't know what I was thinking when I decided to push him out of my mind. It's an impossibility.

I moan as his mouth moves to my neck, twisting my fingers into his hair.

"Don't you know how much I want you?" This shocking confession is a whisper against my shoulder.

His lips resume their torment again, capturing a moan in my throat, not giving me an ounce of space or chance to tell him to show me.

Josh pushes me back until my butt hits the frame of my bed. Effortlessly, he lifts me onto it. Climbing up next to me, he leans me back onto the pillows. I gasp as his hands reach down and pull my shirt off, then reach over his shoulders to strip his off in one fluid motion.

He looks me over, starting at my legs and working up to my face, running his hand along the side of my body, grazing over my breast, before landing on my cheek, leaning in to kiss me gently.

"I won't push you. I won't ask for anything you're not ready to give." Easily, he reads the worry burning in my mind.

The truth is, I'm not sure I'd stop him. I don't even want to. If he tried to go further than last time, I'm fairly certain I'd let him and not regret a second of it.

Josh rests gently on top of me, his skin like fire against mine, burning me from the outside straight through to my soul. Gently, he runs his fingers down the center of my chest, down my stomach, stopping at the button of my pants. Leaning down, he starts kissing my neck, down along my bra line while his hand works at the button and zipper on my jeans, fingers sliding inside once he's undone them.

Instantly, I'm wet between my thighs. It was only a few days ago when I had experienced such euphoric pleasure at the hands of this man, but it feels like an eternity.

"You can always tell me to stop, Lex. Just know that." His breath is a warm caress against my neck as he murmurs his words.

I don't stop him or flinch as he pushes my panties aside, his breath heavy as he rolls his head to kiss my stomach, a growl escaping him as he slides in one finger, then another.

Tangling into his hair, I pull his head up, his mouth claiming mine, pushing it open as his tongue slides in.

As his fingers move faster, I have to break away to breathe. There's a noise bubbling in my chest, little squeaks coming from my throat as they try to burst out around my heavy breaths.

With a few more hurried strokes, I'm tugging at his hair as his lips find my throat, and I cry out.

Josh kisses back up my neck, finding my mouth, kissing tenderly, hand moving out from my pants to my lower back, turning me to my side and pulling me tight against him.

"I want more." It's all I can manage to say.

A sad look flashes across his eyes as he rolls away from me, off the bed, hand lingering on my thigh.

Running his flat palm down the side of my body, he leans down, resting his head on my hip. "We can't, Lexie. We just... we can't."

I can feel his hesitation, in both his words and his actions.

"I have to go. I don't want to. God, you know I don't want to. But I have to." Bending down, he kisses the skin at my hip, down the bone, over to my navel. Warm breath tickles my stomach as he sighs against it.

Hooking my fingers under his chin, I tilt his face up to meet mine. There's such sadness in his eyes.

Smoothing the hair from my face, he gently strokes my cheek with the back of his hand. Leaning into his touch, my lips trace along his fingers.

Closing in, he brushes his mouth across mine, resting our foreheads together. "Please know, I don't want to go right now. It's taking all of my power to leave you."

"Then don't. Don't leave. Stay here, stay with me."

Groaning, he presses his head harder against mine, his hand gently running down my side. "I can't," he breathes.

A sigh escapes me as I seal my eyes closed. "I know."

Josh presses his lips to mine, as if his life depends on this kiss. It's loaded with such a strong sense of desperation, like he senses he's losing me.

But he's not losing me. He has me, all of me. I can't deny that anymore. I know I'm losing him, though. I know this is going to be another mistake, another several days we don't talk. Another several days my heart aches.

When he pulls back, he searches my eyes, thumb softly sliding across my lower lip. "Please don't cry." He must see the mist making my vision blur.

"I'm not. I'm fine. I understand. Just please. Please don't say it. Please don't say it was a mistake, or that it shouldn't have happened. Just please. Don't." Shaking my head slightly,

I will the tears away. I won't be able to stand it if he says those words right now.

Josh hangs his head again, hair gently brushing my cheek, and his lips are like butterflies along my jaw.

My eyelids stay clamped together. I can't watch him walk out. I can't watch him turn his back on me, again. So I keep them closed even after I hear the door click. I keep them closed after the tears start flowing.

CHAPTER 18

L ying in bed, facing the wall, I'm wide awake—it seems sleep has evaded me altogether. There's such turmoil within me. I can't stop thinking about Josh. I can't stop my body from responding when he's nearby. He's popping up in my dreams nightly. And Liam not only has no idea, but is barely getting my attention.

My heart skips a beat as the tone that I set as Josh's rings on my desk.

Josh: Will you come over? I know I shouldn't be asking. I know you have a boyfriend and it's against the rules. I just…I need to see you.

My hand flies to my chest to keep my heart from trying to escape. Does he want something from me? It's one in the morning, after all. Is this some sort of booty call? Honestly, I don't even care. It's been four days since we last exchanged words. Four days since he last touched me. The most I've gotten is a sidelong glance in class.

Josh: I don't expect anything. I don't want anything but to be close to you. Please. I'll leave my door unlocked for ten minutes. If you don't come, I'll understand.

I throw my covers off faster than a girl with a boyfriend,

who is not the one texting to come over, should. Putting on my slippers, I speed walk down the hallway as quietly as I can.

With my hand on the knob, I pause. Am I really about to do this? This man is always running hot and cold. What if I go in and then he doesn't talk to me for two weeks? What if he *does* expect something sexual to happen? What about Liam?

Thinking about Liam makes me heave a breath. He has no idea that I even talk to Josh outside of class or dorm related things. He has no idea that we've gotten to know each other well over the past few weeks. He certainly has no idea about the other things Josh and I have done together, especially since I'm not doing them with Liam.

But I can't help the yearning;I can't resist the need I feel to be near Josh. So,I open the door and walk in.

It's dark, but I can see the smile that spreads across Josh's face as he scooches closer to the wall, holding up the covers for me. Stepping out of my slippers, I climb in next to him, laying with my back to his chest.

He doesn't say anything as he moves to press his body against mine. He doesn't say anything as he wraps his arm tightly around me, pulling me closer, and kissing my head. He doesn't say anything as I drift off into a deeper sleep than I've had in weeks.

WHEN I WAKE UP, IT TAKES ME A MINUTE TO REMEMBER WHERE I am. There's a freshness in my mind and bones that I haven't felt since school started. Remembering the night before and how I fell asleep, a feeling of safety falls over me like a warm blanket. I felt it as I drifted off last night too.

It's quickly chased away as I realize there's nobody behind me in the bed, that I'm alone. Looking around, I find Josh, tall frame, sitting in his chair, head down, legs outstretched in the middle of the room.

Sitting up slowly, I prepare myself, knowing this isn't going to go well. "Good morning."

All he does is huff in response. I guess he disagrees. Shaking his head, he rests it in his hands. "I shouldn't have asked you to come over. It was a moment of weakness. I'd had a bad day, I just nee—wanted, wanted to be near you. I shouldn't have. Nothing's changed; we still can't be together. You're not mine." His jaw tightens at the last part, agony twisting in his voice. His eyes lift to meet mine, torment and longing in them.

"You didn't force me to come down here. For all you knew, I was asleep. I came on my own. I made the choice."

"I gave you the option. I invited you. It was a mistake. It was weakness on my part."

All I can do is shake my head, tears welling in my eyes, as my heart starts to ache. This is what I was afraid of. I should have known better. I *had* known better, but I came anyway. Because I can't deny the longing and want that I have for Josh.

Hopping off the bed, I slide on my slippers and walk to the door.

"I'll go, then. Don't worry about it, we can just pretend this didn't happen too. Just like all of the other amazing things that have happened between us so far that I'm supposed to forget, to push aside." Freezing with my hand on the knob, I'm unable to bring myself to leave. There's a burning in my back and I know Josh's eyes are on me. Turning around, I find he's now standing, a little closer than he had been.

There's nothing but a heavy silence between us, a heated stare from Josh mixed with something I can't identify. Putting my head down, I shake it, tears popping from the corners of my eyes, hair flying loose around my face. Looking up at the ceiling, I push out a shaky breath, willing my tears to cease, and turn to leave.

"Lexie." There's a gruffness in his voice, a firmness that stops me, but I don't turn around. I'm not sure I can look at him. "I just, we can't. I want to, God, you know I want to. But there's too much risk. Too much to lose. For both of us."

Spinning around to face him, the tears are streaming freely now. "Too much at risk? Don't you understand what I'm risking just being here with you? It's not just my place at this school. It's not just your job. I'm in a *relationship*. I have a boyfriend. A boyfriend who has no idea that I see you, that I think about you, that I dream about you. That I long to be with you every single damn day. He has no idea I'm with him only because I can't be with you." I gasp as the realization hits me.

It's not that I don't like Liam; I do. Just not nearly as much as I like Josh. At first, I started things with Liam because he was sweet and charming. He seemed like the perfect first boyfriend for somebody like me. Especially because he was willing to be patient with me, take things at my pace. But it hasn't been anything like what I expected from a relationship. And I'm pretty sure I've broken every rule in the relationship handbook.

When Josh and I first met, he was so hot and cold, to a point I often thought he hated me. But as things progressed, as we spent more time together, I realized I'm only with Liam because the rules won't let me be with Josh. Some part of me, a bad part, is holding on to Liam for the day I'm able to break away from Josh's hold on me.

I'm a horrible person. It feels like somebody punched me in the stomach and knocked all the air from my lungs.

Josh stands there, head hung, completely silent. I'm not sure what I expect him to say; he's already said plenty, as has his silence. Part of me wants him to come wipe my tears, hold me close, tell me it'll all be okay. But I know that's not going to happen; it's just a dream that's never going to be reality.

So, I leave. I walk out the door and turn my back on him.

CHAPTER 19

"Get dressed! We're going to a Halloween party!" Brit yells as she comes bursting into the room. She's been out scrambling for something to do tonight since her field hockey friends had to cancel the party they'd planned for this weekend. The frustration she feels that Liam's out of town, for Halloween weekend no less, seems a little misplaced, and I chalk it up to not having something to do.

"What?" I'm not really in the mood for a party. It's been over a week since I've seen Josh, aside from poorly hidden glances in class. It's been almost as much time since I've seen Liam. And yet only one bothers me and leaves behind a sharp pain in my heart. Despite my constant self-talks, I still want to be with him. And I realize that I need to break up with Liam. As soon as I can.

"A party. Get ready. Come on, we should leave soon." She starts throwing clothes onto her bed, all brightly colored. And tiny.

"Where are we going for this?"

"Off campus, for Halloween. Going to be huge. They host every year and it's always awesome. I can't believe I forgot."

Perhaps idiotically, I let Brittney help me pick out some

clothes. She insists on a pleated mini skirt and top. "I don't know, Brit. I feel like it's just a big sign that I'm open for business."

"And?"

"And I'm not! I have a boyfriend." For now. I do enough bad girlfriend things without dressing like I'm looking for more.

She shrugs. "It doesn't matter. You're not going to be doing anything but looking good for a party. Besides, he's out of town anyway, so it's his fault for missing this sexiness."

"Why this?" I run my hand down the outfit.

"You're a teacher; it's a play on it by turning you into a dirty schoolgirl. Always a fun time." Brittney winks at me as she glides lip gloss across her lips.

I roll my eyes at her. "Fine, let's just go."

Brit's right, it's a *huge* gathering. The house itself is pretty big too, one of the larger ones I've been to. I've been tugging on the hem of my skirt every few minutes, to which Brittney's response is to slap my hand away. I keep running into people I know; it seems like everybody is here.

And everybody happens to include Josh.

Brit and I are standing in the kitchen when I see him walk in, shaking hands with people as he walks through. I hate the way my heart picks up in speed, that I can hear the pounding in my ears and that my panties are instantly wet. I hate that my body reacts to him at all. Everything would be so much easier if it didn't.

He catches my eye as he walks toward the kitchen.

"I'm going to go find a bathroom." Not taking my eyes off him, I talk to Brittney from the corner of my mouth.

She nods as I slip away. His gaze follows me as I walk upstairs.

I'm strolling slowly in the dark of the second floor. It's quiet up here, the guests being regulated to downstairs. I shouldn't be up here, but Brittney's words from one of the first parties she's brought me to flow through my mind. *When they open up their house to strangers, no room is off limits unless it's locked.*

This is where he finds me. Before I know what's happening, I'm being tugged into the nearest room. Josh's hand is on the side of my face, pushing me up against the wall as his lips find mine.

I break free and push him away. But I don't make a move from my spot.

A wide smile spans his face as he moves back into my bubble. His mouth closes on mine, one hand still on my face, while the other finds my hip, and he pulls me against him.

I can't fight it anymore, I don't want to. Tightness seeps from my body as I loosen, roping my arms around his neck, pulling him to me as I fall against the plaster, my mouth parting for his. I gasp as his hand starts moving slowly up the inside of my shirt.

His hands on my bare skin ignite embers throughout my body. I know this is wrong, that he's going to end this at any moment, but I don't want that moment to come.

I don't stop him as his hand works its way higher up my shirt, tongue curling against mine. I don't stop him as he slips his fingers under the edge of my bra. I know I won't stop him for anything. I'd let him do whatever he wants with me, right here in this random bedroom, and it still won't be enough.

Moving his mouth to my neck, kissing, sucking, biting, a moan rises from somewhere inside me. Without realizing what I'm doing, I lift my leg to wrap around his waist, something I probably shouldn't be doing in a skirt. His responding groan lets me know I'm doing something right.

Sliding his hands down, he quickly lifts me, wrapping my other leg around his waist, his mouth back to mine, kissing me like he's about to devour me. It's like he can't get enough of me either. One hand glides down and back up my leg, slowly inching closer and closer to the throbbing spot between my thighs.

With a sharp inhalation, I pull away as his finger slips the edge of my panties to the side. Meeting his intense gaze, I whisper, "We're in an open bedroom, at a party."

His dark eyes bore into mine, nothing but desire behind them. He also hasn't moved his hand from its hold. "Should we stop?"

"No," I breathe the word out. I don't even have to think about it. My body won't let me say no, because it's been too many days since I last talked to him, last felt him. Ever since that night, it's all been downhill from there. It would be impossible for me to say no at this point.

I don't even know why I stopped him to begin with, except the voice in my head that fears we might get caught. It got the better of me for a minute.

I have no second thoughts as he slowly slides in one finger, quickly followed by another. There are no thoughts about the party downstairs or that anybody can catch us, no thoughts about Liam, no thoughts about anything except Josh and how desperately I want him. All of him.

And I have no second thoughts as his fingers start moving inside me, slowly at first. As I make tiny moans and sighs, my lips turn more aggressive, pressing firmer against his, my teeth grazing his lip every so often. It makes his fingers move faster, with more pressure.

Bucking against him, I wrap my fingers in his hair, pulling at the strands gently. His mouth is pressed against my neck, and I thank everything above that the music is loud enough to drown me out as I scream his name.

"Fuck, you're so sexy," Josh whispers against my neck, fingers still inside me. Slowly removing them, he sets me on my feet as I smooth my skirt. Tipping his head down, he kisses me tenderly, resting his forehead against mine.

Then he sighs, dropping his head to hang on my shoulder, one hand on the doorframe by my ear. We stay in silence for a moment, my fingers resting at his collar. The slam of a door draws our attention, and while we don't pull away from each other, Josh's jaw tenses. "I should go. This, this shouldn't have happened. I'm sorry." His tone is always so resolute, so robotic. It's like he practices in front of the mirror every day but doesn't really believe it himself.

Grabbing hold of his shirt, I refuse to let him leave. With a dark stare and confusion overtaking his features, he looks down at me. His height might intimidate me on other days, but he just gave me an orgasm in the middle of a raging party. Any intimidation he may have brought me is long since passed.

Standing against the wall, he fully boxes me in. All I want to do is push up on my toes and feel his lips on mine again, but I know that won't happen. My fingers are still tangled in his shirt, anchoring him to me.

Taking a chance, a complete shot in the dark, I slide one hand down his chest. His eyes grow wide as I keep mine locked on his, hoping they're stronger than I feel. When I get to the top of his jeans, he grabs my wrist, stopping me.

"No, Lexie." There's gravel in his voice, the words coming out strained.

"Why won't you let me touch you?"

"Because if you do, I won't be able to stop myself. And I need to be able to do that." Josh puts my hand by my side, leaving the other still twisted into his shirt.

"Why can't you just let me be like those other girls?" The ones he uses once and discards.

"Because I can't." Josh's voice is low and tight, and he won't look at me.

"Why not? Maybe I want to be."

"*I* don't want you to be. You're not that type of girl."

With both hands, I pull him against me, pressing my body firmly against his.

He closes his eyes as his breathing becomes labored.

"I can be that type of girl." There's a desperation in my voice that almost matches the one that's deep in my bones.

Opening his eyes, there's fire raging in them. Forcefully, he takes my hands in his, pulling them from his shirt, breaking my hold on him. "I don't want you to be. Don't you get it, Lexie? I like you just how you are, who you are."

"But who I am doesn't seem to be enough for you. I'd rather just be a quick hookup and be done." Ice trickles through my veins at the thought of that being it, especially because it's not at all what I want.

"That's not what I need from you, Lexie. God, don't you get it? I care about you. This? Right here? The only reason it keeps happening is because I can't keep myself away from you. But it's not fair to you, and I'm sorry I'm too weak to stop it."

Before I can even tell him I'm not sorry, that I wanted it to happen, want it to continue to happen, he steps through the door and is gone. I can do nothing but stand here, alone, against the wall as he walks off, watching him until he's nothing but a shadow. The familiar ache returns to my chest. It had been momentarily eased by his presence.

After a few deep breaths and a quick smooth of my hair, I go back to the party, looking all around for him, but his tall frame is nowhere to be seen.

"What happened to your neck?"

I jump as Brittney appears next to me. "Huh?"

"You've got a mark...on your neck." Pointing to my right side, her finger almost touches my skin.

My hand flies to it. It's where Josh's mouth had been just minutes before. I run to the bathroom to look at it. Sure enough, there's a big red oval. There's no way I'm going to be able to hide this from Liam.

"Just say it's a burn mark from a straightening iron. That's what I've done." I turn to Brittney—who had silently followed me into the bathroom—with pleading eyes. She holds up her hands in peace. "I don't know anything. I didn't see anything, I didn't hear anything, or anyone, but I know a hickey when I see one."

"Yeah, and I'm pretty sure Liam will too," I mumble as I lean over the sink to get a better look.

"Yeah, he probably will. But like I said, straightening iron. We can try to cover it up tomorrow. I've had a lot of practice."

I can only nod, dread swirling in me as I think of how very wrong this situation is. "Come on, let's go back to the dorm. We'll try once or twice before tomorrow, so if we don't get it right, you can at least straighten your hair."

One thing I like about Brittney is that she doesn't judge. She can admit she's made her own share of mistakes over the years, and even the semester.

But right now, I see judgment in her eyes. I can feel it rolling off of her in waves.

Our walk back to campus is filled with silence. Out of the corner of my eye, I keep catching her staring at me. A few times, it seems like she's about to say something but decides against it. I don't look right at her, hoping she won't see my gaze sliding in her direction. She has every right to judge. I have a hickey on my neck from a guy who is *not* my boyfriend, a guy who I can get in a lot of trouble for being with.

Stopping dead in my tracks, I extend my arm out to Brittney. "Brit, please. You *can't* tell anybody." I hope my eyes are showing the urgency and pleading, clawing to escape me.

"I won't. You know I won't. But you need to be careful. If the wrong person saw you, or found you two together, you could both get in a lot of trouble."

"I know. Trust me, I know. I just…we can't seem to stay away from each other. Even though we both try."

"Well, maybe you both need to try a little harder." There's an edge to her voice that I haven't heard before. It makes me take a step back as my blood slows and my throat dries.

She takes a deep breath. "Look, I know how he feels about

you. That day I went to *study* a few weeks ago?" I remember it well and have tried very hard to forget it. She had come back looking disappointed, and we never spoke of it.

"He asked me about you. I thought I was going to be *studying*, but really, all he did was ask me about you. Repeatedly."

The ice that had overtaken me quickly thaws, and I warm like I'm in a sauna. My mouth is wet again, somehow recreating the taste of peppermint that always seems to linger in Josh's mouth. "Why didn't you ever tell me that?"

"Because I was mad! And jealous!" Her hands fly into the air as she yells. "I thought I was going down to hook up with the most gorgeous guy on campus that everybody hopes to be picked for, and instead, he just asked me about you."

And I had no idea. In fact, when she went down, I thought he hated me. It had been before anything really happened between us, and all I got was the ever-changing sides of Josh. Not that that's changed much, but back then, I thought it was hate with a few instances of kindness.

"I'm sorry. I didn't know." My voice is low, but I'm rippling with shock.

She sighs heavily. "It's not your fault. But be careful. I don't care what you do. If you two want to mess around, fine. If you want to be together, fine. I don't approve that you're doing it behind Liam's back. I'm cool to sleep around, but I draw the line at either person being part of a relationship. That's your choice, though. Just don't get caught. It would be bad for both of you."

"I know. We know. It's all he keeps telling me. But I keep finding myself in these positions with him. He lets me in, brings me close, and then he pushes me away as quickly as he pulled me in. The constant back and forth is giving me whiplash. But I can't stop myself. I don't want to." Looking up at the sky, the twinkling stars blur as tears well in my eyes. "I don't know what to do, Brit."

Putting her arm around my shoulder, she pulls me into a

hug. "It'll be okay. I know it's hard. But I think you need to try to stay away from Josh. It's a fine line you're walking. One mistake and it's over. And then there's Liam."

Liam. Another problem for another day. I'm emotionally drained and already feeling anticipation bubbling in my stomach as I think about seeing Josh again.

"Let's just get back to the dorm and try to cover that. We'll give a trial run so we know if we need to try to straighten your hair before Liam gets home." Brittney turns, keeping her arm over my shoulder, and starts walking again.

"I probably won't see him until Monday."

"Let's be sure, just in case."

I nod and we finish the trek back. We're walking through the door to our room within ten minutes, where I quickly change out of my skirt, feeling guilt and longing at the same time. Utterly exhausted, I postpone Brit's plan of concealing the mark and just crash in bed.

I'd barely had anything to drink, but everything is spinning out of control.

***

"You let him WHAT?!" Lauren's voice fills my ear and causes me to wince as she rises to a painful volume. I'm sitting on my bed for my weekly Lauren call, which I thought about avoiding altogether.

"I let him fi—"

"I heard you the first time! I'm just shocked is all."

"And here I thought you'd be happy for me," I mumble the words as I pick at the intentional fray on my jeans.

"Happy for you? Lex, you were in a bedroom at a party! Anybody could have seen you or heard you. Are you in the middle of some sort of crisis or something? Do you need me to come out there?" Her voice is bordering on hysterical, and I can imagine the crazed look on her face.

My eyes flutter closed as my heart drops. "No, of course not. I'm breaking out of my shell like you've always wanted." I don't convince myself any more than I'll convince her.

"Lex, I want you to have experience with somebody who makes you happy." There's a new tenderness in her voice that makes me hate myself even more.

"He does." The lie feels sour on my tongue. He makes me happy when we're together, which is far less frequent than not.

"He doesn't. I'm not saying Liam is right either, but, Lex. Josh just turns around and hurts you. Let me guess, you already haven't heard from him in the two days since this happened?" I hate that she's right. I let my silence speak for me. The loud sigh that flows through the phone line ruffles my insides.

"Lexie, you know I'm just worried about you. And not even the trouble you can get in. I'm worried about your feelings, your heart. I can hear in your voice there's a lot more than just physical things going on here, that you are at least falling for him. I don't want you to get hurt."

"I know, Laur. I want to say I know what I'm getting myself into, but I don't. Every time he shuts me out, it hurts. But I just…I can't." There's nothing more to say. It's that simple. I can't not be around him. My head falls to my free hand.

"You need to go on the pill. Like yesterday."

My face burns as I turn toward the wall. "Why?"

"Why? Are you really asking me that? Lexie, you've let him finger you three times now, slept *in his room*, all over the course of what, two weeks? Less? I see this progressing very quickly and I want you to be prepared. Don't leave it up to him."

Sucking in a deep breath, I hold it for a beat before puffing it out loudly, allowing that to be my answer.

"You need to break up with Liam." There's a decisiveness in her voice that I appreciate right now.

"I know." My chin falls to my chest as I answer quietly.

"Like now. It's not fair to him."

"How do I do that? He's done nothing wrong. He's been patient, gentle."

"I don't know. Maybe use that party from a few weeks ago where he tried to get you to stay. Say you thought you could move past it, but it's been eating away at you, that you're nervous that all at once, it won't be enough for him." It's not the worst idea.

"Is that fair? To blame him?" Rolling some strings through my fingers keeps the shakiness at bay. The thought of breaking up with Liam terrifies me.

"Is what you're doing fair?" Ouch. I'm not usually on this end of the morality conversation.

"No. And trust me, I hate myself for it. I just don't know how to break up with him. I've never had to before."

"I can't help you there. It's never easy. But you need to and you know that. Don't wait too much longer. Especially because you and I both know if Josh comes back between now and then, you'll be all too keen to let him feel you up, no matter where you are."

Guilt and shame pang through my entire body with an ache settling in my stomach. She's absolutely right. "I'll just have to avoid him until then. Not that it's hard, I'm pretty sure he's taken it as a job to avoid me like the plague after these moments."

"One thing I can say is that he seems just as infatuated with you. Maybe more. I mean, he invited you to his room. I still can't even believe that he did that. And didn't even try to make a move on you. That's never happened in my experience."

I'd told Lauren about the night he invited me down. Which also led me to tell her about the time he kept me in his room after I walked back drunk from Liam's. I had kept my eyes trained on Brittney as she overheard the conversation, her eyes slowly widening and her brows rising as she learned more of the depth, and complications, of the relationship Josh and I have.

"It's all so confusing, Laur."

"If there was no rule, nothing stopping you from being together, would you want to be?"

"Yes." I don't hesitate for a second. There's zero doubt in my mind.

"Despite his reputation? I mean, he has a *lot* of experience."

"I don't care."

"I hope you can figure something out. At least how to push him out of your mind. Maybe if you really dive into it with Liam. Have you considered going further with him?"

The thought has crossed my mind. But I don't want to. It makes me queasy. I'm not interested in his hands all over me, I don't crave it. When I think of him touching me the way Josh has, I immediately push the thought away. Due to this fact, I've been avoiding Liam more than I should because when he kisses me, I wish it's Josh. *I'm a terrible person for even having thoughts like this.*

"Yeah, I have considered it. I don't think it would help."

"You know what you have to do, then."

"Yeah. I do." Dread settles like a weight in my stomach, knowing I have to have a difficult conversation with a guy who's been nothing but sweet to me, including putting up with me distancing myself from him in recent weeks.

Hanging up with Lauren, I curl under the covers to drown in self-misery for a little while. But it's not long before I fall asleep and dream about the person causing me both pain and pleasure.

CHAPTER 20

Brit: *Guy coming over, I'll be a little while.*

Great, just what I need. I've already been at the library for two hours and my eyes are crossing. *A little while* in Brittney land is more like another two hours.

Leaving my stuff at the table, I walk into the café to grab a coffee. It's going to be a long wait, so I'll need some caffeine to keep me going.

Returning to my spot, I stretch my neck and check my phone to see if I've heard from Liam. We've exchanged a few texts back and forth today, I told him I'd be at the library for a while, though once I got here, I was ready to leave. Now I don't really have much choice but to stay.

I can't see Liam. I'm too much of a coward to break up with him, so I've been avoiding talking to him, instead sinking myself into homework. As much as I thought about trying to make things work with him, my heart just isn't in it. It's not fair to him to keep stringing him along when I know I won't get there, when I'm already there with somebody else.

Even if I can't have that person.

There's nothing left to distract me except my thoughts. Outside of class and quick glances in the hallway, I haven't seen Josh in five days. Not that I'm keeping track or anything. Except maybe I am. I'm acutely aware of exactly how long it's been since we spoke and even more aware of how long it's been since he last touched me. My body longs for his hands on me, even just the graze of his arm against mine.

Shaking my head, I urge away the thoughts. Though, I don't want to push them away. I want to will them into existence. But it always ends in heartbreak. Always ends in him telling me it was a mistake, that we can't be together. It makes it nearly impossible to see glimpses of him in the hallway.

Barely anything has been registering in English class. Instead, I spend my time staring at his perfect back, imagining my fingers tangling in his hair as his lips meet mine. And then the thought of his lips moving down my body to kiss my—

I startle myself with a gasp. "Okay, Lexie, time to focus. Josh isn't right for you. Time to let him go." Maybe saying it one more time will help.

Focusing on the work in front of me proves to be impossible, but I'm not putting my all into it. Giving up on writing my paper and the research that goes with it, I check the time, noting I likely have at least another forty-five minutes. Making another attempt at studying for history, I still can't concentrate, finding myself rereading the same few sentences over and over again. Leaving my things, but taking my coffee, I wander up a floor to the fiction section.

I need a break. A mental one. I need to escape to a world that isn't real, that isn't mine, just for a little while.

Easily finding a favorite that I've read over and over again, I know it will quickly take me away. Tucking it under my arm, I bring it back to my table, closing up my books and putting them into my bag as I settle in and start reading.

The sound of the metal café door shutting makes me jump upright in my chair. The book had done exactly what I wanted it to and took me away from my thoughts. Checking my phone, I realize it's midnight. Over an hour has passed.

Setting the book down, I grab my bag to leave. Brit *should* be done by now.

The brisk night air greets me, sending a shiver tearing through my body as I walk through the library doors. As I approach the main path back to my side of campus, I squint at a tall, dark figure, with rounded shoulders and hanging arms, stumbling and walking in anything but a straight line.

As he gets closer and moves right past me, not even noticing my existence, I hear him mumbling incoherently to himself. From what I've observed, he's clearly drunk. "Josh?"

Whipping around, he almost falls over in the process. "Lexie!" he yells, way too loudly.

"Hey there. What's going on here? Can I help you get back to the dorm?" Holding my hands toward him, I talk slowly and am sure to enunciate every word. I've never seen him drunk before. It's a little unnerving.

"I'm fine. I'm good. I'm drunk."

"I can see that. Here, let me help you." Taking his arm, I put it around my shoulder.

Josh leans into me a bit, causing me to stumble to the side slightly. Since he's taller and heavier than I am, and solid muscle, he could easily take me down if he trips. I'm going to have to take this slow to make sure that doesn't happen.

"You don't have to."

"It's okay, I don't mind." Despite the heartache that usually follows, it's nice to be so close to him, even though he reeks of alcohol instead of his usual pleasant musky scent. Besides, he's saved me drunk more than once. I feel like I at least owe him that. "What happened? Why are you so blitzed in the middle of the week?" It's only Wednesday, after all.

"I went over to a friend's room to ease my broken heart." Though slurring a bit, he's still mostly understandable. All the years of going out with Lauren have trained my ear to understand the inebriated pretty well.

SHAYNA ASTOR

"Your broken heart? Who knew you even had a heart?" Smiling, I tilt my face up to his, hoping he knows I'm joking.

"*You* have my heart." Mine slams against my ribs. "And it was smashed tonight. I saw the black scrunchie on your door handle. I know what it means. You. You and *Liam*." He says Liam's name with such disdain that I can feel the hatred licking across my skin.

"I'm not sure what you saw, but I've been at the library all night. I haven't been back to my room since after dinner."

Stopping dead in his tracks, he turns to look at me, arm sliding off my shoulders to rest at his side. "You haven't?"

I shake my head. "No, I haven't. It was Brit, she was...entertaining."

The look of relief that spreads across his face is undeniable. He runs a hand over his jaw. And starts laughing. So hard he's doubled over, tears welling in the corners of his eyes. I can't help but laugh along with him.

"I just got hammered, because I was so sure that you were in there with Liam, that I had to drown it all out." He's so out of breath, he can barely talk. "And now that I know you weren't, all I want to do is take you in my arms and kiss you, but I can't! Because we're in the middle of the quad, and if the wrong person saw, it'd be all over." He starts laughing again.

But it really isn't funny, and I don't join him this time. Josh stops, his face serious, no smile left in sight and jaw tight as he realizes how not amusing it is. He starts walking again, cocking his head toward the dorms as he passes me, hands in his pockets. Taking a few quick steps, I'm able to catch up, noticing he doesn't seem to need my support anymore, the gravity of the situation sobering him. We walk silently for a few minutes.

"I haven't—Liam and I—we haven't. Liam and I have only kissed." I don't know why I'm sharing this with him. It isn't his business. But part of me needs him to know that I've

196

only kissed Liam, that anything beyond that has been with him and only him. That my firsts are still his and his only.

I hadn't noticed how tense he's been until his muscles relax, his shoulders lowering.

When he glances at me, there's the slightest glimmer of hope in his eyes, a tiny smile gracing across his face. "Thanks for telling me."

I know it doesn't matter. It doesn't make a difference if Liam and I are sleeping together or not. Josh and I can't be together. It's that simple.

Though, really, it's anything but.

Josh opens the doors for me, fumbling a little getting the key in the lock. He refuses my help and walks me upstairs. There's no scrunchie on my doorknob, which I'm thankful for, because it's late and I'm tired from studying for hours, just wanting to crawl under my covers and not have to worry about Brit and her guest.

"Well, good night." I turn to look at him before opening the door.

Josh leans down slowly and places a gentle kiss on my lips. "Good night."

I'm frozen in place as he walks away. He just kissed me in the open. I know it was a risk, I know he knows it was a risk. And he did it anyway. I watch him shuffle down to his room, turning to look at me once more before disappearing inside.

I THOUGHT THAT MAYBE JOSH WAS OPENING UP TO ME AGAIN. I was wrong. We don't see each other much in the dorm, seeming to always miss each other. Or more likely, it's artfully designed by him. The one time we're both in the hallway, he doesn't even acknowledge my existence. Not even when my heart is singing out to his so loud even the angels can hear it.

In class, the following day, he ignores me. Same story,

different beginning. I decide to take one piece of Lauren's advice and see if I can put some focus into Liam. It may be easier than breaking up with him.

It's how I find myself in his suite on Saturday, three days after Josh's confession in the quad and a week after Lauren's advice. "Thanks for letting me come over again. I just had to get out of there." Things with Brittney are great, but I need to not be in the dorm, where Josh is just down the hall. The knowledge that he's so close and yet so far is both soul shattering and stifling.

"Of course! I like having you here. It's nice to finally spend some time together. It's been a little less lately." Liam doesn't even look up from his notes as he talks to me.

"The work is getting to me a bit." Especially when my mind is anywhere but class. The partial lie burns like acid on my tongue.

"Ah, yes, I do remember the last few weeks before finals. How are you feeling about that?"

Not really so good, but I can't tell him that. "Alright, I guess. If I focus in class and study a lot, I should be fine." I put on what I hope is a convincing smile, though, inside I feel anything but confident.

In actuality, I'm really worried about the end of the semester. The thoughts of Josh and how horrible I'm being to Liam are distracting me at every turn. My notes are incredibly lacking, and now it's not just in English. I'm afraid they're missing vital information that I won't be able to do well. If I wasn't so sure he'd say no, I'd ask Josh for help again.

"You will be. You'll find a way."

I smile and nod. It's not a helpful answer. It doesn't make me feel better.

A tall, leggy blonde girl comes bursting through the door and into the suite common room before I can respond. She looks surprised to see me as she turns to Liam with wide eyes. "Uh, hi. We're finishing up that movie tonight if you guys want to join us?" She doesn't even acknowledge that I'm sitting right here.

"Oh, yeah, maybe. Cara, this is my girlfriend, Lexie. Lexie, Cara lives down the hall."

Cara turns to me, a pinched smile on her face and rage in her cobalt eyes. "Nice to meet you. Liam's mentioned you." She gives me a quick once-over, and I'm sure I hear a derisive snort before she turns her attention back to Liam. "Oh, and, by the way, we were wrong about Patty. She is totally hooking up with that guy from her chem class."

Liam shifts in his seat, and I realize I've never seen him be anything but confident until this moment. His discomfort is clear, I just can't pinpoint the reason. His eyes keep flicking back and forth between me and Cara.

"Hey, can I come see you later? I'll let you know about the movie." His voice is tentative as he says this, like he's walking on ice, trying not to break through the surface into the cold abyss.

"Oh, yeah, sure." Her shoulders curl forward, and she loses an inch as she leaves.

"Sorry about that."

"So, you guys are pretty friendly." I don't phrase it as a question.

"Uh, yeah, I guess." He isn't looking at me, eyes trained on the notebook in front of him.

"She just let herself right into your suite." Gesturing toward the door, I take another look at it, almost expecting her to come back in.

"Well, yeah, that's what good friends do. I mean, Brit used to let herself into yours all the time, right?"

"Yeah, but she's Brit, and she's a girl. I wouldn't let Tim just walk in."

"Who's Tim?"

Irritation bubbles beneath the surface of my calm, and I roll my eyes at his question. "He's the guy who lives diagonally across from me. We all hang out sometimes, usually for dinner. You've met him. Four times."

"I'm sorry, it's just hard to keep everyone straight." Liam waves a hand flippantly, like it's something he can't be bothered with.

"A person who lives across from me that I eat with a few times a week that you've met more than once?"

"Look, I said I'm sorry." He's trying to be sincere, but there's a clip to his words and an irritated bite to his tone.

"And you're going to her suite to watch movies?" Honestly, I don't know why I'm so mad; I've done far more and far worse than watch a movie. But I at least have the decency to keep it a secret. Though that's probably much worse.

"It's all of us. All six of us go and all six of them are there too. We sit on opposite couches."

"She likes you."

"What? No, she doesn't."

"She pretended I didn't exist. She likes you." Not to mention she had her hip jutting out and her shoulders far back, so her breasts stood nice and perky. I may not know how to make a come-hither look, but I certainly *know* a fuck-me look when I see it. And she was standing in all sorts of fuck-me stance.

Shrugging, his face pinks. "It doesn't matter. I have you, and I'm happy. She can like me all she wants."

His eyes flit up to the door. I'm really not sure why it matters. My mind spends more time on Josh than it does on Liam. I'm the one having feelings for somebody else. Here I am, sitting with Liam, arguing with him over something stupid, all because I can't get my mind off Josh for more than a few hours. Maybe I'm just projecting.

"I'm going to go." Jumping to my feet, I start to gather my things. At this point, I'd rather worry about Josh being down the hall than stay here for another second.

"What? Over that? Lexie, I'm sorry, okay. I can't control how she feels."

"No, it's fine, I'm fine. I just want to go back to my room." There's suddenly a jittery feeling working through my body, and I won't be able to keep still any longer. My thoughts have barely been staying away from my own dorm anyway, I may as well just wrap myself in the blanket of misery.

"Can I walk you back? It's dark."

"No, it's fine, it's like ten feet door to door." I wave my hand toward the hallway, not looking up at Liam.

He hesitates. "Okay. If you're sure you'll be alright."

I give him a tight smile. "I will be. I promise." He's either forgetting I've made the walk in the dark, drunk, or he just feels bad about what's transpired here.

Liam stands and gives me a quick peck on the lips. "Call me tomorrow?"

"Yeah, sure. Go watch the movie with Cara. I'm fine, it's good. I'll talk to you tomorrow."

Hugging my books to my chest, I walk out. Out into the darkness, out into the night. I want to be alone. I want to scream. I need to just clear my head for a little while.

MY MUSIC IS ON FULL BLAST, BASS THUMPING, FILLING THE cabin of my car. A knock on my window makes me jump and shriek, a hand flying to my chest to keep my heart from escaping my body. I open my eyes to see Josh peering in.

"What the hell are you doing?" As soon as my window is down, he reaches in and cranks the volume way down with a quick flick of the dial. No 'hi', no 'haven't seen you in a while.'

"I'm listening to music and relaxing. Why?"

"It's late and dark out here. It's not safe for you to be alone in your car with the music all the way up and your eyes closed. Any maniac can come over."

SHAYNA ASTOR

"Case in point." I glare at him. "Why do you care anyway?" A look of hurt flashes across his eyes. It's so fast I'm not even sure if I had seen it or if I imagined it. On some level, I do feel bad because he's told me, more than once, that he does care about me. But the silent treatment always makes me second-guess it.

And right now, I'm hurting and upset. Part of me wants to take that out on somebody else. It's not like he doesn't deserve it, at least a little bit.

"Ya know, I'm getting a little tired of having to tell you that I care about you." *And I'm getting kind of tired of him telling me goodbye.* His eyes narrow, scrutinizing my face. "You've been crying."

Shit, he noticed. "I don't know what you're talking about."

"Don't lie to me. You've been crying. What happened? Did he do something to you? Did he hurt you?" His jaw tenses and his hand balls into a fist at his side as he looks over toward the dorms.

"What? Liam? No, he didn't hurt me." The fact that Cara is clearly into him, and possibly even that it's mutual, in no way affects me. It's a disappointing realization that this is where I've let things get to.

"Did he…push you? In any way?"

I almost don't understand what he says through gritted teeth. Part of me wonders if he's even going to wait for an answer or just haul off to find and beat the crap out of Liam.

"No, he didn't. It's nothing *he* did or didn't do."

"Well, somebody upset you." He doesn't catch my subtlety that it isn't Liam who's hurt me.

"Nope. I told you. I'm fine." Even though he's never done anything but fool around with me and tell me it shouldn't have happened, I can't tell him it's *his* fault I'm crying. That the back and forth is toying with my emotions more than I can handle. That seeing Liam and Cara just adds more guilt on top of what I already carry day to day.

The burden is getting too heavy to bear.

Sighing, he shakes his head, wisps floating into his eyes. "Let me walk you back to the dorm, at least. Please. It's dark out." His voice is low, so sincere.

I hesitate. Is this just going to be more of me walking in the door, however small of a step, to have it slammed in my face?

But I reach over and turn off the car, taking the hand that he holds outstretched to help me out. We walk back to the dorm in silence, but close enough that his musky scent surrounds me, and every so many steps, our arms brush, sending shock waves reverberating through my body. I've missed this simple touch so much.

When we get back to the building, he holds the doors for me. He may toy with my emotions, but he's always a gentleman. Instead of heading for the stairs, he stops once we're through the double doors.

"Would you...any chance that maybe you'd be interested in getting a cup of coffee with me? I know it's kind of late, but I know you drink coffee any time of day, and midnight meal opened up already."

"Yes," I say faster than I want to. I was just in my car crying over this man, and yet here I am, agreeing within seconds to go sit with him in the dining hall. With the smile that spreads across his face, I know I'll say yes, every time and any time, he ever asks me to go anywhere with him.

"I'm just going to drop these at the desk, and we'll head down." He holds up his books. I hadn't noticed he was carrying any.

Suddenly, my stomach is filled with butterflies. We've been together so many times before, but it's always been a bit more hidden, more secretive. The one time we've been in the dining hall together, we had our books to hide behind, a guise of studying. This is going to be out in the open. I guess it's not too strange for an RA and a resident to eat together.

Seated at the table, our coffees sit untouched, a delicate silence enveloping us. Josh's legs are spread out in front of him, his knee grazing mine. He's staring down at his cup, twirling it slightly in his hand.

Every so often I'll glance up at him. I can tell by the look on his face that he wants to tell me something. Knowing I can't press him, I just wait, fighting the urge to adjust in my seat and tear my cup to pieces.

"I'm sorry." It's so quiet for a minute I think I'm hearing things. But I look up and notice his dark eyes on me, sadness behind them.

"About what?"

"The other night. I shouldn't have—I'm sorry you saw me so drunk. And the reason behind it." The reason behind it has been replaying over and over in my mind, his words, the relief on his face when he realized it wasn't me in the room.

"Oh." It's all I can say. I'm not sorry for it. I don't regret what I told him.

"It's not fair or right to you. To say those things, to do *those* things. The rules haven't changed. I'm still not right for you. I need to stop. Stop pulling you in one day to push you away the next. You should be with Liam. Liam's a good choice."

"Liam is a good choice. He doesn't do the things to me that you do. But he also doesn't see me the way you do." I take his hand in mine. I make sure it's slight and hidden behind the napkin holder, though there are very few people in the dining hall with us.

Josh's eyes flick up to mine. There's an undeniable longing in them, something I recognize so well because I see it in my own when I look in the mirror. I know Liam is the better choice. He's kind, generous, funny, and he likes me. And most importantly, he's somebody that I *can* be with, since he's available. While Josh, well, Josh is not. Plain and simple.

But I don't want Liam. I don't dream about Liam. I don't burn for Liam.

We sit for a few minutes, holding hands lightly, sipping our coffees but not looking at each other. Josh pulls his hand out of mine, pressing the heels of his palms into his eyes before he slides his hands down his face. He looks tired, worn. "Let me walk you upstairs."

That's it, the end of our time. He doesn't have anything to say. No response to me. I know this is going to be another thing we shouldn't have done, another time we shouldn't have spent together. Another mistake.

Dropping me off at my room, his hand grazes my lower back as he walks away. I watch him head down the hall and slide into his room, not looking back once. I feel the click of his door through my entire body.

I wonder how long it will be until he lets me in again.

CHAPTER 21

I'm confused. I'm lost. My head and heart are being pulled in two different directions. One pulls to Josh, the other knows Liam is a better choice. An available choice.

But they war with each other, because no agreement can be reached. If I'm being honest with myself, I know that no matter how much I dive into a relationship with Liam, he can never make me feel how Josh does. Even knowing that heartache will follow, I still look forward to seeing Josh, and because of that, I avoid Liam.

I need to break up with him; I should have weeks ago. But I'm a coward, afraid to lose something for nothing.

So I do the only thing I know might help. Throwing on a loose sweater, jeans, and a pair of boots, I head down to the lake. The sun is starting to set, but it doesn't matter. I need to think. I need the understanding of the water.

I've been here for over an hour, the sun leaving a few remaining streaks of orange in the mostly dark sky, when I hear footsteps coming down the shore behind me. I don't need to look up to know it's Josh. I can *feel* his presence.

"What are you doing down here?" Josh's deep voice reverberates through me.

Rolling my eyes, I don't pull my gaze from the lake. "Thinking."

"About what?"

"Us."

"There is no us." His voice is quiet, strained, sad. The words make my blood run cold, slowing in my veins. Out of the corner of my eye, I watch him put his hands in his pockets and kick a stone with the toe of his sneaker. "It's dark out. You shouldn't be here alone."

"What is your obsession with me being out when it's dark? Am I not allowed to leave when it's dark out?"

"It's not safe. You should at least be with somebody."

"Well, if it's really that unsafe, maybe campus should do something. Why do you care anyway?" I look up at him from my spot on the ground, knees still hugged to my chest. I'm only asking why he cares to hurt him.

It's become our thing. I hurt him at the beginning; he hurts me at the end. Every time I know it's going to happen, and yet I just can't help myself.

Pain flashes across his face. "Why do you keep asking me if I care about you? Do you really not know? Why do you think I look out for you so much?"

Swallowing roughly, I try to strengthen my voice. "Why do you keep pushing me away, then?"

"Is that what this has become, Lexie? You hurt me because you know that I'm going to hurt you? Even though I don't ever *want* to hurt you. It's not a simple situation, Lexie. I wish it was. It would be so much easier if I didn't like you, if I wasn't drawn to you like a damn magnet. If I could get myself to just be fucking strong and stay away from you. But it's proven to be impossible even though I've tried so fucking hard."

Stopping for a minute, he takes a deep breath, letting it trail out slowly. "So instead, I lead you on, I track you down and corner you at parties. I invite you into my room, my bed, and then I don't talk to you for days. And those days kill me. I miss you. I long for you. I *ache* for you. And then I can't stand it anymore. I can't stand to not be near you, to not feel you in my arms, to not feel your lips on mine. So I fuck it up again by bringing you close, just to realize that I was selfish to do that to you when I have to push you away again just as soon."

My heart pounds and a shiver wracks my entire body.

"You asked me why I stopped *tutoring* and I said I had my reasons. You're my reason." Turning, he looks at me—really looks at me—for what may be the first time ever.

"I knew you didn't approve, and even if you did, it didn't matter. I don't want anybody but you. I don't want random, meaningless hookups anymore. For three years, I've been just fine not having a girlfriend, not wanting one. Then I met you, and it seems impossible to not be with you. And yet I can't. But I don't want anybody else, not even for a night. I only want you, for however long I can have you, and I'll wait however long it takes for you to truly be mine."

I can do nothing but stare at him. Our eyes are locked on one another. This isn't the first time he's told me he wants me, but this is the first time he's really acknowledged that he knows he's leading me on and hurting me. My heart's hammering so loudly against my breastbone I'm sure he can hear it trying to escape, trying to get to him.

We stay here quietly for a few minutes; me sitting on the ground, arms wrapped around my legs, him standing there with his hands still in his pockets.

"Sit with me?" I don't know what else to say.

Surprisingly, Josh sits down right next to me, so close our arms touch and I can feel his warmth rolling off him in waves similar to the ones in front of us. I welcome it as it's gotten chilly down here by the lake.

"How did you know I'd be here?" I ask, looking over at him.

Taking my hand in his, he turns my wrist up, tracing over the wave tattoo with his thumb.

"You were looking for me?"

"I'm always paying attention to your presence, Lexie. When the sun started setting, I realized I hadn't seen you in a while, so I made a pass by your room. Brit mentioned she hadn't seen you in hours. I tried the library first."

"I needed the forgiveness of the water. I needed to be listened to, judgment free. I needed to find some peace."

"So what do you have?"

Looking over at him, my brow furrows as confusion swirls through my mind.

"Fear, anger, or hurt." His jaw tightens and eyes flicker as he glances down at my wrist again.

Inhaling a deep breath and exhaling it forcefully, I'm shocked he remembers my words from a few weeks ago. "All of the above?"

He hangs his head. "I'm sorry."

"Josh. Josh, look at me."

He does, albeit begrudgingly.

"It's not just your fault. I could tell you no, to stay away. But I don't. You do all the things you said and more, but I always go willingly, happily. And yeah, you tell me it's a mistake and we don't talk for days. But I'd do it all again. Every encounter, every kiss. Every heartache."

Something flashes across his face that I can't make out in the dark. "I should be stronger. More respectful. I mean, fuck, Lex, you have a boyfriend. I've never respected that. Even after having been cheated on. I know how it feels, and yet, here I am."

I look at him with my brow knit together, head tilted to the side.

Josh smirks at me. "You didn't think I just slept around for the fun of it, did you?"

I shrug. "I don't know. Maybe. I wasn't sure, didn't want to ask. That's just how some people are."

Taking a deep breath, he turns to look out at the great

expanse of water in front of us. "I wasn't. I didn't think I ever would be. I came here with my high school girlfriend. We had a…rough…transition. College was new territory.

"We thought we wanted to stay together, but really, we both wanted to find ourselves a bit more, discover who we were outside of our parents' homes, have new experiences. That often meant not with one another. We did different activities, we started different lives. We drifted apart but stayed together. When we went home between the semesters, we were able to sort of rejuvenate our relationship. Returning to campus, we were in a different place, a little closer, but I could feel that it was still strained." He looks down at his hands, which he's wringing.

A feeling of dread over takes me. This is going to become something upsetting, something that hurt him, and the thought makes bile rise in my throat.

"In March, I walked in on her with my roommate, a buddy of Liam's. They didn't even have the decency to lock the damn door." Chuckling, he looks at the stars twinkling above us, still wringing his hands. "I was hurt, I was mad. But I wasn't really surprised. I felt the break-up coming, knew it was on the horizon. But with our history, I was mad she wasn't decent enough, didn't care about me enough, to break up with me *before* she fell into bed with somebody else. I'd even suspected that there *was* somebody else she was interested in. I just didn't expect her to cheat on me."

I'm biting my tongue, literally, a hint of iron flowing across my taste buds. I need to let him finish, to hear his reasoning, to learn more about him.

"That was the day I decided to become an RA. That was the day I decided I didn't want to be in a relationship again, to just have fun. I'm sure you've heard the stories, that I sleep with every girl that comes to my room." He turns to look at me. "I don't. Not even most of them. But I let the talk continue because I don't want somebody thinking I want a relationship. And it was fine, it was going fine. I was having fun, enjoying being single in college. Until you came along and knocked the wind out of me." His gaze intensifies, making my heart stutter.

"The first day I saw you, I knew I wanted you. But that day I came by, and we talked, and I heard the music you had on, I knew I wanted to *be* with you. It rocked me to my core, wanting to be with you so badly. I tried to fight it, the rules being so strict, but I just...I can't." The last word comes out on a breath so quiet it's stolen by the breeze.

"So, I steal moments. Moments I shouldn't be stealing, moments I shouldn't be taking. Moments you should be having with somebody that you want to have them with and who you can be with. I'm being selfish. And I'm sorry."

"I'm not." I don't even let the air settle between us. I've been quiet for too long, and I have so many things to say, so many words that he needs to hear.

"I'm not sorry, Josh. I *do* want those moments with you, only you. That's why I've let them happen. I can say no. You know you're gorgeous and can have any girl you want, but *I am* capable of saying no. The problem is, I don't want to. I know it's wrong. I know I have a boyfriend. But I can't stop myself either. I don't want to. I answer you before I even have a chance to think.

"And if I were to think, I know I would want to say yes even more but would feel guilty knowing I have Liam. And he's a good guy. He's sweet and patient. He doesn't push me into things he thinks I'm not ready for. He's somebody I can have, do have."

Gritting my teeth, I exhale sharply, the memory of Cara still fresh in my mind.

Shaking it from my head, I continue, "But I don't want him like I want you. And I know it's wrong that I'm still with him. I do. But I think I'm scared you're going to disappear for good next time. I fear that every time. And I'm scared to throw away what could be something good with Liam for what can't exist between us." The mere mention of it makes guilt twist through me, wrapping my heart in a vice. Even if I can't be with Josh, even if he disappears, I'm not being fair to Liam, and that notion weighs on me daily.

"I've tried to give him my full attention, to say I'm going to push you out of my mind and focus on Liam. But I can't. Because the second you look at me, it's like you're the only man in the world."

I laugh suddenly and Josh looks at me with scrunched eyebrows, but a light smile on his face. My explanation may not make sense to him, but it's one I have to give. "I've always been a rule follower. Not necessarily all the rules everywhere, but my mom's rules. I went to parties in high school, drank a little, which is obviously illegal. But my mom's rule was to never get in a car if I'd been drinking or with anybody who had, that I could call her any time to come get me and she wouldn't be mad. And I did, more than once, and she was never angry, never gave me a lecture about underage drinking. She said she didn't want me doing anything that could change somebody's life, mine or otherwise."

Looking at the ground, I shift some rocks with the toe of my shoe. "Her rule around intimacy was just to be careful. She said she'd raised her kid, or at least mostly, she didn't want to raise more. Not to do anything that could be life-altering. I think that's part of why I never…" I can't even bring myself to say *had sex*, even though he's been so intimately *there*, more than once.

"But I followed the rules. Hers, at school. Then I come here, and there's one major rule that I so desperately want to just shatter."

This is the most honest we've ever been with each other, the most we've talked about ourselves. We've never really shared our feelings before, at least not this deeply. It has to be the magic of the water.

I watch Josh intently as he starts to open his mouth, then changes his mind.

Shifting slightly, it's as if he wants to do something with his body that he's not sure he should. Finally, he wraps his arm tentatively around my shoulders.

I don't hesitate to lean into him. My head rests against his chest, his arm warm around me, hand resting on my hip. He kisses the top of my head, and we sit in silence, looking out at the lake, hearing the low waves crashing on the rocky shore, letting the water wash away our fears, our anger, our hurt.

We sit for a while, being close, nothing but the sound of the lake washing onto the rocks, watching the moon dance around on the water. "Listen—"

"I know." I don't need to let him continue. "I know that when we walk up that hill and to the dorm, we're just RA and resident again. I know we probably won't talk for days. Or that maybe this will be the time it's really over." I swallow the lump building in my throat. Knowing doesn't make it any easier. And thinking it may be the last time almost shatters me.

Josh puts his hand on the side of my face. Leaning into his touch, a tear escapes from the corner of my eye. He gently rubs it away with the pad of his thumb.

"Just know that if I'm ever lucky enough to have you, to truly have you, I'm never letting you go." His voice is quiet, sincere.

I meet his eyes. It's dark, but I can see the sincerity in them; I can see how much he means it, wants it. I can't decide if that makes things better or worse. When he bends down to kiss me, I don't move away, I don't hesitate, I don't second-guess it. I lean into him, wanting so much more than just his lips on mine, but knowing that I shouldn't even be doing this one thing.

Josh keeps it short and sweet, mouths staying closed. Disappointment surges in my chest. I want him to push my mouth open with his, I want to feel his hands on my body. I want him to make my mind go blank and forget about Liam and the rules and everything else.

He hesitates a minute before pulling away. "Let's just sit here for a little longer, okay?"

All I can do is nod in the darkness, not willing to separate from him just yet. Settling back into his chest, I listen to his heart beating. My eyes droop shut as I try to memorize the sound, knowing it'll be the last I hear it for a while, and wanting it to haunt my thoughts and dreams.

However long we're together by the water, isn't long enough. Not enough to make me happy, and not enough to account for the long stretch of time before I'll be able to be close to him again.

The water didn't do its job tonight. Or maybe it did, and I've already put myself back in the same position. My soul feels weary and tired as my heart pulls toward the person walking an inch to my left. Right now, he feels so close and yet so far.

CHAPTER 22

It's Friday afternoon, and I'm breaking my own routine and checking the mail. Part of me is hoping to get a glimpse of Josh, as I haven't seen him in almost a week. He won't even look my way in class.

"Ah, so you're the lucky girl who got the roommate transfer."

Spinning around, I find Holly, the hall director, standing outside the office door. I've seen her at most twice in the ten weeks I've been here. She's almost like a mythical creature, rarely seen in the wild, and her existence is questionable.

Tucking some curls behind my ear, I try to smile, but it may come across as more of a snarl since I can feel my lip quivering. Nerves bubble in my stomach and a tingling starts to spread through my extremities. Why is she talking to me? Am I in trouble?

"Oh, uh, yeah, I guess so." My voice cracks at the end and I clear my throat, looking all the more guilty. Of what, I don't know, but guilty all the same.

"You know, Josh pushed really hard to get that done." There's a softness to her tone, almost like she's sharing a secret. In a way, she is.

My eyebrows shoot sky high. "Josh?" Just his name sends a burn ricocheting through my body.

"Oh, yeah. He made it a priority. Even went to the housing department to see what could be done. This is my second year being his hall director and I've never seen him take so kindly to a resident. He usually keeps his head down."

"He didn't tell me that." My voice is just above a whisper.

"Do you two know each other well?" Her eyes narrow, and I try to swallow around my suddenly parched throat.

"I mean, he's down the hall from me, but mostly we have a class together. He drove me one day when my car died. That's probably why he pushed it through, didn't want to hear me complain anymore." I need to stop the word vomit. Soon.

"Josh is a nice guy."

"Yeah, he is." My voice is light, airy, distant. Why hadn't he told me?

"Well, congratulations. I saw you at your mailbox and just wanted to say that."

"Thanks." As she's about to step into the office, I stop her. "When did he start doing that? The paperwork push through."

"Oh, it was a few weeks back. Shortly after you submitted it. These things tend to take a long while, so even though he was able to find something, it took him a few weeks. I know he lost track of time now and again. I think he worked late one night in October. Missed a concert or something."

My heart races, breaths come in short bursts and all my blood has pooled at my feet. The concert. He'd been late, said he was doing something. And I had taken a shot at him that it was someone. But he was trying to push it through. Trying to find a way out for *me*.

And yet he hadn't told me. That was weeks ago. We've spent so much more time together since then, though we often aren't talking, at all. Still, why wouldn't he say something? Even when he saw me and Brit celebrating at the desk.

That must be what I felt. Something in me knew the roommate exchange wasn't a random happenstance.

Josh didn't say something for a reason, so the question becomes, do I bring it up? Maybe I'll call Lauren and ask her. Though I doubt she'd know how to handle something like this. Plus, she's not thrilled I'm still spending even an extra second of time with him.

The click of the door shutting draws me from my thoughts, and I find myself alone in the hallway again. Absentmindedly, I toss the few magazines into the trash on my way out of the dorm.

Sunlight assaults my eyes as I squint and flinch, the chill in the air sends a shiver racing down my spine. At least, I think it's the air. I can't really be sure right now.

I walk to Liam's suite like a robot, the consideration of Josh and what he did for me running over and over in my mind. There's a mental filing cabinet that I'm rifling through in my head, trying to figure out all the reasons he's decided to keep it a secret.

Not landing on one, I twist the knob to Liam's suite, letting myself in as I've been instructed to do on numerous occasions.

A loud moan snaps my attention to my present. Taking a breath, I shake myself out, I need to focus.

Wait. What did I just hear?

"Fuck, baby. You feel so Goddamn good taking my dick."

No.

That's Liam's voice. It may be muffled by the thankfully closed door, but I'd know it anywhere. Almost as much as I'd recognize Josh's in a hurricane.

"Oh, God, Liam. I'm...I'm going to come." That voice. I recognize it. My eyes narrow and I try to pull up a memory, any memory, of the voice. Is it from a class? The dorm? The dining hall even?

My stomach plummets to the ground when realization smacks me in the face.

Teeth grinding together, fingers curling into my palms, I stomp over to the door and throw it open as my rage boils over the top.

Cara shrieks and jumps off Liam, yanking the sheet up to cover her naked body, turning crimson.

"Fuck! Lexie. What are you doing?"

"What am *I* doing?! Are you fucking serious, Liam?"

Scrambling off the bed, he starts pulling his clothes on. I avert my eyes, to a derisive snort from Cara, when he stands completely nude.

"You were supposed to call first." The accusation lacing his tone makes my nails dig into my skin.

"Oh, so that would have made a difference? If I had *called* first. What, so you would have had time to get her off of you and out of your room before I showed up? That's the problem here? Not that you've been screwing around behind my back?" Not that I'm not guilty of the same, on some level. But righteous indignation is the only thing I have right now. It helps tamp down the guilt and anger at myself from overpowering me.

"That's not…that's not what I meant." His voice is low and strained as he runs a hand through his hair, unable to lift his eyes from the ground.

"How long has this been happening?"

"A while."

"A few weeks ago, when I said she was interested in you…"

All he does is nod, still unable to meet my eyes.

"So, when you said we could take things slow, you really only said that because you were getting it elsewhere? You've been cheating on me all this time?"

"We were never really a couple, Lexie."

Ice shoots through my body and freezes everything in its path.

"I never asked you to be my girlfriend; we never said we

were exclusive. But you're a very attractive girl. I was okay biding my time."

Any sense of composure I have left snaps like a frayed wire. "Fuck you, Liam." I fight the urge to cross the room and slap him. "And fuck you, whore." I lean to the side so I can see around his body, which is conveniently, or maybe intentionally, blocking Cara's, to point at her.

I don't wait for an answer from either one of them as I storm out, slamming the door shut behind me.

Everything passes by in a blur, thanks to both the speed of my exit and the tears welling in my eyes.

It's not that I was really that interested in Liam, clearly, since I'd been doing so much with Josh and barely giving Liam a thought. No, it's the sheer disrespect for the situation, for me. The irony of it all.

Racing across the driveway, I barely escape a car pulling up in front of the dorm, blaring its horn at me. I wave a dismissive hand as I get to the doors, resting one hand against the cool glass while I yank it open with the other.

I take the stairs two at a time, chest heaving by the time I reach the fourth floor.

Right now, I don't know if I'm happy or upset that Brittney is gone for the night. Part of me feels like I could use her words of wisdom, her comfort, and of course, her unbridled rage to go destroy Liam. But at the same time, I'm worried about a 'told you so'. She'd told me to ask him about being exclusive. I didn't think it was necessary.

I want to act. I need to do something, but there's nothing *to* do. So instead, I wear out the soles of my Converse as I pace back and forth in my small square of a room, waiting for the waves of anger to subside.

CHAPTER 23

The incessant knocking, though I've tried to ignore it, has only gotten louder. Clearly, whoever is on the other side just can't take a hint.

I fling it open. "WHAT?!" Josh stands on the other side. "Oh, God. It's *you*. I don't have time for you right now." I'm too busy burning a hole in the linoleum of my room. I can't add him coming in, just to turn me away to the mix of emotions. "Go away." I push the door to slam it shut.

Stopping it with his hand, he pushes through my arm and into the room, closing the door behind him and locking it. "What happened?"

"It's none of your concern. Please leave."

"I'm not leaving until you talk to me."

Sighing, I stare at the ceiling, tears running from my cheeks down to my neck. In the time it took for me to pace and my pulse to do nothing but quicken to opening the door, a burn set in behind my eyes.

"Okay, fine. You want to know? Here it goes. I just found Liam cheating on me. With a girl from his floor who I've been saying for weeks is interested in him. He denied it over and over. Said he only had eyes for me, that she didn't matter. Yet, here I am, crying over some asshole I don't even really like that much but out of the sheer disrespect and *lies* he told me. Not that it matters, it's not like I've been overly faithful to him." Staring at Josh, I make sure to catch his eye, making sure he knows that I'm referring to all the things that have happened between us.

"I'm sorry," he says quietly.

"Sorry? You're sorry? You should be fucking sorry! It's your fault! Maybe you didn't throw them together, but I wouldn't have been with him if it wasn't for you. I wanted you. I wanted to be with *you*. And you repeatedly, emphatically, told me we couldn't possibly be together. Yet time and time again, you pull me in, give me a tiny glimpse of something, a taste, just to pull it away and tell me again we can't be together. Had that not happened, maybe I would have put my all into Liam."

Hands planted firmly in his pockets, he remains silent. "God, say something!" I've done nothing but scream at him since he walked in, and he hasn't flinched.

His eyes seek mine, and I recognize the sadness and longing in them.

In two seconds, he's across the room, hand in my hair, his mouth closing on mine with so much intensity it steals the air from my lungs. Josh parts my lips with his tongue, gently sliding it over mine. His other arm reaches around my waist, pulling me against him. His heart hammers against my chest, warring with my own.

Josh is who I want; he's all I want. And he's what I can't have.

With my hands firmly on his chest, I push him away. "Why do you keep doing this to me?"

"I don't know what you're talking about."

"Oh, really? You don't?"

"What do you want me to say?" I flinch as he yells. Turning away from me, he puts his hands on the back of my chair, taking a deep breath. His jaw relaxes, though I didn't realize he'd been clenching it. "Do you think I want this? Do you think I want to be doing this to you? I can see how much it hurts you, and that is never my intention. I don't want to hurt you. I don't like hurting you." His voice is calm, pained.

"I saw you come up here and knew you were upset, and I just...I couldn't not come here. I couldn't not check on you, even if that meant turning away later. Every time, I tell myself it will be the last. And every time I know I'm lying." Looking over at me, sadness seeps through his dark eyes.

I don't know what to say, we've sang this song and danced this dance before. So, I choose to say nothing. Crossing the room, I wrap my arms around his neck, pulling him into a kiss.

Josh hesitates for only a moment before his lips crash down on mine, hands sliding in my back pockets and tugging me against him. Gripping my thighs, he lifts me up as I wrap my legs around his waist. Walking me over to the bed, he lays me down, climbing up to hover over me.

We've been in a situation like this before. And it had led to a new point in our strange and twisted relationship. But things had only gone so far. This time, I don't want to stop.

"We won't...we don't have to do anything you don't want to do. I can leave if you want me to." Josh's gaze finds mine, and it's the softest I've ever seen it as he brushes my hair from my forehead.

Instead of answering, I grab his collar with both hands, bringing his mouth back to mine. His body is stiff for a moment before he relaxes, kissing me back with a fierceness I haven't experienced before, the hand not supporting his weight sliding down my body and back up. Moving his lips downward, he kisses along my jaw, my neck, to my collarbone.

With both hands, he tears off my shirt in one swift move-ment, lips back on mine, kissing hungrily as his hands rove down my body to work the buttons of my pants, sliding them off and throwing them to the side.

Josh stops, looking me up and down slowly, fingers running gently up my legs, over my hips, up my stomach, to my chest. Running his thumb tenderly along my bottom lip, he leans in to give me a tender kiss. "You're so beautiful."

The air in my lungs whooshes out, and my need for him expounds.

Tugging him down on me again, with a new sense of urgency behind the kiss, I want to make sure we get somewhere before he decides to leave again.

He reaches behind his back and swiftly pulls his shirt up and over, his lips finding mine again right away.

I trace my fingertips from his shoulders down his perfect chest to his pants. It's here I hesitate for a moment, waiting for him to stop me again. But when Josh slides his lips to my neck, my fingers move almost on their own to start undoing the button of his jeans. Hopping down from the bed, he kicks them off, his boxers with them. My breath catches, the stirring increasing between my legs as I rub my thighs together, wondering what he'd feel like inside me.

Instead of climbing back up on the bed with me, he takes my hands, pulling me up to sitting. Leaning in slowly, he places a gentle kiss on my temple, torturously working his way down to place a tender kiss on my lips, and continuing down along my jaw, my neck, along my collarbone and across my shoulders. Gently, he slides my bra straps down as he reaches his hands behind my back and unhooks my bra, delicately taking it off and tossing it to the side with the rest of the clothes.

Tenderly, he runs his fingers up my arms, across my shoulders and down to cup my breasts. Running his thumbs over my hardened nipples, a gasp catches in my throat as he keeps his eyes locked on mine the whole time, the need between my thighs increasing. Taking a step closer as he tips down, his mouth closes around my nipple as a squeak leaves my lips, my head tilting back so I face the ceiling. Wrapping my arms around his neck, fingers tangling in his hair, I pull him closer to me.

He leans me back on the bed, keeping my nipple between his lips, tongue moving deftly, and removes my panties, adding them to the heap on the floor. As he climbs up to rest over me, he moves his mouth to my neck as he slides a hand down between my thighs, a moan escaping me as he slips his fingers along my wetness.

"Holy shit, Lexie." His breath catches in his throat with a low groan.

Josh has his face buried in my neck as he slowly slides his fingers inside me and starts to move them expertly.

My back peels off the bed, my chest pressing to his. The warmth and hardness of his muscles only increases my pleasure.

As he hooks his fingers inside me, he wraps his lips around my nipple again, tongue flicking along the peak. My grip in his hair tightens as I whimper and whine, writhing beneath him, the pressure building as I breathe heavily.

Suddenly he stops, pushing up to look at me, eyes gentle with something I can't figure out. "I want all of you, but I don't want to do anything you're not ready for."

I pull him into a deep kiss. When I release him, his eyes are still on mine, questioning spreading across his face. "I want this. I want this with you, here, now. I've always wanted this with you." I voice my deepest desires so he knows, so he hears me fully.

Without hesitation, his lips smash against mine as he slowly pushes his erection into me. I cry out at the sliver of pain. It's quickly replaced with sheer pleasure. The feeling of him moving inside me is better than I could have imagined. I, of course, have no sense of comparison, besides his fingers, but it makes my eyes roll in my head.

"Josh," I sigh as my arms rope around his neck, my fingers grabbing at anything they can get traction on; his hair, his back, his shoulders, anything.

"Fuck, Lexie." His words come out strained as his mouth latches on my throat. "You feel so damn good."

With every thrust, I'm whimpering. My brain can't even wrap around how amazing this feels. The pressure builds until I can't contain it any longer, digging my nails into Josh's shoulders as my back arches, and I call out his name.

He presses his forehead against mine as I tremble beneath him, our breath mingling in the space as he continues to move inside me. His lips latch onto my neck as his breath catches and he lets out a small groan before slowing to a stop.

Staying on top of me, he rests his head against the pillow, breathing heavily for a moment before he kisses my shoulder, then hastily kisses his way to my mouth before rolling to his side.

Turning to face him, he smoothes some hair from my face, his eyes searching mine.

"How are you?" A warm sensation crawls lazily through my body as his first words are concern for me.

"I'm good."

"Are you sure?

"I promise. As long as you don't disappear on me." I close my eyes, not wanting to see his reaction.

Instead, his lips brush mine, his hand sliding to my lower back and tugging me against him. When he ends the kiss, I stifle a groan of protest and open my eyes.

"I'm here, Lex. I can't say what's going to happen tomorrow in terms of being together. I won't freeze you out anymore; I can't after this. But for tonight, I'm here."

Shifting to his back, he pushes an arm under my neck and pulls me against him, resting my head on his chest. Somehow, between the time he'd walked in the door and now, I'd forgotten about what had happened earlier in the day with

228

Liam. I'd forgotten about the ache that Josh puts in my chest every time he walks away.

My mind has gone completely blank. All I'm left with is contentment, peace. I don't know what's going to happen next, but I plan to enjoy tonight and this moment.

As his fingers lightly trace up and down my back, he shakes underneath me, and I realize he's laughing.

"What's so funny?" I can't help the smirk that comes to my own face.

"It's just, I never thought this would happen. I wanted it to. I desperately hoped it would even though I knew—I know —I shouldn't. But I'm so damn happy it did."

I kiss his perfect chest. "I am too." And I am. Because despite the back and forth, the hot and cold, the trouble we could both get into, it had been perfect. We aren't supposed to be together; it's forbidden and wrong in many ways. But it's so clear we can't keep ourselves from one another, as much as we've tried.

Squeezing me tightly against him, he puts his fingers under my chin and tilts my face up to look at him. "No matter what may happen, I will always be happy for tonight and thankful for you." Then he places a tender kiss on my lips.

His mention of being thankful reminds me of something I wanted to talk to him about. It's hard to believe it was only hours ago that I found out.

Pulling back, I catch his eye. "I know you're the one who pushed through the roommate switch for me. Why?" Just the thought makes my heart swell. He knew how miserable I was with Kimberly, how hard living with her was for me. I still don't know what he had to do to make it happen, but he did. For me.

Sincerity sweeps across his face, his eyes filled with adoration as he links his fingers with mine. "I wanted to make you happy; I needed to. I hadn't been very nice to you up until that point, and I'd already had a few instances of making you unhappy, of hurting you. I needed to do something to put a smile on your face."

"Why didn't you tell me it was you?"

"I didn't want anything in return. There was no reason for you to know it was me. It was enough for me to see you happy. I needed to know that I put a smile on your face for once. That was enough for me."

Words elude me. I only just found out that he had been the one to push it through. How could I possibly thank him for removing my toxic roommate? Only one thing comes to mind. Laying on top of him, I connect my lips with his. His arms wrap around me, running down my back as he parts my mouth with his, sliding his tongue over mine.

I break away, kissing along his perfect chest, to his collarbone, to his ear. "I want to say thank you. Will you make me happy again?" I whisper as seductively as I can muster.

Josh flips me to my back, a smirk on his face. "Gladly," he says against my lips.

Moving away from my mouth, he runs his slightly parted lips and tongue along my body, leaving a trail of electricity in his wake. When he gets back up to my breasts, he gently cups one while his tongue flicks over the hardened nipple, making me moan and arch toward him. When he closes his teeth over it, I yelp.

As he leans back over me, my body is humming with the need for him again.

Josh runs his thumb down the side of my face, pulling my bottom lip down before closing his mouth over mine. My body molds to his. I want to stay in this room, in this bed, forever.

His tongue slips along mine as his hand cups my breast, fingers rubbing across my nipple. It makes me break the kiss, head tipping back as I pull my lip between my teeth and moan.

Tilting my head back, I see the sheer desire on Josh's face, his fingers still moving against my nipple.

"Again," is all I can say, breathless and desperate.

It doesn't take more than that one word for Josh to ease into me again, his hand finding my hip and pressing down as he moves inside me, faster than the first time. His gaze stays locked on mine as I try to keep my eyes open, biting my lip and grabbing at him. Before things get too far, he pulls away. I look at him with confusion.

"Roll over. On your knees." His voice is husky and filled with grit.

I do as he says, pushing up on my elbows. He runs his hands from my hips up to my shoulders and back down again as he presses into me. The new position makes my breath hitch as surprise wraps my voice.

"Fuck, Lex." His hands are tight at my hips, and he doesn't move, pressed all the way inside me. Ever so slowly, he pulls out before thrusting all the way back in, increasing his speed each time.

Leaving one hand on my hip, he reaches the other one down to tangle in my hair, pulling the slightest bit. Pushing up on my hands, my head tips back as I try hard to swallow the screams I want to release.

One thing you learn living in the dorms is that the walls are thin. Very thin. The last thing we need is for somebody to hear us. I have no idea if anybody saw him come in, but I don't need to draw extra attention to us by everybody hearing the incredible sex we're having.

While my hands are currently supporting me, I have a desperate need to touch him, to feel his muscles cord beneath my fingers. But the pressure's mounting and before I can give it a second thought, I wrap my fist around the sheets as my head drops forward and I choke out a breath, tightening around him.

He gives a low responding groan as his hand grips my hip, fingers digging into the bone, and he slows.

Kissing up my spine, he flicks his tongue along my earlobe, whispering in my ear, "You're so fucking sexy, Lexie."

Pulling away and flopping to his back, he tugs me down against him, drawing tiny circles on my hip while his other hand glides gently up and down the arm I have flung over his chest.

My eyes are drifting shut within minutes. He must feel my eyelashes fluttering against his chest because he leaves a long kiss on my forehead.

"Good night, beautiful." My heart soars. After the entire night, I'm flying high.

"Good night, Josh."

I drift asleep, warm in his embrace, his heartbeat like a lullaby calming me.

THE NEXT MORNING, WHEN I WAKE UP, I HAVE A GIANT SMILE gracing my face. Though I'm sore in places I never have been before, I'm happy. It takes me a moment to realize I don't feel warmth next to me. Sitting up straight, I pull the sheet to my chest.

He's not here. His clothes are gone. Desperately grabbing my phone, I look for any sort of notification from him. Nothing. Hopping down from my bed, I frantically look around for something, anything, that he may have left to explain why I woke up alone after an incredible night together. Because it had been incredible; he and I together had been incredible.

There's nothing.

Me: Where are you? Where did you go?

I wait and wait. I get dressed, checking my phone every few seconds. Nothing. I could wait more, but I don't. Instead, I walk down to his room and knock on the door. It's early still, so the hallway is silent. Maybe Josh came back to his room to sleep and isn't even awake yet, maybe he hadn't heard the phone.

But I have a sinking feeling that isn't what's going on now. I knock again, pressing right up against the door. "Josh. Are you in there? Josh, please. What happened?" I swallow the lump in my throat, biting back the tears that want to burst free. I try the knob. Locked.

This is the last thing I can handle. Going back to my room, I throw some clothes in a bag, grab my keys, and walk down to my car. I drive away from Liam and his betrayal. I drive away from the hotness and coldness of Josh and all its perfectness that's so wrong at the same time, away from the incredible night we had, away from Josh. And I just drive and drive.

CHAPTER 24

"Lexie? What are you doing here?" Lauren's startled face doesn't cause any reaction in me. It probably would if I didn't feel so numb.

"Can I come in?"

"Oh, of course, sorry. I'm just, I'm a little on edge as to what could bring you here unannounced."

"Sorry, I should have called first." The thought hadn't even crossed my mind. Once I got in the car, I just drove. Even though I've never been here, I knew the route. It was a straight shot down the highway, and I drove on autopilot as my mind shut down.

"I mean, it would have been helpful, but it's fine." She closes and locks the door. I take a quick glance around her dorm room, not so different from mine in size, shape, or layout. Thankfully, we're alone. "What happened?"

"Can't I just come see my best friend?" I try to tip my mouth into a grin but fail miserably.

She cocks her head to the side. "Lex."

And that's when I lose control. Shortly into the four-hour drive, I had been able to shut my brain off, the back and forth and worrying about what happened becoming too much to handle. But here, with Lauren, I'm able to let it all go.

She doesn't hesitate to wrap her arms around me and let me cry it all out. Guiding me over to her bed, we climb up and sit against the wall. Leaning into her, she holds me while I cry. We've been in this situation before, only the roles were always reversed.

When the tears finally stop, I sit up. Swiping my hair off my face and behind my shoulders, she keeps her hands there and levels her gaze with mine. "Okay, now that you're all cried out, you need to tell me what happened."

I nod. "I will, I promise. Can we just, can we get some coffee first?" I'd stopped to grab something to eat on my way, but I couldn't take more than one bite, my stomach being in knots. Now, in the comfort of my best friend, I feel both a little hungry and the desperate need for caffeine.

"Yeah, no problem. Do you want to go to the dining hall?"

"Any chance you could just bring something back here?" I ask sheepishly.

"Yeah, of course. I'll be back as soon as I can."

After she leaves, I take a few minutes to look around her dorm room, searching for the comforting hints of my best friend. Running my hand along the gray comforter that has bright circles, a sense of peace cocoons me. We had picked this out together, and even though she's not in the room, seeing her unmistakably *Lauren* clothes in the closet, smelling her sugary perfume, and sensing *her*, it all makes me feel at ease for the first time in hours.

As much as I don't want to, I check my phone. Still crickets from Josh. I can't tell if it makes me feel sadder or more enraged. Everything is muted, numbed.

What I'm sure should be a wide-open gash through my heart, feels like nothing more than a tiny pinprick.

"Okay, coffee and donuts," Lauren says as she comes in and climbs up on the bed next to me, handing me a large coffee and a chocolate donut. Of course, my best friend knows me so well. "Now spill."

And I do. It all comes pouring out. I start at almost the beginning, telling her some things she already knows. That Josh and I had this hot and cold on-and-off thing for weeks, being drawn to each other but that we couldn't be together. That even though we both tried to avoid each other, we just couldn't help ourselves and always ended up thrown back together. I tell her about Liam, how in recent days I tried to put my all into it, to be the good girlfriend, only to find him cheating, though apparently not really cheating, on me. I tell her all the things and firsts Josh and I shared together, including last night. God, had it only been last night? It feels like ages ago.

"And then this morning, he was just gone! No note, no text. It's been hours and I still haven't heard from him. Not a word. He clearly just played the long game and got what he wanted and decided he was out." I play with the lip of my coffee lid as tears start to well in my eyes again.

"First of all, I'm proud of you for putting yourself out there. I know it didn't exactly work out the way you expected."

"The way I expected? Laur, come on. This is a shit show. The guy who I thought was the right pick that I was racked with guilt for messing around on, who I was taking it nice and slow with while going warp speed with somebody else, had been sleeping around behind my back. For weeks. And the guy who I couldn't help but be drawn to, who told me he couldn't help but be drawn to me despite how wrong it was, who I gave myself to in every aspect, ditched me." I wince at the truth of the statement, the pin prick turning to hundreds of needles pressing into the barely beating organ. Trying to eliminate the feeling, I rub at my chest.

"And I gave myself to him happily. In one day, I lost my boyfriend, my virginity to a guy who then discarded me by morning, and who I'm pretty sure I'm in love with and have been since I first met him." My lungs feel like they can't get enough air in them. It hurts. It all hurts.

"Do you regret it?"

My fingers stop fiddling with the lid edge. Do I regret it? "No."

"Well, that's one thing."

"Is it, though? What does that say about me? I'm okay that I cheated on my boyfriend, or at least who I thought was my boyfriend, with a guy who then turns around and ditches me the second he gets laid?"

"It says you found somebody you want. And look, let's not make it seem like you were all wrong for cheating on Liam. I mean, no, it's not right, you shouldn't have done it. But he also cheated on you. Let's not forget that."

"Oh, trust me. I haven't." Bile inches up my throat at the thought.

"And about Josh." She shakes her head. "I think there's more going on there. I mean, after *everything* you shared, the times together, the fun, the sex, which he never once pressured you for. He even pushed through the roommate change for you, just to make you happy. He didn't flaunt it, he didn't boast about it, he didn't even tell you. If he really just wanted to get laid and move on, he easily could have just told you and hoped you'd reward him. But he didn't."

We sit in silence for a few minutes, but I can tell Lauren is holding something back. Thankfully, she tells me without my having to ask. "What I see is a guy who is so incredibly drawn to one girl he absolutely cannot have because the rules are *so* strict. And as a rule lover yourself, I feel like you should understand that. Yes, he went against it, time and time again, but all that should prove is how much he wants to be with you. He was willing to risk so much just for those tiny bits of time."

Lauren adjusts herself on her bed, and I know it's to draw my attention, which I don't give her, my eyes staying glued to my lap. "Sure, he could have just left you alone, let you be and let it lie. But he wanted you so badly he risked it all for you. He stopped sleeping around for you. I think you need to recognize that while he didn't handle this morning the way he should have, he risked a hell of a lot and was only trying to keep you from losing it all."

I had thought of all of that, in the early phase of my drive. But it doesn't change anything. Now I do meet her gaze. "He still left, though. He's been completely MIA. How do you do that? Laur, I gave him all of me, my whole self, everything. He turned his back and left, and I haven't heard a word from him since." Every time I think about his radio silence, my heart cracks a little more.

"I'm not saying he's handled any of this the right way. But I think you need to give him a little more grace. I think you'll find he does the right thing in the end."

"And if he doesn't? I don't know, Laur, maybe I'm just crazy. Despite all the hurt and hot and cold, he makes me feel things I've never felt before."

"Yeah, I bet he does." There's a lightness in tone that she's trying to make a joke, but none of it is amusing right now.

"Not like that. I mean, that too. It was…incredible. But he makes me feel loved; he really listens and respects me. Josh never once pushed for sex or anything. He had me come over just to sleep next to him. He makes me feel wanted, desired."

"Well, if he doesn't fix this, then I'll beat the crap out of him. And of course, find a better-looking guy." Lauren takes a long sip of her coffee like she's solved everything.

"Trust me, there is no such guy on campus." My eyes widen and my fingers continue to pull apart my cup. I should stop before I break it and spill coffee all over her bedspread.

"Now you're just making me jealous."

Suddenly, there's a knock at the door. Lauren jumps up and opens it, a handsome blond on the other side of the door. "Oh, hey, my friend showed up, she needs me right now. I'll call you later?"

"Okay, no problem." He leans down to kiss her temple, whispering something in her ear before backing away, and suddenly, I'm smacked with a memory.

The night before, Josh had brushed hair out of my face, kissed my cheek and temple lightly, then whispered in my ear, "*I love you, Lexie.*" I gasp, hand flying to my mouth. I look wide-eyed at Lauren as she climbs back up on the bed.

"What? What happened?"

"He told me he loves me." It's just above a whisper, forced, as I stare at the bed, my mind trying to pull the memory back into focus.

"HE, WHAT?!"

My eyes narrow as I work hard to solidify the memory. "I think he thought I was sleeping, I basically was, which is why I think I didn't remember until now. Your whatever over there with whoever that guy is, which I want to hear about by the way, reminded me. But if he loves me, why would he leave? Why wouldn't he say something? Why wouldn't he leave a note, text me back. Something." I'm minutes from falling apart again. It's flooding through my body, the sting of rejection everywhere. Part of me is wondering if I imagined his words.

"Probably because he loves you."

"Right, 'cause that makes all the sense in the world."

"Lex, think about it. Think about what could, or probably would, really happen if you two were caught together. Really think about it."

I do. And it isn't good. The rules are set and they're strict. It's happened before, people getting fired or kicked out for having romantic relations with staff. Hooking up here and there happens all the time. It's not that it's allowed, it just isn't caught as easily. Relationships are harder to hide. You spend more time together, you're in each other's rooms more frequently, and of course when you're actually with somebody, the signs of affection in public are much harder to hold back. He's already risked a lot with nights of kisses in hallways and concerts and parties. If somebody had seen us, that would have been it, for both of us. If we were to start a relationship, a real relationship, there's no way we wouldn't be found out. We can't stay away from each other as it is.

"I have to go back," I whisper.

"Yeah."

"I don't even know how to find him. He won't answer my texts, and he didn't answer the door." My mind is already racing at how to get to the bottom of this.

"Maybe he'll be waiting for you. Or maybe he'll get back to you."

"Laur, it's been six hours since I left. Still crickets."

"Stand outside his window blasting music?" She bursts into hysterics and I'm thankful to laugh a little, to feel a little lighter.

One of Lauren's ex-boyfriends had been in a band and played music, loudly, on the front lawn. Of the wrong house. He wasn't the smartest guy she'd dated. He was trying to reenact the scene from "Say Anything", but did it horribly wrong.

"I mean, we did go to that concert together, but I'm not sure drawing the whole dorm's attention to us is the best choice. Not yet at least."

"Maybe you just have to wait him out. First you have to decide if it's worth it. Is anything different?" Lauren rests her head against the wall, and I feel her gaze burning a hole through the top of my head. She's my best friend and I've barely been able to look at her through this confession.

But I glance up now. I need her to see my surety. "No. My feelings for him haven't changed at all through this whole thing. I've known that he's who I want since day one. That hasn't changed, that's not going to change. I don't know how we'll navigate the rules or the risks. But it's worth it to try to figure it out. Being with him is worth every risk."

"Then go get your man!"

I smile, pulling Lauren in for a hug. "I love you. Thank you for always being here for me. I do want to hear all about that guy, though."

"Call me from the car, it'll make the drive go by faster. It's a good story too." Her eyebrows spike up and down a few times.

"Oh, boy. I don't need all the sexy details."

"You most certainly do. You just shared yours, and have I said yet, so proud." Lauren clutches her chest and then pretends to swipe away a tear.

Shaking my head at her, I slide off the bed. "Alright, I'll call you when I get to the highway."

"Bluetooth, right?"

"Yes, Mom." I roll my eyes. Lauren may be a little looser with the boys and partying than I am, but she's always safe otherwise. And car safety is big one for her.

"Love you, Lex."

"You too, Laur."

I give her another giant hug. Pulling away, she runs her finger over my tattoo. Sometimes all it takes is a best friend to put things right.

CHAPTER 25

It turns out I don't have to wait long for Josh. He's standing outside the dorm when I get back. I notice him as soon as I'm out of the parking lot. My pulse skyrockets, but my feet stop completely.

Taking a deep breath, I try to settle myself, shaking away the nerves. His hands reside in his pockets and he's looking down at the ground. He hasn't noticed me yet, and I take a moment to admire him. His hair is a little shaggier than when we first met, hanging in his eyes a bit. That hint of lightness is showing in the setting sun. I know if he were to look up, I'd be met with those beautiful dark eyes. Despite the light coat he has on, you can tell he's toned, thanks to his broad shoulders.

Once I'm within a few feet, he looks up, almost as if he senses me, a smile flashing across his face. As much as I want to smile, to run to him, I force myself to stay strong, biting the inside of my cheek to keep my lips from pulling up.

"Hi." His voice is low, a breathy whisper.

"Why are you out here?" It comes out as sharp as I wanted it to.

"I was hoping to see you. Brit said your keys were gone, and I checked the lot and saw your car was gone too."

"How long have you been out here?"

"I've gone back and forth between inside and out here for a few hours." A few hours. I force myself to keep it cool, not letting him see that makes me want to melt into him.

"Oh."

"Lexie, I'm sorry."

I meet his eyes. In them, I see his sincerity, but I'm not sure what he's sorry for. "Okay."

"Will you talk to me? You're not saying anything." There's desperation coating his words.

"What do you want me to say?"

He takes a step toward me, and I take one back. "Where did you go? Where were you? You just…left."

Shock knocks me back another step and steals my breath. *I* left? "Yeah, I did. After I woke up to you just *gone*, I *left*. I lost my boyfriend and then my virginity to a guy who then disappeared, all in one day. I needed my best friend. I needed to *see* her. So, yes, I left. But not before you did." I hope the rage in my glare matches the one in my tone.

I wait for a response, but nothing comes. No apology, no acknowledgement that it was wrong or any answer as to where he went or what he did. Nothing.

Pivoting on my heel, I start to slowly walk away. As much as I left Lauren's dorm wanting to be with him, at this moment, I'm ready to walk away from him for today, maybe forever. But a little voice inside me wills him to say *something* to make me stay.

"I quit my job today." That's it. Stopping dead in my tracks, I slowly spin around on my toes to face him, eyes wide. "I just walked right into Holly's office, and I quit."

"Why would you do that?" I whisper.

"So I could do this." Josh takes two big strides, and his lips are on mine in an instant, with a gentle forcefulness. His hands cup my face, fingers entangling in my hair. It's the most perfect kiss we've shared.

"You've already done that," I say against his lips as he separates from me but doesn't pull away.

"Yes, but now, I can do it in front of everybody. And I don't have to stop." His lips close on mine again, parting them with his tongue as it slides over mine. Breathless, I back away, out of his arms, though it's hard.

"Explain."

Looping an arm around my waist, he guides me over to one of the benches by the entrance of the dorm and pulls me into his lap. "When I woke up this morning, I was so incredibly happy. I didn't want to let that go, to let you go. I never should have left. Not without leaving a note or something. I'm sorry."

I swallow around the lump rising in my throat, the butterflies fluttering in my chest at his heartfelt tone and apology.

"Freaking out about getting caught got the best of me. It hadn't even occurred to me to ask last night where Brittney was. I was worried about how I was going to get out before other people saw me leaving. But the main thought in my mind was how I could have the same blissful feeling I woke up with this morning, every day, without all the worry that follows."

His grip tightens around me, and he slides me even farther onto his lap.

"So I went to see my buddy, Troy, who lives off campus. He's got a two-bedroom apartment, and he's basically never there because he's almost always over at his girlfriends, for whatever reason. His parents bought it straight out for him. I told him everything—he's a good guy, he'll stay quiet. He offered me the other room. It's a pretty nice place and would basically be mine since he's rarely there."

A slight tremble sets into my extremities and works into my core. His own place? What does that mean for us? It eliminates the need to sneak around, there are no rules to break if he lives on his own, but will I really see him that much if he's not down the hall?

Josh gives an audible swallow, and while it makes my mouth dry out, I run my fingers along his shoulders to encourage him to continue. "I forgot my phone in my hurry. As soon as I got back, I went into Holly's office. I told her that I've developed feelings for a resident. That I know the rules and I'm not going to go against them and that I quit. She asked if you're worth it. I assured her you absolutely are." My heart swells, and I fight back tears.

Taking my chin in his hand, he tilts my face up to meet his. There's sadness and pleading in his expression. "Lexie, I am *so* sorry. I shouldn't have disappeared like that. My intention was to go down to my room and send a quick message to Troy, but he said he was around right then and would be heading out for the weekend within the hour so if I wanted to swing by, it was the time. I had such a one-track mind that I left my phone by accident. I should have come back in and told you."

My body shifts with his deep breath, and his heart hammers against my palm where it sits on his chest. "Please don't hate me. Please don't hate me for leaving you after everything. Last night meant so much to me that I couldn't leave things the way they were. I had to *do* something. And I made a big mistake along the way by just disappearing on you. Making you think I didn't care; that it was something I regretted or didn't want to do. It was anything but that."

My lips press into a tight line, and I take a second to think about what he's actually saying. "So, you packed up your room? When do you move?" I try to sound steady, but I'm still unsure. I want nothing more than for him to take me into his arms and carry me upstairs. But I also don't know what any of this means. Can we be together?

A smile spreads across his face. "That's another bright light. Holly can't be short an RA on that floor. She needs somebody and doesn't have any backups. With so few weeks left in the semester, she won't be able to find one right now. She'll be sure to have somebody for spring, but until then, I can stay."

My head falls and my eyes fill. It will be months before we can be a couple.

Josh puts his finger under my chin, tilting it up to look at him, tears streaming down my face. He gently swipes them away with his thumb, smile in place on his face.

"Why are you smiling? If you're still an RA, we still can't be together."

"That's the best part, Lex. Holly said she normally wouldn't do it, but that she's in such a bind and she can't afford to lose me. She won't stop us or fire me or kick you out. We just need to keep it quiet. We don't necessarily need to sneak around like we have been, but we can't flaunt it either."

"What about all the other RAs, though? Won't they be mad?" I sniffle the tears back, not necessarily trusting or believing in this course of action.

Josh shrugs. "I asked the same question, and she said she'd come up with something if somebody came to her complaining. She'd rather worry about dealing with people one-on-one if the situation arises than tell everybody outright, hoping we aren't found out, and that if we are, others won't be bothered. Or want the same allowances made." He chuckles softly. "I've made some good friends here. They'll stay quiet. They have so far." Looking down at where my legs sit draped over his, he shakes his head. I know it isn't something he's proud of. He's said as much.

All I can do is nod. I'm confused in so many ways. I want to be with Josh. I know that. I've known that from the beginning, but he pushed me away so many times, left without a word after I gave him something so important. Why should I believe this will be different? Sure, he said it's fine to be together, but what if somebody says something and he gets spooked? How do I know he isn't going to change his mind and decide he doesn't want me? What if he decides he likes the no-strings-attached random sex?

"Lexie, please." His voice is pleading, pain breaking through. "I'm sorry. I'll do anything, *anything*. I did all of this for you. For us. So that there can *be* an us. For real, this time. So, I can hold your hand in public, and brush your hair behind your ear." He tucks some curls behind my ear as he says this, fingers lingering on my neck. "So I can kiss you and feel you and not have there be any sense of wrongness to it; no fear of getting caught." Delicately, he runs his fingers down my spine to land on my lower back while his other hand tangles in my hair at the base of my neck, pulling me close for a kiss.

I hesitate, but his words sink in. He may have disappeared, but he quit his job, a job he needs to be able to afford living at school, for me. To be with me. And I know more than anything that all I want is to be with him. So, I stop hesitating and lean into his kiss, hand reaching up to rest against his neck. Recognizing my reaction, he pulls me closer, parting my mouth with his, a tiny moan escaping me. Hardening beneath me, his erection presses into my thigh.

"Let's go up to my room. Let me show you how much you mean to me. Let's stay in there all day," he whispers in my ear.

Trying to fight the way my body feels and reacts to him is futile. I had longed for him for so many weeks, tiny taste after tiny taste. Last night had been incredible, finally a culmination of everything. Sinking my teeth into my lip, I nod.

A giant smile spreads across Josh's face as he takes my hand and helps me off his lap. Wrapping his arms around my waist, he picks me up and spins me around, kissing me as he puts me down, resting his forehead against mine for a moment. Looping his arm around my shoulders, we walk into the dorm, no more fear of being caught.

CHAPTER 26

We make it as far as the stairwell before his lips are on mine, hands cupping my face. He boxes me in against the wall as his tongue slips into my mouth. A tiny moan escapes from my chest as he presses his pelvis to mine.

Running a palm down my body, he slides it over to cover my breast. Arching toward him, I try to bring our bodies flush with each other. He's touched every part of me, and it's never been enough. Last night, the pinnacle of every other time, wasn't enough.

When his fingers graze my waist, they twist into the hem of my shirt as a low growl rises in Josh.

"We need to get upstairs. Now." His voice is deep and gravelly.

Fire ignites throughout my body. "Have you ever had sex in the stairwell?"

"Nope. Never wanted to. Until that night I walked you upstairs after we had coffee. God, I wanted you so bad then." Josh lets his gaze slowly slide down my body, resting an extra second at my breasts and hips. As he raises his eyes to lock on mine, I find them swirling with desire, and it sends a pulsation straight through my body, settling between my legs.

"We're going to go upstairs and you're going to go to your room to get some books before you come down to my room. That will make it look like we're studying. Which we will be, in a way." He twirls one of my curls around his finger as he speaks.

"How so?"

"I plan to study every inch of your body, and how many ways I can make you moan." His breath against my ear sends a shiver racing down my spine, but it wars with the heat burning hotter throughout my body.

With one more deep kiss, Josh backs away and gestures towards the stairs. I start walking up and he immediately follows, staying a few steps below so we're the same height. His fingers easily slip into my back pocket. Every single inch of my skin is tingling with his nearness and the need to have his hands on me.

Once we get to my room, he gives my waist a pinch. "Don't be too long, Lexie." His lips against my temple and the deep rumble of his voice make me rub my thighs together to try to ease some of the pressure residing there.

Before I can ditch the plan and follow him, I walk into my room. The magnetic pull to him strengthens with every step he takes away from me.

Falling against the door as it shuts, a smile pulls so wide across my face my cheeks hurt.

"Where have you been?!"

I jump, and my hand flies to my chest as my heart threatens to beat out of it. I'd forgotten all about Brittney in the excitement.

"Shit, Brit, you scared me."

"I scared *you*? Lexie, I came back this morning, and you were gone! And then you didn't answer me. I've been worried sick about you."

"Some things happened."

Her eyebrow cocks up, almost reaching her hairline as she

crosses her arms against her chest. "What things?"

Taking a deep breath, I drag my feet into the room. I don't want to do anything but be with Josh right now, and at the same time, I know I'm not going anywhere until I talk to Brittney.

Hopping up on my bed, I dive into the conversation. I start with finding Liam in bed with Cara, to which her response is threatening to chop his balls off. When I get to the part about Josh and everything that happened, I'm as light on the details as I can be. My face burns and I play with the hem of my pant leg instead of looking at her.

When I finally finish, she lets out what sounds like a long-held breath. "I mean, I knew *something* was going on with you and Josh. Aside from the party and whatnot. I had a feeling, some sort of something that lingered. But how long? Was it just the party and last night? Have you guys been dating this whole time? I thought after your conversation with Lauren you were going to stop things with Josh."

"Um, that's a little more complicated. We're not dating, never have been. Honestly, I don't know what's going on right now. But things have been going on since we did that project together. And trust me, I tried after that, I really did. It wasn't possible." I glance up just in time to catch her jaw dropping.

"Wow. Uh, that's a while. You've been having sex that long? And you didn't tell me?" Her brow scrunches and it drives a cold icicle through my chest.

"No! No, Brit. It just happened last night. There were those other things we did. None of it was planned, it wasn't expected at all. Every single time he'd say it was a mistake, that we couldn't be together. I don't know, I was scared to tell you." I avert my gaze from her again as I deliver the last part. It's shitty of me and I know it.

"Did you feel like you couldn't trust me?" The pain in her voice collapses my chest and pulls all the air from my lungs.

"No, Brit. It's just, it was so sensitive, such a thin line. And

I thought you knew. At the party, you said to be careful, that you wouldn't tell anybody and you heard my conversation with Lauren that weekend. I guess I didn't think I needed to say more or bring it up again. Because honestly, it should have stopped. It shouldn't have been happening. But neither one of us could hold back."

"I mean, I almost don't know what to say. I'm happy for you, if you're happy. Are you?"

"Honestly? I don't know yet. He quit being an RA, Brit. For me. So we could be together. He waited for me to come back so we could talk. I want to believe him. I want to be with him *so* badly. It's all I've wanted for months. It's why I couldn't tear myself from him, even if it hurt each and every time. To be together? Really and truly be together? It'd be like a dream come true."

"Well, don't let me stop you. Go find out!" She juts her chin toward the door with a smile creeping across her face.

Hopping down from the bed, I pick up whatever random books are strewn across my desk and throw open the door. I walk hurriedly but try to appear discreet. Bouncing on the balls of my feet, I knock on his door. When it doesn't immediately open, my stomach drops to the floor.

But then a hand wraps my waist, and an arm moves around me on the other side, grabbing the door handle. When his chest brushes my back, my head tilts against it. No words are spoken as he opens the door and ushers me inside with a palm against the small of my back.

"Sorry to worry you." Josh closes and locks the door, causing a tremble to set in my bones. "I was supposed to work tonight, but I went and asked somebody to switch with me. I have absolutely every intention of spending the entire day and night with you. If that's okay with you, of course."

"It is." My voice is quiet and weak. I can barely think about anything, except Josh's hands and body on mine for hours and hours on end. It makes it difficult to create words.

"Good." Stepping toward me, he cups my jaw with one hand while the other closes around my hip and pulls me against him. His lips meld to mine and my books fall to the floor as I wrap my arms around his neck and close the gap between our bodies. Walking us toward the bed, he keeps me flush with him, until my back hits the bed frame.

A low growl rolls off his tongue and vibrates down into my chest, rattling through my body. Lifting me with ease, he pushes himself up and hovers over me, not letting his chest touch mine. The thought of his taut muscles, covered by his shirt has me tearing at his clothes, hands flying rapidly over his body, unable to get a hold on anything.

Adjusting his position, Josh straddles my waist, leaning up on his knees as he pulls his shirt off in one smooth motion. My fingers immediately find their way to his perfectly toned chest as my breath halts in my chest, my heart races, and my panties wet. *God, he's amazing.*

One hand rests against my cheek as his thumb brushes along my temple. Leaning down, he gives me a soft kiss. "You're so beautiful, Lexie." His lips lock on mine again as he stretches his legs out, resting his weight against me, his erection pushing into my stomach.

Looping my legs around his waist, I hook my ankles and grind myself against him. I'm seeking friction, pressure, anything. The need to feel him is overwhelming.

With a groan, he pulls his mouth from mine and looks deep into my eyes. "Lexie, I know last night we…I need you to know I don't have any expectations. I certainly have hopes and wants and wishes. But I don't expect anything from you. We can just kiss. We don't even have to do that, we can just be together."

Wrapping my hand around the back of his neck, I pull his face to mine, kissing him fiercely before releasing him. "I came up here with every intention of having sex until I can hardly walk, Josh."

He trembles beneath my touch. "God, Lexie, I don't think you know what you're saying."

"I absolutely do. Josh, you're not the only one who has been wanting and waiting for months. Last night was amazing for me, and while it ended rough with how I woke up, I want a million more. I'd really like to start right now."

Something flickers through his eyes, and I swear it's a flame. I don't have time to think about it as his mouth crashes to mine and he pins my hands above my head.

"Are you sure, Lexie? I don't know there will be any going back. I won't be able to keep myself from you again. So if any part of you doesn't want this, you need to tell me now." His voice is gruff as his gaze rakes over me, his free hand gliding down my side.

When he reaches my hip and stops, I lift my pelvis in response, pressing into him. "Are you going to leave me again?"

"No." The conviction in his voice makes me believe him.

"Then, I'm sure. Absolutely, one hundred percent sure."

He softens but pulls away, sitting on his heels and raking a hand through his hair, making it stand on end. "But, Lex, you were a vir—"

"Yeah, I was a virgin." I push myself up on my elbows to have what appears to be a conversation instead of sex. "In every single sense of the word, aside from kissing. Until last night, until you. I don't regret one second, Josh. The situation was really shitty. I was a bad person, and I made some bad choices. But the ones involving you aren't the bad ones. The ones where I didn't break things off with Liam were. And yeah, he was equally as shitty, possibly more so because he'd been sleeping with Cara and we just fooled around. But that feels like splitting hairs."

As I talk, Josh puts his hands on me again, resting gently on my thighs. He's the only man I've ever allowed to touch me. It just feels so natural. I've never shied from his touch. If anything, I've always craved it, even before I really knew him. Every tiny touch, every little graze of his body against mine, has always ignited the embers residing within me, and each flame burned hotter than before. There could never be enough.

"So are you going to leave again? Are we going to screw around and then you'll kick me out? Let me spend the night and ask me to leave? Will I wake up alone again and you'll come back once you're sure I've left?"

The look of pain in his eyes makes my heart stutter and my arms weaken as they struggle to support me. I don't want to hurt him. I don't want to point out his past mistakes that I know make him feel awful. But I stay strong, partially for myself, to be sure. I know what he said outside. I know what he said a few minutes ago, maybe I consider it a warranty to have him tell me again.

Dropping his head, he shakes it as his hands grip my thighs. "No. No, Lexie, I won't be the one doing that again. I won't leave. I won't ask you to leave. I'm here, I'm in. But I won't force you to stay. I won't ask you to do this if you don't want to. The secrecy is still there in some ways. If it's too much, I understand."

He swallows hard and I'm about to speak when he starts again. "Not that long ago, I told you that if I'm ever lucky enough to truly have you, I'd never let you go. I meant it, still do. So do I have you, Lexie?" Raising his face, he looks at me intently.

"Yeah, Josh, you do. You always have. From that first moment, I've been yours."

Without hesitating, his hand cups my face as his mouth crashes to mine, leaning me back toward the bed. A trail of fire follows the path of his hand as it glides up the inside of my shirt, cupping my breast and tweaking my nipple through my bra.

At the first sound I make, Josh pulls away and tears the

clothes from our bodies, adding them to his shirt in a pile on the floor. I let him undress me, his hurried hands releasing tingles everywhere he touches.

Leaning over me, his gaze bores into mine, then he lays a gentle kiss on my temple and kisses his way along my jaw, down my neck, to my chest. Running his lips along my nipple, it pebbles against his warm breath. Pulling it into his mouth, his tongue starts flicking at the hardened peak as a hand settles between my legs, which part on instinct.

He moans against my chest as he slips along my wetness. Sliding two fingers inside me, hooking them immediately, I arch toward him, my arms wrapping around his head as I tangle into his hair, pulling him closer.

Mewling, I writhe beneath him. "Josh."

The only response I get is a soft hum and frenzied movements. Within minutes, I'm grabbing at his arms, nails digging in, and I scream his name.

Moving from my chest, he nuzzles into my neck, trailing his lips across my tingling skin.

"Fuck, Josh, I'm sorry, I didn't mean to be loud. I forgot, I'm—" He quiets me with a kiss.

"You don't have to apologize, Lexie. We're okay," he murmurs into my hair, lips still trailing my skin, pulling my earlobe between his teeth.

I had momentarily forgotten we don't have to completely sneak around anymore. The notion is freeing, in a way. "Oh, right." As he settles between my legs, I forget about *everything* but feeling him again.

My muscles tense slightly as Josh eases into me. "Relax for me, Lex. Or we can stop."

Shaking my head, I take a deep breath. But the pinch of pain I was anticipating doesn't come as he glides in farther.

"You okay?" He's all the way inside me now, and my only response is to nod feverishly.

Giving a few slow pumps, he gauges my reaction, which is

a slight head tilt and fluttering eyelids. Kissing down my neck and across my collarbone, he starts moving faster and my hands grip his shoulders.

It's even better than last night. Wow, was that really only yesterday? It feels like an eternity. Everything with Josh has always been amazing. I have nothing to compare it to, but I don't have any desire to seek out alternatives, to have my share of 'fun' in college.

As he starts thrusting faster, I squeak and whine with each one. My head tips back and my fingers knead into his solid muscles.

Josh's lips press against my neck with firm pressure and glide to my shoulder and back again. "Fuck, Lexie."

He doesn't need to say more; my sentiments are extremely similar. The familiar sensation starts to build in my lower belly.

Before I can catch up, I'm crying out as my nails drag down his back. Josh latches his mouth to my throat as my chin tips up, his lips resting right over the spot my moan is vibrating against my skin.

He slows his momentum as I give a few last spasms and settle below him, my whole body tingling. I'm barely able to register his lips running over my neck.

"Lexie? You with me, baby?"

I snap my eyes to his as the words register. "Yeah, yeah, I am."

Tilting down, he melds his mouth to mine as he starts moving faster. The pressure is starting to build again as I make small sounds when Josh presses his forehead to mine and his breath catches in his throat with a low groan.

Stilling above me, our breath mingles in sharp bursts.

"Are you okay?" The gentleness in his voice makes me grip him tighter, wanting him closer even though he's practically crushing me. When he starts brushing the tip of his nose along mine, I nearly break.

"Yeah. I'm really good."

Leaving a trail of kisses from my lips to my ear, he rolls to his back and pulls me against him. He draws circles on my hip as I twirl a finger along his chest.

"You really gave up your job for me?" I break the silence we've been blanketed in for the past few minutes.

"I really did. And I should have done it sooner. All the hurt I caused, all the pain. I'm sorry. I can never apologize enough, or truly make it up to you. I know that."

Sighing heavily, he puts a finger under my chin, tilting it up to meet his gaze. "Lexie, I'm in love with you. Like, really, fully in love with you. I think I have been since I came to your room that day and heard you listening to that Allister song."

My heart threatens to fly right out of my chest. "I love you too, Josh."

His muscles loosen beneath me as a harsh breath escapes him. I immediately wonder if he was nervous about my feelings. After all this time, how could he not know? I never pushed him away, I never kicked him out. Time after time of being the one left behind, I came back. It's always been Josh.

"Why were you so mean to me at first?"

"I had to be." Hooking a strand of hair behind my ear, his fingers graze my skin, leaving a trail of tingles. "I didn't want to be, but I thought it would be easier, if you'd turn away, and you wouldn't talk to me anymore."

A distant look settles in his eyes as he glances just beyond my shoulder. "Professor Carp setting us up for the project together…at the time I thought it was the worst thing that could happen, working so closely with you. In the end, it turned out to be the best. It was hard, it was shitty, but that time with you, it was amazing. Every single moment with you has been amazing. Even when I thought I'd finally convinced you to stop being interested, even when you'd ask me why I care, which shattered me every time. Just being close to you was all I wanted. It's all I'll ever want, Lexie."

Snuggling into him, I stretch my arm across his chest. "I probably should have turned away, more than once. But I couldn't. I just couldn't. And now I'm really glad I didn't. I'd be lying if I said I didn't break a little every time you shut me out, but when you let me back in? It was like lighting the darkness."

He squeezes me against him so tightly my breath puffs out. "This isn't just a temporary thing for me, Lex. This isn't…it's not until one of us gets bored. For one, that's not going to happen for me. I've been infatuated with you, and that's never happened to me before. That alone tells me how different you are."

My heart thumps erratically in my chest, igniting a burn that scorches through my body and settles behind my eyes.

Running his fingers along my arm, he kisses the top of my head. "I don't take relationships lightly. So, if we start this, I'm fully in it, fully committed. And because of everything you just experienced, that means we're boyfriend and girlfriend with complete exclusivity. And I *really* fucking hate that I even have to say that." His teeth grit on the last part.

A tear breaks free and drips straight down onto his chest. Josh completely stills beneath me, pushing my shoulders back to look at me.

"Are you crying?" His dark irises and voice are both laced with concern as his fingers tighten into my skin.

"I'm okay," I sniffle. "There was a lot of back and forth for a while, and it just seems a little surreal right now. And I never really thought anybody would want me like that. Nobody has. It's hard to be interested in somebody who's too nervous to talk to them."

"Well, that's their loss. Big time. You're amazing, Lex. And you've never had a problem talking to me. So I'm not sure what you're referring to exactly, but I can't say I'm complaining or upset about it. Because otherwise, I wouldn't have you now. You're not someone that's easy to let go of."

Shaking my head, I turn my eyes up, chasing the tears away. "How are we going to do this, Josh? You graduate in a few months. Then what?" My body tenses and trembles with thoughts of the future, of being without him. He's right, now that we've gotten to this point, there's no going back. My heart wouldn't be able to handle that. It would surely break in two and he'd take half of it with him.

"I'm going to grad school here. Already accepted and confirmed. The program is a minimum of a year and a half. And then, I don't know. I kind of like this area. I could see myself living here. At least temporarily, while you finish school. If that's something you want too."

All I can do is nod, not trusting my voice to remain steady.

Shifting beneath me, Josh pulls me to him so my cheek rests against his chest, my head under his chin. The steady motion of his fingers trailing from my hair down my spine soothes me, and my eyes start to dry. "I have student teaching next semester. And I've heard it can be intense. I'll be off campus, it won't be as easy for us to just run into each other, with no classes together. But I'm going to want you around all the time. I want to come home and see you. I want to spend every weekend together. I want you in my bed as many nights as you're willing to give me. I want this, Lex, I want you. All of you."

"You have me."

I raise as Josh takes a deep breath below me. "I don't want to talk about any of this sad stuff anymore. I don't want to worry about what's so far away. Let's talk about other things."

"Like what?"

"Anything you want."

I twirl my finger along his pectoral for a minute, thinking hard. "This might sound a little weird since we're laying naked in bed together, but I feel like I don't know a lot about you. I mean, I know you have an older brother and older sister, your parents are divorced, you're from New York. And have a solid group of home friends, but I don't know, I guess there's deeper stuff."

"I'll tell you anything you want to know, Lex. I'm an open book. I know I wasn't at first, but now there's nothing stopping me. I want to know everything about you too."

Hm. "What's your favorite color?" Let's start easy.

"Blue. What's yours?" Placing his elbow on his stomach, he props my arm the same way, tracing his fingers along mine.

"Light purple. Like a lilac shade. It's also my favorite flower."

"Well, that's not fair," he grumbles and his fingers still, linking with mine.

"What's not?"

"I can't go to a florist and buy you a bouquet of lilacs."

My heart swells and tears spring to my eyes again as I push up on his chest and look down at him. "You'd buy me flowers?"

Josh's brow pulls together as his hand finds my hip. "Of course, I will Lex. But not lilacs." His voice is low and soft.

"Lilies. I also like lilies."

"Any specific kind?"

"All of them. I haven't met a lily I don't like."

"Okay. Good to know."

"Tell me your best friend's name." I choose to move on to the next question, another easy one, as I snuggle back into his chest and he starts tracing random shapes on my lower back.

"Mason."

"How long have you two been friends?"

"Since diapers, really. With two other friends, Dan and Colin. We still get together when we're home, pretty much every time. We stuck together through everything. We got into trouble sometimes, four guys loose on the town. But they're like my brothers. Sometimes more so than my real brother." His words rumble through my ear, mingling with the thumping of his heart, and it's already become my favorite sound.

I nod my head against his chest, knowing the feeling all too well.

"That's what it's like with you and Lauren, isn't it?" He speaks before I can, stealing the thoughts straight from the tip of my tongue and heating my core at his memory of my best friend's name.

"Yeah. I was actually going to say that." There's so much, so many stories, so much to learn.

"We have time, Lex. This isn't over in an hour, or tonight, or tomorrow. We'll learn all the things. But, for me at least, I feel connected to you. I feel like my body knows yours, my heart. There may be stories, facts, that I don't know yet, but I plan to learn them all."

There's an itchy feeling in my brain that slowly crawls through my body, which makes me squirm.

"What's wrong?"

"I, uh, hm." I'm not exactly sure where to start, how to say what I want to say. Huffing out a puff that flutters some hair from my face, I take a deep breath and go for it. "I want you to teach me how to touch you. In ways that you like, that you will like, that you know you like. I want to make you feel good like you make me feel good." It all comes out in one rushed breath, and now, I want to shrink in on myself until I'm nothing more than a speck of dust.

My head rises and falls with Josh's chest. "I know this may be awkward for you, and I hope to alleviate that. But there's a lot of...exploring left, for both of us. We need to get to know each other physically, what we like and don't like. It's not the same with every partner. It's not one size fits all. It's all about trying things and communicating with each other. Want to try something? Tell me. If I try something and you don't like it, tell me. And the other way too because if you do like it, I'll do it more often. Does that make sense?"

I try to swallow but my throat and mouth are arid.

"I'm not trying to talk down to you or anything. It's just, it can be tricky at first. It's all new and something different to navigate. Things I've done before, but you haven't. I want to be mindful of that, Lex. I don't ever want you to do anything you're not ready for. There's a lot between kissing and sex that we kind of skipped right over. And that's okay, we can get to it, or not. But don't feel like we have to rush to do everything. Or even anything. It's what you want, Lex. I'm letting you take the reins here to make sure you're comfortable."

Josh has always used a different tone with me when we're together. But this one is different from any other I've heard. It's direct, sincere, and full of compassion.

"So does that mean I can touch you now?"

I shake as he laughs beneath me. "Of course, Lex. And trust me, I want you to. The only reason I couldn't let you before is because I knew I wouldn't be able to stop myself from going further. I wouldn't be able to stay away from you. I was doing a pretty terrible job of it, anyway."

"Well then, maybe I shouldn't have listened to you that night." I'm ready to try now, but I'm not sure if I should ask first. I grit my teeth to keep the heat from rising farther than my chest. If I let this embarrass me or show discomfort, Josh will pull back. Not away, not to disappear, but he'll pull on the breaks. I know him well enough to know that. My antsy fingers wiggle against his chest.

"You don't have to ask, Lex." Well, he certainly seems to know *me* well, to know what's going on in my head. Though it's probably because of our conversation.

Sliding my hand down his chest, his rippled abs, I dip it under the sheet and find he's hard again. I hesitate for a second, not sure what to do, then decide *fuck it*, I'm going for it.

Pushing the sheet lower, I turn my gaze to his lower half. Things moved so fast between us, I've never taken the time to really *look* at him before. Pinching my bottom lip between my teeth, I wrap fingers around the base of his cock firmly, but not tight.

Lauren had been all too kind to explain to me the basic mechanics of all things sexual, despite my desperate pleading for her to stop. But talk and practice are very different.

I give a few timid glides of my hand up and down his shaft to get a feel for it. I'm not sure what I was expecting, but it's certainly not as scary as I thought it'd be. Continuing my motions, I increase my speed a little, tilting my head to look at Josh.

His eyes are closed, his brow pinched together. Squeezing my hand, Josh digs his fingers into my hip and a groan leaves his parted lips.

It sends desire swirling through my body and settling between my thighs. I'd love to feel him inside me again, but this is my focus right now. It's enthralling.

I'm about to turn my gaze back down to watch what I'm doing when Josh's other hand moves. It glides through his hair, tugging at the roots.

"Fuck, Lex. This feels so fucking good. Are you sure you've never done this before?" His words are breathy and end with another groan.

His question doesn't really require an answer. I kiss down his chest as I turn back toward my hand wrapped around him, slipping up and down his length.

"Mm, baby, I need you to stop."

"Why?"

"Because I want to fuck you again."

Well, okay, then.

Before I've even fully released him, he has me flat on my back and is hovering over me. His fingers glide through my wetness and he rests his head against my chest as his breath catches in his throat.

"Holy fuck, Lexie. You're *so* wet."

I can't respond as he pushes into me, and the breath is stolen from my lungs. Leaning down, he closes his mouth over mine as he starts to move inside me.

"Josh." His name flies from my mouth as I inhale, like I'm trying to draw him into my lungs, into my soul.

Resting his forehead against mine, Josh increases his momentum, and I tangle my fingers in the wisps at the nape of his neck.

I'm mewling with every thrust, and everything about it is exquisite. The feeling of Josh inside me, his body all around me. It's all intoxicating and heightens my experience, my senses.

His breath on me sends goose bumps rippling across my skin and his low grunts make me clench around him. When his lips cover mine, it pushes me over the edge and my hands tighten, tugging at his hair, nails digging into his back as I squeeze around him, crying out his name, coming so hard my brain tingles.

With a few more thrusts, Josh's hand twists into the sheet by my head and he moans, his breath warm against my cheek. As he slows, he collapses against me.

His chest heaves against mine as feeling starts to return to my body and I can think again. Peppering kisses along my collarbone, Josh rolls to his side.

Sliding to him, he immediately wraps his arm around my shoulders, pulling me tight into his chest and leaving a lingering kiss on my forehead.

"I love you, Lexie."

"I love you too, Josh."

Snuggling into him, my eyes flutter shut. I'm wrapped in the warmth of Josh, the exhaustion of finally ending the back and forth, and pure ease of knowing we're together now.

As I start to fall asleep, all I can think about is how when I wake up this time, he will still be here, happy and with me.

CHAPTER 27

The rest of the weekend goes by in a blur of tangled limbs and bed sheets. We barely leave the room. Every so often, when hunger pangs overtake the ability to do much else, Josh will order food for delivery and get it from the entryway.

At one point on Sunday, there's a knock on the door that wakes us from a midday snooze. Within seconds, my phone buzzes.

Brit: *Thought you could use some refreshments. Have fun ;)*

Grumbling as he throws on a pair of pants, Josh opens the door as minimally as possible, using his body to block the opening for the briefest moment before he pulls in two waters, granola bars, and a pizza.

"At least she takes care of me."

Freezing in place, his eyes darken. "*I* will take care of you."

Sitting up, I pull the sheet against my chest. "Don't be jealous of Brit."

"You're mine now, it's my job to take care of you."

"She's doing something nice for *us*. Let her. It won't last. And it's just pizza."

Grumbling a little more, he puts the pizza on his desk and

gets some plates and napkins from the closet where he keeps food. His room is no bigger than mine, but it only has one bed and one desk, making the space seem larger. He also has twice the closet space.

"What?" Josh's feet glue to the spot when he turns around and sees that I've pulled his shirt over my head.

"I'm not eating pizza naked, Josh. I haven't eaten *anything* naked."

"Doesn't mean I have to like you being clothed."

Settling on my knees, I move to the edge of the bed as he stands in front of me. "Just think about how much fun you'll have undressing me." I loop my arms around his neck as one of his hands grips my waist. The other tucks some hair behind my ear, lightly caressing my cheek in the process.

Josh's eyes turn serious as he looks me over. "How sore are you?"

Sensing he's about to step back, I link my fingers behind his head to keep him close. Moving a few inches toward me, my breasts graze his chest. "A bit. But I meant it when I said I had the intention of not being able to walk."

"That doesn't mean that has to actually happen, Lex." Trailing his fingers down my spine, he tips the other hand under the hem of my shirt and closes it around my hip, thumb rubbing along the bone.

"But we're having fun, we're exploring, we're just enjoying being together."

Taking my hand in his, he brings my knuckles to his lips, gently kissing each one. "We have time, Lex. There's no rush. Things aren't over after this weekend."

"Thanksgiving is Thursday. I have to leave Wednesday."

"I know. And it's going to be hard to be away from you for four days and nights. Especially because I just got you."

Resting my head against his chest, I swallow back the lump rising in my throat and try to will away the sting behind my eyes.

Kissing the top of my head, he winds a hand into my hair, gently massaging my scalp. "We should eat, baby."

"Yeah."

Neither of us pulls away for another minute. Skimming his lips along my hairline, he gives my hip a squeeze and turns away, opening the pizza box and plopping slices on plates.

We've had the TV on for hours, just droning on in the background. It's been nice in the times when we're too tired to talk.

"Is one pizza enough? Should she have brought two?" I bump my shoulder into him as I tease. He's eaten large portions each time we've gotten food. When we got subs, he ate his whole sandwich and half of mine. He even ordered himself two breakfast sandwiches.

"I'm expending a lot of energy. And I'm not exactly a small guy."

"No, no, you certainly are not." Leaning into his side, I take a bite of my pizza. Josh is over six feet tall, broad shouldered, and has tight muscles everywhere. He completely surrounds me when he's over me, fully encases me when he snuggles me, and I always feel incredibly safe.

"I don't want to leave our bubble and go to class tomorrow." There's a wistfulness to my voice.

"I know, I don't either. Will you stay here tonight?"

"Yeah. If you want me to. I mean, I don't want to get in trouble or anything if I'm caught leaving your room in my pajamas." While Josh says Holly gives her seal of approval, it's still a rule set by the school, and the thought of breaking it makes my stomach twist and my skin itch. It doesn't make sense, especially because I've broken so many, including this one.

"I don't care. I don't. I said I'd try to keep things on the quieter side, but none of that matters to me anymore. You do, only you. If they want to kick me out before the end of the semester, let them. If other RAs or residents want to complain that we're in a relationship and not getting penalized, let them. It's a stupid, outdated rule anyway. Nothing would change in what I need to do except you'd be in my bed. Besides, you've been here all weekend."

"Can I get in trouble, though?"

"No. I made sure with Holly that if anything happens, if anybody complains, I'm the one who takes the fall, not you. She assured me she'd douse any fires that arose. I'll protect you, Lex."

He presses a kiss to my temple before hopping off the bed and getting more pizza.

I giggle as I take a small bite. Things have changed so much in just a few short days. I'm dating Josh, we've spent the better part of the weekend in bed, and he hasn't pushed me away once. Not to mention, I'm in love with him, though that's not really a new development.

We finish out our weekend by meeting Brittney for dinner, per my request. Josh keeps his arm over the back of my chair the whole time.

She keeps looking between us and smiling, but we're able to keep the conversation casual.

"That was just the cutest thing I've ever seen." Brittney doesn't even wait for our door to close before she's assaulting me with her breakdown of dinner.

"What are you talking about?"

"Are you kidding? He had his hand around your waist the walk down to and back up from the dining hall, his arm over the chair all through dinner, and the sweetest kiss on your head before he walked away. Not to mention the googoo eyes you two kept giving each other." Her hands land firmly on her hips as she swishes her blonde hair over her shoulder. I'm still struck by the similarity between my two best friends.

"We don't give each other googoo eyes." It comes out as a breathy laugh. We totally do.

"I'm just happy for you, Lexie. I know you were worried

about this, but he seems really head over heels for you. It's cute. And sweet."

"I'm glad you can see that. I was worried about your reaction. I know things started kind of messy and you didn't approve and were disappointed when you went to uh, study with him." Heat rushes my face at the thought of Brittney doing anything even remotely close to what Josh and I have been doing for days.

Brittney waves her hand at me as she moves to lean against her bed. "None of that matters, Lexie. All that matters to me is that you're happy. And you are. Right?"

"Yeah, Brit. I'm really happy. He's talking about the future so much. Grad school, which he's doing here by the way, living here after that." I'm rifling through my drawers for pajamas as I talk to her.

Glancing up at her, I find her hands clasped against her chest, over her heart, mist filling her eyes.

"Don't you dare start crying, Brit. Because then, I will, and we'll never stop."

"I promise I won't. It's just…it's the sort of thing you watch in romantic movies, read in romance novels. And especially after everything with Liam, you deserve the happily ever after." I bite my cheek to fight the laugh that bubbles at the disgust in Brittney's voice as she says Liam's name.

"It's only been a few days, there's no telling what's going to happen."

Tipping her chin up, she nods resolutely. "No, I see it. You two are going to have the cutest little dark-haired babies."

"Okay, now I'm leaving." I'm about to grab my clothes and toiletries from my bed when I freeze and turn to face her. "Are you…are you okay with me spending the night at Josh's? I don't want to ditch you or anything. I've been gone all weekend."

"You're good, babe. Go get your delicious man. I'm fine on my own. May even have somebody over if I won't have to worry about kicking you out. But I want to have dinner every night until we leave. Deal?" She raises an eyebrow at me, and I smile at her acceptance of the drastic change.

"Of course. I'll throw in a coffee too, if you want."

Brittney pushes up onto her bed, leaning on her hands and swinging her feet. "Absolutely. And then we'll figure out a schedule when we get back from the break. I'm sure you guys will want to be together a lot and I understand. Trust me."

My chest fills with warmth at my sweet friend's words. "You're the best, Brit. Really. I'm so lucky to have found a friend like you."

"I know. I'm pretty awesome." Flipping her hair behind her shoulders, she makes a gesture to swipe her hand over each one before laughing. "You're pretty amazing too, Lexie. I'm happy we're friends."

"Me too. Good night, Brit." With a giant smile on my face, I make my way down to Josh's room.

A few people are lingering in the hall, leaning against doorframes in front of open rooms. My shoulders scrunch and an unease rises in my chest as scrutiny seems to follow me.

But the second I get to Josh's room and see him lying back on the bed, eyes on the TV, remote in his hand as he waits for me, my shoulders lower. When he notices my presence and a wide smile breaks across his face, everything within me settles to calm.

"Come in, baby, close the door."

Walking in, I drop my things on the chair near his mini fridge and climb onto the bed, resting my cheek on his chest.

"You tired?" His murmur is low against my forehead.

"A little," I breathe out as my eyes flutter closed.

"What time is your first class tomorrow?"

"Eight."

"Where?"

"Jacoby."

"Do you eat first or just coffee?" The knowledge of my

love for coffee was something that surprised me over the weekend. It had come up in conversation earlier on, but he seemed
to truly grasp the gravity of it.

"Usually coffee and something quick."

"So you can sleep until the last possible second?"

"Yeah. How'd you know?"

"Just a hunch. You seem like you're not really a morning
person."

Even though we spent the whole weekend together, we
drifted in and out of sleep and wakefulness at varying times.
There was no true sense of morning or night, all blurring
together as one long period of time. We slept when we were
tired, ate when we were hungry, and had sex frequently.

"Mmm." All I can do is mumble as my eyelids suddenly
feel like they're filled with sand.

I fall asleep, warm and happy in Josh's arms.

MONDAY MORNING, JOSH WAKES ME UP BY PEPPERING KISSES
over my face, down my neck, and along any exposed skin he
can find. Which is a lot, since the shirt I stole from him has
ridden up to barely cover anything.

When I woke up last night, I apologized for falling asleep,
which he stopped with a kiss and told me it was alright and
then suggested we get ready and go to bed.

"Bed or *bed*?" I had asked coyly.

"Sleep, Lex." His deep chuckle made me stir and clench
my thighs together. "You're clearly exhausted. And you need
to let your body rest."

"I think I can decide for myself and how I feel."

"Not this time. Let me take care of you."

I had acquiesced, mostly because I really was tired.

Resting on his forearms, hovering over me, Josh tips his
face down and connects his mouth to mine. Swiping his

tongue through my lips, he explores my mouth as my hands twist into his hair and I raise off the bed to meld my body to his.

At the first moan, he disconnects from me, sliding his thumb across my lower lip while my body hums for more.

"Good morning, beautiful."

"Good morning."

"I'm going to take you to a *real* breakfast before class. Then I'm going to walk you and pick you up from said class."

"You don't have to do that."

"I know, but I want to."

"What about you? Don't you have something this morning?"

"No, my first class isn't until eleven."

I run my hands up his arms, over his shoulders, and down his chest, squirming at the sight and warmth of his bare skin. "Josh, you should be sleeping. I've been walking to class by myself for weeks. I'm okay."

"I want every second I have with you, Lex. Non-negotiable." With a tiny peck, he starts to push up on his hands, which makes me lace my fingers together behind his neck, trying to keep him close. When he pushes through easily with a chuckle, I huff and pout.

Getting off the bed, he takes my hand, pulling me to sit and spinning me so I'm facing him. With a tug, I'm against the edge of the mattress, and he's standing between my legs.

"I'm giving you twenty minutes to get ready. I told you, Lex, I'm going to take care of you. That includes making sure you eat real food and not just a granola bar for breakfast."

Harrumphing, I make my way down to my room. Josh shows up exactly twenty minutes later and the wide smile on his face makes it impossible not to melt.

Hanging onto his arm as he walks me to class and stealing his warmth highlights my entire morning. There's a lightness in my chest, an ever-present flutter, that makes me smile at random moments and stare at the clock every few seconds.

Two and a half agonizing hours later, I dash out of the building to find Josh leaning against it. My body goes lax as a smile spreads across my face, and warmth so strong it blocks out the chill in the late November air spreads through me.

Throwing his arm over my shoulders, Josh tugs me into his side and kisses the top of my head. The walk back to my dorm has never been so perfect.

Once back to my room, Josh rests his hands along the top of the frame, tipping his body in to leave a small kiss against my lips.

As he stands straighter, one corner of his mouth ticks up. "I have class for a few hours, and I need your help with something when I'm back. Then the rest of the night is whatever you want."

Taking him in, my mouth waters and my thighs clench. His arms are corded with the strain of leaning his weight on them as he tilts into my room. Those few strands of hair are dangling over his forehead, ones I told him over the weekend to absolutely under no circumstance be cut.

"I'll just be here." Pushing up on my toes, I press my lips against his. As I start to lower to flat feet, Josh loops his arm around my waist and tugs me against him, keeping our mouths together and slipping his tongue to meet mine.

When he breaks the kiss, I'm breathless and ready for the day to pass. "See you later, baby."

My next several hours are spent trying to work on papers, but mostly staring at the clock, willing the numbers to tick by faster. TV, music, reading, none of it distracts my mind from the jitters that run through my body and make my knee bounce endlessly.

Josh didn't say how long a few hours was, and I didn't think to ask.

The buzz of my phone excites me so much I nearly drop

it, trying to retrieve it from the spot on my desk. My shoulders slump when I see it's from Lauren, but once I open it, my lips turn up. Distracted by the back and forth with Lauren, I nearly jump when there's a knock at my door.

Turning, I leap up when I note it's Josh leaning against the frame, smile spread across his lips, laundry basket against his hip.

My brow furrows as I look at it. Laundry? He wants to do laundry?

"Come on, beautiful."

Once we're down in the laundry room, I notice that Josh has his sheets and I'm immediately thrown to the first time we were down here together. Like that first time, we're completely alone.

"Would you mind getting the sheets in for me?"

Rolling my eyes at his request, I step up to the washer as he moves aside. As soon as the sheets and detergent are in, Josh rests his hands against the washer on either side of me, pressing his front to my back. He runs his nose through the side of my hair. From deep in his chest, he releases a hum that rumbles from him straight down into my core.

My head tips back to rest against his shoulder.

Placing his hands on my hips, Josh turns me around and lifts me onto the machine. His palms land on my knees and slide up to my thighs, tugging me to the edge and pushing my legs apart as he steps forward to stand between them.

Leaning forward, hands back on the washer, he runs his nose along my jaw. My arms wrap around his neck, my legs around his waist. Josh starts kissing down my neck, and I wish we were anywhere else than a public room.

Licking along the shell of my ear, Josh pulls the lobe between his teeth. "I want to replace all your bad memories of me with good ones, Lex. I won't be able to do that with everything, like the party, or the times I pushed you away. But I'm hoping a little bit of time here, together, will make you forget how rude I was that first time."

"Josh, it's okay. I understand, you've apologized."

"No, Lex. It's not. I was an asshole. I don't want that to be something in your mind."

"I promise you, it's not. The good times made me keep coming back to you, even if the bad times should have pushed me away."

Instead of answering, he loses his hand in my sea of curls and pulls my mouth to his. Our tongues clash in the middle and I twist my hands into his shirt. Closer, I need him closer.

Understanding my silent request, Josh pulls me into him so I'm barely even on the washer anymore, his erection flush against my throbbing clit.

"You have no idea how badly I want to slip inside you right now, Lex."

My head tips back and I groan at his words. I'm pretty sure I have some idea, since it's all I can think about right now.

Tilting my head back up, he melds his mouth to mine again. I cling to him as we make out in the laundry room, rubbing against his erection and needing so much more.

The dropping of a laundry basket has me jumping and pushing myself away so fast I bite my tongue. When Josh tries to draw me back into him, I shake my head, hopping off the washer.

"The rules, Josh."

"Lexie, I told you, it's fine."

"I'm just not there yet."

A tick sets in Josh's jaw, but he starts the washer, linking his fingers with mine and leads me up to his room.

As we lay in bed at night, on fresh sheets, Josh loops some hair behind my ear and leans on his hand.

"Lexie, about what happened in the laundry room."

"Josh, I—"

"I understand you may need time to feel comfortable, I do. It was so many weeks of me telling you no and pushing you away. But things are different now. Keeping quiet and hiding are not the same thing."

"We were wrapped up in each other, making out on a washing machine." And then promptly came upstairs and had sex twice, letting the sheets sit in the washer for an extended period of time.

"We were also alone."

"At first."

Josh sighs heavily, taking my chin in his fingertips and bringing my mouth to his. A quick kiss is all I get. "Good night, beautiful."

Snuggling into his chest, he wraps an arm tight around my waist. There are things I should be saying, ways I should be adjusting and changing. But I don't know how. Sneaking around is one thing. Blatantly ignoring a rule, flaunting it, is entirely different. I'm not sure how to make the tingling anxiety it brings me to subside.

All I know is that Josh makes me feel safe and loved. That I'll have to find it within myself because the look of defeat in his eyes just a moment ago nearly broke my heart.

CHAPTER 28

Walking out to the parking lot hand in hand with Josh Tuesday afternoon, a weight is slowly settling in my stomach. Thanksgiving is two days away and these past few days together have been nothing short of amazing. It just feels like it's going to be impossible to suddenly be away from him for four.

There's zero discussion that he's driving me to class today. It doesn't need to be voiced. As I slide into my seat, his familiar musky scent wafts into my nose and my body relaxes as comfort washes over me.

Resting my head against the seat back, I stare out the window, the corners of my lips pulled down.

Josh squeezes my hand as he merges onto the highway. "What's the matter, baby?"

Shaking away the fog, I turn back to him with a tight smile. "Nothing. I'm fine."

He glances over at me a few brief times. "You're not. Talk to me. What's up?"

"I'm just thinking about tomorrow." As a resident, I have to be out by one. It's a five-hour drive home.

"I don't want you to worry about it, Lex. It's just a few

days. And then we'll be back on Sunday and things will be like what they are now."

Chewing the inside of my lip, I nod. I don't want to bring up the fact that it's only a few weeks until the winter break and that that's far longer, spanning a few weeks versus days.

When we get to class, Josh pulls me to the back of the room, taking two seats in the corner and moving them closer together. Our legs cross and his arm rests comfortably around the back of my chair.

I try to pay attention to Professor Carp and take notes, my notebook sitting open in front of me, but keep getting distracted by Josh.

Every few minutes, he touches me or leans forward and whispers in my ear.

"You look beautiful today."

"I'm lucky you're mine."

"I can't wait to kiss you."

At one point, he leans in and nibbles my earlobe, whispering again before pulling back. "I'm dying to feel you."

The reactions I've been trying to suppress burst free, and I squirm in my seat, tilting my body more toward his.

I'd be worried about getting caught if Professor Carp wasn't so focused on the whiteboard in front of her and there weren't four rows of tables ahead of us.

More tiny touches on my thigh, brushing my hair back, trailing fingers down my spine, and more whispered words build my anticipation as class draws to an end.

Once released, I spin to Josh. "That wasn't very funny, mister."

"I'm sorry, was that distracting?" The pulling up of one side of his lips gives away the teasing his tone didn't.

Getting to the car, Josh pins me against it, his hips pressed against mine as his hand slides up my body and closes gently around my throat, his thumb skimming along my jaw as he seals his mouth over mine.

I grant his tongue access immediately as he uses it to explore my mouth. When a moan rises in my chest, Josh separates his lips from mine, moving his hand to rest against my breastbone.

With another small kiss but no words, Josh pulls away and opens my door for me.

We talk about Thanksgiving on our drive back to campus, but all my mind can focus on are the things he said during class.

As we're walking back to the dorm, we encounter somebody I would have been happy to have never seen again.

Liam walks past us, his arm around Cara, snorting on his way by and murmuring something that sounds like, "Of course."

Josh's entire body tenses next to me, and he spins around. I desperately make an effort to hold him back by grabbing his hand tighter.

"Excuse me?" he growls at Liam, who stops at his words.

Whipping around, he faces us, disdain on his face and dripping off his words. "You fucking heard me. It figures a slut like *her* is with a guy like *you*."

Josh yanks his hand from mine, despite my tugging and trying to hold him back.

"Josh, no." I try to plead with him, but it's pointless.

With three big strides toward Liam, he throws a solid right hook. Liam reels back, stumbling a bit, hand on his jaw. He's bent over and spits blood.

Josh gets low so Liam can see his face. "That was for her." He points back toward me but doesn't turn around.

I had tried to stop Josh, thinking it wouldn't be worth it to go after Liam, that it would only cause more issues. But it was incredibly gratifying.

"You going to let him fight your battles for you?" Liam asks, peering around Josh, hand on his jaw.

"Yeah, I am, because he's doing a better job of it than I

281

could." Taking the few steps forward, I link my fingers with Josh's, on the hand he's not shaking out.

We turn and start to walk toward the dorm, Cara standing behind Liam, watching with wide eyes. I can't let her get out unscathed.

I spin on my toes, a chipper smile on my face. "Oh, and Liam? I saw her making out with your roommate yesterday. Right outside the dorm."

Josh lets go of my hand and throws his arm over my shoulders. "Don't ever fucking talk to her again." Steering me away from the parking lot, we walk in silence until we hit the sidewalk. "I've wanted to do that for a long time. Did you really see her making out with somebody?"

"Nope. But she doesn't get a pass either. At the very least, it may cause a fight." Pausing, I look over at his other hand, which he's flexing and opening repeatedly. A small smile tugs at my lips. "Hurt your hand?"

"No."

"Mhm. Sure, tough guy. Let's get you some ice." Resting my hand on Josh's chest, I lean into him.

Tightening his arm around my shoulders, he pulls me in and kisses the top of my head.

Once we're upstairs and Josh has ice sitting over his already bruised knuckles, while my head lays in his lap, he speaks, "I told you I'd protect you, Lex. That includes your honor, your heart. If I can get a little retribution for you from assholes like that, *especially* when he walks by mumbling bullshit with his arm around another girl, I'm going to."

"So are you going to be my knight in shining armor now or something?"

I want to bring up the fact that Liam didn't really do anything we didn't, that I'm just as guilty, but I know what Josh would hang on is the fact that he led me on for months, patiently waiting for me to give him my body.

"In a manner of speaking, I guess so."

"Hmm. You'd look good in armor." The thought has a heat settling between my thighs.

"How long do I have to keep this ice on?" There's a huskiness to his tone that only makes me squirm with need.

"Until your hand stops hurting."

"But I can't touch you if I have ice on my hand."

Turning my head up to face him, I catch the naked desire in his eyes. "You can wait a few minutes."

"Actually, I'm not really sure I can."

"How's your hand?"

"Good enough."

Sliding out from under me, he jumps up and flips himself to lay over me, hands on either side of my face. With one arm, he loops around my waist and pulls me toward the middle of the bed. Resting on his forearms, he dips his pelvis down, dragging his erection against my heavy clit.

During our weekend of exploration and fun, Josh made it part of his mission to make me comfortable with both talking about sex and various terminology. He wouldn't laugh when I heated, wouldn't point out my bright red face.

"I just want you to be comfortable, Lex. With me, with this, with all of it. That includes being able to talk about it," he'd said at one point.

Getting my mind back to the current situation, my hands rest against his chest, slowly gliding up to cup his neck.

We get stuck in a moment, staring into each other's eyes. There's so much chemistry, undeniable desire and pull. It makes me burn from the inside out, and I need to feel his lips.

Before I can tug him down or rise to meet him, he crashes his mouth to mine. When his tongue slips along the seam of my lips, I immediately open, granting him access as I twist my fingers into his hair and the collar of his shirt. Space is my enemy right now.

When a moan eases from my throat, Josh straightens up, his hands reaching over his head to tear off his shirt before

283

diving for the hem of mine. The button on my jeans is flicked open just as quickly.

As I trail my hands over his breathtakingly toned chest, Josh slides his hand under the hem of my pants and into my panties.

"Holy fuck, Lex." His voice hitches on a groan as his fingers find my soaking entrance.

Taking his face in my hands, I bring his lips to mine briefly before holding his face above mine. "It's kind of a turn on when you defend my honor."

A strangled moan is the only response I get as his fingers dive inside of me, my hips bucking up toward his.

Kissing along the edge of my bra, he angrily tears at the cup, grumbling, "Stupid fucking...I should have taken this off."

I try to sit up, but Josh pushes my shoulder firmly against the bed, hooking his fingers and moving them furiously inside me. It causes my spine to peel off the bed as my nails dig into his bare back. My head lifts and then slams right back to the mattress. "Fuck," I whine. "Josh. God. Fuck."

Abandoning his mission at my chest, he trails his parted lips down my abdomen, gently blowing air along my skin. It prickles as he moves lower and lower.

Once he's reached my pants, he removes his fingers— much to my dismay and verbal protest—and quickly tears them off. Placing tender kisses along the hem of my panties, his fingers hook under the waistband and pulls them straight off.

As they fall to the floor, Josh settles himself between my legs, kissing up the inside of my thigh. My muscles are tight and shaking as apprehension wraps around my chest.

The second his tongue lays a long stripe through my wetness, all the tightness seeps out of me. The more his tongue laves at me, the looser my muscles become, my hands diving to his head as my fingers twist into his hair. I need him closer.

Josh loops my legs over his shoulders, palming my thighs and spreading them more.

I tug at his hair harder as he moans against me. When he closes his mouth over my clit, I nearly levitate off the bed. It's the most amazing sensation I've ever felt, and my body starts to tremble, and tears spring to my eyes as my chest heaves and the familiar pressure quickly builds in my lower belly.

The room is filled with my screams of pleasure as I shake and tingle all over.

Josh runs his tongue in a steady path, down one thigh, back up, along my pussy, and down the other thigh before continuing the circuit. He does this until my body has stilled, though the tingles still remain everywhere, including my fuzzy head.

Kissing up my stomach, he settles above me, leaning on his elbows as he swipes some hair from my forehead. "Do you want to stop here?"

I roll my head from side to side.

"Lex. Don't push yourself. Let's stop." He starts to roll away from me, but I grip onto his shoulders, keeping him in place.

I'm too exhausted from the most intense orgasm I've ever had to talk to him, but I trail my fingers down his chest to his pants. Reaching a little farther than comfortable, I run my hand along his erection and squeeze.

His eyes fall shut and his head tips back. "Are you sure?"

"Mhm."

Standing and ditching his pants and boxers, he's over me again in a second. Slowly, he eases into me and our breath catches at the same time.

Dipping his head, Josh kisses along my jaw as he starts to move inside me. Sliding his lips to my ear, his low breaths make a shiver run through me. "I love you, Lex."

Moaning, I twist my fingers into his hair and pull his mouth to mine. I don't want to tell him with words; I want to show him with my body.

As our tongues tangle and war, he starts thrusting harder and faster as our breathing increases, our bodies moving together with the rhythm of his hips.

Leaning on his elbow, he kisses down my neck and chest until he wraps his lips around my nipple.

My back leaves the bed as his tongue flicks along the hardened peak.

Everything starts to fade around me and all I can focus on is Josh surrounding me, infiltrating every sense and possessing me.

"Josh, Josh, Josh." My chanting his name makes him move faster, until he can't keep his mouth at my breast anymore, moving to reposition in the crook of my neck.

His heavy breaths shift my hair as he pumps into me hard and fast. Every stroke makes me whimper and whine, and not at all quietly.

Readjusting and looping his arms underneath me, hands wrapping up to cup my shoulders from behind, Josh's thrusts take on a new angle. It only takes three before I tighten around him, nails digging into and dragging down his back as I scream.

That's when the bang on the wall comes.

Josh slows but doesn't stop as he glances in the direction and a smile lights his face, a low laugh coming from his chest. It's quickly overtaken by an uptick of his lip, a scrunch of his brow, and a low moan as his head dips to my shoulder with a shortened breath.

As our chests heave together and our hearts pound against one another, I trail my fingertips up and down his back.

Once our breathing starts to level out, he kisses the crook of my neck and rolls to his back, pulling me to his side immediately.

Snuggling into him, I reach to hold his shoulder as he runs his fingers over my hair.

"Did somebody really knock on the wall?" I ask incredulously as my stomach flutters.

"Uh, yeah. I think they did."

Shrinking into him, pin pricks poke throughout my whole body. It doesn't help that this causes Josh to laugh.

"It's not funny, Josh!"

"It is…a little bit."

"No. No, it's not."

"Relax, Lex."

"I don't want to get in trouble." The fact that I'm barely comfortable enough to think about telling somebody I'm having sex, yet people just heard it loud and clear, is another story entirely.

"You won't. I told you, I'll protect you."

"But Holly said to keep it quiet."

"Yeah, well, things happen. Don't worry, nothing will come of it."

Huffing out a breath, I trace his collarbone with my fingertips. When I shiver, he pulls a fleece blanket over us.

"I don't like this blanket."

"What? Why?" His voice is laced with shock.

"It has a giant moose on it! It's terrifying."

"Moose blanket is awesome."

"Moose blanket is terrifying."

Sighing heavily, Josh turns to kiss my forehead. "Moose blanket will go."

"Don't get rid of it just for me, just don't, you know, use it when I'm around."

"It's fine. Moose blanket has seen better days, anyway." We're quiet for a few minutes, enjoying just being together and soft touches.

"What time do you have to leave tomorrow?"

I startle at the sound of his voice. "By one. I promised Brit breakfast."

He grumbles, "Fine. But only because she's your best friend. But I get you until you have to leave."

"Deal. She's leaving from breakfast anyway."

"Wait. How far is your parents'? Five hours?" His hand stills on my hip.

"Yeah, why?"

"So you'll be driving in the dark?"

I shake my head against his chest. "Not this whole dark thing again. It will only be for a little bit of the drive. It won't be too bad."

"I don't know that I like that idea."

"You'd rather spend less time with me and have me leave earlier just to avoid me driving after the sun goes down?"

"Yeah, maybe."

"What is your obsession with me and the dark? Seriously, please explain this to me."

"You're a gorgeous girl, Lexie. Driving is dangerous by itself, and in the dark, even more so. Bad things can happen when people think they can't be seen. I worry about you. I just want to keep you safe. I always have. I know for a while I did the lion's share of the hurting. But I wanted to keep you safe in any way I could. Now it's every way I can. Because I fucking love you, Lexie, and that's what that means. That I protect you from anything and everything I'm capable of." Adoration crashes through my body as his words sink in.

I want to answer, but I don't know what to say to that. Besides one thing. "I love you too."

"I'd drive you myself if I could. Just know that."

"I do." Somehow, it wasn't necessary for him to say it for me to know.

"You should have dinner alone with Brit tonight. It'll give you a chance to be just you two before the long weekend.

288

Things are different now; you won't be together all the time and I've occupied a lot of it these past few days."

I squeeze into him as appreciation spreads through me like sunshine. I know he wants to spend all of his free time with me, because I feel the same way. But I love that he recognizes my need to be alone with my best friend. Well, my college one at least.

"Thank you. That'll be nice, and I know she'll be thankful for it."

Tightening his arms around me, he settles into the bed. "You can text her to let her know, just in case she made other plans. But not yet. I get your undivided attention for a little longer."

Who can argue with that?

CHAPTER 29

"**Y**ou're the talk of the dorm, you know."

My fork clangs to my plate as my stomach bottoms out. "I'm sorry, say that again."

"You're the talk of the dorm. Like everybody knows you and Josh are together." Brittney gestures her hands toward me nonchalantly, but this news is anything but casual.

"How?"

"Well, I mean for one, you're not exactly quiet." Her devilish smile peeks at me as she looks through her long lashes. "And let me just say, I'm so proud." Brittney puts a hand to her chest like she's a proud mama.

"Really, Brit?"

"I knew you just needed the right guy."

"Okay, but seriously, back to this being talked about. How bad is it?" My heartbeat is erratic, and it feels like I can't take a deep enough breath.

"It's not bad at all, Lexie. People are just jealous, of you *and* him." She waves me off as though she didn't just drop a bombshell.

My brows snap together. "Wait, him? Why?"

"You were noticed. By a few guys. But it doesn't matter,

you wouldn't have gone for them anyway. I knew you were a goner as soon as you saw Josh." The way she shakes her head makes me think she's disappointed in the fact I didn't have fun looking around.

"What are they saying?" I eye my mac and cheese, no longer hungry and push the plate away.

"It's nothing bad, Lexie. Trust me, I wouldn't stand for it anyway. Some are jealous, wishing they could be you or him and saying inappropriate things about being above or under either of you. Otherwise, they're just saying that you two appear to be together." She stabs a piece of lettuce with her fork and eyes it dubiously before popping it in her mouth.

"Nothing about the rules or how it's unfair or that we're getting special treatment?"

"No. Everybody thinks that's a stupid rule anyway. And not just because of you and Josh."

I start to pick apart my dinner roll.

"Lexie." The firmness in her voice pulls my attention and my eyes dash up to hers. "Everything's fine. Nobody's mad at you, nobody's complaining. Just be happy."

Words escape me, but I nod and look back at the table, noticing the incredible mess I made. Jumping straighter in my chair, I wipe the crumbs into my hand and brush them onto my plate. I hate leaving a mess behind.

There's a shakiness in my movements, a jitteriness settled into my bones.

Sighing, Brittney wipes her hands and stands. "Come on." We clear our trays and walk toward the exit. "Coffee?"

"No." I'm far too uneasy to add coffee to the mix. I'd be a ball of quivering mess in the corner.

She laughs lightly. "Alright, my very neurotic friend, let's get you back to your man. Maybe he can talk some sense into you."

I follow her into our room, still needing to pack.

"Not going to see him?" She eyes me wearily. "Don't let

the talk disrupt your life, Lexie. I promise, nobody is giving it a second thought."

"It's not that." *Entirely*. "I just need to pack for tomorrow. I'd rather be ready to go so I can spend my time with him and then leave instead of still having to get this part done."

"If you say so. Don't let me disturb you." Hopping up onto her bed, she flips open a magazine.

Taking a deep breath to quell my nerves, I bend over my desk and shake my mouse, my laptop jumping to life. Music will help.

I'm trying to figure out how many more things I need to pack when there's a rap at the door.

Spinning around, I find Josh leaning against the door-frame, a smile on his face. It makes all the tension slide straight down to my feet and out of my body. The tightness that had been wrapped around my ribs is gone, as though somebody untied a ribbon that was holding them snuggly.

"Good evening, ladies." The deep timber of his voice always rattles my insides.

"Well, don't just stand there! I don't bite," Brittney calls from her bed, not even moving or glancing away from her magazine. "Hard," she mumbles so low I hope only I can hear her.

Hanging his head and chuckling, Josh walks into the room, pressing a small kiss against my neck.

"I'm just getting myself packed for tomorrow," I tell him in a low voice.

"And avoiding you," Brittney interjects.

I turn to her, eyes wide as my face heats. "Brittney!"

"What? I had a feeling you weren't going to tell him. Somebody needs to calm your crazy, and it's clear I didn't do a good job." She shrugs but still doesn't look up her magazine.

A finger plants itself under my chin and tilts up to meet

Josh's scrunched brow and dark eyes. "Avoiding me? What happened?"

"I'm not *avoiding* you. Just, taking a few minutes apart. I was thinking maybe I'd wait until later to come back."

"Why?"

"I have things to do here. Packing, seeing Brittney." My voice is low, airy, fake.

"I'm good!" she pipes in, not helping my case.

"Lex. Talk to me."

Trying to fight against his finger, I attempt to look down at my shuffling feet. But he won't let me get away. "People are talking. About us."

"So?"

"So? What about the rule?"

"I already told you, Lex, that's taken care of." When he doesn't like the look on my face, he drops my chin, wrapping his arm around my waist and pulling me into his chest. His other hand sinks into my forest of hair as he scratches at my scalp. "We're not breaking any rules, Lex. We've been given an exception."

"And a damn cute one," Brittney chimes in again, and when I glance over at her, she's still focused on her magazine, though I don't think she's turned a single page.

"Relax. Please. Trust me."

Nodding, I press my cheek firmer against his chest. His arms tighten in response, pulling me closer.

Josh rests his lips against the top of my head, his breath fluttery in my hair. Leaving a trail of kisses toward my ear, his voice is low and husky. "Let's go back to my room and spend some time together. Okay?"

I nod against him, not wanting to move from this safe haven I've found myself in.

With a final squeeze, he slowly lowers his arms from around me, keeping one loose around my waist as he guides me toward the door. "If I don't see you before you leave, have a good Thanksgiving, Brit." He looks over his shoulder in her direction.

"You too, Josh. Lexie, see you in the morning?"

"Um, yeah." I plan to follow through on my agreement of seeing her; I'm just not sure if I'll be back for clothes or not.

We make our way to his room, and he quietly closes the door and flicks the lock, leading me over to the bed with his hand on my lower back. He flops down, toeing his shoes off, and pulls me to him.

I quickly curl back into my safe space, resting my cheek against his chest as his arms engulf me and his chin rests on my head.

"Let's spend some time together, watch some TV. I don't want you worrying about this anymore, Lex. We're together, if you want to be, no repercussions heading our way. No matter what."

"But you said we need to keep it quiet."

"Lex, I know Brit has her ear everywhere, but so do I. Not a single person has said anything remotely negative, about either of us. There's been no mention of complaining. I even checked in with Holly, who said everything's fine. And I double-checked that you'd be safe if anything was brought to her attention. She assured me, again, that you're not going to be penalized in any way. So, tell me, Lex, do you want to be with me? Or is the talking too much for you?" There's an irritation to his voice that I understand, but it hurts all the same.

"I'm not a rule-breaker, Josh. In fact, being here and being with you and all the circumstances surrounding it are the only times I've really done that. It's all catching up to me at once."

"I know. But I think we're a little past that point now, don't you?" I feel his head turn as if he's trying to see my face. "I need to know, Lex. I need to know if you don't want to do this, if it's too much for you to cope with, or if it makes you too uncomfortable. I don't want to have to convince you to be my girlfriend if you don't want to be."

Turning and shifting so my hand rests on his chest, I raise up to look at him. "It's not that, Josh. I do. More than anything, I want to be with you."

His hand slides from my shoulder, down to rest against my lower back, while the other cradles the back of his head. "Can you handle it? The talking? I won't be here next semester. I don't know if that's going to make a difference for you or not. Maybe it won't matter as much if we're not living in the same place, if we're not breaking a rule anymore."

"It doesn't matter if I can or can't. I want this, I want you, so I'll have to figure out a way to live with it."

"I don't want you to live with it, Lex. I don't want you on edge all the time." His fingers slip under the hem of my shirt and start running along my skin.

"I have to. Because the alternative is not being with you. And I can't…I can't…"

"You can't what?" His tone has calmed, now low and soothing as his finger continues to glide along my back.

"I can't live without you. It's live with it or live without you. I can't do that, not now, not after everything."

His hand cups the back of my neck as he pulls me down, my mouth crashing into his. My lips instantly part, our tongues meeting in the middle.

I start to throw my leg over his lap, but he stops me, a firm hand on my hip as he ends the kiss.

"Let's just lay here for a little while. I think you need some reassurance right now, and you're not going to get that from sex. Or at least not the kind of reassurance I want you to have."

"I'm not sure what you mean."

"I don't want you thinking this is just about sex, Lex. That's not why I want to be with you. Or at least it's not the only reason. It's an added perk. But right now, I only want to hold you and watch some TV and relax together before you leave tomorrow. This is our last night together for a few days."

"That's why I thought you'd want to have sex."

"I'm not saying I don't. I'm just saying, it's not all I want to do."

Comfort settles over me like a warm blanket as I snuggle into his chest, my leg shifting over his.

When he starts running his hands down my hair, every so often pulling a curl straight as his fingers trail down my spine, my eyelids start to feel leaden.

I hadn't felt tired before we came down here. But being in Josh's presence, wrapped in his embrace, allows my muscles to loosen, my mind to go blank. There are no heavy thoughts weighing me down.

It's easy, comforting, and exactly what I need.

At some point later in the night, I'm awoken by Josh slipping out from under me.

Frantic, I push myself to sitting. "What's going on?"

Brushing his knuckles down my cheek, he tucks some hair behind my ear. "Shh, baby, it's okay. You fell asleep. I'm just adjusting you. I wanted to brush my teeth."

"Oh." Sagging back down, I'm almost doubled over. "I'm sorry, I didn't mean to fall asleep."

"It's okay, Lex, that's why you're here."

"No, I'm here to spend time with you and have sex."

"Lex, you're here to be with me, whatever that means. I'm gonna go now."

"Okay. I will too."

"I'll leave the door unlocked."

Shuffling my way to my room, I open the door as quietly as I can. I should have looked at the clock before I left Josh's room.

The lights are on, but Brittney is nowhere to be found.

I bump into her on my way to the bathroom.

"Busy night?" The innuendo in her words is impossible to miss.

"No, I fell asleep."

"You fell asleep? With that laying next to you?" Her jaw hangs open for an exaggerated minute.

"Under me, but yes."

"Just when I thought we were getting somewhere. What am I going to do with you?" She shakes her head as her lips turn down.

"Trust me, Brit, there's nothing lacking in that area. I just, I feel comfortable around him, safe. It allowed me to relax and drift off."

"Aw, that's really sweet, actually. Okay, I'll let you go. Don't forget the morning!"

"I know, Josh does too. I'll see you then. Good night."

"Night," she singsongs as she dances away.

I'm about a foot from the bathroom when a hand wraps around my upper arm and tugs me backward. A shriek dies in my throat when I see Brittney's wide, twinkling eyes.

"I forgot to tell you." Her gossip-look is planted firmly on her face. "Kimberly got kicked out of her dorm."

"She did? For what?" My level to give a shit about her is very low, but there has to be a reason for it, and after all the trouble she put me through, I am curious as to what that could be.

Looking from side to side, she leans in, so I do the same. "Dealing."

"Drugs?" I practically shout it in the very quiet hallway.

"Yes, Lexie. Drugs. That's why she wanted to be in a single room! She didn't want anybody interfering. She was caught shortly after she moved. You know those few late nights she was randomly gone? Turns out, she was meeting a customer somewhere since she had a roommate." It's a good thing I've learned to speak Brittney and keep up with how fast she talks, because otherwise, I surely would have missed some of the juicy details.

"Wow. Just…wow." No other words can come to mind, as it's gone completely blank at this discovery.

"Thought you'd like to know. I just heard earlier tonight." Pressing her fingertips to her lips, she spins and walks away.

"Yeah, thanks," I say to nobody as she's already gone.

By the time I trudge my way back to Josh's, I realize I've forgotten pajamas. I grumble at the thought of going back to my room.

He walks in just as I'm getting my slippers back on. "Where are you going?"

"I forgot pajamas."

"Nonsense."

"Listen, I want to get naked too, but I'm actually tired and worried about the drive tomorrow so I'm not sure—"

"Lex, stop. Your choices aren't pajamas or naked. And I'm not making any moves tonight anyway. We're sleeping." Rifling through his shirts, he pulls one out. "Here."

I'm not sure why the thought never occurred to me, especially since I've slept in them before. I blame being half asleep and the drama Brittney was all too happy to share. My body sags in relief as I strip and toss his shirt on. It falls to mid-thigh. I hold my arms out to my sides and spin from side to side. "Well? How do I look?"

"Sexy as sin. Now get in bed." Reaching over his shoulders, he pulls his shirt over his head, shucking his pants and climbing in.

I follow suit, moving over him to slide between his body and the wall.

Wrapping an arm around my waist, he yanks me toward him and my back hits his hard chest. Josh peppers a trail of soft kisses along my shoulder, the back of my neck, and up to my ear. "Good night, Lex. I love you."

"I love you too, Josh."

A twitch wracks my body, which makes my eyes pop open. "Hey, Josh?"

"Yeah, baby."

Rolling in his arms, I turn to face him, resting a hand against his bare chest. "I ran into Brit in the hallway. She said Kimberly got kicked out for dealing drugs. Did you know that?"

"I'd heard something about it, yeah. I didn't think you cared, or I would have said something."

"I mean, on some level, no, I don't. On the level that she made my life miserable, I do. Did you know when she lived here?"

"Did I know? No, I wasn't sure. Did I suspect? Yes. That's another part of why I pushed through the transfer. If she was caught, and it was only a matter of time, then you would have been questioned too. I couldn't let you get mixed up in all that nonsense." Trailing a finger along my hairline and down my back, he places a tiny kiss on the tip of my nose.

"Thank you." It's not enough, and it's not just for the roommate transfer. There are a million things I want to thank Josh for, and loving me tops that list. But right now, with exhaustion weighing down my mind and love surging through me, I have no other words.

Sensing my inability to think, Josh tips my chin up and brushes his lips against mine before twisting his hand into my hair. The scratching at my scalp and twirling of my curls has my body sinking into the mattress.

I'm back to sleep within minutes.

Sometime in the wee hours of the morning, the sun just poking through a light haze, I wake up and find Josh and I have separated. It seems like a pretty impressive feat, considering how tiny these beds are. He's on his back, arm flung over his eyes. I'm immediately thrown back to the night I slept here after my drunken escapade in Liam's dorm.

But this time, instead of slinking out, I curl into Josh's bare chest. He makes the slightest humming sound and wraps his arm tight around my waist, pulling me into his side, and kisses the top of my head.

WE BOTH JOLT UPRIGHT AT THE KNOCK ON THE DOOR. Rubbing my hand against my chest, I try to contain my pounding heart. It's partially from the fear of being woken up, and partially from the impending doom of being caught in Josh's room.

Running a hand down his face, Josh shakes his head and swings his legs over the edge of the bed, sliding off and pulling on a pair of pants. He cracks the door as he yanks a shirt over his head.

I shrink back under the blankets, pulling the sheet completely over my head, creating my own little fortress.

The voices are low murmurs, nothing I can make out, but Josh releases a deep, throaty laugh that lights my body on fire. If he's laughing, I'm probably not in trouble, but I stay under my blanket anyway.

"And tell Lexie I said to have a nice Thanksgiving. I can't wait to meet her." The male voice is definitely louder this time, clearly on purpose.

"Get the fuck out of here, man. I'll see you, Sunday." By the tone of his voice and the breathiness behind it, I know Josh is smiling, fighting back a laugh.

When the door clicks shut and the lock bolts, I tug the sheet tighter around my head. The huff from Josh makes me curl in on myself, drawing my knees to my chest.

He pulls at the sheet, but I grip until my knuckles are white. Instead, he lifts the side and slides in. "Mind if I join you?" As he does, he unfurls my fingers from the sheet and links them with his.

"It was just Matt, baby. He's dodging out early, has a flight to catch."

"He said my name."

"Yeah, 'cause he knows you're here. He's seen us together, way before anything happened."

I suddenly realize that I don't know any of the other RAs. In a lineup, I could maybe point out two. And who Matt is smacks into the forefront of my mind. He was the one on the couch with Josh the night I came back from Liam's. He was also part of the trio who split up the dorm party.

"And he's not mad?"

"No, he's not. He has a girlfriend who lives off campus. He's happy for me, for us. Matt knew way before anything even happened that I had it bad for you."

"How?" My face scrunches as I try to riddle out his meaning.

"Said he could see it in the way I look at you, the way my gaze finds you the second you walk in. We were actually talking about you the night that you showed up plastered." Josh's jaw ticks at the memory and his hand trails down my side. "When I got back downstairs, he wasn't at all surprised that I had put you in my bed. Fuck, *I* was still shocked by my audacity and bossiness. But I needed to know you were okay, and he understood that. Anticipated it. That's why he helped me get you out of the dorm party a week later."

"So, I guess he's a good friend, then?"

"Yeah. He really is. I want you to meet him, like, officially. All my friends really."

"I've never really seen you hang out with anybody."

"That's on purpose, Lex. Remember that night in the quad? I have a friend in the mid-campus dorms. So, I went there to get wasted."

All I can do is hum. "I look forward to meeting them. All of them."

His smile damn near breaks me in half. Sidling up to him,

I settle into his chest, my forehead resting right over his heart. Sliding his hand up under the hem of my shirt, he feathers his fingers on my lower back.

"Speaking of friends, you have breakfast with Brit."

"I'd rather stay with you." It slips from my mouth before I can stop it and instantly regret it. I love Brit; she's become the most important person to me here. Well, maybe second most now.

"You need to go. Don't let me detract from your friendship."

"I know. And I won't. Just, a few more minutes."

Twenty minutes later, I'm walking into my room to find Brit at her computer. She jumps up immediately.

"I need five minutes to change and then we're good to go eat." I gesture at my clothes as I talk and quickly pull out clean ones.

Breakfast is as fun as it always is. I'm able to give Brittney my full attention and laugh at all her jokes. In the few days I've been solely focused on Josh, she's been busy trying to find her own "boytoy" as she so eloquently put it.

"Listen, Lexie, I know it's only a few days, but things are going to be different when you get back. They have been since that night. And it's okay, I get it and I want you to be happy. Just...try to make time for me. Please?"

"Of course, Brit. I love you. You're my best friend here. I don't want things with Josh to change that. I know he doesn't either. And while he's moving off campus, he'll be student teaching next semester, so he'll be gone all day. I'll still be around a ton, I promise."

"Girls' night?" She tips her shoulder in my direction as she wraps her hands around her coffee cup.

"For sure, girls' night. Your social schedule will be way more demanding than mine, so you let me know what night you want to do and I'll be there."

Once we get back upstairs, I follow her into our room,

finishing my packing and popping up on the bed to watch as Brittney flies around the room, tossing stuff randomly in the general vicinity of her duffel on her bed, eliciting a chuckle from me.

"I have to leave like a half hour ago. My mom's going to be *so mad*." Her eyes are wide, and her voice is frantic.

"How far of a drive is it?"

"It's only like four hours, which isn't too bad. Yours is five, right?"

"Yeah. I actually haven't ever done it myself. I'm a little nervous." I worry my lip between my teeth.

"Good music. Lots of coffee. Stop when you need to take a break." She's still talking as she speeds around the room. Stopping at her bed, she shoves everything inside, barely folded, and zips it up, throwing it over her shoulder. Brittney takes a few steps toward me, throws her arm around my shoulder and pulls me into a hug.

"Bye, Lexie. Have a great Thanksgiving! Tell Lauren I said hi. I'll see you Sunday."

"You too, Brit. I'll see you then. Drive safe!" I have to yell the last part as she's already out the door.

Hopping off the bed, I glance at my computer. I have at most three hours until I need to leave. Shutting it down, I pack it up, double-checking my duffel and making sure I'm ready to go.

Taking a deep breath and letting it out, my shoulders slumping, I walk down to Josh's room, trying to keep the sting from burning my eyes.

My hand raises and lowers. Should I still be knocking? I mean, it's not my room, but he's made it clear he wants me here as much as possible. Do I just walk in? No, my mother taught me manners, and manners require knocking.

The door is thrown open after two short raps. Josh's broad smile makes the burn heighten and my chin starts to tremble. It tears the corners of Josh's mouth down.

"Hey. Hey now. No crying." He wraps me in his arms as a sob breaks free. "It's only a few days, Lex. Nothing's going to change."

"I know. I feel silly, I do. It's just, I feel like we just connected. After most of the semester, we're finally together, and now when we're in this great place, we're going to be apart." I'm pathetic and I'll be lucky if he still wants to be with me after this long weekend. Nobody wants to be with somebody who's this needy. Right?

"I know. Baby, I know. But really, it will go by so fast. We'll talk every day. And Sunday will be here before you know it and then I'm not letting you out of my sight, except for classes."

"Okay." It's all I can say around the tightness of my throat. My behavior feels ridiculous, and the urge to hide from myself is strong. But I want Josh to know how much he means to me, how much I care for him, that it's causing me to be this upset even though it will only be a few days.

And I am excited to be going home. I haven't seen my parents since they left. Lauren has said she won't believe that I'm really alright until she has her eyes on me since the last time she saw me, I was so distraught.

Leading me to the bed, he climbs up, opening his arms for me as he lays on his side. Sliding against him, I twist my fingers into his shirt as I breathe deep. The musky scent instantly draws a peacefulness out of hiding.

With a gentle finger, Josh tilts my chin up as his lips brush mine. Soft, tender. Then they do it again, just as soft.

His lips brush over mine again and again and again, until they start to lose the softness and linger a little longer. His hand slides from the back of my neck down my spine, cupping my ass as I rub my thighs together and tilt my pelvis toward his.

Josh's mouth moves against mine, his tongue gliding along

the seam of my lips. Parting them, my tongue dips out to meet his.

Rolling me to my back, Josh hovers over me, his chest barely brushing mine. Cupping my jaw, he caresses the apple of my cheek, leaning down to leave slow, tender kisses along my hairline, working his way down until he finds my lips.

As he explores my mouth, his hand gliding down my side, mine twist into the back of his shirt. No amount of closeness is ever enough. Right now, there are far too many clothes separating us.

"Josh." His name rolling off my tongue is like the sweetest sin. Never could I have imagined something like this. Both the feelings of love, his nearness, and the sheer pleasure his body brings mine.

"Lex." My name murmured against my neck is the most amazing sound I've ever heard.

Tipping my head back, I give him more access to slide his open mouth along my neck.

The bed dips on either side of me as he pushes himself up to his knees, pulling off his shirt, revealing the mouthwatering muscles beneath.

Mine.

Scooping an arm behind my back, he pulls me up to sit on his legs, hands gliding under the hem of my shirt and igniting little fires across my skin. I'm still amazed at how somebody who had been so harsh to me early on can be so tender. It's part of his personality to be strong, tough, hard. But peeling away the layers, and now wherever I'm involved, he's the gentlest person I've ever met.

His dark eyes meet mine and I'm sure the love and lust swirling through his are matching in mine. Our stare breaks off as my shirt is lifted over my head. I was so entranced I hadn't even noticed him removing it.

"I love you, Lex."

"I love you too, Josh." My hands are resting gently against

his shoulders, our gazes locked on each other's. I don't even look away as he unhooks my bra, gliding the straps down my arms. Releasing my hold, I let him toss it to the floor.

Gliding his hands from my wrists to my shoulders and down, he cups my bare breasts and takes my nipples between his fingers.

My head tips back as a moan rises in my throat and Josh makes the smallest adjustment with his hips.

His fingers start making quick work of my button and zipper as mine fly to his pants to do the same.

Laying me back, Josh leaves a trail of tender kisses from my collarbone down my stomach, giving each nipple some attention and sucking it between his lips on his way. Once he reaches the top of my pants, he kisses along the waistband before pulling them off.

When he runs out of space, he gets off the bed, removing his pants and boxers before running his palms up my legs and pulling off my panties.

Everything is moving in slow motion, the anticipation filling the air like we're trapped in a balloon.

Kissing up my leg, Josh shifts and settles between my legs. He starts with tender kisses before running his tongue right up my slit and swirling it around my clit. Adding more pressure, he repeats the circuit. Up, swirl, down. Up, swirl, down. Each time, with more and more pressure.

When he closes his lips around my throbbing clit, it's like an exorcism is being performed on my soul as I arch off the bed.

"Fuck." It comes out as a whine as I can barely breathe. When he slides two fingers inside me, I'm pretty sure my breath stops altogether.

As he hooks his fingers and combines that with the licking and sucking of my clit, my body takes over, arching and bucking toward him, needing more.

Squeaks start to break through with every breath, and my

hands search for something to grab on to, but can't settle anywhere as my body starts to tremble. As my fingers twist into Josh's hair and a moan rises in my chest, a responding groan comes from him, and I'm thrown over the cliff, my body shuddering, with his name a whisper on my lips. It's all I can manage to get out as my lungs struggle to fill.

I barely feel the kisses Josh lays on my skin due to the tingling that's all through my body. As he hovers over me, he brushes some hair from my face, a smile spanning his and a hand resting on my hip.

"You okay, baby?"

I nod slowly, my eyes hooded.

Josh starts kissing gently along my chest. "I'm okay if you want to stop."

"No. It's going to be four long days. I want to feel you before we're apart."

Groaning, he rolls his head against my breastbone, taking my nipple between his teeth before gliding over me and lining himself up at my entrance.

Slipping through my wetness, he teases me, running up, around my sensitive clit, and back down, just barely sliding in the littlest bit.

"Josh. Please."

"Do you need me, Lex?"

"Yes."

Josh locks his mouth on mine and hums softly, the vibrations rattling through my body.

I'm ready to stop the kiss and beg for more when he pushes into me with one long, slow slide until he's all the way inside.

"God, I love the way you look under me, Lex." His hand wraps around my hip as he starts moving.

After a few thrusts, he takes my hands in his, linking our fingers, and holding them above my head as he starts pumping into me harder and faster.

My back peels off the bed toward him, and I want to feel every inch of skin I can. I need his heat on me.

Every thrust has me moaning and panting. My fingers tingle with the need to touch him, grab at him, scrape my nails across his shoulders, down his back. But they're still trapped under his.

With a slight adjustment to his hips, I tighten around him as I cry out, squeezing his hands in mine. A few more hurried thrusts as I work through my orgasm sets off Josh's.

Resting his forehead against mine, we come down together.

Sliding one of his hands up my arm, he runs the pad of his thumb across my lower lip, down my chin, and my throat, before cupping my neck.

Pressing a small kiss on the tip of my nose, he pulls out and rolls off me, turning on his side with his cheek resting on his hand.

When I turn to meet his eyes, my chin quivers again.

Hooking some hair behind my ear, Josh leans in and leaves a kiss on my forehead. "Don't cry, baby. It's only a few days. It will go by fast, I promise."

"I know. Can...can we just stay like this for a little while?"

"Of course, baby. Anything you want."

Two hours later, we're down at my car, bags in the trunk, as I avoid sliding into the driver's seat.

My foot tips to the side as I work my lip between my teeth, hands resting on Josh's waist as I look up at him.

Tears spring free without warning.

The corner of his mouth tips down as he cups my face and kisses away the tears making tracks down my cheeks.

"I'll miss you, Lex. But we'll be back before you know it. Please don't cry. I'm already going to worry about you driving home; I don't want the added concern of you driving while crying."

"I'll be okay." I'm not entirely sure I believe myself and

twist my fingers into his shirt, holding on just a little tighter for a little longer. I know I need to leave to be home before driving too much in the dark.

"Please drive carefully. Stop when you need to. Call me if you need to."

"Won't you be driving too?"

"My car may be old and junky, but I do have Bluetooth."

"Oh, right. I always forget about that." I pretty much never talk in the car; it's not something that's ever been for me that I rarely even turn mine on.

"Call me when you get home, so I know you made it safely."

"I will." My voice is barely above a whisper.

"Music loud, stop for coffee."

Not trusting the tears staying at bay, I nod.

Josh presses his mouth against mine for a long, lingering kiss, leaving another one on the tip of my nose and another on my forehead. "I love you, Lex."

"I love you too." My heart tugs painfully as he backs away from me, and I slide into the seat, starting the car.

With one hand in his back pocket, he raises the other as I drive away.

Four days. It's only four days. After all the time wanting him and not being able to have him, you can survive four days.

CHAPTER 30

"Laur, I feel ridiculous!" I throw my arms out across the table in front of me, banging my head on my elbows a few times before propping them up and resting my chin in my hands.

"Why?" Lauren asks, before popping her spoon in her mouth.

"Because I *miss* him, and it's only been a day."

"That's not ridiculous, Lex, that's adorable. And sweet. It makes sense to miss him if you love him."

Taking a big spoonful of pie, I shove it into my mouth. Lauren and I are bundled up on my porch, eating our dessert with steaming cups of coffee. While we do Thanksgiving with our respective families, tradition is for us to have dessert together.

She's been here for four hours—with lots of whining, and both three pieces of pie and cups of coffee each.

"I'm sorry, I'm doing too much complaining," I grumble as I stare at the darkness around us.

"It's okay, Lex. This is new for you and I'm glad you're so deliriously happy." She talks through a mouthful of pumpkin pie.

"I don't know if I'd go *that* far." I swirl my spoon through the whipped cream on my plate, eyes cast down.

"Did you or did you not start to cry when you were telling me about how things have been the past week and that you can't wait to see him again."

My shoulders hunch, and heat tickles the nape of my neck. "Okay, point taken."

"It's utterly adorable, though. I need to see a picture."

My eyes widen in realization. "I don't have one."

"Well, text him and ask for a selfie!" Lauren straightens on her side of the picnic table, curling toward me, excitement swirling through her bright blues.

"He's not that kind of guy. He won't do that."

"I'm sure he would for you."

"No, it's weird. I don't need him to think I'm more pathetic than I already am."

"I doubt he would think that, but fine." Lauren shrugs and turns back to her pie.

Waving my spoon in the air, I change the subject. "Enough about me and Josh. Talk to me about something else. Ooo, tell me about you and your guy."

"Not much to tell since you visited, really. Nick's great. Sweet, caring, a gentleman who opens doors and things. And the sex is fantastic." Her eyes grow wide as she snaps her head up from her plate to meet my gaze. "The sex, Lexie. How is the freaking sex?"

"Laur, no. Come on." My face is burning at the thought of having to talk to her about it. Josh may have made me more comfortable, but really, it's only when talking to him about our sex life.

"Uh-uh. No way. You're my friend and I love you and I respect your boundaries, but you have to give me something, anything."

"Amazing," I sigh, quickly followed by a blush.

"Eeek! I'm so excited for you." Giddily, she bounces in her

seat. Her eyes quickly narrow as she looks at me. "What's wrong?"

"He hasn't called today. He said we'd talk every day." God, I'm so pathetic.

"Well, it's only"— flicking out her watch, she takes a look — "hm, it's eleven. Shit, is it really that late already? But you have to give him a little slack. It's Thanksgiving. I haven't heard from Nick since this morning."

"But you heard from him."

"Don't stress it, Lex. If you don't hear from him by tomorrow night, maybe give him a call. You could have also picked up the phone earlier today or tonight, ya know."

"I know, I do. I just won't want to seem desperate. I cried, Laur. Fucking cried before getting into my car to come home for *four* days. He doesn't need me hounding him on the phone too." I crash my head to my arm again, resting against the table briefly to stamp out my frustration with myself.

"I'm sure he liked that you got upset. It shows how much you love him."

"Maybe." Pushing the rest of my pie around my plate, I stare into the mush. I've lost interest in eating.

"What's really going on here, Lex?"

"What do you mean?"

"Something more is going on than that you're worried he doesn't miss you. It's been a hectic and chaotic day, and I know that you know he loves you. So, what's *really* going on in your head?" I hate how well she knows me sometimes.

Sighing, I realize there's no point in holding back. "I don't know what I'm doing. I don't know what to expect. At all."

"I mean, that's understandable. It's your first real relationship. What does Josh say?"

"I haven't told him." I hang my head, anticipating the onslaught that I know is coming.

"No. No way, Lexie. Do not sabotage yourself here. You need to talk to him and let him know how you're feeling so that he can work through this with you. You're going to drive yourself crazy second guessing everything you do instead of being happy. And it's clear that Josh makes you very happy. I mean you—"

"How do you know he makes me ha—"

"Stop. Don't even go there." Lauren holds up a finger close to my face. We play this game of interruption a lot in serious conversations. It's part of our dynamic and it always works for us. "We've been best friends for most of our lives. I know you better than anybody. I can see in your face when you talk about him, the lilt in your voice, the shine in your eyes, how much you love him and how happy he makes you. From the sounds of it, it's very mutual. So please, for the love of God, just talk to the man. I'm sure he'll be understanding. Relax and stop worrying."

She glares at me with an expectant stare until I raise my hands and accept.

"How'd it go with your parents?" Lauren slowly pulls the spoon from her mouth as she looks at me with slightly raised brows, clearly trying to distract me.

I lift a shoulder as I mush my pie into a mountain. "Fine, I guess. I told them both about Josh, that he exists. Dad was only really worried about how he treats me. Which, of course, means I only told him about the nice parts, like holding doors, protecting me. I left out that he punched Liam."

A laugh rises at the memory. "Oh, and you know Dad was super impressed that he changed my battery for me."

"Of course. I think dads everywhere would like a guy who does that for his daughter. How about your mom?"

"She just wanted to know if I was happy. We talked a little more after Dad went to bed. She wanted to make sure I'm being safe."

A half hour later, after Lauren nearly squeezes me to death saying goodbye despite our plans to spend the next day together online shopping, I'm moping around my room. That last cup of coffee only added to the jitters wracking my body, making me on edge and unable to settle.

I want to call Josh, but it's late. College kids or not, I don't want to disturb his family time or wake him up if he's already gone to bed.

Finishing up brushing my teeth, I hear my phone ringing in my room and go flying to pick it up, nearly dropping it on the floor.

"Hello?" I'm breathless as a hand flies to my chest to calm my racing heart.

"Hey, baby."

"Hi." For some reason, I don't know what to say. "It's late." That isn't it.

"I know. I'm sorry. Did I wake you up?"

"No, no. I just meant I'm surprised to be hearing from you." I twiddle an old lanyard between my thumb and forefinger as I stand near my bookshelf. It still hangs where I tied it from the latticework at the top, a testament to my summers at the day camp I had worked at for years.

"I told you I'd call every day. Today got away from me a bit and my brother's been giving me a hard time. But I just wanted to hear your voice. I miss you."

My whole body warms and loosens at his sweet words. "You do?"

"Of course, I do, Lex. Why, do you not miss me?" There's a hint of hurt to his tone and it slices right through me.

"Oh, I do. A lot." Flopping onto my bed, I fall back and turn my head to the side, pulling up an image of Josh so I can imagine he's with me and not hundreds of miles away.

"Well, why wouldn't I miss you?"

"I don't know." Probably because I was a silly crying girl when we said goodbye.

"I do, Lex. So much. I miss you in my arms, I miss your lips on mine." He hesitates and I wonder if he's touching his mouth like I am mine. "Did you know that at night when we drift away from each other, you make this little whining noise and then scoot closer to me and fall back asleep?" The way he says it, I can imagine the smirk on his face.

"I do not." I loop hair behind my ear like I would if he could see me.

"Every night. It's adorable." Silence spans the phone for a moment. "Why don't you come back early Sunday? Meet me there in the morning."

"I'm not allowed back until three." My pulse is fluttering in my neck, the spot Josh likes to kiss, especially in moments like this when it's racing so fast, he can feel it against his lips. It's robbing me of any coherent thoughts. Why would I deny extra time with him?

"I'll sneak you in."

"I don't want you to get in trouble."

"What are they going to do, fire me?" He ends on a snort.

"Good point, I guess," I mumble. "Okay, yeah, I'll meet you there. But what if I'm seen?" The telltale bubbling of anxiety in my stomach sends a tingling through my limbs and I chew on my lip.

"We'll spend the extra time in my room, or go eat. Or we can order delivery and I'll pick it up. I just want to be with you, Lex."

"I want that too." Hesitating for a moment, I consider not saying anything. "I've told everybody about you."

"Oh, yeah?" There's a teasing to his words and I can hear his smile in his tone.

"Of course. Why, have you not talked about me?" My brows pull together and the anxiety bubbles over to full force, sending a shudder through my body.

"Oh no, of course, I have. To anybody who will listen. My mom, my friends, my cousins. My brother's sick of it. I'm talking about you constantly."

"Really? And what sort of things are you telling them?" I

flatten on my bed so I'm staring at the sticky stars still on my ceiling from when I was ten.

"Anything, everything. That you're beautiful and smart and funny—"

"I'm not funny."

A huff resounds in my ears. "Maybe not intentionally, Lex, but you are. You have a good taste in music, you're sweet and caring, you're humble."

"Humble?" My brow arches, as this isn't a word I'd use to describe myself.

"I seem to recall you didn't want to speak up during our project because you didn't want to step on my toes. Humble. And I find your reading habits *very* sexy." The grit in his voice makes me rub my thighs together, and my longing for him increases twofold.

"You told them my reading habits are sexy?"

"Not in so many words. Mostly just that I appreciate them and find them attractive." We're both silent for a beat. "I also told them that I love you. Which is really all they need to know."

"I love you too." My body loosens and sinks into the mattress.

"You'll come early Sunday?"

"I'll come early Sunday."

"Were you on your way to bed?"

"Kind of. I wasn't really sure what else to do with myself." Even as I say it, my fingers play with the fringe on my blanket.

"You can call me too, Lex. I don't know why you think this whole thing is one-sided when I very clearly pursued you, even when I shouldn't have."

Narrowing my eyes, I give it a moment of thought. "You're right. I know you are. I'm sorry, it's all a little new to me. When I was with Li—" Stopping short, I clear my throat. "I've never had somebody really be interested in *me*. I feel like I

317

don't know how to navigate the waters and don't want to seem too clingy."

"By calling me 'cause you miss me? Oh, baby, that's not clingy. And if it is, then consider me just as clingy as you. It's okay to want to talk to each other when we're apart, and it's okay to be a little sad right now. Just like it's okay for me to ask you to meet me there early. There are no rules here, Lex. If you want to call me, then call. If I want to see you, I'm going to do my damndest to do that."

"I don't like not having rules, not having clear guidance of what to expect." Switching hands with the phone, I tilt my eyes back to ease the sudden onslaught of tears. I don't understand where they're coming from except my unease at the very unknown waters I'm treading in.

"I know. How about this, what if we set our own? There really are none, Lex, but we can set some if it will make you feel better. And really, they're just day to day things, but we can say they're rules if you want to."

My heart picks up tempo at his thoughtfulness. "Yeah. Yeah, I think I'd like that."

"Okay. I have some. And these are in no particular order. If we're not together and want to talk, then we call. I feel like I shouldn't have to say this, but I'll reiterate, we're exclusive, so nobody else. You're *mine,* and I'm yours. You are welcome in my room whenever you want, and you can come to my apartment whenever you want. We need to talk to each other if something bothers us. Communication. It needs to be open and honest. Any rules on your end?" Josh says it all rapid fire and the late hour paired with the swirling of my mind require a minute for me to catch up and absorb his words.

He's mine. And I am unequivocally his.

"Um, I don't know. What about things going forward?"

"Let's make them and change them as we go. Deal?"

"Yeah. Thank you."

"I want this to work, Lex. I need it to. So I'll do anything I need to make you happy, keep you happy."

I'm able to fill my lungs for the first time all day and release a hefty, content sigh. "I love you."

"I love you too." Just as he finishes talking, there's a light knock at the door as Mom opens it and pokes her head in.

I lean up on my elbows to talk to her, my eyes narrowing as I take her tight face. "Hang on, Josh," I mumble into the phone and hold it against the comforter. "Hey, Mom."

"Hi, sweetie. I'm sorry to bother you, I just heard voices and wanted to check in."

"Oh, sorry, was I being too loud?" My eyebrow quirks up. I'm pretty sure that despite my not entirely put together brain, I was being fairly quiet.

"No, sweetheart, you're fine." Instead of leaving, she lingers, hand still on the doorknob.

"Did you want to talk or something?"

"Actually, yes. I know it's late and you're on the phone, but yes, I want to."

"Um, okay. Give me a second." Sitting up fully, I turn my back on Mom, putting the phone back to my ear. "Hey, uh, my mom wants to talk? So I have to go."

"Okay, no problem. Sleep well, beautiful. I love you, and I'll talk to you tomorrow."

"I love you too. Night." Hanging up causes a heaviness to settle into my chest. It was so nice to hear from him, but it makes the longing and pull even stronger. Taking a deep breath, I turn to Mom, sliding onto the edge of my bed and cupping my phone between my hands, as though I can hold on to a tiny piece of Josh.

"What's up, Mom?"

Walking slowly into the room, she comes to sit next to me. "I just want to talk a little about Josh. I know we chatted a little last night while we cooked, but you know how crazed I get, how chaotic it is. I'm a little more level-headed now."

"Oh." Relief sprawls through me. It may be premature, but I was expecting something different. "What would you like to know?"

"Tell me about him, tell me about you. Do you have a picture? I'd love to know what he looks like."

"I don't, and Lauren's already scolded me for that. But I promise to send you one when I do have it." Thinking back on what we talked about last night, I don't really feel like I left any stone unturned, so I wait for her to continue.

"That would be greatly appreciated. I guess I have a few concerns that I just want to address." She pauses and I look over at her to see her eyes trained on the threadbare carpet, her mouth a thin line. "Are you sure he's not just using you for your body?"

My eyes grow wide as my eyebrows shoot to my hairline and I try to contain the choke stealing my air. "I'm not really sure how far into this you want me to go, Mom."

She narrows her eyes and purses her lips, the crease lines deepening in her forehead.

"How about this? I'll give you as few details as I can." I would never talk to my mom about sex, but I feel like she needs to at least know I'm having it. "He certainly had the opportunity to make it that way. But he didn't. Things between us did not start well or perfect or even right. But he loves me, and I love him."

"I'm going to say something I know may make you uncomfortable, but I'm your mother and I need peace of mind. I assume you're having sex. It's college, and I would expect it because while you're smart and a rule-follower, you're not a nun. Are you at least being safe?" She pins me with the stare I grew up knowing as her truth serum. It was enough to make me confess my crimes at any time. I realize it may as well be my own eyes staring back at me, but the steeliness of the gaze gets me.

"I went on the pill a few months ago." My face burns, and

heat prickles the back of my neck. This conversation is making me want to squirm. But I need to show strength in front of Mom, or she'll think I'm not ready for this. And all I am is ready. "Mom. I really love him. And if this isn't love, then I don't ever want to know what love is because what I feel for Josh, with Josh, it's...amazing."

"I just want to make sure you're being safe, Alexis. With your body and your heart."

"I know. I am. And if he were to break my heart someday, it'd be worth it for what I feel now."

When she's about to speak again, I start first, "Mom, I know you have your hesitations, and I want you to meet him, I do. But he keeps showing me how much he's learned over the semester, how much he knows me and loves me."

"I just want you to be happy."

"I am, Mom. I really am. Please don't worry about me. And tell Daddy that Josh treats me well. Please. I know it's a concern of his and I'd tell him myself, but honestly, it's a little embarrassing to talk to him about my boyfriend."

She continues to look at me for a minute, her gaze intent on mine. "There's something else. Something you're unsure of."

I swallow around the giant lump that's lodged in my throat. "How do you know?"

"I'm your mother, Alexis. I can tell."

"It's just, I don't know. It's not what I expected. I mean, I found somebody I love right from the beginning. Granted, we weren't together for most of that time except for stolen moments, but still. We broke a pretty major rule which worried me a little, but mostly, I feel so lost on what to do and how to navigate."

"Hm. I can understand how that would be difficult for you. All I ask is that you consider our conversation on the drive up to school. Sometimes, you need to do things that make you happy and let the journey guide you, Alexis. You're already at this point. I just don't want you to second-guess and jeopardize the happiness you've found."

"Okay, Mom."

"Good night, sweetheart. I love you."

"Love you too, Mom."

As she leaves, her words, which are very similar to Lauren's, swirl through my mind. The more the thoughts wind through the weeds in my brain, the more they pull them free, and I know what I have to do.

CHAPTER 31

A s I get out of my car, Josh strides toward me with a speed to his step, hands in his pockets, a wide smile stretching across his face.

Dropping my bag, I take off at a run. He's just gotten to the edge of the parking lot when I reach him, jumping and leaping into him and looping my legs around his waist, my arms around his neck.

Josh catches me with an "oomf" and stumbles back a step before he wraps his arms around my middle, a hand resting against my ass.

"Hi," he murmurs as he leans his head back, using one hand to remove the curls from my face.

"Hi." I don't give him a chance to say more as I take his face between my hands and press my mouth to his.

His fingers tighten in my hair as his lips move against mine, sliding his tongue into my mouth.

Leaving a kiss against my lips, he places another, and another, before moving to my temple, my neck, my cheek, until he lands against my ear. "Somebody missed me."

A shudder runs through me at the deep baritone of his voice. "A lot."

"That was quite the hello. What happened to being nervous about getting in trouble for breaking the rules?"

"I don't care. I don't care anymore. I just want to be with you, no matter what."

Josh hasn't stopped smiling since the moment he saw me, but now, a glint takes over his dark eyes.

"I'm happy to hear you came to that realization. You ready to go upstairs?"

"Mhm." I completely understand his sudden change, sudden need, to get me in the building and into his room.

Groaning as he lowers me to the ground, he links his fingers with mine and walks back toward my car, scooping my bag off the ground and throwing the strap over his shoulder.

"So, while I'm glad you don't care as much about getting caught, you're really *not* allowed to be here. They could tell you to leave; it's supposed to be just RAs until this evening."

Bristling and rolling my shoulders, I try not to let the anxiety overwhelm me as a flutter settles in my chest and I try to tamp it down with a deep breath. Josh notices my reaction and loops his arm around my waist, tugging me into his side.

"How are you getting me in, then?"

"I propped the side door." He says it like it's no big thing.

"The what?"

"The side door. How do you think underage kids get so much alcohol in? Especially those who don't live in the dorms on weekends when we're down by the doors."

Huh. Good question. "I guess I never thought about it."

"I love that about you." He kisses my temple and squeezes my hip. I'm glad my naïveté is endearing to him.

Before we even make it upstairs, my phone pings six times. Once locked inside Josh's room, I pull it from my pocket.

Lauren: *Pic?*

Lauren: *Picture?*

Lauren: *Picture please?*

Lauren: *Come on. I know you're back. Give me something!*

Lauren: *I'm losing my mind Lex!*
Lauren: *PICTURE!*

Giggling to myself, I shake my head.

"What's so funny?" Josh steps behind me, sliding his arms around my waist as he looks over my shoulder.

"Oh, Lauren's just dying a little bit, wanting a picture of you. I didn't have any over the break and she's about to go crazy. Do you mind?"

"Of course not, baby. I want you to have pictures of us. I want them too. We were just a little busy before." Josh winks at me and my panties just about melt off my body.

Tightening his arms, he presses his cheek to mine as I flick open my camera. We take a few of us smiling before he turns to kiss my cheek.

His lips continue their path along my skin as I send a few pictures to Lauren, her response coming through immediately.

Lauren: *First of all...holy hell! He's gorgeous Lex. Good job! Second of all, you two will have the cutest dark-haired babies! I love you!*

I laugh before tossing my phone to the desk as Josh takes my chin in his hand, tipping it back and to the side, exposing my neck as he drags his parted mouth along it.

"What's so funny?" he murmurs against my shoulder as he kisses across it.

"Nothing. Just something Lauren said that Brit had also said. Not important." I'm far too focused on his mouth against me as my need for him keeps heightening.

As he slips the collar of my shirt off my shoulder and kisses along my skin, my head lolls back against his chest. When one hand glides up my shirt and cups my breast, squeezing and tweaking my nipple, a low moan releases from my parted lips as need settles between my thighs.

"Now, Lex, I know I've told you we don't need to keep quiet anymore. But I do actually need that today. You're not supposed to be here. They could ask you to leave for a few hours, and I don't want to spend a single second away from you. Think you can do that, baby?" The huskiness in his voice is alluring on a molecular level as my entire being lights on fire.

"I don't know, but I really want to try." It's a breathy response as my chest heaves in anticipation.

"Good. Because while I missed seeing you, hearing your voice, feeling you in my arms, I'd be lying if I said I didn't miss your body too." Josh's fingertips slip under the waistband of my jeans when my eyes flip open, and I step out of his hold.

His hands are left hanging in the air, and his mouth is agape. "What just happened, Lex?"

"I'm sorry. I want to talk."

"Um, okay. Does it have to be *right* now?" Narrowing his eyes on me, he straightens his posture.

"I'd like it to be. And then we can spend the rest of the day in bed." Taking a step forward, I run my hands up his chest, slipping one under the collar of his shirt to run along the smooth warmth. "Besides, if we wait until people are back, I can be as loud as I want."

His eyes shut as he slips his thumbs through my belt loops and yanks my pelvis against his. "If that's really what you want, but understand what you're doing to me right now."

"Oh, trust me, I do." It'd be impossible not to feel his erection pressing into my stomach.

With a grumble, Josh sits on the bed and pulls me with him, turning me so we're facing each other and looping my legs over his.

"So, I wanted to explain my sudden lack of concern for the rules. Because the thought process is important for you to understand."

"Okay. I'm listening." Josh rests his hands on my hips, his thumbs running along the skin just above the band of my jeans.

"I talked to my mom and Lauren this weekend. And they both had similar things to say about me needing to just let go and be happy, which I agree with. But on my very long drive back this morning, I realized that I was really just hiding behind the rule."

Josh's eyes narrow as he pulls his hands from my waist and runs them down my thighs to rest on my knees. "Then why?"

"I've been a horrible person and made big mistakes recently." When his eyebrows shoot up, I quickly correct myself, resting on a hand on his chest to find his heart thumping sporadically. "Not being with you. But being with you while also being with Liam. Or at least thinking I was. In my mind, he and I were in a relationship. Now that may not have been a mutual agreement or understanding, but that's how I saw it. So, to me, being with you was basically wrong. Where I had really messed up, was not breaking things off with Liam. I should have done it the first time you and I kissed."

Turning away, I pull the inside of my lip between my teeth for a minute before turning back. "I never really had a lot of guys who showed interest in me. I sat in the shadows a lot, despite Lauren being in the spotlight and me being her right-hand girl. So, when one guy actually did show that interest, whatever his reasons and motives were, I went with it. I felt like some of Liam's shortcomings were something I was just accepting, or thought were part of a relationship, since nobody's perfect. You were so hot and cold, I didn't know what to make of it.

"It shouldn't have mattered. I didn't want to be with Liam, and I knew that even before we kissed. That was my mistake. I was just worried that even if we tried this, you'd leave me at some point, and at least Liam had been interested. Call it naiveté or inexperience or whatever you want."

Stealing a glance at Josh, I find his gaze intently on me, his mouth pressed into a line. I can't read his face and my throat dries instantly.

"I-I maybe didn't express myself right."

"I get it, Lex. I do. I'm not mad. Not at you anyway.

Listen, Liam is a jackass, and while I'm forever grateful he didn't see what a catch you are, I can understand your thought process. High school relationships are...different. Some of it has to do with the pool of people you have, some of it is simply a matter of age. Here, we're more like adults, not fully, but more so. You make more choices, more mistakes." Josh runs his palms up and down my legs, looping down to my lower back and up to my knees.

"I don't think you're a bad person, Lexie. You maybe didn't do things the right way, but that doesn't make you a bad person. We all encounter times in our life where we have a choice to make, and we don't always make the right one. Now I hope you don't and will never regret choosing to be with me, despite the way it started and how it happened."

I run my hand along Josh's jaw. "I could never. Josh, truly, I could never regret that. No matter what happens."

"What do you mean by that?"

"I, um, I guess part of me has been worried about being like a sparkler." I fight the urge to swoop my hair behind my ear, my surest tell of discomfort.

His hands grip my knees. "A sparkler? Like, the things at the Fourth of July?"

"Yeah."

"Explain."

"So, Lauren and I have done them at every Fourth since we were like six and her brother, Theo, showed us. And on my drive back, I was thinking about our friendship and just how she's always led me in the right direction. Somehow my mind ended up on the sparklers and I realized I've been afraid we were going to burn hot and bright quickly before fizzling out. That was where the fear had resided all along. The hesitation."

Josh nods slowly before taking my hands in his. "I understand that. But, Lex, things can cool off and we can still be happy. It doesn't have to be burning hot to be love. While love and sex go hand in hand, they don't have to be the same intensity. There are a lot of phases of life, and while the urgency and frequency of sex may wax and wane, what you hope is that the love doesn't."

"That's very wise advice from a twenty-one-year-old college senior."

"I have two married older siblings. They were very happy to share their fountains of knowledge with me." He smiles briefly before his features harden. "Do you love me, Lex?"

"I've never been in love before. So honestly, I don't know. But if what I feel for you *isn't* love, then I don't ever want to be in love. Because I can't imagine feeling stronger for somebody else. And I think that's what scares me a little bit. That love came with the physical." That's the part I didn't tell my mom, I couldn't really. I'm not entirely sure it's true because I've been drawn to Josh since the beginning, and on far more than just a physical level.

"It didn't, Lex. Not for me. I loved you way before I touched you. I know it may sound crazy, I do, but I couldn't get you out of my head after that first meeting. Being mean and pushing you away damn near killed me and there were so many times I almost said fuck it all and gave you everything."

My heart gallops and a burning settles behind my eyes. "Really?"

"Yeah, really." Josh tucks some curls behind my ear, cupping my jaw as he pulls me close for a kiss.

"I can't tell you what's going to happen in the future, Lex. But what I can say is that I'm madly in love with you and don't see how that could ever change. And that I want to work as hard as I have to, to keep you."

Adjusting my position so I'm seated fully in Josh's lap, I lean into his chest and wrap my legs around his waist. His arms immediately close around me and he hooks a hand into my hair, fingers massaging my scalp.

"So, I don't want to scare you or anything, but Brit and Lauren both said we'd make beautiful dark-haired babies."

I shake with his laughter, and my cheek vibrates with the humming that rumbles through his chest. "I suppose we would. Just, not yet. At least a few years."

"Oh, of course." The certainty in his words—the talk of a few years in the future—makes all worry drift away.

Unhooking my legs from around him, Josh lies back, keeping me against his chest, my cheek and palm resting against it, and our legs twining together.

Being in Josh's arms has quickly become my favorite place to be. It was long before we became official, but now it feels better, knowing I can fully relax and don't have to wait for the other shoe to drop or for him to push me away later. A calmness takes over my body, the anxiety is quelled, and the worries cease.

"You tired, baby?" His lips brush my forehead, and his breath caresses warm puffs across my face.

"A little." It comes out a mumble and barely two words.

"Take a nap. I'll be here the whole time."

"I want to spend time with you." I can't even open my eyes as I say it.

"We have all the time in the world, Lex."

"Mm. That sounds nice."

When he starts playing with my hair, taking tendrils and pulling them straight while trailing his fingers down my back, I lose my fight with sleep.

All the time in the world sounds nice, and I dream about babies with dark hair.

EPILOGUE

T*en Years Later*
        Frantically, I dash down the stairs, putting the back on the pearl earring Josh bought me for our anniversary three years ago. "Josh?"

He walks out from around the corner of the living room, stealing my breath as I take in his suit. His dark eyes twinkle as he looks at me, his hair side swept on top.

Damn, my husband is sexy.

"Mom here yet?" I ask as I rifle through my purse on the entryway table.

"No."

Freezing, I spin to look at him. "No? Really?"

Sliding his hands into his pant pockets, he nods, lips pressed into a line.

"Huh. We're going to be late." I take a deep breath to quell the uneasiness trying to rise within me.

"I'm okay with that. I don't even want to go."

"But it's *your* ten-year reunion."

"I know. And I have zero interest in seeing anybody. The only person I wanted to keep in touch with from college is the gorgeous woman standing in front of me."

After ten years, he still knows exactly what to say to make me weak in the knees.

"What about all those who came before me?"

Taking a few steps across the foyer, he stands in front of me, his musky cologne swirling in my nose. It smells familiar. It smells like home.

"Are you going to give me a hard time about them forever? We've been together for ten years, married for five, have two beautiful dark-haired children, and"—he leans down, wrapping a hand to my lower back as he draws me to him, lips against my ear— "I make you come every night."

I shiver and rub my thighs together as he chuckles at my reaction. "I like to tease. It's fun for me. And you like to do...*that*."

Sliding my hands up his chest, I twist my fingers into his lapels and pull him down so his lips can cover mine. One of his hands cups my neck, thumb resting along my jaw. Even in heels, he still towers over me.

We break apart at the sound of the door opening, but don't separate, or lower our hands. Our intense stare doesn't cease either.

"Mimi's here!" Four thundering feet come echoing from the living room, drawing my attention from Josh.

His hand slides to wrap around my waist as I turn, not allowing me to leave his side as he pulls me against it.

My shoulders slump when I take in the sight in front of me.

"Mom, I told you that you can't bring fast food every time you come over." I fight the urge to give Josh a scowl as I shake with his silent laughter.

"Nonsense. That's what grandmas are for. Spoiling their very special grandchildren."

"Thank you, Mimi!" my children squeal in unison as they take their kids meals and scamper off to the kitchen.

"Mom, really. Maddie's only two. She doesn't need all that."

Tightening his grip on my waist, Josh talks low against my temple, "Baby, it's fine every once in a while. Let her spoil them, because then she'll babysit even more and spoil *us* with more nights out."

Letting out a huff, I relax into his side, resulting in a long kiss along my hairline as he slides his hand along my arm.

"So you two are off to the reunion? Excited, Josh?"

"Not really. But if Lex wants to go, I'll go."

"Nobody you kept in touch with?"

I shift with his body as he lifts his shoulder. "A few, but they won't be there."

Resting my hand on his chest, I turn to face him. "Oh, actually, Brit decided to go. So, Jim will be there."

His eyebrows rise at my words. "Oh. Well, that's a nice surprise, actually."

"Alright, well, you two get going. I don't want you to be late. I know you wanted me here twenty minutes ago, but Alexis, you always have me come before you actually need me and the line at the drive through was long. You two have fun! I'll see you when you get back." Mom pats Josh on the shoulder as she moves past us.

Craning my neck over my shoulder, I watch Mom disappear into the kitchen, her sugary sweet voice that she has only for my children filtering through the hallway.

"Go ahead." The murmur is low next to me.

"What?" I turn my attention back to Josh.

"Go say goodbye. I know that's what you want to do right now." He jerks his head toward the kitchen.

"Don't you?"

"I did while you were getting ready. Hugs and kisses and a story."

"With voices?" Josh does the best character voices.

"Of course." One corner of his mouth ticks up and my panties soak. God, he's still so sexy.

Pushing up on my toes, I give him a quick peck on the cheek and try to walk slowly to the kitchen. Perching against the archway, a wide smile pulls at my face. Maddie is sitting on her knees to reach the table and Lucas reaches over to help her squeeze ketchup for her fries. He may be four, but he's a great big brother.

A hand slides across my stomach, and soft lips touch my neck. But I can't tear my eyes from the back of their dark heads. Maddie's curls fall in a dark sheet, much like my own. And I can't help but note that Lucas needs a haircut, his hair curling up at the ends around his ears as he shakes some wisps from his eyes.

"We should go, baby. They'll be fine. They love your mom."

"I know. It's just tonight. We owe everything to Bleeker. Our whole lives."

Josh's other arm joins the first across my stomach as he leans down, resting his chin on my shoulder. "Yeah. We do. So, let's go see some old friends, have a few drinks, and enjoy a fun night."

"Okay. Give me one second." Slipping from his hold, I place gentle kisses on the tops of my babies' heads. "Thanks, Mom."

"You two have fun. Don't worry about us, we're going to fly a secret space mission to Mars when we're done." Mom looks at my kids with a bigger smile than I think I've ever seen, and I know she's living her best life with them.

"Mimi! It's not a secret if Mommy knows," Lucas whines.

"Oops, I didn't hear anything!" I quickly cover my ears with my hands as I back out of the kitchen.

Josh isn't in the house when I leave the kitchen, so I know he's already waiting in the car. Taking a deep breath, I join him.

Once I'm settled, he takes my hand and kisses my knuckles. "Ready?"

"Yeah. Let's do it."

We stayed in the general area of Bleeker after I graduated, now living about an hour away from the campus. In the years since we graduated, a small hotel was built on the premises, which is the location for tonight's event.

"You excited to see Brit? It's been a while since they moved."

Brittney ended up marrying one of Josh's old RA coworkers. I hadn't even met him until my second semester there, as they'd worked together the year before. He helped Josh move and Brit happened to be "helping" too. They hit it off immediately.

We all lived near each other and spent a lot of time together while Brittney and I finished school and for a few years after. But about three years ago, they moved to Connecticut. It's not terribly far, but it's more than a day trip.

"Yeah. It'll be nice to see them again. It's been a while since we've all gotten together."

"Maybe we can take a little vacation out there this summer? Get the kids together. And one to Lauren, too. Or maybe somewhere we can rent a house, and everybody can come to us."

Leaning my head back in my seat, I look over at my sweet, handsome husband. Sometimes I feel like he's still trying to make up for the hurt he caused ten years ago. But after all this time, he *has* to know that he's made up for it a thousand times over. That he shows me he loves me every single day.

"That sounds really nice."

By the time we get to campus, we're a half an hour late. Not that there's anything to start really, or that the time was overly important.

"Hey. It's fine. It's just people mingling, nothing that

335

requires us to be here right at that start." Josh squeezes my hand and rubs his thumb along the back of it.

"I know. I just like to be on time."

"I know, baby. We'll make the most of it."

Before we get to the front door, Josh stops, tugging at my hand where our fingers are linked.

When I stop and turn to him, he gives a small yank, and I fall into him.

Looping some curls behind my ear with one hand, the other rests low on my back, fingertips brushing the top of my ass.

"I have a little surprise for you."

My heart races and butterflies flutter through my veins. "Oh, really?"

"I booked us a room here tonight. I already asked your mom to stay over. And we have bags in the trunk."

My eyebrows shoot to my hairline. "You did all of that without talking to me?"

"I thought it'd be a nice surprise. And if you really don't want to stay, we don't have to. I understand if you want to be home with the kids. I just thought we don't get a lot of time to be just us anymore and that it might be nice to have more than just the time surrounded by other people."

Pushing up on my toes, I link my fingers behind his neck and meld my lips to his. "I think that's a great surprise. I, um, I have one of my own, actually."

"Oh, really?" There's a gravel in his voice and I know what he's thinking, but he's wrong.

"Yeah. I wasn't necessarily going to tell you tonight, but, I don't know, I guess there's no reason to wait." Taking a deep breath, I try to calm the shakiness wanting to invade my body. "I'm pregnant." For some reason, that never gets easier to say. Even to the man I love.

"What? You're…we're…pregnant?" He has the same reaction every time. It's like he can't find the words, losing all ability to form a coherent thought. And like every other time, when I nod, the biggest, brightest smile breaks across his face, and he pulls me into his arms, spinning me around.

Putting me down, he peppers kisses along my forehead, my cheeks, my jaw, anywhere he can reach that's not covered by the hands cupping my face. "I love you. I love you so much, Lex."

"I love you too, Josh. So, you're happy?" This is the third time we're having the exact same exchange.

"So fucking happy, Lex. How could I not be? Another baby? Another little bit of you and little bit of me? What about that wouldn't make me happy?"

"I mean, I'm not exactly the easiest pregnant wife."

Tipping his face to the sky, he releases a single rough laugh before turning his face back to mine. "No, no, you certainly are not. But it's all worth it. I'll get you a thousand jars of olives, an entire orchard worth of apples, a million bags of Goldfish. Whatever you want."

"Even at two in the morning?"

"Where's this sudden doubt coming from? Have I not done it all twice before? I seem to recall going out once at three AM to try to find you a strawberry banana smoothie." Ah, yes, the infamous smoothie run from hell. I think all of our friends know that story. I didn't get my smoothie. And may or may not have, but definitely did, burst into tears and cry myself to sleep in Josh's arms over it.

"You have, but we're weary and worn now. Three AM feels different when you have not one but *two* needy kids at home. Especially when said kids are up at six-thirty every morning."

"I'll do anything for you, Lex. Always. *Especially* when you're doing something so amazing for me."

Taking a step forward, I fall into his chest, sliding my arms under his suit jacket and up his back, my eyes closing as I take a deep inhale. *Home.*

His lips press and linger on my top of my head. "Do you want to go in still? Or right up to the room and rest? How are you feeling?"

I don't move from my safe space, wrapped in Josh's arms and pressed against him. "Mostly fine."

"Tired?"

"Yeah."

"I was wondering why you were falling asleep on the couch every night. I thought the kids were just tiring you out with the extra outside time since the weather is so nice lately." Josh twirls a lock of hair around his finger while the other hand rubs up and down my back.

"It certainly doesn't help."

"How long have you known?"

"Officially? About a week. Unofficially? About three."

"I'm going to let go of the fact that you didn't feel a need to tell me."

Guilt wraps briefly around my chest, tightening it like a corset. "I wanted to surprise you. I had some things planned, was going to involve Lucas and Maddie, but, well, you know I'm not always good at following through with those things. Plus, I figured a surprise for a surprise."

"Yours is way better than mine."

"Well, I very much appreciate yours. I'm looking forward to some alone time."

"Do you still want to go in? We can just go up to our room. Or home, even, if that's what you want. You know I don't want to be here." When he repeats himself, I realize I never answered him before.

"Let's go in for a while. I want to see Brit. Plus, anybody who's here from that year. Let them see we may have broken the rule but we're long term, we're still together, and happy."

"So fucking happy." Josh tilts my face back with one hand on my chin, beaming down at me as he holds me against him. "I'm still so in love with you, Lex. Even ten years later."

"The feeling is mutual, Josh."

"Everything we have, everything you've given me, it's beyond the dreams I ever could have imagined. I had no doubt I wanted to be with you for the rest of my days, but this life we have, that we've built, it's beyond anything I could have hoped for." Josh's eyes cloud over for a moment, and I know he's lost in memories.

"Those first few years were hard for us, Lex. Between school and me student teaching and then finding a job and starting...I was tired more than I wasn't. That meant I couldn't give you the full attention and love I wanted and needed to. It wouldn't have surprised me then if you left me, especially because we argued, a lot. But you didn't; you stuck by me. You spent nights alone in my bed while I stayed up working. You waited patiently by the phone for me when I got out of work hours later than expected after grading papers and parent phone calls."

The memories make bile spiral in my stomach, and I know it's not morning sickness. I hate thinking of those times and often try not to. There was a period of time I wasn't sure we were going to make it to the next week, let alone several more years.

We had finally fallen into a routine of Josh working and getting home at a normal hour, allowing us to spend time together, when I started the craziness of student teaching. It was quickly followed by grad school and securing my own job, where we started the chaos all over again. It wasn't quite as difficult; Josh was able to help me find my footing, support me, encourage me.

The biggest difference was that I started my career being pregnant, left when Lucas was born, and haven't gone back since.

Cupping my shoulders, Josh lets out a heavy sigh and makes sure our eyes are locked on each other's. "Thank you, Lexie. For everything you've done, everything you've given me, all you've loved me through. I know those years weren't easy on you. I only hope I followed through on my promise to make it worth your time, your effort, your love."

My head cants to the side, sure I didn't hear him correctly. He *hopes*? "Josh, of course you have." I wrap my fingers around his wrists. "You've given me just as much. You showed me what it's like to love and be loved. A family. I was an inexperienced and naïve girl with expectations about college and a set of rules to follow. But you never saw me like that, and you showed me it's okay to break the rules sometimes."

A smile cuts across his face with a light laugh as he rests his forehead against mine before brushing his lips across my own. "I love you."

"I love you too."

"Hey, lovebirds! Get a room!" We both laugh, but don't separate at the sound of Brittney's voice.

When I feel her behind me, I pull away from Josh's grasp to give my friend a giant hug.

"I have to say though, guys, you two give me hope."

"You and Jim aren't so far behind us."

Hooking my arm through hers, like she did all those years ago, we walk toward the reunion, the boys following behind as they reminisce about some of the things they did as RAs.

Once inside the hotel, I look around. This wasn't here when I went to Bleeker, when all of our memories started. It's beautiful, and a testament to time passing, things changing.

With my best friend to my left, and my husband standing to my right, arm looped around my waist, contentment wraps around me. It's warm, light, and soothing.

It took me almost nineteen years, but I realized that some rules are worth breaking.

THE END

CONTENT WARNING

The following is an unedited preview and subject to change.

The preview contains the following content warnings: mature language, sexual situations, mental struggles including depression, self harm, rage issues, and attempted suicide.

The full length novel contains the content warnings above, in addition to: anxiety, attending therapy, explicit sexual scenes, abandonment, drug and alcohol abuse, promiscuous behavior, and nonconsensual intercourse.

Both are intended for readers age 18 and older.

PREVIEW OF OWN ME

The light flicks on, chasing away the all encompassing darkness. I raise my head from my hands to see Zane standing with his fingers still on the switch, taking in the scene. Me, sitting on the cool tile of the kitchen, knees to my chest, heels of my hands to my eyes. Knife on the floor.

He's kneeling in front of me in half a second, grabbing my wrists and pulling them out straight, looking them up and down, turning them over.

"What happened? Are you okay? Did you cut?" His voice is low, trying to be calm, but I hear the slightest hint of panic seeping through.

"No. But I want to," I whisper.

Crossing my arms against my chest, he curls around me, pulling me into his lap and wrapping his arms tightly around my waist. I let myself feel his strength. I wish I could steal it, or at least just borrow some. I'm weak. So much weaker than he is.

We have similar problems, similar demons. But he's learned to control his urges better than I have. He doesn't end up awake at two in the morning fighting himself like I do. At

343

least not anymore. This isn't the first time this month. It's not even the first time this week.

"It's okay. I've got you." His deep voice is low against my ear.

Breathe. Close your eyes. Take in the moment. Go to where you feel comfortable, safe. The only problem with the directions my psychologist gave me when we practiced the exercise, is that I don't know where that place is. Zane makes me feel safe, but I refuse to use him as my grounding visual.

Instead, I keep my eyes open, looking around to find five things I can see. *Toaster, magnet, coffee pot, moon, knife.* My stomach roils at the thought.

Deep breath, keep going. Four things I can hear. *Zane's heart, the tick of the clock, the hum of the fridge, the wind.*

Three things I can touch. *Zane's warm skin, the cool tiled floor, water from the faucet.*

Two things I can smell. *Soap, fresh coffee.*

One thing I can taste. *Tangy iron.* A shudder wracks my body.

"Are you doing your grounding exercise?"

"It's not working." It comes out through gritted teeth.

"Focus on me. See, hear, touch, smell...and taste." With a firm finger under my chin, he tilts my head up as his mouth meets mine, forcing it open as his tongue slips in. Mint crosses my taste buds as my hand splays open over his chest. It's a dual touch sensation, his warmth and the steady beating of his heart beneath my palm.

Zane understands me in a way no boyfriend before him ever had or ever could. I hate that he does because I don't want him having the same internal struggle that I do. But it's what makes us work as a couple. It's also what makes us toxic together. Kind of like how they say addicts shouldn't date each other. Sometimes if one of us falls off the bandwagon the other does too.

When we moved in together we had strict rules. No breakables of any kind, including glasses and dishes. We eat off paper or plastic dishes and only have plastic cups. No vases of any kind. We learned the hard way that mirrors aren't safe either when Zane connected his fist with one.

At the beginning, he locked up the knives, keeping the key with him at all times. My therapist had recently recommended he remove the locks so I learn self control. It isn't working.

When Zane urgently says "Jules" and shakes me I snap to. Great, I'm dissociating too. When had he stopped kissing me?

"Huh?"

Pain, I feel pain in my shoulders. Zane's hands are gripping me so firmly it hurts. I try to shrug him off but it only makes his grip tighten until I wince, making him realize how strong of a grip he has on me. It's like he's trying to hold onto my sanity for me.

"Feel the pain Jules. Focus on it. Let it be enough."

Closing my eyes, I take more deep breaths. *Nails digging into my skin, warmth rolling off his body, mint lingering in my mouth, clean linen tingling my nose, a heartbeat.* At the moment I don't know who's heart I'm hearing, mine or his, but I try to focus on the steadiness of it. In the blackness behind my eyelids, I pull up visions of flower fields, the beach, a snowy mountain. Any place that may hold calm. Instead, my mind wants to come back to this apartment.

It seems to be working, as my shoulders start to slump against Zane's hands. He starts rubbing small circles wherever he can. I keep my eyes closed, trying to focus on his fingers, even willing myself to think about all the things they can do to my body. But that just brings up other impulses.

Shivers tingle through me as Zane slides his hand up my neck and into my hair, massaging my scalp. It's two fold. It feels incredible and helps ease the tension from my taut muscles. But it's also a move he uses when he's trying to get me to take my pants off. I'm not really sure what his motive is at the moment.

When he tangles his fingers in my hair and pulls my head back as he closes his mouth over mine, it becomes clear.

His lips are hungry on mine, tongue forceful in my mouth. Without words he's begging me to relinquish my body to him, to give him everything so he can clear the darkness. It's worked before, more than once.

But tonight feels different, darker, harder. Even as his hand slips up my shirt, all I can think of is shiny metal gliding across my arm. The pinch, the sting. The *feeling*. It was a hard day with my psychologist. Sometimes those make for the hardest nights. They bring up all sorts of feelings you've tried to bury for years.

Then at one thirty in the morning you realize they're not so dead and buried anymore and find yourself standing in the kitchen holding a knife to your arm fighting yourself not to do it while the tiny voice in your head eggs you on. *Do it. You'll feel better. This pain will take away that pain, the hatred, the numbness.* But it never does. It's temporary, fleeting. And then you're left with the reminder of how stupid you were, how weak.

I have to tell Dr. Ptansky if I cut. I don't have to tell her if I have sex, at least not if it's with Zane. Sex with your boyfriend is not self destructive. Sex in the bathroom at a bar with a man you just met, especially while in a relationship, is. But in the two years Zane and I have been together I've never once even come close to cheating on him. Dr. Ptansky calls it progress. I call it finally being satisfied in bed.

It helps when that person understands you and doesn't belittle you. Even that they know when to add a little pain to the pleasure. In more ways than one, Zane just gets me.

A whimper rising from my own chest brings me back to what my body is doing. At some point I straddled Zane's lap and his mouth is against my throat, both hands cupping my breasts. He'd pushed away from the counter, his back now resting against the fridge. Great, I dissociated again.

Focus, focus, focus. Has Zane not had a shirt on this whole time? I'm usually much more aware of his naked physique.

"If I get up will you follow me to the bedroom?" His voice is low and gravelly.

Will I? I don't know. I want to. Oh, I so want to. But I'm also acutely aware of exactly where the knife is and how it would be to grab it. His hands on me feels so good, but I don't want pleasure. I want pain. I need it. It gives me a reason to hate myself, it reminds me I'm not numb, that I can feel something.

"Yes."

"You hesitated." Grabbing my wrists from behind his head he pulls them forward, his grip tight. He leans away as I try to kiss him again. "It's not worth it Jules. Whatever you're thinking, it's not worth it."

"You don't know that."

"I *do* know that. Don't do it. Come to bed with me, let me distract you. Feel me, not the pain."

I nod. "Okay."

Sliding me off his lap, he goes to stand, but he's not careful enough. He doesn't keep control of my hands and before he can stop me, I throw myself across the kitchen and grab the knife, dragging it across my forearm and watching the dark liquid blossom.

I barely hear the knife clank to the floor or Zane screaming behind me, suddenly at my side pressing something to my skin, blackness invading my vision. As I fall into darkness, I have one last thought.

Pain.

Jules and Zane's story will be coming to you in the spring of 2022.
Pre-order Own Me today

ACKNOWLEDGMENTS

What an amazing journey it's been to get here. With that, comes many thanks.

To my amazing husband and children:
Thank you so much for your time, your effort, your sacrifices while I wrote. I would not be here without your understanding and love.

Not only did you give me your full support and understanding that sometimes I just needed time to write or edit, but you helped me at every turn. From reading the book and giving input, to helping me when I had a question with which line worked better, to helping promote the book. You've been nothing short of amazing and I can never thank you enough.

We did it!

To my soul sister, Garnet Christie:
Where do I even start? You've been on this entire journey with me and have cheered me on every single step of the way. From that very first, terrible, bottom of the drawer story, to everything that's yet to come, you've been my cheerleader. Every time I thought I wasn't good enough, wanted to quit, you were there pushing me on. This book would not exist without you. I am so thankful for you and that we have gone from writing partners, to amazing friends.

To Amy Kaybach and Rachel Lehan, the other two integral pieces of my team:

How can I begin to thank either of you for your time, dedication, and advice? You've both been absolutely incredible women to work with, and have become good friends. It means so much that I can come to you with a question related to my story, that you'll read any change and give your input, and that we can talk about *life* even when not related to writing! I couldn't do it without either of you!

To my bestie, Joelle Lynn:

You have been through every step of this process with me. From hearing me talk about writing nonstop, to helping me decide which book to start with, to beta reading this one for me when I was short on time, you've been amazing. Not to mention, through all of that, you've been a huge supporter. I'm so excited that we get to share this journey together, even if on slightly different paths.

Jemma Ryken and Cathryn Carter:

Thank you both so much for your support, help, advice and of course the time to read through and comment on a work such as this. I appreciate your input so much and have loved working with both of you!

To my parents and brother:

Thank you for your continued support of my passion, for checking in on the process, for asking questions, and for encouraging me to keep going.

To my amazing editors Zainab and Mackenzie:

This book would not be what it is without you and your input. Thank you for helping me learn how to be a better writer, adjusting my words, and most importantly, keeping my voice my own.

Thank you the amazing **Coffin Print Designs** for my stunning cover!

To my ARC team:

Your time and effort does not go unnoticed. Thank you for reading my novel before it hit the public and for your gracious reviews. I know it's not always easy to find the words, but it's all so appreciated.

And most importantly, to the readers:

Thank you for taking a chance on a new author. I know it can be difficult to see a new name and say "hey let me try that" but it is so beyond appreciated, I cannot begin to find the words. I write because it's my passion, but I publish because I want to share my words with all of you. I hope you enjoyed reading it, as much as I enjoyed writing it.

ABOUT THE AUTHOR

Shayna Astor is a romance author who loves writing sweet love stories, with a lot of spice. When she's not writing, she's probably watching The Office with a cup of coffee, spending time with her kids, or playing video games with her husband.

Stalk me for all the latest updates, teasers for upcoming novels, giveaways, and all the goods on what's coming next!

Instagram @shayna.astor.author
TikTok @shayna.astor.author
Facebook Group Shayna's Coffee Corner
Website www.shaynaastor.com

Made in the USA
Middletown, DE
06 April 2022

63685818R10215